ASMARAÑA

a novel by
Adam Creagan

CHAPTER 1

A horde of intrusive thoughts gather in the distance. These unexpected anxieties create storm clouds on the horizon of Asmara's mind. Swirling panic stirs up winds which push the dark mass to the front of her consciousness.

Like a bombing raid, the negative notions detonate in her head. It's impossible to deflect them all. The thunderous impact of insecurities becomes a chanting chorus: "You are going crazy. You are going crazy."

Now that a path has been flattened by the assault, an army of her self-loathing sentiments prepares to march forward against her.

There is no obvious trigger for this onset as tonight has been a relaxed evening with friends. The arrival of the cruel shroud makes her fear its contours will harden into a permanent fixture around her.

Asmara tugs on the invisible mask and it has not yet suctioned to her face. If she is able to slip fingers of hope beneath its edges the seal will not hold. She pries the rotten filter from her eyes and rays of light shine through the storm. This illumination shows an empty battlefield. The marching sounds are not getting any closer and they soon recede.

It is evident what is happening. There are so many barbarians of doubt at the gate of her consciousness that they can't get in. Their hostile messages are imposed on each other, turning the signals into diluted static and weakening their potency. As for distress about mental illness and going crazy, those stability killers cannot sink their hooks into her. The rusted barbs have been dulled from overuse.

With the storm dissolving, the anxiety beasts remain lodged together at a distant entry point in her mind. They begin to howl. These insecurities will soon start feeding on each other in frustration. The cannibalism of negative thoughts will continue until one is left. Then it will starve.

At least Asmara hopes so.

Every panic attack in her life felt as if it would be the one which never went away. Her nightmare scenario is these cycles of dread increase in frequency until they connect on both ends, forming a continuous state of terror.

This attack had a fast onset. It also dissipated at a record pace. The emotional whiplash transpired within a span of one minute and it all took place as she noticed a hole in the wooden stage at The Naomi. It's not clear why merely looking at the circular portal in this San Francisco music venue had such a negative initial effect. The platform's ordinary hole for wiring and cables has no obvious correlation with the fright it produced.

Bizarre.

And... what's this?

The tiny trapdoor in the stage emits an altogether different wavelength. It provides her with visions—detailed images of a performance grand finale in the near future.

The spontaneous idea comes to her with a pleasing jolt. It entails not quite a magic trick but more of a climactic stunt. This is the live birth of an elaborate plan brimming with ambition. It demands she attend to it and take action.

As she reviews the concept, Asmara shakes her head in disbelief for its details bear no resemblance to her usual spectrum of daydreams. However, she is not complaining and is intrigued by this visitor.

. . . .

Once a month The Naomi switches up its live music schedule and hosts an open mic night for literary types. Stories, narrative comedy, and spoken word are featured and each speaker gets five minutes on stage. The event is called Word Bound and, in Asmara's estimation, it makes for an above-average night out with lively readings in front of a receptive crowd. Tonight is a normal bar night at The Naomi and no stage act is scheduled.

Asmara has attended Word Bound twice before and considered reading one of her stories on stage but was never inspired to follow through. *Why in the hell would I read in front of a crowd?* Now she has her answer. Asmara's new plan which hatched is preposterous yet it contains a parallel benefit—the stunt itself and a live reading are intertwined. One can't happen without the other. It's an opportunity to share her writing. She will get her words off of the page and into the world around her, where they can live and breathe, or die, on their own.

Asmara's Word Bound conception is that, during her live set, an accomplice beneath the stage will feed a tube through the hole she observed tonight and run it up into her pant leg. The long tube will continue upward under her shirt where it will stop below her collar. The audience can't know what's going on—this has to be done with stealth, baggy clothes, and incremental movement.

Hold on.

Pants won't work. The entire effect will be ruined if people stare at the serpentine bulge up her leg. She's going to have to wear a floor-length skirt. *Damn.* She never wears a skirt and the one she owns, a relic from college, isn't long enough. A thrift store visit is on the agenda for this week.

Her friends will be perplexed by the sight of her in a skirt the night of the show, but no matter. The attire is not suspicious enough to indicate what's in store. No one will anticipate that during the closing moments of her reading, with the tube having arrived beneath her collar unnoticed, a syringe-style plunger at the bottom of the device will be pressed upward, pushing a live tarantula out from under her shirt and spilling the hairy creature onto her face.

Asmara will allow the spider to crawl on her as she finishes telling her story. She will calmly walk off stage with the beast clinging to her.

It's going to be pure theatrics. A strange climax. This stunt is so out of place for a night of Word Bound there will be a beauty to how ridiculous it is. Sublimely unnecessary, one might say. Of course she'd like to craft a memorable experience for the audience, but that's secondary. Even if her act bombs on stage and she is met with bored, blank stares, there is more than success or failure at play here. This is an exhilarating plan, at least to her, and it arrived in a surge of inspiration. She isn't going to let it dissipate like so many other ideas she's had.

That is what this is about—ending the losing streak of repeatedly having creative, energizing moments and never doing anything about them. There is no specific outcome she's aiming for. It is not a goal to have a video recording of the show spur viral fame. She just wants to be the type of person to see a plan through to the end, no matter the results. Whether this is a good or bad idea will be determined, but it's a big idea. The concept emerged from a fertile place within her—a landscape simmering with more surprises.

Perhaps someday she will look back on the absurd night of a tarantula on her face and view it as an essential springboard in her life. A true turning point. That is the effect she's seeking.

. . . .

Asmara's two friends talk between themselves and she times her head nods to appear engaged. Her mind is not present because it's racing through spider stunt logistics. From the table where they are seated she steals glances at the empty stage where Word Bound will be held in one week.

Her friends share a chuckle over a comment and Asmara is so preoccupied with her idea she misjudges their cues. She unloads a laugh without hearing what they said.

"Ha! Ha!" Like two gunshots.

Asmara's friends swivel their heads in her direction. Damage control: time to join the group with actual words. Half-heard conversation hangs in the air and the talk involves food. She gathers a random anecdote and launches it forward.

"I know, I ate a huge Azteca burrito yesterday," Asmara says. "I felt like a giant snake that needs three days to digest a meal. I had to unhinge my jaw to eat this thing."

The two friends both grin. A good sign.

"I wanted a warm rock to lie on afterward. I might get a terrarium heat lamp in my apartment. I'll lay under it after every meal."

Their smiles give way to a laugh. Asmara bought herself more non-speaking time to let her mind wander.

. . . .

She'll need to find a compromise between the size of the tarantula and the tube diameter. The spider will hopefully be coaxed to scrunch its legs together to fit into the tube. Safety is essential as it is lifted on top of the plunger like an elevator. It'd be horrific if Asmara's grand finale involved a dead spider flopping out of her collar.

There are more hurdles ahead but one looms large: her written material. What will she read on stage? Asmara writes for herself and sharing will be difficult. She has dozens of short stories written both longhand and typed into her laptop. Her stories are cryptic, semi-autobiographical and constantly being revised. None of them feature a spider.

Asmara pictures a forensic detective analyzing her papers for clues after she is found dead from tarantula bites.

She is not opposed to having a readership for those stories which don't embarrass her. But an audience listening to her words on stage? And spoken in her own shrill, rooster-like voice? That is not what her writing is intended for.

Asmara reflects on old story ideas which may be primed for resurrection at Word Bound. As she sifts through her mental catalog, doubt creeps in. The region of her mind which employs logic had been generous and allowed her to enjoy this daydream, but it has had enough. The fantasy of performing on stage is about to get strangled and it will be a quick death. There are pangs of disappointment already.

This spider stunt of yours? It will never happen. You don't have it in you.

Asmara lingers on the thought of letting this idea go, same as all the others which faded away. The concept was probably never hers to begin with. This inspiration she encountered is pre-existing—a wider frequency of impulsive creation she stumbled into. These wavelengths are broadcast from place to place, searching for a receptive person. The individual must not only be a creator but a conduit—someone who will recognize the idea, act on it, and give it life. Someone other than herself.

And yet.

She pushes back. And pushes some more.

What if she *is* the correct conduit this time?

Asmara uses the weight of her doubts against themselves by acknowledging their threats head-on. They lumber toward her and are easy to dodge. These misgivings topple from their own momentum. She engages in the martial arts of confidence.

There will be more rounds of similar doubt ahead, of course. Asmara is determined to resist them again and again. As for now, she expects herself to be on stage at Word Bound in seven days and her performance is going to end with a peculiar eight-legged flourish.

. . . .

Asmara is at The Naomi tonight with her friends Sarah and Gillian. They all went to UC Davis together and graduated the same year. None of the three have used their English degrees in the seven years which have followed. Sarah does sales for a small winery. Gillian does administrative work for a physical therapist. And Asmara is unemployed. Kind of. It's more of a purgatory as she distances herself from the years she spent managing a screenprinting shop. Her position was not horrible and she liked the responsibilities, but the job was not fulfilling anymore.

One of her other friends, Dylan, said he is "almost positive" he can get her a job in content aggregation at the tech company where he works. The startup is an app and website which pairs freelance writers and artists to showcase their talents for hire. Asmara was told she would be reviewing submissions, copy-editing articles, and writing biographies of the contributors. Anything even remotely creative and where she gets to write is ideal. Dylan has promised to contact her about the job within days and Asmara pretends she's enjoying a vacation in the meantime—a vacation with a toxic cloud of anxious uncertainty hovering above.

Every few months the three women make an effort to meet since they all live in the Bay Area. Sarah and Gillian are in Oakland and Asmara lives in San Francisco. Their bond is nowhere near what it was in college and these visits are more about routine friendship maintenance. The women used to form a tight triangle and their energy would bounce off each other and amplify. They're not sure how to rekindle the fire or even if they should try.

Tonight they near the two-hour mark of chatting and the conversation slow down is apparent. Sarah and Gillian are talking about a show they've been binge-watching—a dramatic series about closeted gay people navigating life in Iran. This type of "favorite show" banter is common but Asmara can't relate. She's in the overlooked minority who has no shows to speak of, favorite or otherwise.

As she listens to her friends describe a scene where a private nightclub is raided by Iranian police (the captain of which finds his son in half-naked attendance), Asmara's attention lifts above the conversation. She swivels her head right to left, as both a genuine neck stretch and a way to conduct a room survey. While she scans the bar to determine if anything has happened since she last looked, Asmara makes eye contact with a man leaning against a far wall. He is with two other guys and a woman.

Maintaining his gaze with Asmara, the unknown man lifts a beer, stops short of his mouth and tips the bottle back in her direction, as if he acknowledges her. He says something to his group and they turn in unison toward her and give a synchronized head nod.

On an ordinary night out, Asmara hopes for a unique "something happens" moment—anything where the occasion earns a memory stamp to contrast with other featureless nights. The tarantula Word Bound idea has already placed an imprint onto this evening.

With the group of four strangers walking toward Asmara's table, it is apparent this night is not done revealing itself.

CHAPTER 2

The newcomers stride up to Asmara's table and form a semi-circle around it. They cast an imposing presence for a split second. Smiles and a meek wave by the woman of their group indicate these are not homicidal mutants.

Emerged from the shadows, this crew is an odd mix. Asmara develops instant bird associations for them. Two of the guys are pudgy with similar rounded dimensions. They are the penguins. The woman is rail thin and towers at six feet. She is the stork. And the guy who first made eye contact with Asmara, he is a peacock, for he displays a maroon scarf wrapped around his neck. Classifying him as a turkey might make more sense but she's sticking with peacock.

There is a second unfortunate accessory in his possession. He has one hand rested on an upright skateboard, as if it's a cane.

A winter scarf indoors? A skateboard in a bar?

These red flags flap and send a foul breeze toward Asmara.

"Hey," the peacock says, addressing Asmara. "I'm pretty sure I've met you. So, I dragged my friends across the bar to find out."

Asmara is certain she's never seen this guy but he's elevated the night into something more than it was one minute earlier. "We've met? I'm not sure. Where would that have been?"

"It was either at my work or Don DeLyon's house."

"Who?"

"Don DeLyon."

Asmara laughs. "What kind of name is that? Is it real?"

"Yeah... Wait. I forgot Don is his nickname."

"We're talking about a guy? Isn't Dawn a woman's name?"

"It's spelled D-O-N. Like a mafia don."

"You realize the name you're saying sounds like 'dandelion,' right?"

"Yeah, that's why his nickname is a joke among friends. Damn it. I can't remember his real name right now."

Sarah tries to convey words within laughter. "What is happening here? Is this a prank?"

"No. I swear he's real. I'm not feeding you some pick-up line."

The peacock turns to his companions for help but his flock gives him two blank stares and one shrug.

Asmara narrows down the possibilities. "I've never met a Don in my life, I assure you."

"Maybe it was at my work. Have you been to One Track Mind in Oakland?"

"The bike store? I've heard of it but I have not stepped foot in there."

"Really? I still feel like I've met you. Weird. Oh, man."

"Well, I don't know what to tell you... Man."

The peacock doesn't appear mortified but a nervous smile grows across his face. He wants to avoid the walk of shame back across the bar in social defeat.

"All right, enough," Asmara says in a mock-serious voice. "I need to see a photo of this girl you've mistaken me for. Any way you can find one?"

The Peacock and his companions relax.

"Whenever I'm told I look like someone, it's never flattering," Asmara says. "I get shown their photo and it tends to be, like, a basset hound."

"I have a hunch who I confused you with. The woman is friends with a guy I know. Let me look in my phone for a photo."

"I am joking. You don't need to find her."

"No, I've got this. You're going to be blown away by the similarity. And she's no basset hound. Although, I heard she has a good sense of smell."

As he examines his phone, Gillian keeps the talk moving. "So, where are you all from?"

"These three are here in SF," the peacock says, without looking up. "I'm in Oakland. We all work together."

A flurry of name exchanges commence. Asmara struggles with retaining new names and sometimes the voice sound waves never even reach her ears. However, when the peacock contributes his greeting she chisels it into cerebral stone. His name is Ryan.

Asmara finds him well-positioned on the threshold of being cute. He's *almost* there for her. If he speaks intelligently and, one hopes, is funny as well, he'll cross over. His scarf and skateboard cast a shadow over the equation.

Ryan appears to inhabit the same late-twenties age as Asmara and her friends. In fact, Asmara is a few weeks away from reluctantly departing her twenties. The baptism into her third decade is soured with restless unease, especially about her unemployment.

"Pull up some seats," Sarah says.

The flock reaches around for unoccupied chairs. It's settled—some fresh blood and new faces were in the cards for tonight.

"That's quite a scarf," Asmara says to Ryan, who takes a break from his phone—an act she regards as encouraging.

"Yeah, it's a joke I have with Amy," he says, motioning toward the tall girl. "It's her scarf."

"Isn't it too warm for indoors?"

"Yes, it is. And it itches, too. I wore it as a dare. Amy insisted girls like guys who wear something other than jeans and a sweatshirt. And since that's what I had on tonight she told me to add her scarf."

Asmara feasts on these delicious details. It matters that Ryan has a female friend who cares enough to decorate him and present him to her lady tribe.

"Has it gotten you any attention yet?" Asmara asks.

"No."

"Well, good luck."

"Women will gravitate to him," Amy says. "The scarf will be like a pussy whip, I'm telling you."

Hmm, vulgarity. Amy has entered the ring in foul-mouthed glory. The barriers of decorum are crumbling and Asmara finishes them off.

"You have to clarify," Asmara says. "Which definition of pussy whip are you using?"

The two penguins are smiling.

"A good scarf shows a guy cares about his appearance," Amy says. "Some women will be attracted toward that. So, it's like a pussy whip."

"Sorry, Amy. I have to take issue with your wording."

"Why?"

"A pussy whip is an expression for what a woman uses against a guy to keep him in check. It means she controls him. That's the common usage of the phrase."

"Yeah, but the way I'm saying it works, too."

"If your contention is this scarf has the power of gathering pussy like a magnet, the metaphor doesn't work. Whips re-direct or corral animals, but whips are not associated with bringing something directly toward you. In fact, it keeps things away."

"What about Indiana Jones?" a penguin says. "Didn't he grab things with his whip?"

"That's in a movie," Asmara says. "No, you cannot grab things with a whip. Even if you managed to wrap the whip around something, when you wrench it back toward you it will be like a missile in your direction."

"Did you guys know the crack of a whip is the sound barrier being broken?" says the other penguin. "It's a small sonic boom."

His trivia is ignored.

"Maybe pussy whip has different regional meanings," Amy says. "I'm saying it correctly like where I grew up."

"If you're talking about bringing something toward you," Asmara says, "I hereby declare the scarf Ryan is wearing is not a pussy whip but a pussy lasso, as seen with cowboys who wrangle livestock."

Thoughtful head nods around the table indicate the distinction is worth pondering. Amy even rubs her chin.

"Let me see that thing," Asmara says to Ryan.

He slips the scarf off his neck and hands it to her. Everyone knows what's coming as she ties a wide loop-knot at one end of the garment. They laugh anyway when she swings her arm in a circle, creating a lasso spin with the scarf levitating above the table like a helicopter blade.

"Now *this* will get you all the kitty you want," Asmara says.

The knot unravels after three spins around the table and Asmara has a hard time keeping the scarf aloft. On its dying orbit the wool accessory clips the top of Sarah's beer, knocking it over. The impact sprays fat beer droplets across the faces of both penguins. A yellow tide of spilled drink races across the table toward Ryan. Showing agility, and a desire to avoid soiling the crotch of his pants with beer, Ryan leaps from a seated position. He escapes as the frothy wave turns into a waterfall from the table's edge.

Everyone gasps and all eyes go to Asmara. She is obligated to speak first.

"I... I don't regret a thing."

CHAPTER 3

The beer-bath laughter generates energy at the table. Conversation flows easily. When another round of drinks is suggested, Asmara and her two friends decline but they are happy to continue chatting with this new group.

It turns out the four coworkers are celebrating the near-finish of a new One Track Mind bike shop in San Francisco, the first branch outside of Oakland. Asmara determines the penguins are named David and Seth. They are both married (not to each other, which would have been incredible) and they are both doing structural engineering work during the building's remodel. Amy is the store manager and Asmara isn't sure what job Ryan has at the shop. It would be easy to blurt out, "So, Ryan, what do you do?" But she considers the question a cheap and sometimes rude short-cut.

Asmara is frustrated by Ryan's position at the table. She has to raise her voice over the crossfire of two other discussions filling the air. An opportunity for musical chairs arises when Sarah takes a phone call outside. Ryan gets up and sits next to Asmara as they enter their own world. They take a conversational stroll together down a wide, breezy path of topics. From favorite concerts to sleep disorders (they both have a father who sleepwalks), and from today's weather to childhood injuries (they both have scars from miscalculations on a jungle gym). They also explore the great philosophical question of the region: is San Francisco ever going to be like it was before? No, is the answer they arrive at.

But maybe it'll be even *better* than it was before.

"SF is over," one of the penguins interjects while eavesdropping. "It's not coming back."

"Whatever," Ryan says. "People complain about every city. In his day, Caligula probably whined that the vomit-piss-orgies in Rome were more fun ten years earlier."

The penguin blinks a few times and turns away without comprehension. Asmara gives her first unrestrained laugh of the night.

. . . .

A solid half hour goes by with Asmara and Ryan immersed in each other. The only time the spell is broken is when Gillian sends her a toothy grin wider than any great white shark could manage.

Even though this experience with Ryan is like entering a romantic-comedy screenplay, Asmara plots how to wind things down. Ending the night on a high note is crucial instead of squeezing dry every drop of positive energy. She wants to preserve this glowing representation of herself she crafted.

Asmara engages with the rest of the table and gives cues she will be departing soon. Ryan's attention returns to his phone and he announces, "Found her. I've got a photo of the woman who I thought you were across the bar."

"All right, let's see this chick," Asmara says.

He raises his phone and the screen reveals... a basset hound.

"I'm just playing. Can I get your number? "

. . . .

After two more series of prolonged farewells, Asmara stands and announces it's time for her to go. Her eyes round the table while she gives personalized goodbyes to everyone, making sure to save Ryan for last. Once her gaze is upon him, she does her best to summon a look of both confidence and sultriness. The result is her confused eyebrows rise and fall independent of each other.

Sarah and Gillian plan on staying longer and they offer to walk outside with Asmara for a proper send-off. As they exit The Naomi a frosty chill broadsides them.

All three women are wide-eyed with excitement about Ryan. Juicy details will be shared at a later date, now it is hugs goodbye. Sarah and Gillian head back into The Naomi and Asmara remains on the sidewalk, acclimating to the change in environment. Her body and mind downshift from social stimulation back to the familiar hum of her private realm. It is liberating to have the vast night sky above her, even if city lights try to banish the darkness.

Asmara does not own a car. This is by choice and without regrets. Although, on a night like this, she wants to summon those regrets and rub them together for heat. If and when she moves somewhere requiring car ownership, she will purchase a horseless carriage. Until that change, she regards public transit as part of city living. A ride-share option is a phone-tap away but Asmara uses discipline and prepares for a healthy six-block walk to the subway.

Her journey lasts one footstep before her attention is drawn to three guys who are out front of The Naomi. They finish their cigarettes and are about to go into the venue. This trio is under-dressed for the cold and they bounce in place, looking like engine pistons, as they try to keep warm.

There is a thin cigarette disposal bin behind the smokers. Asmara hopes they are near the receptacle precisely for its intended use. However, the three guys each flick their cigarette butts in a high arc toward the street. These pinpoint red embers act as cruel shooting stars, traveling in the opposite direction of where Asmara wanted them to go. If she had one wish, she would skip world peace and instead have these guys eat those cigarette filters.

Asmara is non-confrontational, especially with strangers. She is able to count on two fingers—her thumb and index finger touching tips, forming a zero—the number of times she's scolded someone on the street for littering.

Tonight is different.

"There's a place for cigarette butts behind you," Asmara says, pointing toward the bin. A rush of howling air echoes in her ears. Probably adrenaline. Or maybe it's the ghosts of ten thousand litterers past, being called to judgment.

The three guys pivot toward her. They are in their mid-twenties and they all have freckles. The one closest to her has a tattoo creeping from under his collar onto his neck. It is a tentacle.

Two seconds have passed since she voiced her comment and Asmara imagines booking a plane ticket to her parents' home in Oregon and slipping into her childhood bed before these guys react.

"What was that?" the neck-tatted one says.

Asmara draws in a breath of cold air. "I'm just saying, The Naomi staff placed the receptacle for smokers to use," she says. "It's there so people don't throw cigarettes into the street."

"The Naomi staff, huh?" the neck-tatted one says. "That's me. I work here."

His accent is funny. He sounds Australian.

Asmara is undeterred by his employment. It makes his littering even worse. She continues her flat gaze into his eyes.

"Ah, you're probably right..." the neck-tatted guy mumbles.

He bounds over to the street, scoops up the three cigarette stumps and jogs back. He deposits the butts down the bin's slender neck where the smoldering embers are deprived of oxygen and extinguish themselves.

The neck-tatted guy turns to face Asmara.

"Eh, it's an excuse a child would use," he says, his Australian accent revealed. "But doesn't everyone toss cigs about? Like, everywhere?"

"It's true, most people drop them on the ground," Asmara says. "But tonight you didn't. I want to say thanks."

He gives Asmara a long look, perhaps trying to figure out this strange woman and her futile crusade, and he flashes a grin.

"Well, all right. Glad I could help."

The three guys return to The Naomi. Its front door is designed to prevent itself from slamming shut. During the last inches of its swinging motion before closing, the hinges catch and slow the door to a crawl. Asmara glances inside through the gap between the door and its frame as a digital clock on the wall turns from 11:59 p.m. to 12:00 a.m.

CHAPTER 4

(Eight days later)

The story ends here. Of all places.

With each step as she enters the darkened garage, Asmara's heartbeat churns with growing intensity. There is a percussive impact against the wall of her chest as blood transfers in and out.

Asmara can't allow herself to die of a heart attack before she finishes what she's here to do. Death in that manner would mean she failed, thus igniting an inferno of evil. Her demise must come in another way more specific. It is the only way to extinguish the flame.

Or, to be more accurate, to stop the flood.

There's little time left. The apocalypse is imminent.

She blindly pats her hand along the wall in search of a light switch. A jab in the palm locates the fixture and she flips the light on to reveal a small garage with no vehicle inside. Garbage cans are congregated in a corner and boxes are stacked along both walls. Within this confined space it is easy to locate the blue toolbox sitting on a shelf at eye-level. The rusted box is covered with cobwebs and dust. There is no handle on top where one should be—it probably broke off ages ago. Asmara grabs each side of the casing and lifts it off the shelf. Gravity takes over and carries the dead weight toward the garage floor. She pulls back before the toolbox reaches concrete and a single metallic chime rings out.

Asmara listens to determine if the noise alerted anyone in the adjacent home. All that is heard are the hydraulics of her heartbeat.

She kneels in front of the toolbox, two latches separating her from what's contained inside. A finger-flick will determine if the world is able to be saved or whether it will be swept away.

Asmara unhooks both latches and the toolbox splits open. There is a tray on either side of the interior, each filled with nails and screws. At the bottom is a pile of various tools: screwdrivers, pliers, a hammer, and other devices. It's what is not there which causes Asmara to recoil.

Oh, my God. There's nothing here. There is no way of stopping it now.

At this point, a heart attack would put her out of her misery, yet it would not halt her transformation.

Lowering her face further into the toolbox, a thin black bag comes into view. It had been concealed beneath a tray. As she cradles the bag in her hand, Asmara's relief is spiked with despair. She tilts the rigid plastic sheath downward and two rods ease into her free hand. They are each nine inches long and have a maroon-gray color. The rods emit an aura which suggests they contain a dormant threat. Raising the deadly artifacts closer to her face, a musty odor stings her nostrils. She assumed their curved surface would have labeling but she finds none. Even a skull and crossbones warning would be confirmation.

These should say "TNT," right?

Or maybe "Danger: dynamite."

One stick has what appears to be a fuse projecting off the end. It is a dead give-away she holds dynamite. The other rod has no fuse. By chance, a roll of electrical tape is in the toolbox. She scrapes her fingernail along the black, inch-wide tape and peels off a long strip. She binds the dynamite sticks together. It is not unreasonable to believe the fuse-carrying stick will trigger an explosion in the other one as well.

Asmara does not have a sense of scale for the fireball these rods will create. Surely, the two sticks will be enough to finish the task at hand. Flesh and bone do not put up much resistance to superheated shock waves which pulverize stone. She has one chance at this and when the dynamite explodes it needs to be a final act. Nothing may remain which will allow the evil to survive.

The rods jostle and vibrate. Asmara tries to hold them tightly. Viewed up close, the rods are not moving themselves—it's her arms which shake out of fear.

Her grip on the dynamite relents and she places the sticks on the ground. The tremors and clawed hands are not her body betraying her. It is the opposite: these are acts of self preservation. Asmara's anatomy is trying to save itself from her demented thoughts.

She finds the torn edge of the electrical tape and unwinds a long strand, leaving it connected to the roll. Asmara pats the length of tape against her forehead in a horizontal line above her eyebrows. She circles the tape around her head, sticking it on top of her hair in the back and passing the roll from hand to hand as it crosses her face. With each cycle, a fresh black ribbon is laid across her forehead. As the tape makes its third time around, she reaches for the dynamite with her other hand, and presses the two sticks vertically against her right temple. The fuse dangles by her mouth and brushes against her lips.

There is no longer any shaking in her arms—they have surrendered. She continues taping around her head in the same manner as before, adding new layers of black streaks and securing the dynamite against her face. After finishing the obscene headband—a perverse crown of her own annihilation—Asmara tears off the tape and puts the roll down. She no longer needs to contemplate or even look at the dynamite. It's just... there. It is part of her and waits for whenever she is ready.

There is an undercurrent of sorrow to this situation but Asmara bears a colossal weight of responsibility. Saving all life on planet Earth is an honor. How many could ever make such a claim? Maybe fate chose her for how she would respond to this moment.

Asmara won't feel a thing when her body disintegrates—it is her friends and family who will endure the pain. They will never understand the reasoning for this sacrifice. Even if she had an opportunity to explain, no one would believe her. It would come across as the rambling of a delusional maniac.

Perhaps that's exactly what I am.

Asmara holds the cigarette lighter she brought to ignite the fuse. She is still on her knees and the discomfort of the concrete floor creeps upward. All she wants to do is experience the intake and release of deep breaths a few more times. There are beautiful nuances to breathing when it's a countdown to the end of your life.

The calming effect is short lived. Like an alarm which receded into background noise and rose again more shrill than ever, her thoughts speed up. She cannot postpone this act any longer. A planet-killing evil is at the door and Asmara herself *is* the door. She is a portal which must be closed.

Facing her own mortality, Asmara hopes her life will flash in front of her eyes. Every twist of fate would be displayed, showing how she stumbled into this crisis and is not at fault. Yet no such lifetime retrospective appears. Instead, her mind retraces the past week. A handful of recent decisions by her could have created vastly different outcomes. In each of these alternate realities, she would live a normal life. The concept of igniting a dynamite head-detonator would have been unthinkable. Now it is inevitable.

She has reached the end of a hellish path.

Of all the opportunities to have avoided this dead end, two stand out.

I should have never read that story at Word Bound.

And I should have never put that fucking spider on my face.

CHAPTER 5

(Eight days earlier)

Observing a clock as it turns to 12:00 a.m. would carry no meaning most other nights, but on this evening its significance shines. For Asmara, tonight's stroke of midnight entails a fresh start. Word Bound, the spider stunt, meeting Ryan—something happened tonight at The Naomi.

Asmara appreciates the quiet grandeur of our planet finishing a rotation on its axis and the conclusion of a day. She has a vision of Earth hurtling through space, a cosmic grain of sand with a veneer of atmosphere surrounding it. The thin blue shield protects us from waves of radiation and the icy vacuum of space. Life's successful evolution on this rock had odds stacked against it in the range of billions of planets to one. And here we are, riding atop the astronomical lottery ticket.

This fleeting moment of awe is, of course, already gone.

Ugh, I'm hungry. I gotta go to the bathroom, too.

It would be logical to re-enter The Naomi and use their bathroom but Asmara just exited the venue with high-note grace. She doesn't want to join the line of women inside waiting to relieve themselves.

Her digestive tract gives fair warning: she has a fifteen-minute window of time before emergency evacuation is required. Even though it's late, a suitable spot is next to the subway station where she's headed. It's a twenty-four-hour coffee and donut shop. The bathroom is appallingly unmaintained but it is convenient to use before descending into the toilet-less tunnels. She'll grab a snack there as well—a lemon poppyseed muffin she likes. It is devoid of nutrition and looks like it was squeezed out of a tube onto a conveyor belt. Still, it mimics food in that it occupies otherwise empty space in her stomach.

She starts walking.

Her strides not only create body heat but they enliven brain activity as well. Disjointed half-thoughts of Word Bound, a tarantula, and the faces of the group she was with tonight swirl in and out of focus. Ryan is at the forefront of this blizzard. She needs to pace herself on how much she thinks about him or her mind may spin away.

. . . .

Within two blocks Asmara is at the edge of the Tenderloin—the grimiest neighborhood in San Francisco. At its worst, this area is not merely downtrodden, it is a hellscape of addiction and mental illness.

Asmara knew that walking a direct line from The Naomi to the subway would involve the Tenderloin. She is determined to *not* avoid this rough patch of the city. She believes a steady flow of regular pedestrian foot traffic might help the neighborhood. Asmara does her part by hauling ass straight through these mean streets tonight.

Unthinking muscle memory in her arm lifts up her phone for no reason. The battery has zero charge and the zombie device demands a resurrection soon.

From out of the shadows, a voice. "Got a dollar?"

Asmara shakes her head "no" and has not a clue who spoke to her.

Twenty steps later a group of people are sprawled on the sidewalk in various slumped positions. One guy lays horizontal with his limbs extended as if he's making a snow angel on dry cement. The five are having a grand time as they are in the middle of a big laugh, even the horizontal guy. The group consists of four men and one woman and all wear what appears to be rags. These people are either naturally impervious to the cold or numb to it from the bottles of liquor lined against the wall. The glass containers form a miniature city skyline which glimmers from the streetlight above.

"Har-huh! Har-huh!" The woman of the group has a laugh like she's gargling pebbles.

As Asmara passes by, the woman throws an arm around the man she's leaning against, pulls him toward herself, and kisses the top of his greasy head with an emphatic "Mmm-whah!" The woman playfully shoves the guy back into his previous position against the wall.

Asmara guesses the kiss recipient is the one who said something funny and he received his rightful reward. It was a nice moment and the scene paralleled her own evening: they both were a social gathering among peers and included drinks, laughs, and flirtation.

She keeps walking and the lights of Market Street ahead of her serve as a beacon. The thoroughfare means she will be enjoying intestinal relief soon. This biological requirement is likely to involve sheer euphoria. Leaving the bonds of Earth and soaring above the city in joyous satisfaction will be a real possibility.

"Are you a cop?" Another voice from the shadows.

A hunched, old man emerges into the light and his limbs are all at unnatural angles. He shuffles toward her with pigeon-toed feet. One arm is raised to his shoulder with his wrist dangling limp at the elbow. It's as if he has an arm draped over an imaginary friend.

This poor individual has been contorted by some full-body disability, the likes of which Asmara has not seen before.

"You look like you're fresh out of the police academy," he says. "You out here walking your first undercover beat?"

The questions are not hostile for they are spoken with a smile. His face brightens in surprise as she slows to a stop.

"Nah, you're too pretty to be a cop," he says. "The way your hands are jammed into your jacket—cops walk like that. You gotta loosen up, baby."

The form of her upper-body is standard posture to Asmara, especially on a cold night. She takes her hands out of the jacket and lets them drop to her sides.

"How about like this?" she asks.

The man leans back to appraise the adjustment.

"I changed my mind," he says. "You know, the Tenderloin don't play. Out here maybe a lady *should* walk like a cop. It'll keep the wolves away. Get them hands back in there!"

It was an amusing reversal and Asmara gives a smile, aware of what comes next.

"Hey..." he says, his voice becoming low and serious.

As predictable as a sunset.

"Any chance you gotta extra buck?"

Asmara never developed a consistent philosophy with panhandling. She generally declines without deliberation. There are times, however, when her defenses get lowered.

"Yeah, I got a buck," she says.

Asmara dips her hand into her pants pocket and pulls out a ten-dollar bill. They both stare at it for a moment. It's the only cash she has tonight.

Damn it. There goes my muffin.

Asmara once read about poverty voyeurism—exposing oneself to destitution to feel the rush of relief as you re-enter your life of comfort. Maybe this ten-spot is the price of admission.

She hands him the bill.

"I couldn't take the whole thing from you," he says, digging around in his jacket. He drops into her palm two filthy dollar bills which are crumpled into balls. They look like dark-green bird eggs.

"That's my way of saying thanks," the man says.

The idea of receiving cash back from her charitable gesture strikes Asmara as not just unusual, but unprecedented.

"Cool. I'm gonna grab a muffin," Asmara says as she closes a fist around the money.

CHAPTER 6

A warm rush of air ushers Asmara into the coffeeshop. Savory smells of fried donuts circulate around her. It explains why this dingy establishment has not invested in decor or a flashy storefront—they don't need to. A jet stream of enticing aromas convince people they crave sugary fuel.

Asmara scans the food selection. It is a scene of anti-health. There does not appear to be a single natural ingredient in this place.

Not so fast.

A lonely basket on the far counter has ancient-looking apples and oranges in it. The mummified fruits were last stirred from their still-life composition during the Loma Prieta earthquake in 1989.

Asmara eyes the glass display case in search of a muffin. The old woman behind the counter frowns either with impatience in the moment or displeasure at the world itself, or both. There is one lemon poppyseed muffin which stands tall among the field of glazed donuts. Asmara orders and pays with the two wadded-up dollars she was handed on the street. The bills resist being flattened and act as if they want to curl back up like a pair of armadillos.

The old woman is not amused as she tries palm-pressing the cash into submission so they're able to slide into the cash register.

"Hrrm," the woman grunts, her frown becoming even more pronounced.

Asmara leaves the muffin on the counter as she does not want to risk contamination in the bathroom. "I'm going to leave this here for second. I'll be right back."

"Hrrm."

. . . .

After attending to her needs, Asmara exits the bathroom back into the brightly-lit coffee shop. Her prediction of euphoric flight doesn't come to pass but she does feel like she played Frisbee with God, received a neck massage from an angel, and has returned to Earth reborn.

The woman behind the counter gives her a wary expression, as if Asmara did drugs.

Deal with it, lady. I AM high.

Asmara grabs the muffin and takes a seat.

A nearby table has a mound of newspapers and magazines strewn about. Most everyone stares at their phone these days (three other people in the coffeeshop are doing just that), so it is refreshing to have printed material free for customers. A science magazine catches her eye with its cover showing a radiant, detailed photo of a planet. To be exact, it is a moon of a planet. Its name is Europa and it orbits Jupiter. She is informed of this because the cover copy reads:

"EUROPA—Ten exclusive images from the Caerus space probe inside. Jupiter's moon may be the most interesting place in our solar system. Move over, Earth!"

Somewhere, perhaps everywhere, astronomers are cringing at those words. Even by the standards of hyperbole used to sell magazines, to call this unexplored moon more interesting than Earth is a quantum leap of speculation, not to mention an ungrateful cheap-shot against our home planet. The obnoxious cover tries to manipulate her into inspecting the magazine further and it succeeds as she grabs the issue.

Europa shines brilliantly against the featureless backdrop of space. With no context for its size, the perfect sphere looks like a luminescent white marble streaked with a network of thin brown lines and reddish smudges. There's no cloudy atmosphere to conceal the moon's icy surface, so the web of cracks are an intimate view at another world laid bare, or at least its frozen eggshell.

While soaking in the cover image, Asmara's memory gets sparked about this space mission. It had been in the news months ago when the unmanned Caerus probe had successfully locked into orbit around Europa and sent back images. The event was big news at first and she read about it with sheer fascination. However, the news cycle has to move along and Asmara doesn't recall seeing anything about the mission again.

This journey to a Jupiterian moon required a decade of planning, half a billion dollars, and six years of travel to cross 390 million miles. There also was exquisite, rocket-fueled mathematical precision necessary to cozy into Europa's orbit. However, the space-exploration triumph was no match for mankind's short attention span. The world forgot about Caerus soon after it reached its destination.

The exclusive photos inside the magazine aren't much different than the cover. There's only so many ways to capture images when you're in orbit around a celestial body. It boggles her mind that this is not a computer-generated simulation of Europa, nor the fanciful guesswork of an artist. She is viewing one of Jupiter's moons as it exists and how it would be seen with the naked eye. Amazing.

Asmara jumps around within the article and speed reads some sidebars. Even if these spacecraft were cheap (which they're not) and you launched one hundred of them every year for a decade (which is not feasible), it would *still* be a miraculous, hail-Mary bullseye to hurl a Volkswagen-sized probe into space and have it join a gentle dance around Europa.

On either side of the magazine, remnants of her muffin lay scattered on the table. Asmara devoured the whole thing without enjoying a single bite. There is a weight in her belly but the sensation is an illusion of nourishment. As her stomach tries to digest this processed lump it will realize it has been swindled. Demand for real food will produce an angry growl soon.

It's time to head home.

Asmara has an impulse to take this magazine with her. The Europa article captured her attention and she would like to read into it more. Asmara flips back to the cover and a small subscription sticker reads "All-Nite Quality Coffee." After years of visiting this place and polluting its bathroom, she never knew the coffeeshop's proper name.

Asmara abhors theft, even at this mundane level. If everyone stole the reading material, the coffeeshop would stop providing it. One option is to ask the woman behind the counter if the magazine can be borrowed, but that would create maximum awkwardness. Asmara pictures the woman's frown becoming so severe at the request her face falls off.

How about I borrow it without asking?

There is an ethical issue in turning the reading table into a personal library. However, the dilemma doesn't produce enough guilt to make her abort the plan. The magazine is concealed in her jacket as she strides toward the door.

"All right, thank you," Asmara says with cheer as she exits the shop. She moves briskly and hopes for a head start in case an anti-theft alarm starts shrieking or a shotgun blast tries to stop this daring heist.

The old woman behind the counter looks up.

"Hrrm."

CHAPTER 7

Within seconds of leaving the coffeeshop, Asmara bounds down the nearby subway stairs to catch a train home. The cold air doesn't get a chance to harass her before she slips into the warm underground network. She half-wished the old woman would have chased her for stealing the magazine. The only adrenaline rush now is the gamble of what kind of weirdos may be lurking in the tube below.

Local SF bus routes give her travel options but the Bay Area Rapid Transit train lines, serving the wider region, will take her in the same direction sooner. Any train going East suits her, so she's in a good position for a speedy lift to the Embarcadero station. From there she has a pleasant walk to her apartment at the base of Telegraph Hill.

An electronic display states an Antioch train arrives in two minutes. Her tense shoulder muscles loosen.

A scattering of people are spaced across the station platform, giving each other maximum room to avoid human interaction. No weirdos in the bunch. Subway hours were extended last year and most late-night riders have a peaceful dignity, giving the tunnel a monastery feel.

The train arrives.

She picks a seat near the door and sits bolt upright. There's three stops until her station so she doesn't want to slouch into long-commute mode. As the train gains speed, her body sways and visions of her eventful evening bounce in her head. At one of the stations, the doors open and no one enters or exits her train car. But a voice cries out.

"Yo! You gotta run!"

A lanky teenager has materialized outside the train's open door and he shouts at his friends as they hurry toward him. It appears he is much faster than his companions because they have eighty feet to go. He leans his back into one side of the train's doorframe and extends his leg against the other side. He prepares to resist the closing door. Behind him, two teen boys give an honest effort as they sprint through the station. If they were strolling toward the train or, God forbid, sauntering, Asmara would be annoyed. The real issue will be the ear-piercing shriek the train unleashes when a door is held ajar. And the alarm is coming, right about...

"EEEEEEEEEPPP!"

The teens stumble into the train, pushing the door-holder's raised leg aside like a turnstile. With clanking gears, the door angrily closes behind them, as if it knew transit rules were broken.

Gasping laughter overtakes the trio of boys.

"Ahh! I'm outta shape."

"I've never seen you run before!" the door-holder says. "Not even once!"

He does an impression of his friend's frantic running. As an impartial witness, Asmara notes the mimicry is accurate.

The train starts moving and certain details of the station catch her eye. Something's not right. This isn't Montgomery—her second-to-last stop. It's Embarcadero.

Those kids distracted me. I missed my stop.

Embarcadero is SF's last subway station before the train continues to Oakland. She has committed to a three-and-a-half-mile long tunnel ride beneath the San Francisco Bay. The journey is fifteen minutes, one way. With the waiting time to catch a returning train and the extra ride itself, she added forty minutes to her commute.

In an attempt to blame anyone other than herself, Asmara glares at the boys who are still laughing like hyenas. She is upset for a few seconds and the feeling passes. It's not difficult to catch a returning train.

Conceding this tunnel has kidnapped her for the next fifteen minutes, the unexpected reroute perks up her energy. She takes stock of the train cabin to observe what kind of people are heading to Oakland tonight. She doesn't complete a full glance over her seat before her head whips back forward.

Is that him?

The guy was looking down during her first glimpse, so she risks another head turn. Asmara peeks over her seat as the man makes eye contact with her.

She is staring straight at Ryan.

Asmara swivels forward again, panics at the poor decision, and turns back with a smile to match the one he is giving.

"Hey!" she says.

"Hi!"

Ryan stands up from his seat and, carrying the skateboard he had earlier, sits next to her.

"What's up?" he says.

"Not much. Nice to see you again."

Asmara hopes the train's harsh, unforgiving light is flattering to her. His eyes are striking when seen up close. There is something peculiar about them she cannot place.

"I didn't expect to see you again so soon," she says. "Sorry for the double take I gave you. I wasn't sure if that was you."

"Ha, no worries. So, where did you go after The Naomi?"

"I went to a coffeeshop, read for a while, and then hopped on the train. What about you? Did the scarf work any magic for you?"

"Hey, I got your number didn't I?"

"Yes, you did."

"I'm joking. There's no pressure. We can hopefully hang out. I barely meet people anymore and you seem cool."

To Asmara, somewhere in his statement might reside an insult. She doesn't analyze it.

"Your two friends are nice," Ryan says.

"I've known them since college. We try to meet up in order to not drift apart. So, you were with your bike-shop crew tonight?"

"Yeah. I see Amy a lot, so it wasn't unusual to be with her. However, it was strange to go out with the two contractor guys doing our remodel. We've been working hard on the new store and we wanted to grab a drink."

Now is a good opening for her to ask what Ryan does at the bike store but she lets it pass. Maybe they will forge a years-long relationship without ever inquiring about each others' employment.

"So," he says. "What do you do, Asmara?"

You gotta be kidding.

"Well, I managed a screen-printing business for a long time. I'm now waiting to find out if I got a job at this website app-thing which features freelance writers and artists."

"Nice. Sounds cool."

See, that wasn't so bad.

"So," he says. "You're not working now?"

For fuck's sake!

"No, I'm enjoying a break in between the two jobs. It feels good to not be shackled for a change."

"Enjoy your time off. I hope you get the gig. You might be... wait," Ryan pauses in thought. "Earlier tonight you said you lived in SF. Why are you going to the East Bay?"

"This is embarrassing, but I missed my stop."

"Really? You're not supposed to go to Oakland?"

"No. I'll grab a train back to SF after the tunnel."

Ryan's face migrates into a grimace.

"What?" Asmara asks.

He keeps making the damned face. "You may still have a chance."

Ryan yanks his phone from his pocket. "It's past one o'clock," he says. "You might have a problem."

"Why?"

"The last train heading to SF left Oakland ten minutes ago. There are no more trains running in either direction tonight."

"You're not serious."

"I am. There's a maintenance project in the tunnel all weekend. They've had notices about it for weeks. You didn't hear the conductor on the intercom at Embarcadero? He said last stop, no returning trains."

"I didn't hear that."

Asmara had heard noise coming from the train's speakers but to her it was a mumbling robot.

Ryan gets out of his seat and leans toward a sheet of paper taped near the door. Like an optical illusion coming into focus, more of these same flyers throughout the cabin emerge from nothingness. Or, more likely, they were present the whole time and escaped her attention.

"Yeah," Ryan says, peering at the updated schedule. "There are no trains in either direction until Sunday night."

"Unbelievable."

"Don't worry," Ryan says. "We'll get you back to SF. You can get a ride share."

"My phone is dead. I have no cash for a cab."

"I'll order a ride for you. No problem."

Having Ryan witness her flounder in modern-life's quicksand aggravates Asmara, but none of this is existential.

"West Oakland is my stop," Ryan says. "Let's get off there."

There is more light talk between them about The Naomi and how Asmara convinced a guy to properly dispose of cigarette butts. The moment they reach the West Oakland station, Ryan starts tapping on his phone.

"Yikes. My battery is also low."

They are the only two to exit the train. As they stand outside on the platform, the cold air confirms to Asmara this night has stretched too long. Her bed calls to her with a siren song from across the bay. Or maybe it's the wind.

Ryan develops a faster phone-tapping pace. "Okay, so where are you going in SF? I'm worried my battery isn't even..."

His eyes bulge. "Ugh! My phone died. I swear."

He stares at the expired device in his hand and shows her the blank screen. "I can give you a ride. I have a car at my place, I just didn't drive it tonight."

"You mean you'd drive all the way to SF, drop me off, and come back to Oakland? No, I couldn't have you do that. I'll find someone who has a phone charger."

The absurdity of her words float in the air of this desolate train platform.

"There's no way I'm leaving you here," Ryan says.

He exhales in a manner which indicates impatience.

"Thank you so much," Asmara says. "Let's go."

CHAPTER 8

Asmara and Ryan are a few hundred feet out of the train station when he puts his skateboard down, stands on it, and rolls alongside her. She is surprised the board doesn't produce the usual clickety-clack noises. Ryan explains how soft wheels are quieter.

When she does not look at his feet, there is an effect that he levitates like a floating genie. His skateboard is the magic carpet ride.

This scenario might have been embarrassing—her an adult woman escorted by a grown man on a skateboard. Yet he is so at ease on the board it calms her insecurities. It's likely if Ryan knew she had a problem with his skateboard, he would be unmoved. That would be something she needs to sort out, not him.

"How long have you been skating?" Asmara asks.

"My whole life," he says. "I've slowed down, though. As soon as I hit thirty, my body started unraveling. My injuries don't heal anymore, they pile on top of each other."

Ryan serves, on a skateboard platter, a chance for Asmara to ask his age. Even though she was near to him on the train, it is difficult to pinpoint how old he is. She will shudder in disappointment if he declares an elderly number above thirty-five.

"I'm not surprised skating gets tougher as you age," Asmara says. "Imagine how you'll feel at forty. How old are you now?"

Maybe he already is forty. What will we talk about? Ronald Reagan? The 1988 Olympics?

He opens his mouth to speak.

Say any number under forty and I'll marry you, you son of a bitch.

"I'm thirty-two," he says.

She expects Ryan to ask her age but he doesn't.

"I live on the end of this block," he says. "We're almost there."

Their pace of movement keeps Asmara's blood flowing and the night chill loses its bite. They are on a quiet residential street. He steps off the skateboard and lets it coast to a stop in front of her.

"Do you want to take a spin?" he asks.

Asmara is indifferent to the contraption but it's an opportunity to show she's not a delicate bore. She steps on the board, gives a push and rolls along. There is motion but no real thrill. It's as captivating as the moving sidewalk at an airport.

"After all these years, do you still have fun on this?" she asks.

"I like being on the board, but I can't do a fraction of what I used to do."

"So, most of the fun is in the tricks?"

"Yeah. A lot of the satisfaction is learning new challenges and figuring out board control. It involves painful trial and error."

"How many tricks can you do?"

"Ha! I've never been asked that. It hasn't occurred to me to add them up."

"Maybe I should learn one trick and you will be inspired to learn new ones yourself. Does me not dying count as a trick?""

"Definitely." He stops in the middle of the road. "We're here."

Asmara is not sure what "here" consists of. They look in the direction of where a house would logically be located. However, a large oak tree with low-hanging branches obscures the area. There is also no outdoor lighting at this address.

Ryan notices her hesitation. "Yeah, it's kind of dark. I need to get the front light fixed. And the tree is... Uh."

He looks around at the row of parked cars down the street. She follows his lead, unclear of what she's scouting for.

Ryan runs his fingers through his hair. "Ho. Lee. Shit."

"What? Just say it."

"I forgot that I let my roommate borrow my car tonight."

Asmara sighs. The longer they are forced together like this the more likely they will become irritated with each other. It's tough to smile through an unnaturally prolonged first impression.

She's also disappointed he has a roommate. But considering she has one herself, as does most of her unmarried friends in the expensive Bay Area, she can't hold it against him.

"When is he coming back?" Asmara asks.

"He's staying at his girlfriend's place tonight. He's not coming back until tomorrow."

The twists of this unusual night have included one suspicious turn too many. Asmara does not consider herself paranoid but since she's stranded outside the unlit home of a guy she met three hours ago, she needs to monitor her safety.

Could a psychopath orchestrate tonight's chain of events, leading up to me entering his dark house?

"I'll tell you what," Ryan says. "Let's charge your phone and we'll get you a ride share. You can either wait inside, or if you don't want to go into my spooky haunted house, you can wait out here."

He again anticipated her concerns. This soothing ability was perhaps honed by outwitting his previous murder victims, whose skulls are stacked in the backyard.

"Another option," he says, "and I will throw this out there, is you can stay over. I have a pull-out bed in the living room. I'll have my car back in the morning and I can give you a ride."

Asmara is too much in shock at those words to risk-assess the situation. Ryan speaks up again. "I'm not an idiot. You have every right to be hesitant and I'm not offended. We also can charge your phone and have you take a photo of my face and my driver's license. You can send the images to people you know, explaining how you're ensuring your safety at a stranger's house. What kind of dangerous maniac would I be if I allowed all that evidence?"

"It would mean you're an incompetent maniac," she says. "And those are the scariest maniacs of all."

He pulls out his wallet and removes his driver's license. "Here, take it. Snap a photo of it when your phone's ready."

She takes note of his full name. "Ryan Q Smith? That's the most fake name I've ever seen. If you're going to kidnap people you've got to get a better fake ID."

"Ha! Honestly, if there's any other steps I can take to put your mind at ease, please let me know."

The personality wavelength he's been emitting all night makes it impossible to view him as a threat. She's sold.

"Okay, I'll stay," Asmara says. "I'd normally never do this. However, I can tell you're a decent guy and I appreciate the offer."

His face shows a flicker of happy surprise but he masks it with calm confidence. "All right, there's plenty of blankets for you. Previous guests all said the pull-out is comfortable. This will be fine."

"Is your middle name really the letter Q?"

"Yeah, it is. I have weird parents."

They walk toward the large tree, duck beneath low branches, and there is indeed a one-story house on the other side. Ryan opens the front door and before he turns on the light Asmara says a prayer to the patron saint of bachelors with messy homes. Saint Chore Calendar guides wayward men toward presentable living conditions.

Please don't be a shithole...

The home interior fills with light and Asmara is relieved at the appearance of a tidy living room. No wrinkled posters thumbtacked to the wall, no dirty dishes piled around a video game console. He has nice furnishings and even a couple of tasteful house plants. There is a large and well-stocked bookshelf against the wall.

"Are you hungry or would you like any water?" Ryan asks.

"No, thanks. I'm going to crash."

"Me, too."

Ryan pulls on the couch frame and it flattens into a bed. As he completes the transformation his strong forearms catch Asmara's attention. He walks into a nearby room and emerges with an enormous pile of blankets. They're even folded.

"Thank you," Asmara says. "I do have one request, though. Can I borrow some toothpaste or mouthwash?"

"Sure. I have an extra toothbrush still in its package."

"That would be nice. Do you want to hear something crazy?"

"Of course."

"People don't believe me, but I've never forgotten to clean my teeth before I went to bed. Not once in my life."

"I don't want to be responsible for breaking the streak tonight."

Ryan walks down the hall as Asmara spreads the blankets on the bed. Sleep is imminent. And yet... might something happen tonight between them? If her three-year drought is ever going to end it might as well be in the clean home of a cute guy she would like to date anyway.

No, it's too soon. There is an absurdity in that she contemplated if he was dangerous one minute ago.

"These are for you," Ryan says, handing her toothpaste and a packaged toothbrush.

As she reaches to take the items Asmara tries to give him a flirtatious look. She aborts the mission for his eyes are bloodshot and half-closed.

"I left a light on in the hallway," Ryan says. "There's a bathroom on the left."

"Sounds good."

"I wake up around eight but I'll get up earlier if you want."

"No, that should work."

"My roommate will be back in the morning. I'll give you a ride then. Also, there's a phone charger under the table."

"You've handled everything. Thanks again so much."

"No problem," he says, displaying a new smile variation from the other ones she has seen tonight.

Is that something? Is that my opening?

"Goodnight," Ryan says as he turns and walks down the hall.

. . . .

After brushing her teeth, Asmara lays down on the pull-out bed and burrows into the mountain of blankets. Like a power grid which is shut down methodically in sections, parts of her brain signal goodnight as they turn off the lights.

A mutinous stray thought catches her attention. It is a reminder that when she was young and slept in new places, especially ones with doors and hallways all around, she tends to have bad dreams. There's a loss of sleep security for her when a room has this much potential for people to enter and exit. It's been years since this was an issue, but the seed has been planted for a self-fulfilling bad dream.

The nightmare gathers steam as it prepares for showtime. Her best hope is to outmaneuver the bad dream by falling deep into REM sleep before the nightmare sinks in its hooks.

The ominous visions close in as she fades to black.

Tomorrow will reveal if she avoided the dreadful visitation.

CHAPTER 9

Asmara is wrenched out of sleep and catapulted into a wide-awake state by the noise of two kitchen plates colliding.

She has to prod her memory to recollect how she arrived in the unfamiliar room. A montage of her previous night plays out—from The Naomi to the train to Ryan's place in Oakland.

From her perspective, she had surrendered to sleep a moment ago. During a mere eye blink the room went from dark to now filled with sunlight. Blue skies are visible through the living room window. Asmara sits upright on the pull-out bed and cranes her neck toward the kitchen where the crash came from. Ryan peeks around the corner.

"Sorry," he says. "I was trying to be quiet and I instead hit those plates. So much for letting you sleep in."

"It's fine."

He holds up a box of waffles. "I'm about to get started on some food if you're interested."

The frozen carbohydrates are not a romantic sensual meal, but it's better than him pouring two bowls of children's cereal. "Sure, I'll eat. Thanks."

Asmara breaks free of the bed and folds the blankets. Her creaky limbs are stubborn and the movements are hard labor.

A dream lingers in her thoughts. It doesn't have the eerie aftershock of a nightmare. It's just... a vision. The details are out of focus.

Before she heads to the kitchen Asmara eyes the bathroom door. She would normally give herself an appraisal in the mirror, yet this morning her swagger outweighs any insecurity. Asmara and her tousled hair bounce into the kitchen.

"Be honest," she says. "Did you bang those plates together on purpose because I was snoring?"

"I would never do that. Well, I would do it if you were annoying and a dude. You are neither of those things."

Ryan is wearing snug shorts. "Is your upper body as hairy as your legs?" she asks.

"Geez. You don't like my Chewbacca limbs?"

"I was just curious."

"Well, my fur coat is my business but, no, I don't consider it unusually thick up top. By the way, I texted my roommate and he'll be back soon with my car."

"All righty."

"How did you sleep?"

"I had a strange dream. I sense it, although the details are vague."

"If you don't remember soon, it's going to fade away. Sometimes a reference will pop up while you're awake and spark memories of the dream."

"Yeah, I was hoping for that."

"Let me throw out some ideas. Maybe one will help you remember."

"I don't think that will work. Who does this?"

"In the dream, were you flying?"

"No."

"Falling?"

"No."

"Being chased?"

"Let me think... No."

"Was I in it?"

"No."

"Were you at The Naomi?"

"No."

"On the train?"

"No."

"How about..."

"Wait! Yeah, part of the dream was on the train. You're right. How did you do that?"

"I guessed but there's logic to it as well. I figured some part of last night would sneak into your dream. So, how was the train incorporated into the mix?"

"It's hard to describe. I was in the tunnel between SF and Oakland. The train was empty except for myself and one other woman... Ah, weird. It's coming to me."

The dream memory, which had been disintegrating, cobbles itself back together. The other woman on the train is looking out a window. An ominous energy hangs in the enclosed space. Asmara approaches her from behind to make contact. She doesn't want to interact with this person but the dream commands it. With each step, a sense of dread adds weight to her legs. There is an excruciating build-up of tension as the reveal nears. Asmara reaches to touch the woman's shoulder and the stranger whips her head around...

Gasp!

Back in the kitchen, her heart races. Asmara shivers in revulsion.

"Shit," she barks out loud. "I *did* have a nightmare."

"You sound surprised."

"When I was young and slept in rooms with open doors and hallways I would get bad dreams. I thought I outgrew the habit but I guess not."

"What about this other passenger? How did it become a nightmare?"

Asmara doesn't want to describe how the woman's face was not human. It was covered in giant, brown hairs—as big as porcupine quills. Where her mouth should be, she had grinding mandibles instead of a jaw. Protruding from this orifice were six-inch-long hooked fangs. The stranger also had a series of reflective black orbs for eyes, like a spider.

A tarantula.

"Oh, it was nothing," Asmara says to Ryan. "It was... strange. "

. . . .

Ryan and Asmara dance around each other in the kitchen as he gathers breakfast items and she moves out of his way. She should sit at the table and give him room but she likes this close proximity. He doesn't appear to mind the crowded space, either. It is obvious she should offer to lend a hand, but Asmara enjoys watching him prepare the food. At one point she blocks his way and he puts his hands on her bare forearms to swivel past her. The warm contact is over in an instant and yet their first touch is significant. She finds herself craving more.

They are soon seated and biting into waffles and fruit. It occurs to Asmara she never did help with breakfast. Ryan waves off her apology with a swipe of his fork.

After they finish eating and cleaning dishes they head to the living room. Conversation has been steady and it is light in nature so Asmara doesn't have to analyze everything said. By spending an intimate morning in his home, she has leapfrogged several relationship steps. As a bonus, she entered this comfort zone without the baggage of hooking up with him last night.

While continuing to talk, Asmara stands and investigates his bookshelf. "You're a reader," she says. "Are these books a mix of you and your roommate's?"

"Those are mine. I've known Evan for three years and he's never cracked open a book."

She traces her finger along the titles and they are a broad mix of fiction and non-fiction. Asmara spots a section of books which consist of old-looking horror and science fiction paperbacks.

"You read those when you were in high school, didn't you?" she asks, pointing at the grouped genres.

"Even earlier," he says. "Middle school. What? You think I'm too old to be reading *Blood Moon Paradox?* Werewolves versus vampires never gets old. Just ask Shakespeare."

A thin book among the others is out of place. Asmara pulls it from the shelf and it appears to be cheaply self-published, weighing in at ninety pages or less. There is no art on the cover, only block letters colored yellow on dark gray. The author's name jumps out before she reads the title.

By Ryan Smith. That's odd, but there's thousands of these guys.

Asmara lifts the book to show Ryan the coincidence and his face makes a pinched reaction—as if he's stifling the pain of a knife wound.

It's his. He wrote this!

She reads the cover title out loud. *"Rain Rising Over An Oakland Horizon* by Ryan Smith."

Ryan's face has an unrestrained grimace, stuck in place like a stone gargoyle. Without using words, he's begging her to slip the book back on the shelf.

"Here's the deal," she says. "I'm taking this and I'm going to read it. I'll finish it by tomorrow. You cannot stop me."

"Please, no. It's truly bad."

"I don't care."

"Of all the books, you had to grab that one. I was an idiot when I wrote it."

"How old were you?"

"I was twenty-two. I printed one hundred copies my senior year of college."

"Really? That's awesome."

"It's an inflated short story bursting at the seams with filler. That thing is garbage. I was pretending to be a writer at the time."

"If you finished it and printed it, that's not pretending. This will be a time capsule back into your mind when you were that age."

"That's exactly why I don't want you to read it."

Asmara is sympathetic to Ryan's concern because she has written stories she'd never share. And yet, tough luck for him. This is the risk you run if your self-published work is on display in your living room.

"I was a bitter, angry guy back then," Ryan says.

"At twenty-two?"

"Yeah. I was sour about everything. I was into a lot of pessimism porn."

"Yuck. What's that?"

"It's not actual porn. It's the thing where you read articles and seek viewpoints about how humans are rotten and mankind is a mistake. You wallow in negativity."

"And you start to almost enjoy feeling bad, right?"

"Exactly. My dumb book is a real Debbie Downer. You won't get past page fifteen without throwing it across the room. There's a bunch of typos in it, as well."

Asmara slides her palm across the bland, gray cover. She has been warned about its contents and perhaps he is not indulging in false modesty. He comes across as sincere that the book is terrible.

Ah, so be it.

It's a short read and it'll be fun to wander around the mind of a young Ryan, even if he managed to become jaded at a young age. She's just thrilled he's a reader and a writer.

"I'm going to borrow this book anyway," Asmara says. "I will take into account you were a sullen author at the time you wrote it. I won't hold it against you."

"Okay."

"You seem content and even like an upbeat guy. What made you stop being so angry?"

Ryan's eyes narrow. He's either trying to formulate a response tailored for her or he's never considered the question until now.

"I had to change. The anger nearly killed me."

CHAPTER 10

Before Asmara follows up on Ryan's morbid statement there is a rumble on the street outside followed by a familiar "thwack!"

It's a skateboard.

Asmara steps toward the window and, in the daylight, the front-yard tree has clearance which she is able to see through. She spots a skinny boy in his mid-teens, baseball hat pulled low over his face, jogging to catch a skateboard which escaped from him. The boy scoops up the board and hops on for another ride. He crouches low and another "thwack" is emitted as the board rotates beneath him—unsuccessfully, for he is again chasing the wayward device.

Asmara has seen this routine among skaters. This is how they learn to manipulate those things and it must be a tedious endeavor.

"Hey, there's a skater out here," Asmara says to Ryan.

"Yeah, that's my neighbor."

"How are you sure without looking?"

"I'm sure of it."

The boy stomps his foot on the disobedient board to secure it from rolling away and he pulls out a phone. His thumbs twitch a series of taps.

A phone vibrates behind Asmara and she turns. Ryan reads a message and writes a response of his own.

"How random," she says. "The kid out front sent a text and your phone buzzed right after."

"Yeah, I know. She messaged me."

"She? No, this skater out front is a boy."

"That's Zoe. She's a girl. I hope you don't mind but she's coming over."

Asmara peers through the window again and the teen with a skateboard is walking toward Ryan's house.

"Don't worry, she's a cool kid," Ryan says. "I used to see her skate by herself. I felt bad and started rolling around with her. Now we're buddies."

Asmara warms at the thought of Ryan giving attention to a neglected neighborhood tomboy. Amid the glow, however, she is not thrilled about meeting a teenager. It is often an obnoxious age.

"With this kid," Asmara says, "do you view it like a mentorship?"

"Not at all. There's no schedule and it's not like I'm doing charity. I just like skating with her."

"How old is she?"

"Uh, I don't know."

"How could you not know?"

"I never asked. Or maybe I asked and forgot. Oh, she's in ninth grade. So, whatever age that is."

The front door flings open without a knock, Zoe marches in and she leans her skateboard against the wall. It's not until the girl does a diving flop onto the couch that she sees Asmara. Zoe looks over at Ryan and breaks into a grin. He shakes his head in disapproval at whatever she is thinking or about to say. She snorts a laugh.

"I'm sorry," Zoe says. "I've never seen Ryan have a girl over before."

Her skateboard crashes onto the ground after tumbling over.

So far, so annoying.

"I'm Zoe."

"Hi, I'm Asmara."

"I live across the street. Ryan said he was going to take me skating today, that's why I came over."

"Sounds like fun."

"He used to be a really good skater. I bet he didn't tell you that."

"No, he didn't."

"He never admits it to anyone so I do the bragging for him. There's videos of him online."

Zoe takes off her hat and throws it on the coffee table. As her chin-length hair tumbles down, her boyishness recedes.

"So, what do you do?" Zoe asks.

There's that damn question. From a ninth grader, no less.

"I'm hoping to start work on this app which pairs together artists and writers."

"Nice. So you're not working now?"

Asmara almost growls. Words come out instead. "I have things going on, but I'm mostly waiting for that gig."

"Cool. I'm making a website in my media class."

"What is it about?"

"You know how you see cars that have been keyed? Like, deliberate scratches through the paint?"

"Yeah."

"Well, I'm finding as many of them as I can, taking photos of the damage, and I'm interviewing the car owners to see how it happened. Then I'm making an online spreadsheet of the results."

Asmara wasn't expecting to be impressed by a middle school project, but the idea has a nice hook. Whenever she sees those thin lines cleaved into a car's exterior she has been curious what prompted the vandalism.

"Did you come up with the idea on your own?"

"Yup. We were asked to report on something in our community which doesn't get enough attention and I came up with that."

"You walk up to people and ask how it happened?"

"Yeah. Or I leave a note which explains the project and asks them to call me." She reaches in her pocket and pulls out paper slips. "I'm creating a list of all the different reasons for the scratches. I have twenty-six responses so far."

"What a cool project. How many people call you from the notes you leave?"

"Not many. It's better to wait until they arrive back at their car and ask them in person. It helps because I speak Spanish. Mexicans are the most willing to tell the stories about how they got keyed."

"What are the reasons they tell you?"

"Some people say they don't know why it happened. Others bought a used car that already had scratches. The main reasons are parking disputes. I sometimes get a crazy story about who did it and why. Those usually involve a crazy boyfriend or girlfriend."

"Have you had any bad experiences collecting data?"

"One time a guy asked me if I'm a cop and he wasn't kidding. That's hilarious, the idea of a cop being my age."

"Ha! I got asked if I was cop last night, too. So, I know how you feel."

They harmonize a laugh together.

. . . .

Through the window, two cars are seen pulling in front of the house. Asmara guesses one must be Ryan's roommate. A young man hops out of the first car and notices her in the window. He gives the stranger in his home a quizzical look—maybe he's never seen Ryan bring a girl home, either.

"I think your roommate is here," Asmara says.

Ryan walks up to the window and nods in agreement as the guy dangles car keys in his hand. The keys are placed above the driver's side door and Ryan gives a thumbs up. Instead of a reciprocal thumb, the guy in the street gives an exaggerated double first pump. It is a "congratulations on bringing a girl home" seal of approval. The guy slips into the passenger side of the other car and it speeds off.

"That was lame," Ryan says. "Sorry about that."

"Yeah, not very subtle with me standing right here."

"I'll tell him nothing happened. I promise. I can text him."

"Don't worry about it. He must have been in a hurry."

"No, he's inconsiderate. He couldn't walk to hand me the keys, now I have to go get them."

Ryan leaves through the front door and heads toward his car. Asmara turns from the window and is startled by Zoe who is beside her.

"Do you want to see something awesome?" Zoe asks.

"Yes, I do."

Zoe goes to the bookshelf, pulls out a large hardcover and flips through it. The book is filled with skateboarding photos.

"Here," Zoe says. She walks up to Asmara displaying her find and shoves the book forward. A single photo covers the two-page spread but Asmara is not clear what she is looking at. It's a downtown setting— the foreground is filled with marble and concrete. The background is a wall of overlapping buildings. Within this urban environment a skateboarder hovers high in the air.

"What do you think?" Zoe says.

"I don't know. It looks like it would be difficult."

"Do you recognize anything?"

"No. Should I?"

"That's Ryan!"

Asmara calibrates the facial features and adjusts for age.

It is him.

"For God's sake," Ryan says as he returns through the door and spots them holding the book. "Zoe, I don't need a cheerleader."

"The photo is sick. You should be proud of it."

"It is pretty sick," Asmara adds, semi-confident in her usage of the word.

"Ryan, tell her the story behind it," Zoe says.

"No."

"Okay, I will. So, ten years ago Ryan ollied from that ledge there," Zoe points to a spot on the photo, "to that ledge over there. It's in downtown San Francisco by City Hall."

With the helpful cues, the image starts to make sense to Asmara.

"The ledge he lands on is very skinny," Zoe says. "It's only as wide as his wheels. He rode the ledge to the end and hopped off, all while going super fast."

"Cool."

"The best part is that skaters have been trying to duplicate what he did for a decade and no one has done it. The trick is called Ryan's Line to this day."

"That's amazing. What an accomplishment."

Asmara reads the photo caption out loud. "Mr. Smith forges his spot in skate history with Ryan's Line and the Holy Grail of psycho roll-aways."

"Ryan, tell her about the contest," Zoe says.

By the time he says "no" Zoe has already continued. "A skate company held a contest at the spot and they offered one thousand bucks to anyone who could do Ryan's Line. No one could do it. Not even pro skaters."

"Ryan, I've learned a lot about you this morning," Asmara says. "You wrote a novel. You did an epic skateboard trick. What other treasures will this bookshelf reveal?"

"It's not a novel," Ryan says. "And that trick was the only memorable thing I did on a skateboard."

Zoe's eyes grow big. "Ryan, you wrote a book?!"

"Oh, no."

. . . .

Asmara finds herself inspired by Ryan. His book is an intellectual achievement and his skate stunt is a physical triumph. They're both legacies of some sort, no matter how much modesty he drapes over them. Asmara guesses Ryan didn't wait for perfect motivation—he charged forward. At Word Bound in six days, Asmara plans to make a leap of her own.

Zoe is back at the bookshelf, looking for Ryan's novel. He tries to convince her it's not there.

"Asmara, did he really write a book?" Zoe says. "What is it called? He won't tell me its name."

The book in question is where Asmara last placed it—on top of the coffee table which is four feet away from Zoe. Asmara flashes her eyes onto the book and snaps them back to Zoe's gaze.

"Um, I don't know where his book is."

After a eureka moment, Zoe lunges for the book but Ryan anticipated her attack. He gets one hand firmly onto the cover while she gets both hands on the other side, albeit with a weak grip. A tug-of-war commences.

"Please! Who cares? Let me read it," Zoe says.

"No, you're too young."

"Okay, I won't read it. But let me look at it."

Zoe changes her strategy of tugging backwards and instead lifts the book up and down in a crank motion. Her new approach loosens his grip.

Sensing defeat is near, Ryan no longer plays fair. He takes his free arm and gives Zoe a healthy shove. When she hits the couch behind her, pillows go airborne and bounce off her head. She gasps in shock at this personal foul while hair falls across her face. With a gulp of air, she inhales a clump of her hair and spits it out.

"Pfflt! Ugh!"

Ryan bursts out laughing. Zoe follows, then Asmara.

Man, I'm glad I went to The Naomi last night.

. . . .

Ryan rummages through the trunk of his car while Asmara hops into the shotgun seat. Zoe sits in the back. The clean interior is another sign Ryan is more mature than indicated by his skateboard and friendship with a ninth grader.

"You know what?" Ryan says. "Asmara, are you in a hurry to get home or can you wait a few minutes as I do something?"

"No problem. What's up?"

"I'd like to put new wheels on this board and I can't find my tools. Zoe, can I use a wrench from your house?"

"Sure."

The three head over to Zoe's house across the street. Ryan takes a seat on a low brick wall as Zoe goes into the garage to get a wrench. A side door to the home opens and a middle-aged man walks out.

"Hi, Mario," Ryan says.

"Hey, Ryan. How are you?" the man replies with accented English.

"Good. This is my friend Asmara. Asmara, this is Zoe's dad, Mario."

The two share a wave and a greeting.

Mario gives a lingering look at each of them. He does not appear upset but he evaluates the grown adults his daughter spends time with. Asmara doesn't blame him one bit.

"Did Zoe tell you I was taking her skating today?" Ryan says. "We're going to go south of SF. We'll be back later this afternoon."

"No, she didn't say that to me but I'm glad she's going to have fun."

"Oh. I always tell her to ask for your permission first."

"It's not a problem, Ryan."

Zoe exits the garage and pauses at the sight of her father. He speaks first. "No me dijiste que ibas a la ciudad hoy."

"Yes, I did," Zoe says. "Te lo dine cuando sali de la casa. You didn't listen."

"Esta bien, quiero que te diviertas. Call me if you need anything."

Asmara is fascinated as Zoe talks to her father in Spanish and English. The language center in Zoe's brain must be crackling with vitality, while Asmara's monolingual neurons are like a wad of chewing gum.

As Mario enters his home, a woman appears in the doorway to survey the scene. While the door closes behind them, Mario mutters to the woman in Spanish.

After a pause, Ryan cringes and turns to Zoe.

"Ouch," he says. "Did your dad say: 'At least he knows some women his own age?'"

"Pretty much," she replies. "Don't worry. He likes you or he wouldn't let me skate with you."

Zoe hands Ryan the wrench she took from the garage.

"Wrong size," he says.

"That's the only one I could find."

"I know you have a crescent wrench. Can I grab the toolbox?"

"Sure."

Ryan heads toward the garage.

"Hold on," Zoe says. "You're talking about the gray toolbox near the door, right?"

"Yeah."

"Okay, you can grab that one but do *not* grab the blue toolbox on the shelf. We're not supposed to touch that one."

"Why not?"

Zoe casts a glance toward the door where her father had last been. "Because, he has sticks of dynamite in there."

CHAPTER 11

With the crescent wrench having proved effective and the new skateboard wheels transplanted, Ryan rolls alongside Asmara and Zoe as they head toward his car. He deposits the board into the trunk while Asmara and Zoe take their seats. Ryan slides in, fires up the engine and they depart.

The sticks of dynamite remain undisturbed in Mario's garage. Zoe explains her dad had a rock quarry job long ago and he brought home a couple of explosives. Asmara guesses that act involved few legal and safety considerations. For function, but mostly for fun, Mario was going to use the dynamite to destroy an old wooden shack he inherited in the desert. He never wound up doing it and the sticks have remained in the garage ever since.

"We should blow something up," Ryan says as he eases the car onto Telegraph Avenue.

"Careful. Even joking about that could get you into trouble," Asmara says.

"I have an idea," Zoe chimes in. "How about we wait until Halloween and make a pumpkin pyramid and explode them all?"

"We will need a long fuse," Ryan says. "Dynamite isn't just a big firecracker. It's a bomb. I'm not lighting the fuse unless it's a mile long."

"What about the plunger device?" Asmara says. "You know, the red box with a handle they press down when they demolish a building?"

"Aren't those only in cartoons?" Zoe asks.

"No, they're real," Ryan says. "I'm sure Home Depot has those in their 'Blowing Shit Up' department. Asmara can run in and grab one."

"I'm on it."

Ryan turns up the volume to his stereo which had been producing musical background noise. "I love this part."

To Asmara, it is like any other generic guitar solo.

"I swear the guitar is communicating something here," Ryan says. "It's not merely notes or chords. Something is being said through the guitar to the listener."

Ryan turns it up even more. "Do you hear it?"

"The guitar is mimicking words? I don't notice that," Asmara says.

"No, it's not trying to speak English. It's like a parallel language. I can almost comprehend it."

Ryan's enthusiasm compels Asmara to listen more intently. The music attempts to stimulate emotion in her but no connection is made.

"I think I know what it's about," Zoe says. "The guitar is talking about being in love with another guitar. They miss each other."

Ryan adjusts in his seat, deep in contemplation. "If there's a better theory than that, I don't know what it'd be."

They slow to a stop and Ryan parallel parks. They've arrived in front of a bicycle shop. It is One Track Mind, where Ryan works.

"What's up? Are you going to work today?" Asmara asks.

"We were one block away and I realized I should swing by. We have a new manager and I need to show him a change to our inventory spreadsheet. It'll take less than two minutes."

"You have to explain things to your new boss?"

Ryan smiles and Zoe burps up a laugh in the back seat.

"What?" Asmara asks. "What did I say?"

"He's not my boss. I hired him. I own One Track Mind."

He walks into the store and Asmara is surprised by her strong reaction upon learning he's a business owner. Up until now, it was promising for Ryan to merely have a clean apartment. At no point has she picked up on the vibe he has a lot of money—hell, he has a roommate. Regardless, Asmara doesn't care about his money. It's his ambition she is attracted to.

Ryan appears again and settles into the driver's seat.

"That was fast," Asmara says.

"Yeah, he figured it out on his own."

Ryan tosses a T-shirt into Asmara's lap and throws another one to Zoe in the back. "These arrived. Our logo got redesigned."

The shirts are white with black print on them. The logo says "One Track Mind" written in a paintbrush style and there is a smaller "Oakland, CA" beneath it. Each capital letter "O" is represented as a bike wheel.

"Awesome. I can have this?" Zoe says.

"Of course," Ryan says as he starts up the car. They merge into traffic and head west toward the Bay Bridge.

There are rustling noises and Asmara's headrest gets thumped by what must be an elbow. She turns and Zoe is proudly wearing her new One Track Mind shirt. The garment is way too big on her.

"It's sick!" Zoe exclaims.

Ryan gives a half-turn toward the backseat and Asmara gets a close look at his face as he is bathed in sunlight.

There is something about his eyes.

. . . .

After going through the highway toll booth, the road ahead is a straight shot to San Francisco with no intersections or stoplights. They climb the gradual arc of the Bay Bridge. The surrounding water is lovely on this bright day. However, the full effect of the bay's beauty is on the second half of the bridge.

They proceed into the heart of the small, rocky Yerba Buena Island in the middle of the bay. The short tunnel, connecting the two expanses of bridge, swallows their car and spits it back into sunlight. San Francisco's city skyline bursts into view. Even though Asmara is a local and has crossed the bridge countless times, it's impossible for her not to be impressed.

The towering wall of downtown buildings are nicely contrasted with the looming natural giant of Mount Tam, the grassy hills of the Marin Headlands, and Angel Island. The Golden Gate Bridge shines on the northern side of the San Francisco peninsula. Nothing is distant from Asmara's vantage point. These landmarks are huddled together in an embrace of the bay's perimeter, forming an amphitheater around the water. There's twenty or more sailboats within view, all of them leaning hard into the wind generated off the Pacific Ocean. The water shimmers with white-cap waves which blink in and out of existence.

Asmara's trance gets deflated by a joyless, practical matter that needs attending to.

"So, Asmara," Ryan says. "What exit should I take for you?"

Buzzkill.

She wishes the bridge was a forty-mile expanse over these same waters, with the city forever imminent but never arriving. Or perhaps there will be a non-injury accident ahead of them on the bridge, shutting down traffic and leaving them stranded with the view and each others' company.

"Well," Asmara says. Long pause. "Uhhm, take the first exit to Embarcadero and go to Bay street."

Her "uhhm" is a disappointed sigh. It is a desperate signal she isn't ready to end their time together, yet she has no idea how to prolong it.

"Okay, Bay street. Got it," Ryan says.

Maybe I could grab his wheel and cause the accident I'm hoping for?

The next ten seconds are filled with the hum of bridge traffic until Ryan demonstrates his intuition. "I understand if you want to go home after your long night," he says, "but we're going on a hike to a ditch by the airport if you want to join us."

Asmara would love to continue this adventure with him into the afternoon, but the reality of his offer sinks in. They're going skateboarding. In a ditch. By the airport.

"A ditch? I'm... I'm...," she says, struggling to visualize the endeavor.

"I know you don't skate," Ryan says. "It'll be fun, anyway. It's a cool spot to hike to."

The fact he's making an effort to entice her is almost enough to make Asmara want to go.

"Hate to pressure you," Ryan says, "but you've got until this next exit to decide. If you're going to pass on the hike, I want to get you home. Otherwise, we're kidnapping you for the day."

The off-ramp is fast approaching.

"You should come with us," Zoe says. "It'll be awesome."

"We'll also go to a taqueria afterwards," Ryan says.

"I'm in," Asmara says, hearing the ingredient she was looking for.

Zoe and Ryan let out a "Yes!" in unison.

A warmth of group inclusion washes over her. Ryan turns the music up and gives the gas pedal a little punch.

Rock music fills the car. Guitars and drums combine forces to electrify the air.

Apropos of nothing, other than a conversation he was having in his head, Ryan says, "I bet those dynamite sticks are so old they're duds now, anyway."

CHAPTER 12

The highway is such an efficient route away from downtown that the city recedes at an accelerating rate. In less than twenty minutes, they've achieved escape velocity from urban areas and head toward the natural landscape of San Bruno Mountain. This grassy giant is covered in coastal shrubs and most days it appears like a series of large hills to Asmara rather than an actual mountain. Today, the ridge goes halfway to the sun.

Ryan navigates through an industrial area at the base of the looming mounds. He parks behind a derelict warehouse covered in graffiti. Every window in the building is broken and there's litter everywhere. Amid the scrawl of spray-paint tags, there is one mural which states "No Place Like Home" in cursive script above a rendering of Earth floating in space.

Ryan and Zoe exit the vehicle and have an air of quiet determination.

"You didn't need to drive all the way out here to rob me," Asmara says. "You could have done it in Oakland."

"As if you have cash on you," Ryan says.

Ryan and Zoe start marching up the hill through tall grass.

"There's no trail?" she shouts up them.

"Not really," Ryan says. "It isn't that bad."

"Is this a mafia hit on me from Don DeLyon? Is there a shallow grave waiting for me up there?"

He doesn't laugh. "C'mon, join us."

She jogs up behind them and matches her pace to theirs. Asmara enjoys trail hiking but trudging through wild-growth terrain is another matter. Her feet disappear into the grass with each step. This blind process is unnerving and it's a small victory every time she doesn't twist an ankle. The undergrowth threatens to conceal a squirming mass of snakes and ticks.

Ten minutes into the hike, large shrubs begin to dot the hillside. One hundred yards beyond that a forest line awaits, although it's more a grove of trees rather than a sprawling wilderness.

Voices arise ahead of them. Next comes a wooden "thwack!" It's the second time today she's encountered the unmistakable call of a skateboard. One of the unseen skaters erupts with a loud belch. It has the specific resonance of a beer burp.

Abandoned buildings, trespassing, beer drinking. What an ideal field trip for a middle schooler.

Zoe and Ryan squeeze through a gap between shrubs. Asmara follows and a wide clearance opens up. As Ryan described, their destination is indeed an old concrete drainage ditch.

There are four guys on the other side of the banked pit. Two stand on their boards and the other two are sitting and drinking beers. They are in their mid-twenties and as they evaluate Asmara and her companions there is no apparent enthusiasm for visitors.

"What's going on?" one of them murmurs.

"What's up?" Ryan says. He gets no reply. To be fair, he never did declare what was going on.

Zoe places her skateboard on the edge of the ditch and stomps her foot on the tail. She has gotten the attention of the other skaters. Maybe they figured she was a little sister tagging along.

Rolling into the ditch, Zoe picks up speed. She zips through the flat-bottom and hits the other side's banked incline. Her momentum sends her flying out of the ditch and her board floats from under her in a shared trajectory. She grabs the board with her hand mid-air and lands confidently on her feet in the grass.

"Aw, this ditch is perfect!" she says.

It must have been a test run for her. The four skaters all smile.

Ryan is next to drop in. Instead of flying out of the other side he carves through a steep corner and gains more speed. He hits the top of the far bank, grinding his skateboard's trucks against the concrete lip of the ditch. The harsh friction makes a loud noise. Three of the strangers give a "yeah!" of approval. The fourth guy contributes a belch while raising his beer can in a salute.

Asmara imagines she's watching a tribal gatekeeper ceremony which is required to ride the sacred ditch.

One of the four guys summons Asmara with a wave. Since Ryan is heading in that direction anyway, she joins the group. Zoe is busy rolling around, getting more comfortable with the terrain. Her too-large One Track Mind shirt ripples like a flag in the wind.

"Where did you guys park?" Ryan asks the skate crew. "I didn't see your car down there."

"We hiked over the hill," one of them says. "I live on that side so we made a full day out of coming here to skate."

"Whoa, I've never heard of someone doing that."

"Your friend is ripping," the stranger says, nodding toward Zoe as she catches her first grind in the ditch. The guys let out a cheer and Asmara follows with a howl of her own (which includes an embarrassing voice-crack).

The belch guy lifts up an unopened beer and extends it to Ryan and Asmara. They both shake their head "no" and he shrugs before opening the can for himself.

"Do you come to this spot much?" one of the skaters asks Ryan.

"Maybe once a year. That keeps it special, though, because it remains fun every time."

Ryan turns around, jumps on his board and rolls into the ditch. "It's like seeing an old flame," he says over his shoulder as he accelerates down the bank.

Inspired by the fresh energy brought by Ryan and Zoe, all four of the other skaters gather their boards and line up on the ditch's edge.

Asmara sits at the base of a smooth rock and overlooks the scene. The skaters take turns dropping into the ditch and a rhythm develops. They are each trying a unique skate maneuver at the top of the tallest bank. There are numerous failed attempts for each of these tricks, evident by a runaway board or a tumble down the slope. However, when they successfully stay on the board during a showcase stunt, a victorious roar is shared by all.

For Asmara, it is a pleasing show, especially because Zoe is treated as an equal. She has earned her spot by pushing herself, taking spills, getting up and trying again.

. . . .

After a steady streak of skating, the energy dissipates. One guy after another bows out of the session and sits down in exhaustion next to Asmara. The last two standing are Ryan and Zoe. She struggles with an elusive trick on top of the tall bank. After numerous failed attempts, her face shows defeat. There doesn't appear to be a trace of fun involved anymore. Ryan walks over to the seated group. He, too, has had enough.

All eyes are on Zoe as she rolls into the ditch. The crack of the board's tail sends the skateboard into a rotation while she hovers above it. Zoe returns both her feet onto the griptape. Success! She rolls backward down the ditch and Asmara prepares to holler in celebration. However, Zoe's balance is off and this margin of error magnifies. Her efforts to remain upright are doomed. Zoe crashes and rolls like a ragdoll.

She hops up, grabs her board, and jogs toward where the group is sitting. There is more anger than agony in her demeanor. She throws the board aside and sprawls face first into the grass. The back of her once-clean white shirt is streaked with dirt and there are holes where the ditch gnawed through. Her elbow has a streak of blood oozing from a fresh wound.

"I almost had it!" Zoe shouts down into the grass.

"If it makes you feel better," one of the skaters says to Zoe, "I've never landed one of those and I've been skating longer than you've been alive."

Zoe springs upright off the grass and marches to her board. She heads toward the ditch as a chorus of calm encouragement follows her.

"You got it." "This is the one." "Get it."

She descends. The stage is set for a cinematic conclusion where she scores the game-winning touchdown, or at least the skateboard equivalent. She pops her board at the top of the far wall. Even Asmara's untrained eyes have learned this is a promising attempt.

Zoe's feet land on top of the board. She rolls backwards down the ditch... only to get splattered with a brutal impact, this time worse than the first slam.

"Fuck!" Zoe yells.

With board in hand, she sprints back up the ditch. She is trying to get in another try before pain and stiffness overtake her. Red specks of blood are distributed throughout the front of her shirt.

The moment Zoe finishes her run up the ditch she jumps on her board to head back down. She rumbles up the opposing bank, flips her board, and slips onto her backside. The fall includes an awkward tumble with a head bonk on the concrete.

Another "Fuck!" is shouted toward the sky.

She walks back up the bank, slower this time and with a limp.

Shouldn't this be stopped? Is this normal? Isn't it supposed to be fun?

Zoe rolls in again and speeds toward the far side. She coasts up the incline, sends her board spinning beneath her, and lands squarely on top of the griptape. Her body language oozes confidence, as if this roll-away is golden. Sure enough, her center of balance is spot on for a smooth ride down the bank.

Asmara wants to celebrate with a shout but she waits for a cue from the guys. They remain silent. Each skater gets off the grass and they stand to greet Zoe. She is on her way toward them and her face displays total shock. Her vision locks in on the group awaiting her and she breaks into a cartoonish, face-contorting smile. She is euphoric as the cheers start. All four guys start hollering and Asmara joins the fun. High fives connect with such velocity they sound like firecrackers. During a back-slap hug, Zoe dribbles her blood across the shirt of one of the guys. He shakes his head and is more amused than upset.

Zoe collapses into the grass in the same spot as she did before but this time she is face up, looking at the sky and laughing in rapid bursts.

The thrill of a successful trick must be infectious among skaters because the guys are high fiving each other. This exchange signifies the formal end of the session. One of the guys gives Ryan a farewell handshake and a look of recognition causes the skater's head to snap back.

"Dude," the skater says, "are you the Ryan's Line guy?"

Ryan gives a wince of disappointment, as if he is not a fan of re-hashing the skate stunt story. "Yeah, that's me."

"Dude!" The skater shouts, using the singular to address his three friends. "This is the guy who ollied the gap by City Hall, the one with the crazy roll-away."

"Ryan's Line?"

"Yeah!"

They crowd near Ryan and a round of skate talk commences. He's peppered with questions about the event.

Ryan keeps his answers short. Asmara starts to tune out the interrogation but one question leaps out at her.

"I have to ask," beer belch guy says. "I heard you lost an eye in a car accident but someone else said it was a gunshot. I was wondering..."

Asmara gives a small gasp she hopes Ryan didn't hear.

The skater's friends cringe at the personal nature of the question. "Dude," one of them says. "What the fuck, man?"

"I'm sorry," beer belch guy says. "I was just curious. You don't have to answer."

Ryan appears unmoved and lets an extended silence linger.

"I'm baffled you would know anything about me," he says. "But, yeah, I was shot in the eye."

This time Asmara fully gasps and she's certain he hears it.

"Although, I prefer not to get into details," he says. "Sorry, guys."

CHAPTER 13

As they plod through tall grass back toward the car, Asmara tries not to dwell on the fact a bullet once entered Ryan's eye socket and extinguished half his sight. At some point she will find out how this incident transpired. For now she does not want to make wild guesses.

"How many ticks do you think we have crawling on us?" Asmara asks.

"I'd say there's nine on each of us," Ryan says.

"When we get back to the car let's groom each other in a row like monkeys do," Zoe says.

"Sure, but keep in mind monkeys eat the ticks when they do that."

"Gross."

Their hiking pace picks up as the pull of gravity tugs them down the hill. Even with socks, shoes, and pants on, Asmara's ankles are mauled by a gauntlet of sharp vegetation.

They reach the car and are relieved the windows are intact. Skateboards go into the trunk, clothing is brushed by hand to remove clingy plant-life, and the trio hops into the vehicle.

Ryan pulls the car out from behind the condemned building and they drive through the corridor of warehouses.

Asmara has continuous irritation on her ankles. She lifts her pant legs and every inch of her socks are embedded with burrs and other stowaways.

"Look at this shit," she pleads to Ryan.

He glimpses down and laughs.

She slides off each sock and the plant debris gives a few final scratches. "I am literally going to have to throw these socks away."

"Literally?!" Ryan says and cackles some more.

Zoe, riding high from her successful skate stunt, has residual adrenaline she needs to purge from her system. She rolls her window down and lets out a wordless shout. Ryan gives the car horn a few blasts to help with the exorcism of her restless energy.

"Oh, yeah," Zoe says, as the window goes up and the outside wind quiets down. "We never did check for ticks, did we?"

. . . .

That veggie burrito is alluring. The damn thing is flirting with her.

A construction worker, with his hard hat on, receives his order in front of Asmara. She was going to pick something lighter to eat but his delicious brick of food sways her decision.

Ryan steps to the taqueria counter and turns toward Zoe. "I'm paying for yours because you're a rock star for landing that trick."

He points at Asmara. "And I'm paying for yours because you're a broke-ass who has no cash."

All three place their orders and take a seat by the window overlooking Mission Street. Ryan and Zoe both have faint splotches of dried grime and sweat on their faces from skating. Asmara wishes she had taken a dusty tumble in the ditch, to be aligned with the gang.

"I'm gonna wash my hands," Ryan says. "You should too, Zoe."

"Sure thing, Dad."

Ryan walks away and Zoe turns her attention to Asmara. "You know, I hope you keep hanging out with Ryan because he's a good guy. He could use a girlfriend."

"Why do you say he needs a girlfriend?"

"I think it would make him happier. He's not depressed or anything but he could use a change in his life."

"He's twice your age. Do you know him that well to talk about him like this?"

"Yeah. I do."

"All from skateboarding?"

"Kind of. Whenever we go somewhere we talk about stuff."

Ryan returns and he's holding a large tray with their baskets of food and three glasses of water. Zoe pours some of the water into her cupped hand. She puts the glass down and slides her hands one over the other, dripping water onto the floor.

Asmara drips water into her hands as well. "The proper way to clean is like how raccoons do it," she says, swirling her hands together, mimicking the animals' meticulous paw ritual. "They're the kings of handwashing."

Zoe offers her own imitation of a raccoon and bares her teeth for extra effect.

The next few minutes consist of the soft noises of tortillas, rice, and vegetables being chewed.

At a certain point, Asmara evaluates her companions. She blurts out what's on her mind before she can stop herself.

"Are you familiar with Word Bound at The Naomi?"

"The open-mic night?" Ryan says.

"Yeah. I'm going to do a reading on stage there in a few days."

"That's awesome. What are you going to read?"

"One of my short stories."

What Ryan says next gives Asmara a happy buzz. "Can I come watch you?"

"Yes. Of course."

"When you stole my book you never said you were a writer."

"The thing is, reading one of my stories isn't the main reason why I want to go on stage."

"What's the real reason?"

Here we go.

"Last night I had a crazy idea while we were at The Naomi. During my set, I'm going to have an accomplice hidden beneath the stage. They're going to secretly run a long tube through a hole in the stage which will go under my skirt and up to my shirt collar. The audience won't see a thing. When my story is about to conclude, the assistant will push a plunger through the tube..."

Asmara pauses to magnify the reveal.

"...and a tarantula will be forced out from under my shirt. It will crawl on my face as I finish the reading."

There is no reaction. Ryan and Zoe continue to blink while looking vacantly at Asmara. She may as well have been reading the ingredients from a cereal box.

Maybe my pitch needs a visual aid?

"And I will walk off stage with the spider on my face."

The blank stares continue.

At last, something happens—Ryan's eyes gaze upwards while lost in thought. While Asmara awaits what he has to say, Zoe speaks first.

"Will the spider get hurt?"

"Nope. I will take every safety precaution."

Ryan's eyes come back down to meet Asmara's.

"I just... I just..." he says.

"You just what?"

"I dig it. I swear. But what are you going for? What result?"

"I'm aiming for a weird, memorable finale. However, more so, I want to see if I can go through with this idea, start to finish. That's my goal."

"I respect that. However, to lift the spider through the tube, you're thinking the plunger will be like pushing a syringe, right?"

"Yeah."

"Well, for a tube to reach from beneath the stage to your collar it will have to be around five feet tall. The plunger will need to be that tall as well. However, the stage at The Naomi is three feet tall."

"I was thinking the tube could be bendy. It will be fed through the hole at an angle."

"No. You're going to want a rigid tube which goes straight upward. I don't know of any five-foot-long flexible tubes that have a plunger.

Besides, the more twists in the pipe the more likely the spider will get crushed in a corner. You're going to want the spider to go on a slow, straight lift with a rigid tube."

"Yeah, there's a bunch of logistics I haven't worked out yet."

Ryan's eyes turn upward in thought again. "I've got it. You will need two tubes, each two-and-a-half feet. At that length they can go vertically straight through the hole. Once the first one is under your skirt, the second tube will connect to it beneath the stage. The whole five-foot unit can be pushed up to your collar. The plunger will connect last and will require two pieces which attach together as well."

Asmara follows the logic but has a hard time picturing every detail. Maybe she needs the visual aid.

Ryan takes a bite of his burrito and chews while in contemplation. "After we finish eating, do you want to know where we're going?"

"Where?"

"We're heading to The Naomi."

"What? No. I want to move forward and I'd love your help, but let's take a breather first."

"The Naomi is on the way to your place. It'll be a quick stop."

"I don't know..."

"You need to ask their management if you can even do this in the first place. And you need to examine the stage to see if your idea will work."

Asmara turns to Zoe. "What do you think?"

"I think it's a great idea. Let's go to The Naomi."

"Cool. I guess we can swing by there."

"One more thing," Zoe says. "I want to be the one beneath the stage pushing the spider on to your face."

CHAPTER 14

Asmara finds it peculiar to be standing outside The Naomi in broad daylight. She associates the place as a nightlife venue.

"Zoe can come in with us, right?" Ryan asks. "They're not going to kick her out because it's a bar?"

"She should be fine since they're serving lunch," Asmara says.

The three enter and Asmara is surprised by how different the interior looks during the day. Natural light flooding in through the windows creates a more revealing atmosphere than the shadowy realm at night.

When this establishment is dimly lit in the evening it gives off a well-worn charm. In bright light it borders on being a dump.

The Naomi is close to empty except for a group of people eating lunch at two tables pushed together. With their white hair and an average age around seventy, these diners are a far cry from the crowd last night in this same room.

"Weird," Ryan says. "For senior citizens this is a happening lunch spot."

"It's like an alternate universe in here during the day," Asmara says.

The only visible employee is a late-twenties red-haired woman behind the bar. Asmara greets her with a smile. "Hi."

"What can I do for you?"

"I have a couple of questions about the next Word Bound."

"Sure, let's hear them."

"I was hoping to give a reading and I wasn't sure how to get involved."

"You're talking to the right person. I started Word Bound and I handle the line-up."

"Oh, that's great. It's a cool event."

"Thanks. It's not like I invented the concept of live readings. My boss wanted some non-music events and I convinced him to try Word Bound."

"Good call."

"So, all we ask for is a synopsis of what you're going to talk about. The Naomi has a website and there's a Word Bound tab you submit through. It allows us to form the night's line-up."

"That makes sense."

"You can send the email but, out of curiosity, what kind of reading did you have in mind for that night?"

"Well..."

A young man emerges from a kitchen door behind the bar. Asmara has seen this person before. The tentacle tattoo crawling up his neck is hard to forget.

"You're back," he says in his Australian accent. "You're not checking on where I throw my cigarettes, are you?"

"No. I thought you and your friends were tourists last night."

"You're two-thirds correct. Those were friends of mine visiting from Australia. I've lived in SF for a few years and have been working here the whole time."

"James is the manager," the red-haired woman says.

"Yesterday, you were in the right," James says to Asmara. "I'm gonna dispose of cigs proper from here on out."

Holy smokes. My litter intervention worked.

"What brings you back here today?" he asks.

"She wants to present at Word Bound," the red-haired woman says.

"Yes, I do," Asmara says, "and I'm glad the manager is here because I want to include a wild stunt at the end of my reading."

"Hmm. I'm listening."

Asmara gives a concise pitch of her tarantula idea. She presents the concept as a fun, unexpected twist to Word Bound. James and the red-haired woman remain expressionless, as if there is a time delay before Asmara's words reach them.

"It will all be tied together—my story and the surprise ending."

Still no reaction. She might as well be talking to the burrito she ate.

"I figure it'll be a theatrical, ridiculous addition to Word Bound."

If Asmara was ever going to concede this is a dumb idea, now would be the time. Instead she gives one last push.

"It's gonna be fucking awesome," she says.

James tilts his head upward in thought, much like Ryan's reaction when he heard the idea. His eyes come back down. "Sure, go for it."

"Yeah, I love the idea as well," the red-haired woman says.

"Really? That's awesome. Thanks so much."

"I suggest you do a test beforehand," James says. "It can't be thrown together the night of Word Bound."

"I agree. We were hoping to examine the stage today."

"Go ahead, take a look. I'm intrigued if this will work."

Asmara waves over Ryan and Zoe. "These are my friends."

Greetings are exchanged. Elizabeth is the name of the red-haired woman. The group talks for a bit and they head over to the stage. At three feet tall, it will be tough to operate under this platform.

"The access under there is backstage," James says. "Follow me."

They walk through a door into The Naomi's kitchen area. Once they round another corner they are behind the stage. The wide wooden base of the structure protrudes through the wall. At knee-level, there are two hatches which look like big cabinet doors.

"I can't remember the last time I opened these," James says. "It's been a forgotten storage area."

He swings open the doors and the dark tomb inside is exposed. A lonesome dustball bounces out of the disturbed crypt on a wave of circulating air. The whole group crouches to get a better view beneath the stage. Inside, there are stacks of tables with their hinged legs flattened as well as dozens of metal folding chairs.

"Oh, that's right," the manager says, "we got new chairs and tables a long time ago and we jammed the old ones under here."

Ryan activates his phone into a flashlight and illuminates the area. The only information to be gleaned is the space is cramped and dusty.

"What do you think?" Asmara says.

"I think a lot of effort will be needed to get the stuff out of there," Ryan says.

"Since I like your weird plan," James says, "and since you showed such concern about littering in front of The Naomi, I'll be happy to help you. We can stack this stuff in our other storage area."

Asmara has the sensation of being at an actual crossroads. Coming to the venue and getting permission from management is a crucial first step in her plan. However, that is talk and talking is easy. If she accepts the labor of this group around her, she will be obligated to pursue her Word Bound performance to its conclusion.

"All right," Asmara says, "let's do this."

James claps his hands together in anticipation of the grunt work about to commence. Ryan and Zoe plan a work flow strategy.

Elizabeth pulls her hair back in a ponytail. "I'll rotate my help between here and out front with the diners."

"I can't thank you all enough," Asmara says. "And since this is my stupid idea, I'll be under the stage, sliding out the items toward you."

She gives her clothes a light hand-stroke of sympathy before they endure this dusty indignity.

. . . .

Due to entangled table legs, the first items blocking the entryway put up a fight and are difficult to move. With a lot of brute yanking, Ryan and James break the inertia of this logjam. After an area is cleared, Asmara crawls on her knees beneath the stage. The group forms an efficient daisy chain which has Asmara in the lead. She slides tables and chairs through the hatch and everyone else carries the items to the spare storage area.

For Asmara, the process is a filthy endeavor and there is a moment (when her thumb gets pinched in a folding chair) in which the absurdity of her situation amuses her. One inspiring sight is how Zoe runs back and forth to move as many items as possible. Zoe is not merely being a good sport about this workload, she loves it.

After twenty minutes of activity, Ryan shines his phone flashlight beneath the stage to get a sense of their progress. With a sheen of sweat across her forehead, Asmara is disappointed to find herself still surrounded by tables and chairs. The prospect of another half-hour in this large coffin makes her want to surrender the Word Bound stunt idea.

"How are you doing in there?" Ryan asks.

"Not so good. We've barely made a dent."

"There's enough room for two of us now, I'm coming in."

Ryan crawls like a dog into the space. He wastes no time and the lifting and sliding begins again. His contribution to the moving system makes a noticeable difference. They are in the home stretch when the stage's interior walls come into view.

"Asmara, look," Ryan says, pointing behind her.

She turns and a solid shaft of white light beams through a hole in the stage—the same hole which caught her attention last night and started this chain of events. Now unobstructed, the hole produces a spotlight circle on the ground next to her. The vertical light column cleaves through the darkness and a blizzard of dust swirls within its borders.

An echo of the mysterious panic attack she suffered when she first saw this stage portal drifts into her thoughts. *Was that a warning of sorts?*

Asmara runs her hand through the light rays and catches the spotlight in her palm, raising the bright circle off of the ground. Ryan scoots toward her and extends his hand to grasp the light himself. She moves her arm aside, handing the light off to him. As they sit in silence, he carries the spotlight up to the hole it originates from.

"I wasn't sure," he says, "but I think this will work."

Asmara is so lost in the strangeness of the moment—kneeling under a dark stage with a man she met last night—that she isn't sure of the context of his statement. She replies anyway.

"Yeah, I think it will all work out."

CHAPTER 15

Ryan turns onto Asmara's street and she scans the block in search of her roommate's car. The presence or absence of Lisa's vehicle sets the stage for Asmara's attitude when she arrives home. For the past year, the two women have had a decent system of living together—a mix of friendliness and independence—and yet Asmara cherishes having the apartment to herself. There's no doubt Lisa enjoys the same freedom whenever she is alone.

Lisa's car is not here. Fantastic.

"You can drop me off by the street light," Asmara says to Ryan. "I live on the second floor of that building."

He pulls over to the curb and gives a look of apprehension. "Is there any chance I can use your bathroom?"

"Of course, no problem."

Asmara tries to recall the cleanliness of her apartment when she left home yesterday. Her and Lisa keep the common areas tidy even if her bedroom is in a state of laundry-strewn disarray.

"I have to go to the bathroom, too," Zoe says.

"Sure. Come on up."

"I'm glad Ryan said something because I've been dying back here. Just so you know, it's number one, not number two."

"Both numbers are fine. Let's go."

They exit the car, enter the building's lobby and wind their way up the staircase to Asmara's apartment. The front door gets unlocked and, after hearing "down the hall, to the right," Zoe gallops to the bathroom.

"You asked first but I really gotta go," she shouts to Ryan as the bathroom door slams shut.

He frowns at the injustice of it all.

"Can I urinate in your kitchen sink?" Ryan asks Asmara. "Or are you one of those uptight, neat freaks about stuff like that?"

"Not funny. Would you like something to drink? A giant glass of water straight to your bladder perhaps?"

"Not funny. Now we're even."

Ryan spots a framed painting in the hallway and pivots toward it. Despite there being a range of art and photos on every wall, most people who enter Asmara's apartment gravitate toward this piece. Her friend Sarah, who she was with last night, painted it during one of her creative outbursts. The art is abstract and contains a storm of kaleidoscopic colors. Asmara isn't sure how anyone could examine the piece and *not* see a representation of the San Francisco skyline.

"What do you see?" Asmara asks, hoping Ryan doesn't botch this easy ink-blot test.

"An embrace. Between a man and a woman. At first I thought they were grieving. Now I see they're in love. The scene is happy, not sad."

She's never heard that one before. There was one visitor—he was ten years old—who perceived an octopus fighting a robot among the colors. The monstrous scenario the boy saw is more plausible than a romantic hug between two humans.

"Yes," Ryan says, "they're intertwined. He's taller than her and he's colored gray. He's on the left."

Ryan holds his finger to the painting to trace where the supposed male figure is. Asmara is not persuaded.

"Since he's looking down, you're only seeing part of his face," Ryan says. "But his arm is around her waist."

If she wants to play along, Asmara will admit there is an apparent limb jutting out of a misshapen torso. It might be one of those octopus tentacles the boy noticed.

"He's holding her," Ryan says, still using his finger to give a guided tour. "Do you see her, in blue?"

This painting Asmara has viewed hundreds of times—one in which she has never seen anything except the San Francisco skyline—shifts before her eyes. Even though the paint on the canvas does not move, it undergoes a metamorphosis.

And there they are—the man and woman. In an embrace. Swirling within blues and grays.

"Whoa. She's touching his forearm," Asmara says. "Her eyes are closed. And her hair is long."

"Yes," Ryan says. "You got it. Her hair is the best part."

"That is so cool to see this painting in a new way. It's such a..."

A key rattles in the lock of the front door. Lisa is home. Asmara didn't even get to enjoy a brief illusion of having her own apartment. At least now a third party will meet Ryan and confirm he is not an hallucination.

Asmara is not concerned about Lisa's opinion of her non-existent love life, but bringing home this male companion is an exciting change of pace.

The front door opens and Lisa pauses mid-stride at the sight of a strange man in the hallway.

"Um, hi there," she says.

"Hi, I'm Ryan. I'm with Asmara."

"Really? Okay. I'm Lisa."

The bitch had to say "really?"

Asmara positions herself to be more visible.

"Oh, there you are," Lisa says. "How are you?"

"Good. I had a crazy mix-up yesterday and got stranded in Oakland. I spent the night over there."

"Whoa. Bummer."

"Yeah. I'll tell you about it later. Ryan was nice enough to help me out and he gave me a ride back today."

With the brief summary to go on, the gears are working behind Lisa's eyes. She ponders the delicious possibility Asmara spent the night at a guy's house.

The intrigue is broken as a toilet flushes and the bathroom door opens. Suctioning water echoes in the hall. It is obvious no hands were washed. A boyish-looking teen joins the group with her filthy, over-sized T-shirt. She motions with a jerk of her thumb back toward the bathroom.

"It's all yours," she says to Ryan.

"I'm sorry," Ryan says to Lisa, as he shuffles backwards in haste. "I have to go."

He disappears with the click of a door and the three females are left standing in the hallway. Zoe gives a blank look at Lisa.

"Have you ever heard of Ryan's Line?"

CHAPTER 16

Asmara's introversion activates. Her welcoming castle bridge is withdrawn, fences go up. She looks forward to being alone in order to digest the past night and day. Lisa went to her room and Ryan and Zoe discuss their drive back to Oakland. Solitude is near.

"This has been fun," Ryan says to Asmara, signaling his departure.

"Yeah, what a day," Asmara says. "Also, I know this Naomi plan of mine is crazy. I won't be offended if you don't want to be involved."

"Your idea sounded far-fetched. But since you were willing to clear out the space beneath the stage, that's when I knew you were for real. What happens from here?"

"I'll plan a rehearsal and buy a tarantula. I also need to see which tube system is feasible. Your input helped today."

They step out of the apartment into the main hallway. Zoe senses Asmara and Ryan prefer time alone and she hastens her exit.

"I'm glad you came out with us today," Zoe says, while giving Asmara a hug. "And it's so cool you're gonna do this spider thing on stage."

"Thank you," Asmara says. "It was awesome watching you skate and hearing those skater boys cheer you on."

Zoe walks to the stairwell and turns around. "Ryan, I'll see you outside by the car."

The heavy door to the stairs slams shut and Asmara and Ryan share a small sigh together. She prepares for their parting exchange. A platonic hug? A sloppy, open-mouth kiss?

Seconds float by as they enjoy the quiet one-on-one dynamic. The silence keeps unfolding and there is no pressure to break it. At some point they shake their heads with a laugh at the strange fun of it all.

"I should get Zoe back home," Ryan says.

He opens his arms wide and comes in for a hug. Asmara dissolves into his embrace. Their anatomy is flush together. If not for the whisker of space between their pelvic regions, this would qualify as dry humping.

With a quick jostle her arms are empty. Asmara lifts her head and Ryan is halfway down the hall, jogging backwards.

"I'll call you tomorrow," he says.

The door to the stairs slams shut again and Asmara is alone.

. . . .

It's important to not overreact.

As Asmara heads into her apartment, she won't twirl around in place and let out a squeal of elation. No romantic-comedy cliches for her. She does not believe in jinxing, either. It's unlikely there's a cosmic goblin with its finger on the trigger of fate, waiting to ruin good fortune. However, there is logic in not celebrating something before it happens. A dead-end fizzle with Ryan is still a possibility.

To avoid premature exuberance, Asmara keeps her focus on the current agenda: a shower and going to bed.

A sheen of grime she accumulated from the hike and The Naomi washes off in the shower. She dives with a belly flop into her bed.

Since she will be asleep in a minute anyway, Asmara allows her mind to wander. Flashing images of Ryan and Zoe, hiking and skateboarding, all ricochet under her closed eyelids. A curtain of slumber is about to descend when she registers one last image. It's the woman with the spider-face again, from her subway dream.

The fright Asmara had when she first saw the strange figure isn't present this time. In the current fantasy, the two of them are in a still-frame snapshot of time. This mysterious person stands on an empty San Francisco street, facing Asmara. They are in the Tenderloin, with the neighborhood turned into a ghost town. The distance between them obscures the details of her horrifying face, but it is the same woman.

It's no surprise the Word Bound spider stunt would implant itself into Asmara's subconscious. However, this individual facing Asmara is not a symbolic portrayal of stage-fright anxiety. There is a palpable depth beyond that.

The still-frame image breaks its facade as movement arises in the scene. With violent twitching, the hybrid woman shakes her head side-to-side, indicating "no."

Faster and faster the head-shaking continues until her face is nothing but a blur of brown streaks. The woman, now so unhuman she is an "it," emits a high pitch which is part electrical feedback and all distorted shriek.

Asmara manages to pierce through the all-consuming noise and reach a lucid state. Her eyes may be closed but she has not crossed the threshold into sleep. She is wide awake and is aware she laid in bed a few moments ago. Asmara tries to open her eyes to obliterate this unwanted vision but her muscles are paralyzed.

The inexplicable spider figure has appeared in her bad dreams twice. It is following her and, with a certainty Asmara cannot account for, this strange thing has arrived from the future.

CHAPTER 17

Cleaning out The Naomi storage was the first indication Asmara is serious about Word Bound. Further evidence lies in a semi-circle around her. With morning light filling the room, she sits upright in bed, surrounded by printouts of her stories. She will select and edit one of these to fit into her five-minute spoken word set.

All of the material surrounding her had been crammed into a large binder. Her habit, whenever the writing mood strikes, is to dig through these archives and choose a piece for revision. The best, or most tolerable, stories are toward the front of the binder. The rear of the binder is purgatory for banished tales. Asmara is reluctant to read those for fear they will cause death by embarrassment.

This is the first time she has viewed the entirety of her writing output at once. The rejects go into a face-down pile and receive a burial beneath a sweatshirt. The rest are face-up and ready for their chance to shine in this pageant. She searches for darker-themed stories and it's a simple quest because there is only one. *Lightning in Ojai.*

She runs her hands over its nine pages and the contents transmit like braille through her fingertips. Asmara has edited this story for so long she is able to summon the information from memory.

The death of a scientist in Ojai, California, is the hook. He is struck by lightning even though there is not a cloud in the sky. This brilliant innovator was at the forefront of trying to create sentient artificial intelligence. When the man seemingly succeeds, a God-like entity's first act is to kill the scientist with weaponized lightning.

It turns out, artificial intelligence was never reached. Instead, the hyper-compression of data used in the scientist's AI experiments collapsed a dimension of spacetime, similar to how condensed matter can collapse into a black hole. Superintelligence was not created, but a door was opened and something was allowed in—a being of a higher order.

As a final twist, it is shown this alien entity had a noble cause in its murder of the scientist. It calculated Earth cannot sustain the future effects of a hobby the scientist was working on: a surfboard design. He was on the verge of producing a revolutionary surfboard shape which would allow almost anyone to catch a wave. This growth in surfing leads to extraordinary oceanside stress which unravels the planet's ecological health. So, the entity kills the scientist and burns down his surfboard workshop with lightning.

Asmara laughs at the ridiculous premise she wrote years ago. It stems from her surfer uncle who once solemnly warned—"the worst thing that could ever happen is if surfing becomes easy." He was earnest when he said it, as if the insight was deep cautionary wisdom. Her uncle's concern about crowded waves was pure self interest—just a guy who didn't want kooks in his way. But what if his warning was much more? What if surfing became easy and it actually was the worst thing that ever happened? The idea was the seed which sprouted *Lightning in Ojai.*

In terms of Word Bound, her scientist story has nothing to do with a tarantula and yet Asmara is unfazed. She will make the connection work on stage, even if the spider is a metaphor—a signal of encroaching threat.

Asmara starts planning a condensed edit for her five minutes on stage. Her eyes drift along the pages, absorbing entire paragraphs with a glance. The words on the paper start to blur. No, not blur. They vibrate. She blinks her eyes and the visual effect is still there. Asmara gains a compulsion to edit her story in a particular way. It's as if detailed writing instructions are broadcast to her.

Sections of *Lightning in Ojai* volunteer to be deleted. They beg, even. Other pages whisper specific directions to Asmara—change this word here, move that sentence over there. Her eyes get a vigorous rub and the twitching words lie flat on the page. The sentences no longer spasm with life and yet their dormant letters hint at captured energy. There is self-awareness contained on these pages, as if her written words understand they are being observed.

She gathers the scattered papers on her bed in order to return them to the binder. *Lightning in Ojai* will not be exiled with the others. It receives a prime placement on her work desk. The chopping and swapping of the story's contents will be a brutish reconfiguration. Hopefully, the Frankenstein monster will not attack its creator.

As Asmara places the mound of papers back into the binder, one loose sheet catches her eye. This ink-covered page is filled with annotations of her random thoughts and supposedly bright ideas over the years. Most of the entries are free-floating sentences with no context. At the time of their creation, Asmara figured these jewels might shine in a future storyline. However, this treasure trove has devalued over time. Her hurried handwriting is a mess and the legible notes are stone-cold crap.

One scrawl on the two-sided page is circled. She has no recollection of writing it and not a clue what it pertains to.

"There is no waterfall until the flood."

Asmara tries to imagine a storytelling scenario where the sentence would be relevant or make sense. She comes up with nothing. Yet there is something there, in those words, looking back at her.

CHAPTER 18

One day, at a terrible point in the future, Broadway Thai's yellow curry will no longer be a comfort food which soothes Asmara's soul. That day isn't today. As she is handed the take-out box, the smells put her in an aromatherapy trance. It doesn't matter she was not hungry when she phoned in menu item number eleven. Her mood was high and she wanted to get higher so she called her favorite restaurant for a natural fix. Fresh air invigorates her and trudging down the steady slope of Bay Street increases her appetite. Experience has taught that she will be ready to eat when she finishes the return trek after picking up her meal.

Asmara nears home, food baggie in hand. Her stomach sends affirmative signals after being seduced by the curry. Life is good, until the sight of garbage strewn beside her apartment building sours the vibe.

With disdain, her eyes trace along the stripe of litter which has blown against the wall. Asmara lowers herself onto one knee to gather the trash and dispose of it.

She scoops up three salty-snack bags, a daisy chain of fast food wrappers, an empty cigarillo packet, unused napkins and one... *Hey*.

One green slip of legal tender. A dollar bill.

A loose dollar exposed in the wild, devoid of ownership, creates a tantalizing excitement for Asmara. Everyone enjoys finding money but Asmara suspects her reaction is stronger than most.

It is because of Lake Tahoe.

When she was ten years old her family took a weekend trip to the cold-water basin four hours north of San Francisco. A cousin gave her a snorkel and goggles which turned out to be a life-changing decision. Asmara's previous fear of swimming, especially in spooky, fish-filled bodies of water, evaporated while using the headgear. Breathing easily as she explored the blue realm, the mysterious environment of Lake Tahoe was far more stimulating than mundane swimming pools.

During that weekend, Asmara floated face-down, snorkel-up for longer than she spent on land among the beach-dwelling mammals known as her family. A magical memory was the deep-sea treasure she hauled in: four dollars in cash. Each of those discovered one dollar bills had been half-buried vertically into the sand underwater. Their upper halves swayed like seaweed in the current. One find after another, Asmara would sprint up the beach in euphoria to show off her riches and lay the bills on a towel to dry out. She would race back into the water, lest further treasure be plundered by pirates. It was a day of joy and it's the origin of her life-long exaggerated reactions upon finding cash.

The fabulous childhood experience also, upon reflection, was a staged act. It was not until Asmara was well into her twenties and relating the Lake Tahoe story to a friend, that the improbability struck her. How had the papers not disintegrated underwater unless they were freshly placed? Four separate dollar bills each buried halfway into the sand in the same way? Come on...

Reviewing the trip with hindsight, she remembers her father taking periodic dips into the water around where she snorkeled. He obviously provided the bountiful haul.

Asmara never asked her dad about it but the sense of adventure he provided for his daughter that day is an integral part of her.

Years later, here in SF, she examines the dollar buried among litter. She folds it in half to distinguish it from the other bills in her possession.

This one is different.

. . . .

Asmara uses discipline to enjoy the curry at a slow pace instead of diving head-first into the bowl. The plan is to ride this feel-good wave straight into story revisions for Word Bound. Editing has its rewards, but Asmara is not above the pleasures of procrastination. Her phone tempts her with endless distractions. Other hopeful options to avoid writing include a police raid of her apartment or an alien abduction, if either were to randomly occur.

She gives it a minute.

No such luck. Time to edit.

The printed version of *Lightning in Ojai* is in her hands. Her laptop is open and the digital file is ready as well. Pen in hand, Asmara will juggle editing tasks between the two formats.

She sprints through a reading of the nine pages and cringes the whole way. It's an absurd tale, no doubt. Asmara second-guesses the story of a scientist's surfboard design leading to his murder by lightning.

The twisted tale settles in her mind. As it marinates among her critiques, minutes drift by with no inspiration. Not a single editing strategy is devised.

She allows the story to circulate on its own terms—as if it's outside of her body. There, in the air before her, *Lightning in Ojai* changes shape. Its structure, comprised of words, takes on a sleek form like an arrowhead.

Asmara casts aside the printed version of *Lightning in Ojai*. This is unusual because she always uses a pen to write notes before editing on screen. However, her hands have settled on the keyboard and she types. And types.

She's not sure how much time passes, maybe twenty minutes, before she snaps out of her creative zone. A thick mound of completed text glows on the screen. This is not editing. It's stream of consciousness writing.

Again, more typing. More typing.

This doesn't make sense. The story is expanding, which is the opposite of what she intended to do. She is compelled to continue this approach.

Asmara never writes for an hour straight. She's not built that way. And yet she has passed ninety minutes of continuous key pounding. The story is twenty-five pages long now.

A fatigue clouds her mind. Surely, it is time for a break. Her eyes and hands disagree as they shift gears and plunge into editing the story.

The masochism of butchering her written efforts stirs up a perverse thrill. After working hard to write fully-formed thoughts, giving them life, she wields those same powers to banish the excess material forever. These particular sentences she came up with on her laptop have never been arranged before. And if they do not satisfy her they will not be long for this world. She is a merciless judge and her written words plead for consideration before they get edited into oblivion.

It is a bloodbath as paragraphs get annihilated. Their scattered body parts are reconfigured into new sentences. Asmara unleashes a torrent of productive output unlike any she's had before.

Her energy peaks and the keystroke rhythm slows to a halt. She's cooked.

Asmara powers down the laptop and catches a glimpse of the digital clock in the corner of her screen. Right before the computer goes black the display turns from 11:59 p.m. into 12:00 a.m.

CHAPTER 19

When it comes to ex-boyfriends, Asmara keeps nostalgia limited to brief flashbacks. She prefers not to reminisce for too long out of fear the memories will grow dull from overexposure.

Asmara envisions the guys now. All four of them. They were each a positive addition to her life—there wasn't a douchebag in the bunch. The relationships ended with heartache but no hard feelings as lives diverged and sparks faded.

She indulges in this boyfriend excavation of her past because her romantic life is about to rise from the dead. After being alone for so long, cobwebs have formed in the headspace required to be in a relationship. She needs to dust off and reexamine what it means to be a girlfriend because of a text Ryan sent this morning: "When can I see you again? Today please?"

Straight-up courtship. His next correspondence may include "M'lady."

Asmara bottles the exhilaration from the message and plans to continue her morning normally. Ryan's text has a wonderful radiation which seeps out and brightens her mood, but she wants to attend to morning rituals first, then she'll reply.

. . . .

"Europa is the fourth largest of Jupiter's ninety-five moons (yes, ninety-five. Not a typo.) It has an outer crust of ice which is estimated to be twelve miles thick. There is evidence that beneath this icy shell lies a liquid water ocean an average of seventy miles deep. As Europa orbits Jupiter, tidal forces wrench on the satellite and create periodic deformations of the entire celestial body. This tug-of-war of varying intensity creates internal friction which heats the interior of Europa and allows the ocean to remain liquid water instead of freezing over. There may also be thermal vents which release heat from the moon's core. Scientists speculate ice-sheet movements and cracks in the moon's outer shell create a constant interchange of molecules from the surface to the ocean below, possibly including organic chemicals. These observations and theories make Europa a contender for extraterrestrial life in our solar system."

Asmara puts down the magazine she stole from the donut shop. She sips her coffee at the kitchen table and marvels again at the photos of this moon 390 million miles away. She loves awe-inspiring theories such as the possibility of life on Europa because they are based on established science. There is no wild leap into the supernatural to observe that life can emerge on rocks in space. It happened on our planet.

Maybe there's a highly-evolved alien fish on Europa right now reading about the potential for life on the distant blue dot of Earth. Asmara's air-breathing, land-walking existence would be an astonishing science fiction scenario to this creature.

Or what if the Europan aliens evolved before the dawn of humans? Cosmic timeframes are so vast there's a likelihood those watery species on Europa have long-since gone extinct or moved away. The slow speed of planetary evolution never allowed for the two solar neighbors to meet, or even exist, during the same time. There might be abandoned, dead cities underwater on Europa. The fishes there had a good run but their story lies entombed under a sky of ice.

Asmara pours another cup of coffee.

. . . .

As special as Ryan's text was this morning, a polar opposite, antimatter message arrives. Her friend Dylan, who was confident he could get Asmara a job, sent a text saying his boss "...isn't sure if she's gonna hire anyone but she'll think about it"

Those words would normally indicate an unmistakable "no" from the employer, but Dylan's follow-up text gives something to hold on to. "Asmara, I SWEAR they might still hire you. She really is considering it"

This opportunity may have passed by. For now, there is hope in not knowing.

Asmara has a small pile of savings in the bank and she is not going to panic. Yet. Her modest safety net is so threadbare it's more like she's walking on a tightrope. Still, it has psychological value in that she doesn't have to move into her parents' basement.

The brown carpet down there... Please, no.

CHAPTER 20

In her short walk east from her apartment, she has seen three parked cars which have been keyed. There is no chance the scratches were the result of innocent error. These long, thin lines are wounds borne of focused anger. The scars seethe even now.

One of the vehicles belongs to Asmara's neighbor, Inga. She is a nice

Russian woman in her sixties who lives alone across the hall. Her heavily-accented English does not hinder her presentation as an articulate woman. There is a rumor in the building that Inga was an astronomer in Russia.

The two women chat when they cross paths at each other's front door. Asmara has considered inviting her inside but the threshold has not been crossed. Neighbor entanglements need to be approached with caution.

Inga's blue car displays a thin but nasty scratch on the driver's side door. There is a sharp angular path to the eighteen-inch line. It looks intentional to the point of being a hieroglyphic. The vandal had a steady hand. What could the nice immigrant woman have done to deserve such an auto-body attack?

Maybe Inga is in a torrid love triangle with a handsome Moscow spy and a jealous oligarch.

Asmara pulls out her phone and takes a photo of the scratch. Before she sends the image to Ryan she confronts the question looming over her morning: should she meet up with him today or not?

She loves how he is assertive and asked to see her again, but Asmara needs a day to recharge. Her thumbs hammer out a text.

"Hey! Looks like I didn't scare you away after all. These past two days were great. However, I want to relax today and handle some errands. Thank you for the offer and we will meet up before Word Bound"

Asmara proofreads her text before sending. Always. She gets teased by friends because of how formal and lengthy her texts are but she refuses to lower her standards.

She hits send and includes a follow-up message with the car photo. "Also, my neighbor has a car scratch I noticed. Please send this picture to Zoe and I can help contribute data to her school project"

Asmara continues to walk. She is heading to a department store near her old workplace. She is on the hunt for tubes. Beneath every street and within every building there is miles of the stuff. However, she needs to go where this type of piping is sold and where serious men discuss its various properties. For instance: what kind of pipe is ideal to transport a tarantula under her clothes and onto her face?

. . . .

"That is a strange plan," says the store employee.

His eyes lift toward the ceiling, the same reaction everyone has when Asmara describes her tarantula idea. The name tag on his shirt says "Richard."

"The space beneath the stage is three feet tall," Asmara says. "I'm five foot five. So, my friend suggested we place one tube vertically through the hole until there is enough room to connect a second tube which will be tall enough to complete the task."

Richard's eyes come back down.

"The tube only needs to reach your collar, not the top of your head," he says. "That would knock a foot off how much length we need."

Yes. He's paying attention and doesn't think I'm insane.

"Good point," Asmara says. "And the plunger will double the length."

"Follow me."

She matches his determined pace as they zig-zag through several aisles and reach the area she hoped to discover today—an oasis of pipes.

"Take a look at these various widths," he says, "The smaller the diameter, the less likely you'll see it under your clothes. However, that will leave less room for the spider to safely travel."

Wow, this guy REALLY pays attention.

Asmara extracts a three-foot length of pipe from a display box and wields it like a mighty sword. She takes a few slow motion swings and Richard is unamused.

"Excalibur," she says, for no reason.

Asmara raises the hollow pipe to her eye as if it's a telescope and peers at Richard. A close-up of his face fills the light at the end of the tunnel.

"This is as good a width as any," she says. "Um, can I put it under my sweatshirt?"

"Sure," he replies, turning away to give her privacy.

Asmara slides the pipe under her loose-fitting top until it reaches her collar. The rigid beam tugs on her clothing and its cold contact between her breasts is incredibly foreign. However, she is pleased her sweatshirt is not misshapen. There is no tent-pole effect. And when she wears a skirt the night of the show the lower half of her body will conceal the rest of the pipe.

"Does my sweatshirt look unusual?" she asks Richard, who turns to face her.

"No," he says. "The audience at your show will never suspect it."

"Great."

"Also, we have versions of that pipe which have inter-locking adaptions so you can link them."

Richard draws out two more tube samples and demonstrates the twist motion which connects the two pipes. "We don't have rubber-tipped plungers here that are four feet long. We will have to engineer our own."

"Good point."

Asmara runs her hands along the various pipes. The answer to the puzzle reveals itself. She was hung up on the idea of a syringe-style plunger and neglected to consider any tube within a tube will suffice as an "elevator" for the spider. Asmara grabs a sample which appears to fit within the pipe diameter her and Richard decided on.

The smaller hollow tube fits perfectly within the larger one. She slides it in and out and there is no harsh friction or excess wiggle room.

"I'll put duct tape on the top of this interior pipe for the spider to sit on," Asmara says.

"Yes," he says, "you've got yourself a plunger. Clever thinking. How about I cut you two lengths of this new size to match the original two?"

"Perfect."

As Richard heads into the back area there is a sense of accomplishment at how the project is coming together. Momentum is often self-fulfilling. Next up, get a tarantula.

A shiver electrifies her upper body. She is not nervous about Word Bound. She is excited.

Richard returns and walks her to the cash register. "Good luck with the show," he says, as he finishes ringing up her purchase.

"You were a big help, Richard."

"And be careful," he says. "I don't want to read about some tragedy with you at an open-mic night."

Thanks. Dick.

CHAPTER 21

"Your magic trick sounds fun," says Ken, the pet store employee, "but the spider may get injured if forced through a small tube. I'm not comfortable selling one of our animals if I know it's going to be hurt."

"That's my point," Asmara says. "You don't know it will get hurt."

"We're allowed to use discretion who we sell our animals to."

A weight of disappointment sinks in Asmara's stomach. "Aren't you infringing on my constitutional right to buy a tarantula? This country was founded on spider ownership."

Ken smiles. Asmara tries to pry it open wider. "Look," she says, "I like that you care enough about the tarantula to not want it harmed. I'll do a tube test in front of you."

"It's not just the tube that's a risk. If the tarantula falls from any serious height its abdomen will burst and it will die."

Asmara gives Ken a look of earnest resolve. "That's all the more reason for me to be careful. I swear."

Ken at last detects Asmara is an arachnid ally. "All right," he says. "What have you got?"

She shows him the pipes she bought at the hardware store. "Here's the device which will go under my clothes. Do you think the spider will fit through this tube?"

"Let's find out."

They walk through aisles of pet food and an outlandish variety of dog toys. Even a golden retriever puppy would regard this crap as overkill.

After going down a ramp, Ken leads her to a basement with drab cinder-block walls. Warehouse-style metal shelving holds cages and tanks filled with reptiles, amphibians, and some bugs. This store made no effort to showcase the creatures in any enticing way. These beasts are not even on the same pet spectrum as furry bundles of joy like cats and dogs.

"Here is a Chilean Rose Hair tarantula," Ken says, pointing toward a clear plastic tank. "They are known for being docile and easy to handle."

Within the container, there is a bedding of soil and wood chips, a shallow water dish, and an open-fronted plastic lump which mimics a gray rock. Inside the modest lair crouches a dark ball of hair and legs. Its armored body is covered in spike-like hairs. Asmara marvels at how nature crafted such an imposing predator.

A lifelong ease around household spiders allowed her to humanely catch and release them from indoors. She would plop a drinking cup on top of the interlopers, slide paper beneath them and lift the captive up to her eye-level. Asmara would inspect their grotesque and fascinating forms before she passed judgment on their fate. And when she deemed them worthy of continued life and freed them outside—as she did every time— she would bask in her benevolent dominion.

However, those experiences with small spiders did not prepare her for the shadowy ball of exoskeleton facing her now.

"You seem hesitant," Ken says. "All I can say is she almost certainly won't bite you."

"She?"

"Yes. Most of our tarantulas are females."

Ken lifts the fake rock out of the enclosure with the spider inside. "I fed her a fat cricket today, so she's happy and content right now."

He tilts the plastic lump toward his palm and the once-compact ball of legs begins to expand. Two large forelegs stretch out of the rock as they tap and explore Ken's upraised hand.

The rest of the beast spills onto Ken's palm. With all of its limbs extended, the tarantula is twice as big as it initially appeared.

Crawling forward, the spider is on the move but it doesn't get anywhere. Ken alternates his hands as platforms, creating a treadmill for the animal.

"This kind of a spider won't blindly leap," he says. "It always wants to have safe, sure footing. They're very cautious."

The futility of the hand treadmill becomes apparent to the animal and it stops moving.

"Want to take her for a ride?" Ken says.

Asmara rolls up her sleeve to expose bare forearm and Ken tilts the ominous cargo toward her. The spider again sends two exploratory legs to inspect this new landscape. As it taps her flesh, Asmara stifles a gasp. She doesn't have time to react as the tarantula transfers onto her arm. Her instinct is to fling the creature as if it's a red-hot coal. But with each passing second, the interaction becomes more compelling than fearful.

This is so cool.

The trust-building honeymoon between the two species hits a snag when the tarantula adjusts its mandibles, thus giving Asmara a view of its elaborate mouth parts. A pair of sharp, curved fangs descend from its supposed "face" and hover above her bare skin. As if those hooks weren't intimidating enough, it's chilling to note they also pump venom into prey.

"Can I have her walk on my face as a test?"

"When agitated, these spiders fling off hairs which will irritate your eyes. But she is calm now. Let's give it a try."

Ken's hand swoops under the tarantula and he balances the spider next to Asmara's jaw. The creature's now-familiar leg taps on her cheek don't startle Asmara this time. All eight legs make the transition to her face and there is a small tug of gravity as its weight dangles by her mouth. The spider takes a few steps and stops on her right temple. Asmara walks in a circle to get a feel for the passenger. Its sensation on her skin is already routine.

Like an expert tarantula wrangler, Ken brushes his hand across Asmara's face and scoops up the spider. He also picks up the interlaced plastic pipes Asmara purchased this morning. "Take these," he says. "I'm not going to force the animal down the chute but we'll see if she takes the plunge on her own."

Asmara holds the device at a steep angle and Ken tilts his hand toward the top of the pipes. Tarantula leg-taps on the cylinder create a pitter-patter echo as it surveys this strange terrain. Either the spider has an adventurous spirit or it's a dumb critter because the animal chooses to drop into the tube with a fateful descent.

It slip-slides down the tunnel. A scratching sound emanates from the pipe as the tarantula's limbs fail to grip the smooth interior. The spider falls out of the bottom hole and plops safely into Ken's palm. If the creature is terrified or calm, Asmara has no idea, because it squats there like it always does.

"This idea might work," Ken says. "You don't believe in jinxing do you?"

"No."

"Good. You may want to research what to do if the tarantula bites you. Because I don't have a clue."

CHAPTER 22

"Hi Zoe, this is Asmara. Ryan gave me your number. I attached a photo of my neighbor's car scratch. Would this work for your school project?"

Perhaps not surprisingly for a teenager, Zoe's text reply arrives within twenty seconds. "Hey!!! That's cool you thought of me. Sure, I have some basic questions about the scratch. I can either call the person myself or send you the question list"

"Send me the questions. I'll talk to her and report back to you."

"Awesome! Thanks again. :) Are you still going to do your crazy spider plan?"

"Yes, I bought the tarantula and tubes today. I'll have a stage test at The Naomi soon"

"Sick!! Please ask the manager if I can join, even tho it's a 21+ bar night. I promise I won't buy a beer. LOL"

"I'll do that"

"Great! Also, I'm going to Ryan's new bike shop in SF tomorrow. He's gonna pay me to help set up stuff. Maybe you could swing by for a hello??"

Any social invitation, big or small, gives Asmara a nice ray of gratitude. But it's strange to be interacting with a teenager like this.

"I'll text Ryan and see if it's OK for me to bother you two while you work"

"Ha! You don't have to ask. Ryan told me to invite you. He's next to me right now. We're helping my dad clear out our garage"

"All right, it's a deal. I'll see you tomorrow. And make sure Ryan doesn't accidentally blow himself up with your dad's dynamite"

"Not funny :("

. . . .

The tarantula container sits next to folded laundry in Asmara's room. She lays in bed reading the pet-care pamphlet included with purchase.

Most of the advice is obvious—*yeah, no shit, I'm not going to bathe this creature under a sink faucet.*

These suggestions, with their helpful illustrations of a smiling spider, are idiot-proof. *Although they've never met this idiot before.*

Filling the spider's water dish is simple and there will be no cricket sacrifice ritual required, thanks to Ken the pet store employee. He fed the tarantula a meal this morning and Asmara will return the spider back to the store before it needs to feed again.

Regardless, Asmara is committed to this animal's proper care. After a lifetime of catching and releasing spiders, the thought of a fatality would weigh heavy on her.

. . . .

Out comes the most recent draft of *Lightning in Ojai.* Loose hand-written pages surround Asmara's laptop like an altar on her bed. These reference pages stand ready in case she wants to thread older material into the story. Asmara hesitates before reading the updated version on her laptop. It felt good to hammer out those lines yesterday, but in the past her written gold often turned out to be garbage when revisited later.

She dives in.

Asmara swims through the story in a few minutes and does not absorb anything. This happens sometimes. Her mind needs a warm-up before actual reading comprehension takes place.

She sets aside her laptop and reclines on the bed. Her thoughts narrow as she prepares for more focused attention. With a burst of motion which startles herself, Asmara springs upright and yanks the computer toward her face. She reads the story again, although at a more rapid rate than the first time. It makes no sense to do this. She should be reading slowly if she wants the words to gain traction.

She finishes reading *Lightning in Ojai* in half the time of the previous review. Asmara doesn't even take a breath before she starts reading again from the start. The sentences stream by at an even faster pace.

By the fourth time around, this cannot be called "reading" at all. There are just blurry horizontal lines imprinting themselves into her brain.

Asmara's eyes ache and she blinks furiously to appease them. It's as if a direct link has been created between her mind and the story and she cannot break the download.

Hoping to sever the connection, she pries her eyes away from the screen while tossing the laptop to the side. Falling backward from a seated position, Asmara bounces on the mattress and her legs kick toward the ceiling. Loose pages lift up and flutter around her.

Maybe it's an illusion because of the eye strain, but the sheets of paper do not behave like inanimate objects falling naturally onto the bed around her.

Instead, for a few seconds, the pages levitate.

CHAPTER 23

Lisa is a low-conflict roommate but her habit of scattering junk mail by the front door annoys Asmara. The envelopes and coupons are evenly distributed in the area, as if manure was being spread.

It's a small battle Asmara concedes in order to save ammunition for future disputes with Lisa. Although, a full war never arises.

The junk mail is prominent today. As she gathers the items a jingle of keys are heard in the hallway. It's her neighbor Inga, the Russian immigrant, arriving home. Inga's habits are a mystery and Asmara is never sure when the woman is inside her monastery-like apartment. Inga lives alone and if she has family who visits then Asmara has never seen or heard them.

This is a good time to catch Inga and ask about her car getting scratched. Who wouldn't want to contribute a vandalism story into a kid's survey? Worst case scenario, Inga will spit on the floor and mutter an ancient curse.

Asmara opens her door. "Hello, there."

"Oh," Inga replies. "What a nice surprise."

"How are things?"

"I'm fine. I've been at the hospital all day."

"I'm sorry to hear that. I don't want to pry but I hope it's not serious."

Long pause. "It's the usual appointments. They take good care of me."

For Asmara, the car scratch project is trivial now. She isn't sure where to turn the conversation.

"You know," Inga says, "we haven't met in the hallway like this in some time. How is your... friend, Lisa?"

I wonder if she thinks I'm a lesbian.

"Lisa is good. We have different schedules and we don't see each other much."

"Ah, I understand. That must be hard on you two."

Damn. She thinks we're lesbians.

"We manage to make it work. And we get along well when we're home together."

The answer is ambiguous enough. Asmara considers adding lurid lies. *Inga, I must confess I miss the intimacy with my female lover, Lisa, ever since she ordered a gasoline-powered sex toy.*

"Well," Inga says, "I'm not much of an exciting host, but you're always welcome to stop by for tea or a hello."

"Thank you. And the same holds for you at our place as well. We're right across the hall."

Asmara senses an opening to ask about the car scratch but Inga throws a curve ball.

"How about right now?" Inga asks.

"Um. How about what?"

"You coming over. I don't mean to put you on the spot but I'm about to have tea to unwind. And I don't know the next time I'll bump into you like this."

Asmara's reflex is to say no, even though they extended invitations to each other one second ago. Crossing the threshold into her neighbor's world is a massive chasm. Regardless, she is compelled to take the leap.

"Sure," Asmara says. "I'd love to come over."

"Wonderful."

The neighbor's door is opened and Asmara passes the event horizon into uncharted territory.

. . . .

Yup. There it is. Framed on a wall.

Asmara knew this Russian woman's apartment would contain a vintage screenprint poster from her homeland. No grim Communist-era political propaganda here. This graphic design is festive and charming. The illustration displays an orchestra performing in an ornate hall. Russian typography is splashed across the scene.

"Ah, yes," Inga says, as Asmara leans toward the poster. "My parents bought that seventy years ago. They went to a symphony in Moscow when they first started dating."

"That's sweet."

"Can you believe I have no photos of my parents together when they were young? The images were all lost."

"How did it happen?"

"A friend from their church offered to make digital scans of my parents' old photos, for safekeeping. My father reluctantly handed them over. This same fellow who was trying to help out lost the entire photo album. He left it on a bus."

"Left on a bus? I feel sick to my stomach hearing that."

"Yes, it's sad. The friend apologized as much as one person could ever apologize. There's nothing more which can be done."

Asmara frowns from the dismal story.

Inga walks into the kitchen while talking. "As for the poster, now it is like a holy sacrament to me in their honor."

"That's a nice way to put it."

"I only have lemon tea at the moment," Inga says from around the corner. "It's a Russian brand you've probably never heard of."

"Sounds great."

Asmara strolls around the living room. It is tidy to the point of being immaculate. A small table is covered edge-to-edge in prescription pill bottles. Beneath the table is a wicker basket filled with even more pill bottles, but these are empty.

Whatever the medicine aims to accomplish, at a certain point it must be like trying to stop the tide.

"I don't want to embarrass you," Inga says from the kitchen, "but I think it's neat how you agreed to come over."

"It's about time we did this."

"I'm realistic about these things," Inga says as she returns to the living room. "Fun, young women don't want to spend time with their old neighbors. Growing up in Russia, I had aunts and uncles on my street I was obligated to spend time with. I loved them dearly but often I was desperate to visit friends my age."

"Family is important."

"Yes, of course. The tea will be ready soon. Have a seat."

Asmara sits on a chair and its upholstery emits a loud crack, as if the fabric hadn't been sat on in years.

"To be honest," Inga says, taking a seat of her own, "I wouldn't dream of hijacking your time for long. I don't want you to tire of me your first time over here."

"I also limit my time with people," Asmara says. "In fact..."

She stops herself. Does she want to spill romantic gossip about Ryan to her elderly Russian neighbor? The answer would be "hell no" most times but today is different.

"...I met a guy the other night. I don't date often and this has been a whirlwind for me. But I want to monitor our time together in order to keep things exciting."

Inga's eyes open wide and her eyebrows rise halfway up her forehead. *Did I really tell this woman that I don't date often?*

"My point," Asmara says, "is that limiting time with people is sometimes better than overexposure."

"I'm happy for you. I suggest if you like him, you don't want to limit your time too much. Then you're depriving each other."

Inga's eyebrows lower and she points toward a nearby wall. Or more specifically, she points through the wall, across the hallway and in the general direction of Lisa, who is the other half of the presumed lesbian couple. Inga made an assumption Asmara was a lesbian and has been confronted with conflicting information.

She pivots from the subject. "What do you think about the guy in 23E loudly talking on speaker phone?"

"You can hear that, too?" Asmara says. "I believe they are doing a video chat. It helps they're speaking in Chinese because I don't understand what they're saying and I can tune it out easier."

"Their volume is annoying and yet, him and that woman…"

"They seem romantic, right?"

"Yes! I can't comprehend a word of what they say but it's clear they're tender to each other. It's tough to complain about a couple being in love."

"One time I heard him crying while he talked to her. She was crying on the other end as well. I felt guilty listening to them but I figure it's not eavesdropping if you can't understand anything."

Asmara flashes back to riding in Ryan's car on the Bay Bridge yesterday, listening to a particular piece of music. From the back seat, Zoe interpreted the guitar's notes as an expression of its love for another guitar. The music now reminds Asmara of the neighbor in 23E. Perhaps lovesickness produces universal sounds.

From the kitchen, the kettle starts to whistle.

. . . .

The tea is way too sweet. Nevertheless, Asmara consumes three cups and spends an hour chatting with Inga. With each sip, Asmara has to force herself to not wince from the tooth-melting potion.

They talk about apartment life—the adorable brother-sister duo who never tire of riding scooters in the courtyard, the pathetic mailbox lock which can be bypassed with a finger flick (or maybe even a stiff breeze), the eye-watering incense odor which clings to the property manager. They discover they both enjoy Broadway Thai, although they argue about their favorite dishes.

Not once does Inga ask what Asmara does for a living. It's a welcome omission.

The conversation runs its course and lasts longer than they both expected. Inga skips subtlety and gives a loud sigh of exhaustion. Asmara lifts her teacup and takes one last sip of the decadent nectar. She runs her tongue across her teeth expecting to find fresh pot-holed cavities.

Zoe's project. I never asked about the car scratch.

"Before I head back to my place," Asmara says, "I have something unusual to ask you."

"What is it?"

"I know a fourteen-year-old girl in Oakland. A sweet, smart kid. For her middle school project she is conducting a survey on people who have had their car keyed."

"What does that mean?"

"The project is about cars which have been scratched with lines cut into the paint. This is usually done by someone using their keys to do the scratch."

Inga maintains a blank look.

"And, well," Asmara continues, "yesterday I walked by your car and I noticed a scratch down the side."

Inga's eyes narrow.

"It's a somewhat common occurrence," Asmara says, "Cars being keyed, that is. There are rotten people out there who damage other people's vehicles. And for dumb reasons, too."

Inga is still expressionless but a reaction brews inside her.

"I was just wondering," Asmara says, "if you'd be willing to contribute your story to..."

Inga's upper lip curls into a sneer. The gentle creases of her face contort into deep furrows of anger. It is a flash, though. Her expression snaps back into a neutral state.

"How strange," Inga blurts out. Her voice is louder than Asmara expected. "How very strange."

"Did I say something wrong?" Asmara asks. "I didn't mean to offend you."

Inga smiles and beams with a pleasant glow. She has erased the disapproval which turned her face into an angry mask, but something remains altered.

"Honey, I'm not upset at you," Inga says. "It was unusual and I was caught off guard."

"What was unusual?"

"Everything you said."

The words hang in the air. It's as if Asmara is supposed to be painfully aware of something she cannot grasp.

Inga fills her in. "I was just thinking about that car scratch. It appeared in my mind one second before you mentioned it."

"That is odd. What a coincidence."

Inga forces another smile but this one is different than the ones which came before. It is a cold, unfriendly transmission. "It's as if you were reading my mind. Are you able to hear what I'm thinking?"

Asmara is at a loss. Should she stoop so low as to declare she is not, in fact, a psychic vampire who feasts on her neighbor's thoughts?

Inga stopped blinking some time ago. Her stare is relentless.

"I don't think that's possible," Asmara says. "Reading minds, that is. And if it is real, I certainly can't do it."

Inga gives her head a shake and her eyes light up with recognition, as if Asmara had only now walked into the apartment.

Yeah, this woman is nuts.

Their parting minutes are a blur. There's not much Asmara can do to repair this awkward ending. Inga shifts topics by asking if Asmara will scan the old Russian orchestra poster. An archivist friend of hers in Moscow asked for a high-resolution digital version. Inga jokes how Asmara is unlikely to lose the poster during a bus ride between their two front doors.

In a daze, Asmara agrees to the task, thanks Inga for the tea and scurries back to the safety of her home while carrying the poster.

. . . .

It's impossible for Asmara to have known this at the time but, along with her Word Bound performance in four days, the decision to step across the hall and enter Inga's apartment has put the planet on a collision course with total annihilation.

CHAPTER 24

There's nothing wrong with this preliminary act before things get serious. In fact, it would be irresponsible for Asmara to *not* take this step. Her laptop is open and it's time to conduct an internet search of her future boyfriend, Ryan Smith.

He has perhaps launched his own probe of her background as well. Asmara is at ease regarding the modest search results under her name. Ryan might find her running time from a 10k women's race she participated in long ago. Hopefully, he's not judgmental of her snail-like finish time.

Ryan's full name is so common she doesn't bother with a basic search, especially on social media. Key words need to be added. She starts with

"Ryan Smith, Oakland." Articles regarding an Oakland city council member pop up. He has very white teeth and appears to be a nice guy. But he's of no help.

She tries "Ryan Smith, One Track Mind." The bike store's website appears along with customer reviews. There is one promising post from several years ago. "The Bay Area Business Blog chats with the owner of Oakland's newest bike shop."

She clicks the link hoping for an in-depth interview but it's a four-paragraph fluff piece of advertising. There is also an unflattering photo of Ryan with long bangs in his face and acne on his cheeks.

One line in the article gives Asmara another lead in her research. "Ryan Q Smith gained a degree of acclaim in the skateboard world before his passion transitioned into bikes."

Ah, of course. I forgot to add the Q to his name.

Zoe had explained earlier how, in the skateboard world, Ryan's middle initial was used to differentiate him from another Ryan Smith pro skater.

She types in "Ryan Q Smith, skateboarding."

A flood of articles and thumbnail images of a young Ryan pop up. Even though skateboarding is an activity she cares little about, Asmara can't deny this archived attention about Ryan is exciting.

One of the video links says: "Ryan Q Smith, first full part." She clicks the thumbnail icon and is soon disappointed. It contains low-quality VHS footage of a guy cruising around on a skateboard, although she's not sure what else she expected. Punk music strains her laptop speakers and she lunges to hit the mute button. A rapid edit leaps from scene to scene with no connecting theme beyond the board flipping under his feet. The post has a meager 6,104 views, a viral reach which could be surpassed by uploading any amusing cat video.

Asmara scrolls through the other search findings. The phrase "Ryan's Line" is repeated in different posts.

That's right. His famous stunt.

Asmara spots a link which says "Ryan's Line, original edit."

A video pops up and the timeline indicates it's short—fifteen seconds. Asmara is confused by the clip's play count. It reads 3.7 million views, but that can't be right. This is one skateboard trick.

She hits play.

The video begins with Ryan riding his board fast along a skinny ledge, six feet above the sidewalk. Click-clack, click-clack, click-clack. This footage quality is high-definition and crystal clear. Asmara recognizes the downtown plaza environment from the book photo.

The marble slab Ryan is riding on drops out of sight as he reaches its abrupt end. Ryan launches from the tall ledge, flies an outlandish distance through the air—his blue flannel flapping like a superhero cape—and he lands his skateboard on a separate narrow ledge which is about waist-high. Asmara lets loose an audible gasp at how dangerous this maneuver appears to be.

Ryan maintains a steady line as he rolls along the second thin ledge— all while racing at a reckless high speed. His body language shows how gravity conspires with momentum to yank him off the runway. He fights them both to hold a straight path. The struggle is a success as he arrives at the end of the second ledge and hops off onto the sidewalk. Ryan rides out of view from the camera and carries himself, evidently, into skate history.

Although illiterate in the nuances of skateboarding, Asmara was able to translate this particular stunt. The way in which the clip is comprehensible to non-skaters might explain its internet success.

After a fade-to-black effect, the same video of Ryan plays again but in slow motion. His soaring hang-time is more pronounced. His blue flannel flaps with even more cinematic flair. His efforts to not tumble off the second ledge are extra-heroic. It's great stuff.

Beneath the link are related video suggestions. One is listed as a short web documentary where skaters talk about the influence of this single trick. The video is called, *"He Went From Here To There: The legacy of Ryan's Line."* Asmara makes a mental note to watch it later.

She is about to conclude this background check when an item leaps off her computer screen. It is an archived chatroom discussion and the forum's question is savagely blunt:

"Does anyone know how the Ryan's Line guy lost his eye?"

Up until this point, all Asmara knows is a bullet once entered Ryan's skull, deleted his right eye, and somehow he survived the ordeal. She is one click away from learning the crucial details. Was it a no-fault accident? Was he the victim of a violent crime? Or, God forbid, did Ryan partake in some insane mutual combat scenario? Decent people don't often find themselves in a Wild West shoot-out.

If Ryan did have a violent past culminating in his near-death by gunfire, could she get past it?

She pictures him addressing the subject. "Asmara, I know we just met, but what are your thoughts on massive bodily trauma suffered during a justifiable homicide attempt?"

Asmara started this internet search hoping to uncover information on Ryan. Now she is throttled by the ancient adage: be careful what you wish for.

The link teases her by showing twenty-four comments are contained within. That's two dozen opportunities for anonymously-generated bile to be spewed. The remarks in there may be filled with lies and rumors about Ryan's shooting.

This digital portal is a trap. Her relationship with Ryan shouldn't hinge on gossip written by teenage skateboarders. She turns off the laptop and sets the computer aside.

Asmara wonders if there's a Congressional Medal for Superhuman Restraint. She just nominated herself.

CHAPTER 25

Asmara grabs Ryan's book, *Rain Rising Over An Oakland Horizon*, and sits in her favorite reading chair.

Sunlight shines through the window in the living room and the photons feel fabulous. She peels back the cover.

The opening to the story is a free-form conversation between two people driving on the open road. Pages go by with nothing but dialogue. The narrator, who is behind the wheel, and a person sitting in the passenger seat trade viewpoints. These verbal exchanges are rapid, plausible and, as Ryan had warned, often pessimistic. The narrator wallows in nihilistic tropes which would be familiar to any joyless individual who decided life sucks. He touches on the purity of oblivion (nothing is more beautiful than no things). He complains about the lack of consent when one is dragged into existence through birth (no one volunteers to be born). And he whines about how time and entropy will claw back any progress humans make, so, collectively, what's the point in trying?

The narrator's outlook is downbeat but snappy dialogue and injections of humor prevent the story from being insufferable. Maybe Ryan had foreseen he was testing readers' patience at this point in his story because the vibe changes. Ryan mentioned the book's negativity but he had forgotten the wonderful counterpoint he provided in the mysterious character riding shotgun—a man named Omar. Through friendly persuasion, Omar guides the unnamed narrator back from the brink of a pessimism spiral. Moaning about the emptiness of modern life is easy, Omar says, until you decide to sacrifice its benefits. If daily drudgery is so bad, take a long hike and find yourself in a pre-technological age. The wilderness calls out to you and your melancholy, and it'd be happy to eat you alive, one insect bite at a time. If you're lucky enough to survive a few days isolated in nature, there are bountiful grocery stores which await your return to civilization.

As the narrator goes to acrobatic lengths to remain a cynic, it's evident his miserable state is a self-fulfilling choice. Meanwhile, Omar's optimism radiates off the page and becomes infectious for the reader.

Dialogue comes to a halt and descriptive passages of sights from the highway fill the pages. The story perspective alternates between the two characters as they sit in silence and observe the same things passing by their windows.

Now the writing is unleashed. Ryan has real skills, even if he grinds the gears of his own talent here and there.

After one particularly well-written section where the characters pass through a motorcycle rally and they each muse about the bikers' lives, Asmara picks up her phone to write a text to Ryan.

"I'm halfway through *Rain Rising*. I really like it. I want to be more like Omar"

A vibration reply soon stirs her attention.

"Omar... I forgot about him. I haven't read that book since I wrote it"

"My elderly neighbor accused me of reading her mind today. She was not kidding"

"Your neighbor thinks you're a psychic? If you are, what am I thinking about right now?"

"I think that you think I'm a weirdo. Hey, I watched Ryan's Line. Nice jump, bro"

"That stupid clip haunts my life. Oh yeah, I ran into the neck-tattoo Naomi manager today. He said it's OK if we do a Word Bound test under the stage. I was hoping to pick you up tonight and go to the venue. Are you down?"

"Yes"

"Cool. Tell the tarantula to get ready"

CHAPTER 26

The last time Asmara tried to read *Lightning in Ojai* it was as if the sentences observed her instead. Now the words appear like a normal file on her laptop screen.

Scrolling through the story, Asmara calculates it is still too long for the five-minute Word Bound slot. She braces herself for the laborious process of editing. Her assumption is it will take several hours to pare away the excess words like a careful surgeon. However, as she reviews the story on the screen Asmara allows herself to gaze upon the paragraphs themselves—their various shapes, their internal textures formed by letters.

She begins editing, not by analysis, but by instinct. Instead of hacking away written material with a machete or slicing unwanted text with a scalpel, Asmara condenses her story by merely observing it and even *listening* to it. Entire paragraphs highlight themselves and volunteer for obliteration. Other sections whisper how they should be left alone. Massive chunks of her hard-earned prose do not object as they are eliminated.

As hundreds of words dissolve on her laptop, the final story emerges. Asmara goes to The Naomi's website and, as the employee Elizabeth had mentioned, there is a tab for Word Bound. Once clicked, an email window pops up with a notification:

Asmara copies all of *Lightning in Ojai* and pastes it in the email tab. Elizabeth must receive these notices so Asmara addresses her directly.

"Hi Elizabeth, this is Asmara. I'm the one planning the surprise stunt at Word Bound. (Thanks again for helping us clear beneath the stage.) I'm writing you to request a slot for the next event and to send you the full story for review. Please reply if you have any questions. Thank you."

Asmara hits "send" and is struck by a revelation: *Lightning in Ojai* is now alive. The story had been caged in a small world no bigger than her laptop. Now, for the first time, her writing soars through the air, bouncing off cellular towers, and it will soon leap into the mind of someone else.

It occurs to her a more meaningful Patient Zero would be Ryan. He should be the initial infected recipient of *Lightning in Ojai*.

Asmara emails the story to herself in a document. She picks up her phone, sends the attachment to Ryan, and includes a message:

"Since I kidnapped your book, I wanted to share some of my own writing. This story is what I'm going to read at Word Bound. It's a weird one but take a spin"

After years of inertia it is liberating to set her words free. However, reading them out loud on stage might be a disappointment so crushing she collapses into a black hole in front of a startled audience.

Asmara will find out either way in three days.

· ·

She is in a good place. The clothes she chose are no different than if she was meeting friends for dinner. The light touch of makeup is the same effort she would apply before a day of errands. Asmara lays on the couch, waiting for Ryan to pick her up in fifteen minutes. They will then pick-up Zoe at the new bike store.

She is not freaking out and anxiety is not squeezing her like a coiled anaconda. Or at least that's the lie she's telling herself.

Asmara flips through the science magazine again. The photos of

Europa floating in space continue to enchant her. She skips around the article and one passage jumps out.

"Through the lens of astrobiology, it is conceivable simple lifeforms may have arisen in Europa's oceans. From that reasonable hypothesis, it's hard not to let one's imagination run wild. With enough time (something our solar system has plenty of), the forces of evolution could have produced complex lifeforms in the dark depths. The moon's icy shell is so vast and formidable these underwater species might require ages to breach their environmental barrier. Maybe the Europan aliens wouldn't even know there is a boundary to begin with. From their perspective, their solid, icy "sky" is the edge of all known reality, with nothing beyond."

Asmara puts down the magazine and basks in fascination. What a concept—these hypothetical alien fish, believing they are entombed under an infinite dome of ice. Could there be explorers among their species who dream of a dimension past the frozen veil? Perhaps they are deemed heretics by the squid high priests and punished for blasphemy.

She imagines the first revelation when the fish break through Europa's surface and discover the universe beyond. For millennia, humans had a transparent night sky in which to ponder wider existence. The Europans would get a crash course in reality's hard truth—how they had always existed on a frozen pebble rocketing through limitless space.

Her phone vibrates. Ryan is here.

. . . .

"There is the main event," Ryan says as the tarantula cube is loaded into the back seat. "Does he have a name?"

"Nah," Asmara says. "I don't want to get too attached. This is all business. Also, it's a female."

"How about naming her Octavia because eight is..."

Asmara hops into the passenger seat and Ryan's voice trails off as he locks eyes with her. His face beams with affection and she prepares for a potential kiss. A gigantic, unrestrained smile stretches wide across her face. It's all teeth and gumline and nothing like her usual close-mouthed grin. Asmara is embarrassed how she may look like a horse and she swivels her head with a laugh. Ryan puts the car into drive.

Soon they are on Broadway. The next three intersections ahead are visible and they're all green lights.

"I almost kissed you back there," he says.

"I know."

"I'm not trying to be aggressive. These past couple of days with you have been wild. And it keeps going, now with this whole Naomi thing."

"Yeah, this has been fun."

Asmara pulls the seatbelt strap from off her chest. Once her upper-body is free, she lunges from her seat and plants a full-lipped kiss on Ryan's cheek.

"Yes!" he says. "I'll take what I can get."

"That was for letting me stay over in Oakland. And making me breakfast. And introducing me to Zoe. And taking me skating. And helping move stuff beneath the stage. And picking me up tonight."

"No problem. I enjoyed every one of those things as well."

"Oh, and... you can write! I love *Rain Rising* so far. A lot of young people that age over-write but you had a nice, restrained touch."

"I wouldn't know. I remember the overall story but I probably couldn't even recognize my own writing."

"For real, it's good. I like when Omar and the narrator view the same things and have different perspectives."

"I have a news flash: the angry narrator represented me at the time I wrote it."

"Shocking. That's what I figured."

"I included Omar because no one would have read the damn thing if it was just my voice complaining about everything. I had to add some light to the darkness."

"Well, it worked."

"*Lightning in Ojai* was great, too, by the way. It is short, though. I wanted it to keep going."

"Thanks. It's a condensed version of a longer story."

"I was surprised it was science fiction."

"Really? I don't view it as science fiction."

"Oh, come on. A scientist creates artificial intelligence and it zaps him with lightning? That's the definition of science fiction."

"I just viewed it as a weird story. And, actually, the scientist never created artificial intelligence."

"Yeah, you're right. His experiments opened a doorway to another dimension and allowed something to cross over."

Ryan summarizing details of her story gives Asmara satisfaction. It shows he paid attention and didn't skim it.

They glide into a parking spot in front of the new One Track Mind storefront. Although the interior is dimly lit, the place is brimming with bicycles. They walk to the front door.

Asmara doesn't do jealousy. That shade is not part of her personality palette. And yet, she has a sting of insecurity how Ryan owns two stores, made history on his skateboard, and wrote a decent book in his youth—

and she's an unemployed woman hoping an open-mic night will change her life around.

Before Ryan puts his key into the door it swings open. Zoe emerges from inside the store with a grin. She is still wearing the over-sized One Track Mind shirt Ryan gave her. It's been cleaned but small holes from her skate slams are visible.

Zoe comes in low and gives Asmara a tight embrace at waist level. While maintaining the bear hug, she cranes her neck and lifts her big brown eyes. "Did you bring the spider?"

CHAPTER 27

Zoe's foot clips the curb and she staggers onto the sidewalk in front of The Naomi. This would be unremarkable except she holds a plastic cube with delicate spider cargo inside.

Asmara gives Zoe an angry snort.

With the venue looming over her, Asmara is bewildered by the events of these past few days. Different paths have intersected and looped back around.

Zoe lurches toward The Naomi's front door and, for a second time, she stumbles. Asmara produces a growl of disapproval as Zoe hurries inside before she is bombarded with more zoo noises.

They enter the establishment and there are only twelve people spread around the dining area. A flicker of motion sways like a windshield wiper in the corner of Asmara's eye. It's James and Elizabeth waving their arms, trying to get the attention of the three stooges who walked in.

Asmara waves back with the plastic tubing in her hand and it smacks an exit sign above her. The impact is so loud she may have cracked the frame. They all cringe and hustle over to the bar.

"The spider squad is in the building," James says as the group converges. "Shit just got real."

"It's been real," Asmara says.

"To be honest," James says, "as you first pitched the idea I could hear your commitment. That's why I said yes, because you were sincere."

This Australian stranger described one of the outcomes Asmara hoped to generate with the project—a sense of drive which radiates self-confidence. It appears to be manifesting already.

"We're ready to rock," Asmara says. "We've got a tarantula and a transport tube."

"And a teenager," Ryan adds, casting a thumb in Zoe's direction. "Can she assist us during Word Bound if it's a bar night?"

"I'm pretty sure there are exceptions for minors in a case like this," James says. He addresses Zoe. "For legal purposes we're gonna call you a stunt coordinator. Okay, kid?"

"Sure!" Zoe says.

"Great. By the power invested in me by the city of San Francisco, you are hereby granted access to this venue despite being under twenty-one."

"Cool. Do you really have that power?"

"Ha! There is NO power invested in me. You have more legal rights than I do, kid. My immigration status is a mess. I'm technically not even the manager of this bar."

Asmara and Ryan exchange a look of disbelief.

"Relax," James says. "The owner is my good friend. He kept asking me to do more and more work until I ran the place better than he did. For real, though, I'll probably be deported within a few months."

Asmara musters a nervous laugh.

"Don't worry about me," James says. "I've had a blast and wouldn't change a thing."

"We have a surprise for you," Elizabeth says, changing the subject. She presents a plug-in lamp the size of a small toaster.

"During your show, you won't want to bother with flashlights under the stage," she says. "This will cast wide light and free up your hands."

"Amazing," Asmara says. "Good thinking."

"Since your performance will be a tough act to follow, are you okay with going up last at Word Bound?"

"If that works best, it's fine by me."

"All right then," James bellows. "On with the rehearsal! Your monster is ready for its close-up. Follow me."

"By the way," he adds, "did you just break our exit sign back there?"

. . . .

The storage door opens with a creak as its hinges groan from being awakened. All five members of the group crouch low and peer into the dark void.

Elizabeth unwinds the power cord for the lamp and plugs it into an outlet near the hatch. It turns into an orb of diffuse yellow light. Holding the lamp at its base, she extends her arm into the tomb and the interior is illuminated. Dead center in the space is a blanket, a couple of pillows, and two squat, foldable camping chairs.

"No way," Asmara says. "You did this for us?"

"I didn't do much," James says. "This camping stuff was in the back of my truck. The blanket and pillows are for your comfort and to reduce noise. I doubt you're gonna sleep under there."

"I can't thank you enough. You've shown so much support for my ridiculous plan."

Asmara connects the two transport tubes and slides them together. "Before we are cramped beneath the stage, should we do a test lift with the spider out here in the open?"

Zoe puts the plastic cube on the ground and steps away. A silence descends over the backstage area as if Asmara is about to confront a ticking timebomb.

She unsnaps the container's top latch and opens the lid. The tarantula is in its throne room—the hollow lump of fake rock, where it rules over its domain. Asmara sticks her hand into the tank with the hope Zoe's stumbling didn't turn this passive pet into a blood-thirsty flesh biter.

The rock-cave domicile is extracted. She tilts its opening toward her other hand. Someone, it might be Zoe, lets out a gasp as the creature stretches out all eight legs and they each explore Asmara's skin.

Asmara positions the open end of the combined tubes beneath the spider. The tarantula suspects this device does not serve its best interest and all eight legs snag the rim in defiance.

Asmara is about to give the spider a downward poke with her finger when it retracts its legs, slides down the tube and lands on the taped platform within the device. She peers into the hole and the tarantula is alive and waiting for whatever indignity is next. She pushes the bottom tube and slides it upward. The taped platform rises like an elevator until a flurry of spider legs burst from the opening.

"All right," Asmara says. "Proof of concept. "

. . . .

The skirt has the effect of an unwanted visitor, clinging to her. Asmara is more comfortable with a tarantula on her skin than this alien garment. She bought the dark-blue skirt yesterday at a thrift store.

Unaccustomed to fabric flowing behind her every move, she twirls around, like a dog chasing its tail. Her upper clothing for this test is a loose-fitting maroon sweatshirt which will be forgiving in terms of hiding the plastic tube.

Ryan and Zoe, *bless their hearts,* have crawled into the storage space. Bless their immune systems as well, because it's still filthy under there. Asmara stands backstage atop a platform which serves as a loading dock to wheel equipment onto the main stage. She waits for James to unlock the door from the other side which will lead her into the venue.

The muffled noises of Ryan and Zoe sliding into position in the cramped area get punctuated with a loud thump, an "Ow!" from Ryan and laughter from Zoe.

The doorknob rattles and James emerges. "Showtime," he says. "Or, well, rehearsal time."

She steps through the passage from a banal room of stockpiled boxes onto The Naomi's elevated stage. Even though there is no crowd waiting in anticipation, there are sparks of show-business allure. She appreciates how performers of all kinds must get a rush when they enter the spotlight.

Tonight, the audience is a loose collection of disinterested people spread around the venue. The various faces turn their gaze to James and Asmara standing on stage.

"Hi, everyone," James says. "We're doing a test. Don't mind us."

The people in the venue don't appear to mind as they look away with more disregard than before.

James gets on his knees and lowers himself to the hole in the stage. "Can you two hear me?"

"Yes, we're right here," says Ryan's disembodied voice.

"Good. I have to tell you something. If the spider escapes down there I'm locking you both in the storage area until you find it."

James leans in closer to the hole. "I will burn this building to the ground before I have a loose tarantula trying to kill me."

Ryan's thumb pokes out of the hole causing James' head to jerk out of the way.

"We've got you covered," Ryan says. "Loud and clear."

"Fair enough," James says with a laugh as he rises to his feet. Elizabeth has joined them on stage and she carries the spider's container for when the test is over.

Asmara stands over the hole and gazes upon the entirety of the venue. She tries to imagine this interior filled with an audience staring at her. "What is the crowd size on a Word Bound night?"

"Around two hundred people," Elizabeth says. "Plus staff."

Asmara gives a nervous sigh. "James and Elizabeth, can you step onto the main floor and watch as if you were in the audience?"

"You got it," James says as he and Elizabeth hop to the floor. Asmara confirms the hem of her skirt hovers a mere inch off of the stage.

"Okay, Ryan and Zoe, I'm ready whenever you are."

There is shuffling activity and a murmur of talk from her concealed assistants. A loud smack follows as the tube hits the edge of the hole beneath her. She will need these two to be extra quiet during Word Bound.

Contact is first felt on her right calf. The tube grazes her skin and slides upward, charting a path by the curve of her leg. A concern enters her mind, one she is surprised didn't occur to her earlier.

I do NOT want this device touching my vagina.

As the plastic pole continues its climb between her legs, Asmara devises an impromptu strategy. The moment it reaches her inner thigh she will arch her hips backward and lean forward. This movement should nudge the device onto her abdomen thus avoiding a direct poke. Also, the body tilt will create a bagginess in her loose top which will hide the bulge of the tube.

"How is this speed?" Ryan asks through the hole. "Should I lift slower or faster?"

"A little slower."

Asmara tilts her stance and with a slow-motion wiggle of her hips the plastic pipe bypasses her critical lady parts and transfers onto her abdomen. The tube snags the elastic waistband of her skirt and starts lifting it. With a subtle motion Asmara pinches her skirt and tugs downward. This frees the device and allows it to slide up her belly.

To break the awkward silence, Asmara speaks up. "How are things looking to you two?" she says to James and Elizabeth.

"All good here," James says. "Have you guys started yet?"

"Yeah," Elizabeth says. "Let us know what we should be looking for."

It's music to Asmara's ears. "Really? You haven't seen anything odd?"

As she says these words the transport tube slides between her breasts and arrives at her collar. Asmara taps the pole with her foot three times. She didn't coordinate this signal with Ryan but he gets the message and stops lifting.

"Nothing strange at all?" Asmara asks again.

"It looks like you're leaning toward us a bit," Elizabeth says. "But your posture is not too crazy. Have they slid the tube up yet?"

Wow, they don't see it!

Another logistical hurdle of her plan has been leaped. If the tube had looked ridiculous under her clothes, there is no Plan B.

"Asmara," Ryan calls out from beneath the stage, his voice having a hollow echo as it travels up the tube. "Should we raise the spider?"

"Yes. I'm ready."

The pipe jostles against her chest as Ryan and Zoe try to join the tubes together within their confined space.

"I'm now seeing movement under your sweater," Elizabeth says. "Your breasts are bouncing."

"I know!" Ryan yells out, as if his voice is from beyond the grave.

"We're trying to hold it steady."

"We can barely move down here!" Zoe says.

"Stop shouting," Asmara says. "Your voices are blasting up the tube into my face."

A sliding friction rumbles as the interior tube carries its payload upward. All goes quiet and Asmara is certain the top of the lift has been reached beneath her collar. The grand reveal has arrived at its destination.

With an unnerving burst of sensations, the tarantula scurries up her neck in a full sprint and circles around her face twice before stopping square between her eyes. Every inch of skin covering her skull quivers from the flood of unpleasant signals. She is anchored to the stage with the tube under her clothes and can't move. Asmara has never had a stronger urge to scream in her life. No noise is produced because she is terrified of opening her mouth and having this creature insert some part of itself.

"Whooooaaa!" James and Elizabeth each vocalize in harmony, except James ends with "...dude!"

"Oh, no! Is that real?" says a woman's voice from across the room. This is followed by the clatter of utensils hitting plates and a series of gasps from people in the venue.

"My goodness!"

"Oh! Oh! Please, what is that?"

Asmara can't see their reactions because her eyes are covered by a mass of hairy exoskeleton. There is still a crackling static on her face from the numerous leg taps. During its galloping tour around her face, the spider poked her in the eye with one of its legs (not maliciously, she presumes). The eye waters and is half-closed but the discomfort beats getting bitten by the arachnid's fangs.

Having served its purpose, the tube descends from beneath her clothes back into the stage.

"Don't worry, everyone," James says to the small crowd. "This is a safety test for a magic trick."

With a curl of her finger Asmara beckons Elizabeth to come over.

"Do you have the container ready?"

"Yes, the cube is right in front of you."

Asmara blindly lifts her hand to her face and pauses when there is a barrage of taps. The tarantula climbs aboard. Asmara guides her arm into the plastic cube Elizabeth holds, she tilts her wrist, and the spider marches into its rock cave.

As much as a human and a tarantula could ever share emotions, they both savor exhilarated relief.

CHAPTER 28

There are logical reasons why Asmara should conduct another rehearsal. This would allow Ryan and Zoe to practice being more quiet with their tasks beneath the stage. Also, any more revealing errors in the performance may be ironed out. And yet, for Asmara and this spider, they are one and done tonight. The experiment was a messy success.

Asmara is backstage with James and Elizabeth as they greet the two production assistants crawling from the storage space. Zoe has a cobweb embedded in her hair and a smile on her face.

"We could hear everyone out there freak out!" she says.

"It was insane," James says. "The spider bolted out of her collar and ran around her face twice. The other people in the room were tripping."

"We almost lost the spider," Ryan says. "It would have escaped."

Commentary begins to overlap.

"I got poked in the eye by a spider leg."

"No way!"

"One of the guys at the bar said, 'Yo, I have arachnophobia.'"

"I heard him say that, too."

"Ha!"

More war stories and laughs are exchanged as the group migrates out of the backstage room toward the main hall. Asmara stays behind near the storage compartment to unplug the lamp's power cord.

James pokes his head around the corner. "Can you make sure the crawlspace door gets shut? We'll be out front at the bar."

"No problem."

James' footsteps fade as he leaves the area. She bundles the cord around the lamp and takes a moment to enjoy the solitude.

What a night.

Asmara puts the lamp on the ground and unusual muscle strain is required to stand up. Either her back is sore or the pull of gravity increased. Her posture goes rigid and she turns toward the storage opening beneath the stage. There is a visual effect where the black rectangle appears to hover on its own. The doorframe and wall give the passage an ordinary context, and yet... the portal is floating.

The sight is strange but not alarming. Just an illusion.

A suffocating silence envelops the room. It's not enough to say the area became quiet. It's more like the environment is now a vacuum of space. This contained zone is devoid of an atmosphere able to sustain sound waves. Even if she tried to scream, it would be a mere theory in her mind. The friendly chatter which had been bouncing off these walls is incomprehensible now.

A shift occurs. Her eyes are open and yet the details of the room, the elements big and small which make up her immediate surroundings, have dissolved. There is only the black box in front of her.

Okay, now this is alarming.

To ground herself back in reality, Asmara considers the four people in her group who walked away seconds ago. Her perceptions had been integrated with theirs. What changed? There is also a dining area with visitors, all on the other side of a nearby wall.

Except there is no wall now. The dark portal is all that remains.

She pictures Ryan and Zoe in particular. They are so close. Or is that proximity not accurate anymore?

There is a sense those people are now, in a literal way, millions of miles away. Or perhaps much farther. They were not transported anywhere. They are still at The Naomi venue in San Francisco. Asmara is the one who has been extracted. She has taken some sort of leap.

Even if she is on another planet, or out of her mind, the least she can do is try to regain control. She commands her foot to lift and nothing happens. She tries to blink and her eyes remain open.

What the hell is going on?

The floating portal reflects no depth beyond its dark surface. All incoming light is captured and swallowed. However, something stirs within the interior, beyond the threshold. The hidden entity strokes the edges of the passage from its side. It's not a caress of affection, instead it's a gesture of ominous threat. An appetite is being displayed—not just a desire to devour Asmara but also to consume the world she came from. This living thing craves access and it knows a breach of the barrier is inevitable.

A formal name arrives to Asmara. "The guest you have blessed— the Patron." It's a bizarre descriptor. Asmara isn't sure what it means. Patron of what? Either she created the name out of thin air or this being has introduced itself.

Acknowledging how it has now been properly addressed, the Patron presses closer against the veneer of the black rectangle. The outline of its form suggests it is like no living thing on Earth.

A giant pillar bursts through the chasm.

It's as if a solid-black tree trunk crashed in front of Asmara. And yet the cylinder is not a featureless shape—it is a limb with a clawed hand at one end. As the fist unclenches, the sheer span of this demonic arm is revealed. Its palm and outstretched fingers are eight feet wide.

The claw tries to tear through the threshold of the void but instead the inky veneer has coated the fingers in a dark, elastic substance. Stretching but never breaking, the barrier acts as an impenetrable liquid and creates a skin-tight glove around the hand.

The Patron's arm structure is roughly human, although the knuckles are grotesque and bulbous. Each gnarled finger has a pointed nail the size of a large traffic cone. It's unimaginable what this hand is attached to.

Asmara does not recoil as the fingers strive to crush her. Their grip opens and closes inches from her face. The more this God-forsaken claw tries to harm her the more she leans toward the hand in defiance. She will not give in to the delusion because she believes there is no hand from hell. To her, it's a matter of not fearing what isn't there. This is an hallucination. It has to be.

After a broad swipe from the Patron's limb, rushing air breezes her cheeks and her hair stirs. That last bit of effort from the Patron tears a hole in the surface tension of the void. Rays of black light stream out and a wretched smell makes Asmara gag. The rip heals itself quickly and the smell dissipates.

All illusions, hijacking her different senses, Asmara tells herself.

The monstrous hand, still coated in a waxy black substance, stops flailing in its attempt to reach Asmara. This colossus settles into calm resignation after its frenzy of aggression. The hand retreats back into the portal and the surface of the void shudders with turbulence.

In this final spasm of rippling activity, a human face presses against the black sheet from the other side. It is a woman, of normal-sized scale, voicelessly mouthing words beneath the taut elastic material stretched over her head. It would be unwise to trust anything from within the hellhole passageway, yet this figure does not cast a malevolent energy. The stranger shouts a warning but no sounds are emitted.

Even when obscured with an inky mask, the woman is familiar. And now she's gone.

Ambient noise fills Asmara's ears as the normal backstage environment of The Naomi vibrates back into focus. Never has the electric hum of fluorescent lights sounded this good. The dark void which had been threatening to obliterate her has returned into an ordinary stage compartment. It's the same place Ryan and Zoe safely crawled out of a few minutes ago.

Asmara is losing her mind, but reality has not abandoned her yet.

CHAPTER 29

As the car hurtles down nighttime city streets, the stillness of the interior soothes Asmara. This is not pure silence for there are tones within it—musical notes of contentment and relief. Sharing the vehicle's confined space with Ryan and Zoe helps stabilize her. She is able to lean into their support and it prevents her from falling apart.

The tarantula rests in its container, indifferent to these human dynamics. Solitude is sufficient for the creature.

Zoe sits shotgun next to Ryan at the wheel. From the rear seat, Asmara tries to envision what they are thinking as city lights streak by. Their internal worlds must be vast and complex. Asmara makes no claims her troubled innerscape is unique—after all, people fight their own demons every day. However, she doubts these two friends up front would understand the hallucination which tormented her minutes ago.

It would be reasonable for Asmara to seek emergency psychiatric care right now. Instead, she breathes slowly through her nose and enjoys the ride.

Asmara doesn't mind how no one is talking. Part of her wants to underscore the normalcy of the moment by blurting out how everything is fine. *"Yup! No psychopathic visions back here. How about you two up there? Are you completely SANE like I am?"*

The car stops at a red light in the deserted business district of downtown. The intersection is empty.

"Oh," Zoe says, looking out her passenger-side window. "Ryan, can you pull over?"

"Why?"

"I saw some cash laying on the sidewalk back there. It's a few bucks."

Ryan tilts in his seat to peer through the side window. "Really? Well, jump out. There's no cars here."

"I know, but the light is, uh, going to change green. Can you, uh, pull over."

Ryan is suspicious. "There is no one, uh, around. I promise I won't, uh, drive off."

"Dude... There's no money. I made it up. You're ruining my surprise. Just please park over here."

"Fine, I'll pull over."

Ryan takes a right on red, drifts to the curb, and puts the car in park. "Okay. What's my surprise?"

Zoe's hand darts toward the ignition button and she turns off the car.

The engine shivers to a stop. "It's actually a surprise for Asmara," she says, grabbing the key fob from the center console.

As Ryan tries to process this betrayal his face contorts like a slow-motion sneeze. His annoyance takes effort to project.

Zoe howls with laughter at his dramatic facial display. "Ahh! Are you turning into a werewolf?"

All Ryan can muster is one word. His mouth hasn't caught up with his brain yet. "What... What..."

Zoe flings open her door and hops out. She addresses Asmara through the window. "Can I show you something? Ryan, you can come, too."

Asmara figures that if the surprise is worth disabling Ryan's car without his consent then it must have value. She joins Zoe on the sidewalk. A still-speechless Ryan emerges from the vehicle with an aggravated look on his face, if not quite a werewolf transformation.

Zoe jogs toward a nearby office building. "Follow me. Ryan, you never would have stopped if I didn't take your keys. I'm sorry."

Asmara finds herself race walking in anticipation as well. Ryan plods behind them with grumpy reluctance.

They round the corner of the building and enter an urban plaza. There are benches and tree planters scattered throughout the area. Giant blocks of concrete take various stacked forms along a central pathway in a modern art display.

Or is this primitive art?

Zoe runs over to a marble wall at the base of grassy landscaping. She boosts herself up the six-foot-tall slab and, once on top, alternates her footsteps like a tightrope walker on its narrow surface. This balancing act continues until her feet reach the wall's abrupt drop-off. It's as if she walked the plank of a pirate ship and is about to take a plunge. Zoe dangles her toes off this polished cliff and lifts her arms in victory.

Asmara is baffled. *What are we celebrating here?*

One of Zoe's arms drops down and her index finger points at something. This gesture guides Asmara's line of sight over to... another separate ledge a good distance away.

Who cares? Why would... oh! It's Ryan's Line!

"You're killing me, Zoe," Ryan says as he comes around the corner into the plaza.

"I had to show Asmara," Zoe says. "At the red light I realized we were near here. It was fate."

Asmara walks over to the second, shorter ledge Zoe pointed at. This one is four feet tall, thirty feet long and narrow as well. She climbs up top and waves at Zoe as if these two elevated perches were barely visible outposts to each other. Zoe waves back.

"Did you really jump from over there to down here, Ryan?" Asmara asks.

"It's not just the gap which is legendary," Zoe says. "It's how he rode all the way across the ledge you're standing on. That's why he's famous."

"I'm not famous," Ryan mumbles.

"My grandma had a citizenship ceremony close to this plaza," Zoe says. "I took her here to see Ryan's Line. I explained what it was."

"Your immigrant grandma didn't know about my ollie ten years ago? Imagine that," Ryan says.

Asmara had been playing along and feigning her excitement to match Zoe's, but as she calibrates the distance of these ledges she is impressed. If conventional sports have moments of heroism and epic lore, skateboarding does too.

There is a crunch of footsteps and a shadowy figure descends the unlit grassy slope. He's holding a flashlight and the beam cuts like a wand through the darkness.

He steps into the light. "How are you all doing?"

No surprise—a security guard. He appears to be around twenty years old and his uniform is so generic it could be a dollar-store Halloween costume.

"Are we in trouble?" Zoe says.

"No, not at all. The plaza is closed but I can tell you aren't causing problems. I mostly tell homeless people they can't sleep here."

"We'll move along," Ryan says.

"What are you all up to?" the guard asks. "Are you skateboarders?"

"Yeah," Zoe says. "How could you tell?"

"The only people who climb on these ledges and stare at them are skateboarders. Although, it's hella weird because you don't have any skateboards. I've also never seen two girls stand on the ledges. But skater dudes do it all the time."

"Have you ever heard of Ryan's Line?" Zoe asks.

"Nah, what's that?"

"My friend standing right there ollied these two ledges a decade ago and he made skateboard history."

"Shit. I *have* heard about that. I don't skate any more but my cousin is hella good. He told me about a famous trick here but I didn't know it had a name. So, you're Ryan?"

Ryan's eyes are closed and he runs his hands through his hair. He nods awkwardly as if his head is on a lever controlled by someone else.

"Are you okay?" the guard asks.

"He's fine," Zoe says. "He's just turning into a werewolf."

"Ryan is modest about his claim to fame," Asmara says.

"For real, I see skaters scoping out this gap all the time. It's funny, they never ride it. They climb on the ledges and look around like tourists."

"They don't skate it because it's too gnarly and Ryan is too sick," Zoe says.

Asmara wishes this flattery would have some effect on Ryan but his blank expression makes him look like a sullen Sphinx.

"All right," Ryan says. "We're going to head out."

The three start walking back to the car.

"You should be proud, bro," the security guard says from behind them. "If you did a thing on your skateboard ten years ago and people still talk about it—that's hella cool."

Ryan gives a weak fist pump with mock enthusiasm. The guard recoils in confusion at this disrespect.

"There's a documentary about Ryan's Line," Zoe says. "You can find it online."

The guard nods and lifts a thumb up.

Before Asmara turns forward again the guard's upturned thumb of approval transforms into a middle finger.

Asmara is tired of Ryan not taking a compliment. He's being rude and getting flipped off by strangers. To cheer him up, she pivots and gives him a bear hug from the side.

"That guy was nice to you and made a great point," Asmara says into his ribcage. "You *should* be proud... bro."

Ryan stops walking and his body goes rigid. He grabs her wrists and removes them from his waist.

"I'm sorry," he says. "I wish I could explain it."

Asmara is tempted to scream: *"Get over yourself! It's a fucking skateboard trick."* But Ryan speaks first. "I'll tell you someday. I will tell you everything."

"What is the big deal? Did you make a deal with the devil in order to leap between two ledges on a toy?"

Ryan's eyes flick downward. His cryptic non-answer hangs in the air.

"What the hell are you two talking about?" Zoe says. "I've watched the video a thousand times. Ryan is a legend. Case closed."

Zoe dives in for a hug around Ryan and she pushes him forward. "Let's go. This place is haunted with the ghost of Ryan's Line and it bums him out."

As Ryan gets propelled toward the car by Zoe, Asmara adds to the group velocity. All three are soon lumbering in a shared jog together.

This moving unit reaches a sprint until a foot gets stepped on and the tripod collapses into three stumbling, laughing individuals. Zoe uses the momentum of her fall to handspring back on her feet.

"Even if the devil is coming to collect your debt," Zoe says while handing Ryan his car keys, "we still love you."

CHAPTER 30

The car rolls to a stop in front of Asmara's building and Ryan's attention is on the Slow Pour Reading Den across the street. It's a coffeeshop distinct for its floor-to-ceiling bookshelves which are visible through large storefront windows.

"I know it's nine o'clock," Ryan says, "but I'm going to grab a decaf if you have any interest. I won't stay long. I have to get Zoe home."

"Sounds good. I get decaf sometimes as well."

"Are you cool with that?" Ryan asks Zoe.

She's already stepping out of the car and chirps out a "sure."

When Asmara moved into her current apartment, Slow Pour was a nice neighborhood attribute. After a few visits, however, the allure wore off. Their coffee has a weird aftertaste—a cinnamon/metal flavor—and the mountains of books were exposed as a gimmick because it is too dark to read in there.

Once inside, Zoe gravitates to a magazine rack. The tattered titles look years old and some have visible stains. Yellow crumbs hardened onto one magazine cover beg the question of how long have they clung there? And what nasty chemistry keeps them in place?

By the time Ryan and Asmara receive their coffee, Zoe is sitting on the floor and absorbed in a magazine. Her lips move as she reads the words in the article—something presumably about splashing through mud on a mountain bike because it is the featured photo.

Asmara's heart warms at the sight of the girl. These past few days Zoe has adapted to everything. No complaining. Funny commentary. Now here she reads instead of staring at her phone or saying she's bored.

With his coffee in hand, Ryan examines a series of bookshelves which comprise an entire wall. He turns toward the barista, a young man wearing eyeliner and with one dangling earring. "Excuse me, where did you get all these books?"

The man looks up and his earring swings around like a tiny chandelier.

"We get asked that all the time," he says. "A small college library in Hayward had a fire in the 1980s. There was a lot of fire and water damage, as you can imagine. The remaining books were given away for free. So, the owner of Slow Pour brought them here."

"Interesting," Asmara says. "That gives the books a special energy, the fact these all survived a fire."

"I agree," the barista says. "I like to think these books have gratitude and are happy to be around."

Asmara spots an opportunity to suggest brighter lighting in Slow Pour so people can actually read here. And less shitty-tasting coffee might help. But the opening closes.

"If you look over by the mirror," the barista says, "that lower shelf has books with the most fire damage. They have their own unique spirit. They barely made it out alive and have the scars to prove it."

It must be the power of suggestion, but as Asmara kneels in front of the shelf, she hears the steady crackle of burning paper. The sharp odor of smoke fills her nostrils. "Am I tripping or do these books still smell like smoke?"

The barista makes a skeptical face. "Well, 1985 was a long time ago. Perhaps the smell lingers. Or maybe you have superpowers."

As quickly as the sound and smell of burning paper passed through her senses, the phantom effects disappear.

Since the traumatized books have huddled together for survival since 1985, Asmara is loath to disturb them. However, one title catches her eye. *My Very Educated Mother... A Fun Guide to Our Solar System.*

The title's reference is familiar to Asmara. It's a memorization trick to recite the planets around the Sun. The first letter of each planet is represented in the absurd yet easy to remember sentence: "My Very Educated Mother Just Served Us Nine Pies." Mercury, Venus, Earth, Mars, Jupiter, Saturn, Uranus, Neptune, Pluto.

The boys in her sixth grade class constructed their own vulgar sentences in a similar manner. One such ad-lib started as "Mary's Vagina Eats..." but the rest is lost to time.

The cover features an illustration of nine planets swirling around the Sun, each satellite leaving colorful motion blurs in its wake. This book's typography and groovy art scream 1980s, not to mention the material is outdated since Pluto is no longer deemed a planet.

She pries open the book with an audible crack as the binding stretches for the first time since 1985. Flakes of burnt paper float down between the pages. It is like uncovering ancient scrolls from a lost civilization.

As the pages shuffle by, the chapter on Jupiter stands out and

Asmara stops for a look. The book may be forgiven for representing Jupiter's moons as pencil drawings since the Caerus spacecraft and its high-definition photography were decades from launch when this art was created. Europa gets a one-sentence write up: "This icy rock is notable among Jupiter's many moons as it may contain liquid oceans."

Asmara pulls her phone out and takes a photo of the Europa drawing. She's not sure why.

Europa has appeared twice in printed material randomly crossing her path. First the science magazine from All-Nite Quality Coffee and now this charred schoolbook.

Asmara returns *My Very Educated Mother* back to its station within the burn victims unit.

"I love book review blurbs," Ryan says, as he reads the back of a novel pulled from a shelf. "The praise is so dramatic."

"Yeah, every blurb says every book is a masterpiece. What does that one say?"

"Harold McCloud of the Los Angeles Times wrote: '*The Colmenero Conundrum* has reshaped my worldview of what a book can do. This extraordinary thriller has overshadowed my previous literary experiences.'"

"I guess he liked it," Asmara says. "Why didn't you use any cover blurbs for your book *Rain Rising?*"

"Oh, please. Maybe I could have bribed one of my stoner friends to actually read it first. Will you ever print your story *Lightning in Ojai?*"

"It's too short. Maybe I could expand it someday."

"If you need a cover blurb, I'll be happy to write one."

Ryan squints in concentration and opens his eyes with a fresh book review. "After reading *Lightning in Ojai* I had to be resuscitated from cardiac arrest. The perfection of Asmara's prose *literally* stopped my heart... figuratively."

Asmara laughs and summons her own review.

"Upon completion of *Rain Rising,* I flew to England, excavated Shakespeare's corpse and crushed his skull as I proclaimed Ryan Q Smith the true God-King of the English language."

"Ha! You *are* a writer."

Asmara catches a glimpse in the wall mirror. The reflection shows a far corner of the coffeeshop which she hadn't noticed. In the low-light area shown in the mirror is a seated woman with long white hair. The woman looks into the reflection as well, making eye contact with Asmara. There is a delayed reaction as sparks of recognition illuminate this figure.

It's my neighbor. Inga.

Asmara turns away from the mirror. She weighs the costs and benefits of pretending to have not seen Inga. The decision is not Asmara's to make.

"Excuse me," Inga says from across the room. "Miss?"

Asmara pivots toward the woman and feigns a look of surprise. Displaying enthusiasm to see this neighbor is beyond Asmara's acting abilities. "Inga. Hi, there."

As Asmara nears Inga, she is startled how the old woman bounds out of her seat and takes long strides to the center of the coffeeshop. Inga holds a pen and small paperback novel in one hand.

"It *is* you," Inga says, as she gives Asmara a light squeeze on the arm. "I wasn't sure from across the room."

"Yes, my friend wanted to stop by for a coffee."

"I'm glad you're here, Asmara. I wanted to talk to you. It's hard for me to knock on your door and bother you."

"Sure, what's up?"

"I wanted to apologize for how I acted at the end of our recent visit."

"Oh. I don't know what to say."

"My goodness, I can't imagine how you felt when I asked if you were reading my mind. I can be such a fool."

"No, it's fine. We've all had moments where people say what we're thinking."

"I was excited you came over. I love young people. You have an energy that you won't appreciate until you're older. It felt nice to sit and chat with you. And then... And then that thing you asked..."

"The car scratch?"

"Yes. Everything was pleasant but when you asked about the car damage I was shocked. It's all so strange."

"What is strange?"

"You see, Asmara..." Inga leans in and her eyes grow wide, "I may be sick, in my head. Or I may be blessed. It might be a blessing that I don't understand yet."

Oh, no.

"I don't want to burden a young, happy person with my problems," Inga continues, "but I have to ask—why did you want to know about the scratch on my car again?"

"I told you, it is for a student's class assignment." Asmara points to Zoe reading on the floor. "She's sitting right there."

Inga whips her head to inspect the teenage inquisitor who is still lost in a magazine. Asmara winces with regret at identifying Zoe in all of this.

"Her?" Inga says. "Why does a child need to know about my car?"

"Again, I told you—the girl's project is to interview people about how their cars got scratched. There's no evil agenda here. Let's leave her out of this."

Inga looks back at Asmara. The old woman's jaw grinds side to side, her face a display of simmering tension.

"The reason I reacted strongly," Inga says, "is because the car scratch has haunted me."

"Why are you haunted?"

"Because…"

The woman's teeth crunch past each other with bone-rattling force.

"Because I scratched my own car." Inga extends her finger and slices a jagged line through the air. "And I couldn't stop myself."

Asmara's senses tune into a state of threat assessment. How disturbed is this neighbor?

"There's a shape," Inga says, "a line, actually. It keeps appearing. First in my dreams. Then in my everyday thoughts."

"What kind of line?"

"It's just… a line. But not straight. There are turns in it. Four of them. Those angles are everything. If the angles aren't correct, the line means nothing. But when they are present… I can't get it out of my head."

"Inga, if you're not feeling well there are ways to get help."

"The line is a message. There's more to come. I want to ask you something."

This should be lovely.

"Asmara, are you being visited as well? Are you seeing things?"

With a hard swallow, Asmara's throat seizes. Her esophagus stings from the painful contraction.

"Why would…" Asmara croaks out each syllable. "Why would you ask me that?"

"I've been seeing things for years. Decades. I suppressed it for as long as I could, but the kettle is boiling. I believe you're seeing things, too. There is something inside me. I'm afraid it's inside you now."

The flesh across Asmara's scalp tightens. She grasps for a logical explanation. Is this a transmission of mass hysteria? Maybe their apartment building is somehow poisoning them both?

Asmara faces a stark choice: deny her shared insanity with this woman or follow Inga down a rabbit hole which leads to God knows where. She goes all in and it's like stepping off a cliff.

"Yes," Asmara says. "I have been hearing and seeing things."

Inga raises her hands to her face in distress. Her jaw no longer grinds back and forth. "Have you seen the crooked line?" she asks.

"No. There has been no line. But a portal opened yesterday. A doorway. And something tried to get through it."

Inga's eyes blink in utter dismay. Asmara continues. "I could only describe it as a monster. A giant demon. It was like a gateway to hell."

The two women stand silent in the strangeness of their encounter, each trying to process what the other is thinking.

Am I out-crazying this crazy woman?

Inga's eyes narrow into an icy stare. She initiated this lunatic conversation but it apparently went somewhere she did not foresee. Without speaking, Inga walks past Asmara and heads toward the door.

"Hey, that is not fair," Asmara says, grasping Inga by the wrist. "You confided in me how you were seeing things. What is happening to us?"

Inga slaps away the hand holding her and pins Asmara's wrist against her own hip. Even with forceful jostling, Asmara cannot move her arm. Inga locks eyes with Asmara while continuing the restraint and projects a deranged determination straight into her soul. This old woman is unrecognizable as the neighbor across the hall.

Asmara catches a glimpse of the book grasped in Inga's other hand. The novel has fluttered open and there are hundreds of doodles drawn in blue ink over the printed words on the pages. This chaotic scrawl contains repeating patterns of the same angled line. There are different lengths to these lines but they all have the same proportions and the same four crooked turns.

Inga lets go of Asmara, steps out of Slow Pour Reading Den and onto the sidewalk. From a calm evening earlier, the wind has picked up into gusts during the short time in the coffeeshop. Inga is backlit and only her silhouette is displayed. Around her head, long strands of gray hair swirl in the wind, as if they are Medusa's snakes.

"There's no place like home," Inga says, as the coffeeshop's front door closes. "Right, neighbor?"

CHAPTER 31

"Are you comfortable staying in your building tonight?" Ryan asks. "I can drop Zoe off and come back. Or you are welcome to crash at my place in Oakland."

"Thanks," Asmara says. "It sucks that my neighbor is crazy but I can't imagine her breaking into my apartment."

Ryan only caught a glimpse of the exchange the two women had.

Asmara downplayed the confrontation and told Ryan it was her eccentric neighbor acting strange. Zoe was unaware anything happened at all and Inga has long-since walked out of sight.

Back at Ryan's parked car, Asmara removes the spider container. Ryan tosses Zoe his car keys. "It might be best if I walk Asmara to her apartment," he says. "I'll be back in a minute."

Zoe gives a goodbye hug and slides into the passenger seat.

Asmara makes a small noise of complaint about Ryan walking her home but she appreciates his gesture. They stroll to her building in silence and when they enter the lobby Ryan spins her by the shoulders into his chest and gives a deep embrace. A wave of emotional release unwinds through her body and it almost culminates in a loud sob but Asmara holds it in.

"Hey, what happened tonight?" Ryan says. "There's no reason to hide anything from me."

They both recognize the hypocrisy of his words. "Oh, that's right," Ryan says. "I owe you one explanation of how my eye got blasted out of my face and another of how I sold my soul when I ollied between two marble ledges."

"You don't owe me anything," Asmara says. "Anyways, this doesn't feel like the right time to share."

"Here is your chance. You can find out why I'm a one-eyed goblin trying to escape his haunted skateboarding past."

"Stop it. We'll share our stories when I'm not exhausted."

"Understood."

They start walking up the steps to her floor when Asmara stops halfway up the stairwell. She gives him a light poke in the chest. "Are you real?" she asks.

"As in a real person? I sure am. What makes you ask?"

"Strange things have been happening ever since I met you."

"You can't blame me for your weird neighbor."

"You're right. But that woman is a piece in this puzzle I'm trapped in. It's like I am playing a role in some movie I'm not aware of."

"Geez. This is serious, huh?"

"I just want to let you know what's on my mind. The Word Bound night plays a part in all of this. It's a bigger deal to me than you realize. My life is in a rut. I want to create something memorable."

"For someone whose life is in a rut, you are an interesting person. You've made a big impact on both myself and the teenage girl outside. Zoe thinks you are so cool. She has already lined up plans for you to hang out with us."

Even under the cloak of pessimism weighing her down, that is a joy for Asmara to hear.

"You say your recent days have been strange," Ryan says, "how do you think I feel? Did you ever consider that I find you to be mysterious and exciting?"

Asmara has no response. She basks in the compliment.

Ryan's eyes close and his face leans toward hers. A kiss is imminent and Asmara surrenders to the advance as her eyes shut as well. Three seconds pass and no lips arrive. She opens her eyes and Ryan stares at her with a grin. Before Asmara reacts, he bounces his mouth off hers with a high impact, though not unpleasant, close-mouthed kiss. As she recovers from the loud smacker, he swoops back in and the two of them are making out.

For Asmara, it is soul-stirringly fabulous. Beyond the pleasures of nerve endings stimulated around her face and mouth, there are layers to her delight. First is an excitement in the romantic moment itself. Next comes a bone-deep relief in how her intimacy drought has come to an end. Lastly, as her lips press against his, she has hope looking forward.

The kissing slows to a stop and Ryan's head withdraws. Asmara has an ache in her right hand. It's from the clear plastic container she's been gripping the entire time.

"I can't believe we made out while I was holding a tarantula," she says. Asmara bops one more kiss off his lips and they continue up the stairs.

Asmara cannot feel her legs navigate the steps. She might be floating. This stairwell had previously been notable for a repulsive resident who let their pet urinate between floors. Asmara is glad she has a new association for this spot which will supplant the foul memory.

As they reach the hallway leading to her apartment, Asmara puts a finger to her mouth, communicating silence to Ryan lest he summon the psychotic neighbor Inga. They tip-toe down the hall not out of fear of the old woman—it's more like their soft ninja steps are a way of avoiding confrontation altogether. Ryan does a ridiculous high-stride march which almost makes Asmara laugh and blow their cover.

When they are in front of her door, there is a faint thump across the hall. Maybe it's one of the untraceable vibrations the building produces every day. Or perhaps Inga leaned against her door's peephole with a blood-greased chainsaw in hand, ready to mutilate her perceived enemies.

Ryan makes sure Asmara is safely inside her apartment. They exchange soft-talking pleasantries, share one more kiss, and then Asmara is alone.

Her mind and body have reached their limit tonight. After a few footsteps to her room, even standing is too much to ask. She collapses onto her bed, forming a melted pool of anxiety and ecstasy.

It's the first night of her life she forgot to brush her teeth.

．．．．．．．．．．．．．．．．．．．．．．．．．．．

A relaxed four count for each inhalation through the nose. An unhurried four count for each exhalation through the mouth.

Asmara has never meditated in the morning before.

Again, barbarians of stress are at the gates of her mind. They argue over who should enter first and their indecision grants her peace.

Is this a new approach to mental health? To stockpile so many problems that they can't form a line?

Asmara is a novice with meditation and she's never sure when to pull the ripcord to return to an Earth-bound state with open eyes. Perhaps the sensation you've "had enough" or reached a finish line precisely means you need to keep meditating. Regardless, her eyelids open and Asmara glides to a soft landing in the living room's reading chair.

A few more minutes go by of uninterrupted empty thought. At last, it's time for Asmara to scrutinize one of the pressing concerns she can't run from: what in the name of all which is real and unreal, holy and unholy, happened backstage at The Naomi last night?

That sensory input—the dissolved walls, the floating portal, the demon hand—must have been produced in her mind alone. The torment of mental illness she sees on the streets of San Francisco, schizophrenics lashing out at sights unseen by others, must involve similar visions conjured in the brain.

What would have happened if Ryan and the others returned backstage during her ordeal? Would they have witnessed a flesh-and-bone monster's limb, thus confirming the event was real? Or would they have seen an ordinary backstage environment and nothing more than Asmara with a scared look on her face?

She has fragile confidence in the answer. It allows her to integrate back into reality.

Asmara admires the morning light streaking through the window. The walls around her are illuminated with a deep yellow. At this early time of day, the angle of rays shoot into the living room and cast a narrow beam onto a portion of nearby hallway. The natural spotlight happens to land on the abstract painting hanging on the wall, the one featuring a lovers' embrace—if you allow yourself to see it.

She was not aware of this brief time of day in which sunlight falls upon the painting.

It's never looked so beautiful.

CHAPTER 32

Pure brutality. Torture, even. If what Asmara is doing to herself was forcibly applied to another person, the sadist would be imprisoned. As the Grim Reaper's icy embrace wraps around her body like liquid death, her next breath may be her last.

I am NEVER taking a cold shower again.

Asmara has read that cold showers provide a host of health benefits. She questions the data as she cranks a fierce towel rub over herself, trying to generate warmth. The upside to a cold shower is you are grateful you're alive after the cruel downpour, even as your soul shivers.

The bathroom mirror hasn't been cleaned in a while and Asmara swipes her wet hand across the grimy glass, creating a ribbon of clear reflection. She leans in toward her face looking back at her. There is no judgment of beauty. No appraisal of flaws. There is a recognition of survival—not from outlasting a cold shower, but from persevering through her demons.

After everything, you're still here.

Asmara slips into her most comfortable sweatpants and long sleeve shirt, trapping the body heat she feared was gone forever. As she exits the bathroom with a happy hop in her step, a revelation follows—*there might be something to these cold showers after all.*

. . . .

Her phone greets her with a message. It's from Elizabeth at The Naomi.

"Hi Asmara, we're excited for Word Bound. Since you're going to make the night so special we wanted to see if you can design a flyer for the show. You're a creative person, so we figured we'd ask. I'll send you more info if you're interested. Thanks"

Asmara's bloodflow warms even more with a deep satisfaction. Elizabeth asked her to produce the flyer precisely because the spider stunt idea left such an impression. There was never any talk about whether Asmara even has artistic skills.

This is what I'm looking for. Creative risks leading to more opportunities.

The two women exchange texts and Elizabeth sends a link. Asmara opens it on her laptop. As she examines the app, it is a one-stop shop for poster design. She can easily import and arrange images in this interface.

There also are previous Word Bound flyers shown for context. Asmara figures the mechanics behind their designs can be reverse engineered. She has fooled around with design programs in the past and knows the basics.

Somewhere in her closet is a tote bag filled with unused art materials. They are about to come out of retirement.

The laptop gets folded shut and Asmara reclines on her bed. She lets her mind wander, allowing thoughts to arrive and depart on their own terms. These brainwave currents can't be harnessed, but sometimes good ideas float in on their tides. After a few minutes, this ocean of mental activity recedes and a small locket of ideas is stranded on the shore. Asmara is pleased by the treasure of inspiration. The poster concept is settled.

Except for the small matter she's not an artist.

The embrace of her old friend, procrastination, tugs downward and settles her further into the bed. "No, my dear," procrastination says. "The poster can wait. Please rest with me for a while."

She counts to three and springs from the bed's gravity. The momentum carries Asmara stumbling toward her closet. She claws through the accumulated clothing debris and it is like an archaeological dig which reveals a timeline of her past. The tote bag makes an appearance and is exposed to light for the first time in years.

Her roommate Lisa not being home proves beneficial as Asmara turns the kitchen table into an art station. She takes screenshots on her computer from the Ryan's Line video online and their resolution is surprisingly good. Asmara prints out nine enlarged frames of Ryan on her inkjet printer and spreads the images on the table. Inspiration has taken the wheel and she's along for the ride.

Brush strokes commence. Paint is traced along the printed screenshots of Ryan on his skateboard. There's guesswork and risky gambles with each application of acrylic. Blue on his skin. Yellow on his clothes. It looks great. Until it doesn't. Asmara crumples up one piece of paper and tries again, having learned what not to do. She is on auto pilot and every attempt is a learning process. This system continues until she puts the finishing touches on her ninth and final attempt. The once-detailed video image now has a diffuse, abstract appearance. To her, not only is this not bad, it's actually compelling. A savvy observer will recognize how the painting is traced on top of a photo but Asmara doesn't care. She has full confidence in how to produce the remaining visuals: a giant hand, a dark portal, a microphone, lightning, and Europa.

The artistic march continues with more screenshots, printouts and paint-overs. Crumpled papers from failed attempts litter the floor. She had every intention to not get paint on her clothes but both shirt sleeves are criss-crossed with splatters.

After some unknown passage of time, she catches her breath and finds she is both hungry and down to one last image needing to be crafted—Europa. All other assets for the flyer have been created to her liking. She will take camera-phone photos of these finished pieces and assemble them in the design program Elizabeth sent.

While Asmara consumes peanuts and orange juice, there is a simmer of euphoria regarding this poster project. Viewers may not have their minds blown by her work but it has a captivating overall look—no small achievement for someone who wasn't an artist earlier today.

Asmara gulps air between chugs of orange juice, knowing the hollow injection into her stomach will produce a loud belch. Part celebration of artistic paths being blazed, part salute to her roommate Lisa for not being home, a ribcage-rattling burp echoes in the kitchen.

Now, on to Europa.

Asmara goes to her room to fetch the science magazine. The Jupiterian moon will look great floating above her painted visuals. While flipping through the pages, a blurb catches her eye: "Go to our website to download more Europa photos taken by the space probe Caerus."

She visits the website on her laptop and clicks the download link. As she opens one Europa image at a time, Asmara shakes her head in awe at the glorious sphere suspended in darkness. This giant white-brown marble has been locked in a gravity dance with Jupiter for untold eons. The silent frozen satellite is here for Asmara to admire, in vivid color.

Within the download folder is a sub-folder containing fifteen more images labeled "Caerus near-pass sequence." The first image within it contains a relative close-up of Europa compared to the previous photos. There is text imposed on the photo which reads: "This sequence was taken during Caerus' closest pass above Europa."

She read in the magazine that Europa's brown patches are where the moon's ice surface has a higher mineral content. One particular dark slash looks to be a crack in the crust and the deep hue may indicate exposure to the moon's interior. Still in Photoshop, she uses a keyboard command to zoom in. The jagged brown line gets bigger and fills the frame with each keyboard tap. Asmara understands digital resolution enough to know that each zoom advance merely makes the existing pixels bigger. No information is gained past a certain point. She is not going to telescope her way into detailed images of alien cities nor will she be able to read the license plates of their cars. And yet, it is exciting to peer deeper into another world.

Photoshop has limits and only a few magnifications remain before the program displays nothing more than a grid of large squares—the inevitable finish line of any digital image.

The center of the Europan brown patch contains a stripe of solid black and she is allowed three more zooms into the deepest part of the crevasse. Photoshop has no magnifying capability left and, not surprisingly, Asmara faces a frame of solid darkness. She squints, hoping something cool manifests itself, but the black pixels do not oblige with evidence of an underwater civilization. Scrolling up and down through the gouge in the ice, there is nothing but a featureless void.

Until they appear.

Five pixels. Their visual content is almost the same solid black as the surrounding digital grid, but these five squares have a sheen of gray. Their shade difference is so subtle Asmara could have overlooked them. Even if she's looking at a mere ice ridge within the crack, it is an incredible research success. She is truly peering into Europa.

Asmara considers if others have seen this ice ridge but her arrogance must be foolish. The Caerus team probably includes an army of PhD geniuses who use super computers to analyze every pixel the spacecraft captured.

Regardless, she stares at the five squares as if she discovered the beating heart of this moon. The blocks are connected in a vertical zig-zag line, two on the left side, three on the right. She refuses to believe it's a mere camera glitch and she's proud of her investigation.

. . . .

It turns out unstoppable artistic momentum *can* screech to a halt. The poster elements were loaded into the design program. And yet, when they are cobbled together the whole thing looks weird. It's a colorful, messy collage with no shared DNA among the subject matter.

Asmara ponders the craft of writing, of which she is more familiar than visual arts. With story editing you sacrifice previous hard work for the greater good. Paragraphs don't get to stick around only because they were difficult to construct. Applying that logic to the flyer makes her question if she should remove something. The answer: All the damn colors. She spent hours applying a rainbow of acrylic to the images and never asked if the broad palette needed to be there.

A simple setting change evaporates the color vomit and turns the file black and white. She likes the way it looks—understated, though not bland. The poster contains a uniformity which wasn't there with the blizzard of colors.

Something else catches her attention. An opportunity for a final flourish.

Asmara does adjusting in the design program and a new complete poster is sent to Elizabeth. The black and white design looks much the same—a soaring skateboarder screams out hand-painted words into a lightning-electrified microphone held by a giant fist thrust out of a dark portal. Except now Europa floating up top has the only color on the poster with its blend of egg white and reddish-brown.

There are also five gray squares in a zig-zag vertical line imposed on the luminous moon.

CHAPTER 33

Two page turns remain. It's at this point where Asmara gets the same feeling with every book she's ever finished—a crescendo has built and an emotional release awaits. In the past, even mediocre material which was a struggle to slog through earns respect at this end stage.

Rain Rising Over an Oakland Horizon has been a worthwhile read. Ryan's wordplay left an impression on her. The book lacked a propulsive story—the narrator and Omar just drive and talk—but it was never boring. This thin novel was a vessel for Ryan to exercise his writing skills more than a rip-roaring page turner of a tale.

With her eyes absorbing the words eagerly, there is no more paper to peel back. All that remains on the last page is a short stack of paragraphs. The blank space beneath the last words in a book always stir melancholy in Asmara. After hours of enriching, lively sentences communicating to her, the paper becomes voiceless and the story speaks no more.

The closing lines, always important, strike the right chord:

"Omar slings the backpack over his shoulder and his legs ache with gratitude now that they're standing upright instead of crammed in the car. Behind him, a slow crunch of wheels on gravel.

The soft noise of rocky churn rumbles to a stop. A voice, thirty feet away, transforms Omar's despair into elation.

'Let me know when you're going back home. I'll give you a ride.'"

Asmara's chest heaves with a sigh as she closes and hugs the book, a proxy for Ryan himself. A hopeful ending is a great way to conclude this story.

While reading the book, Asmara found herself scouring for subtext and insights into the author. Ryan made it easy to find clues. The two characters were clearly his optimistic and pessimistic sides fighting for control.

She considers sending Ryan a text but this warrants a call. He answers after one ring.

"Hello," Ryan says.

"Hey. I finished *Rain Rising.*"

"You finished wha... Oh, no."

"I loved it. Do me a favor and don't downplay and ridicule your book any more, okay?"

A pause. "All right. I won't."

"You're talented and I hope you write again."

"Thank you. If I think of something to write, maybe I will."

"So, at the time you wrote it, were you consciously presenting yourself as both the narrator and Omar in an allegory of your own struggle with pessimism?"

"Oh, man..."

"No downplay. No ridicule."

"Uh, yeah. The characters reflect one person. Which was me, to an extent."

"I felt hopeful at the end. Optimism wins."

"Glad to hear it. I almost had a dumb surprise ending where you find out the narrator was driving alone the whole time and Omar was in his imagination."

"I was worried about that. It would have been a gimmick."

The phone line goes quiet until Ryan breaks the silence. "Can you believe we made out in a stairwell last night?"

Asmara laughs and gets a warm rush in her arms. "It was great."

"I'm at the bike shop in SF right now. I've been working all morning. I need a break. Can I pick you up?"

"Yeah. Come on by."

. . . .

There is no question the sky is different. Blue hues shine with unique radiance. The way clouds billow into altered states is not random. Each floating shape carries direct meaning to any thoughtful observer. And that seagull up there is flying in a blatant, heart-shaped pattern.

As Asmara stands outside her building waiting for Ryan, she is quite excited about having a boyfriend.

The relationship won't be able to resist time's cruelties—fights, familiarity, doldrums. But she's going to enjoy every stage along the way.

Ryan's car rounds the corner. Asmara steps near the street to meet him and she's in front of her neighbor Inga's parked sedan. The vehicle has the aura of bad voodoo attached to it from its owner. Scratched in the door paint are those troublesome angles—the autograph of a madwoman. Ryan pulls up and Asmara hops into the passenger side.

"Hi, there," he says, reaching over to squeeze her hand. "Why were you staring at that car?"

Asmara gives Ryan a long look, trying to estimate his appetite for insanity. "It's my psycho neighbor's car. Although maybe I'm as strange as she is. There might be a contagious strain of mass hysteria going around."

"If it's mass hysteria, I hope to catch it from you. We'll be together in our own weird world. "

. . . .

Willpower goes a long way. Asmara does her best to convince herself of the romance of this beach walk. The setting is beautiful with the Golden Gate Bridge looming to the north. They're holding delicious ice cream cones and Ryan's periodic hugs and light kisses on her forehead are a joy. But it is too windy for this shit.

The last straw is when Asmara laps up a large helping of vanilla onto her tongue and sand grinds against her teeth. That most recent gust of wind was the one which covered her sugary treat with a million tiny rocks.

She glances at Ryan who examines with a frown his equally ruined chocolate swirl. "We should have stayed in the car, huh?" he shouts over the gale-force winds.

"It's all good!"

Back at Ryan's car in the parking lot, Asmara shivers as she kicks off her shoes and an avalanche of sand pours out. They enter the vehicle and the typhoon howls are reduced to an angry murmur.

As they adjust to the calm interior, there are relieved sighs, sniffles, and the rustle of fabric. They get comfortable and all goes quiet. Even the wind recedes to give these two privacy. Asmara and Ryan lean toward the center console and stare at each other from one foot away. Nervous smiles rise and fall until their faces settle into a tranquil balance.

"I like that you don't look at your phone when you're with me," Ryan says.

CHAPTER 34

The Word Bound panic arrives in waves. Asmara focuses on keeping her head above anxiety waters but this is made difficult when sharks circle below. The predators beneath her are the vicious doubts she has about her stage act.

Asmara is back at her apartment, seated in the reading chair. Her brief afternoon with Ryan was fabulous. They chatted softly in his car at the beach and she loved it. However, a nagging fear gnaws away at her—the single stage rehearsal with the tarantula might not have been enough to establish proof of concept. The successful test yesterday could be a one-in-ten fluke and failure is the actual norm. Any more attempts may lead to a dead spider, a venomous bite, or some other fiasco.

She also re-read *Lightning in Ojai* and its allure has dimmed. The story is bizarre. Will people enjoy listening to it?

Another sour ingredient which spoiled Asmara's confidence is the weak response Elizabeth gave about the Word Bound poster. Elizabeth's text regarding the art submission was a mere: "Got it. Thanks"

The reply might as well have said: "God, it sucks."

Asmara didn't expect to be pampered with an adoring art critique hand-job, but one compliment tug on her ego would be nice.

The insecurities about this Word Bound event layer on top of each other until their weight presses down. As pressure builds, a full-fledged panic attack nears. Anxiety is a monster which looms behind Asmara, casting its shadow in front of her, always reminding her of its presence.

This panic compression takes an unexpected turn, though, as the grinding weight produces a diamond—a spark of insight.

The gray squares on Europa.

They need to be examined again. Right now.

Those five pixels are going to remain squares no matter how intensely she observes them. A staring contest will not produce new details, she understands that. But a compulsion demands she take another look.

Asmara grabs her laptop. In Photoshop, she opens the first picture from the Caerus fly-by sequence of Europa. The file is zoomed in to its maximum capacity and the zig-zag gray squares are found. Her insight does not involve scrutinizing this totem pole of blocks, hoping it will confess its nature. Instead, she is going to inspect every remaining picture from the fifteen-shot sequence.

The second photo is opened and she spots the same dark streak on the moon's surface where she made her initial discovery. Asmara magnifies her way deep into the crevasse. Her screen fills with solid black as she scrolls up and down through the interior realm, looking for the series of squares. They are nowhere to be found.

Damn it.

She zooms out to get her bearings on the moon's landscape. Maybe her virtual dive was into the wrong surface crack? Nope. That's the one.

With keyboard commands, she plunges back into the icy valley and enters sheer darkness. Scrolling. Scrolling.

There they are!

Five gray pixels, and they're in a different order. Instead of the original alternating pixels going left-right-left-right-left, this second photo of descending squares has them in attached clumps—left-left-right-right-right.

Asmara looks up from the laptop and returns to the Earth-based apartment around her. It is jarring to go from extraterrestrial exploration back to her flea-market chair.

As expected, thoughts trickle in which are laced with skepticism. The photos contain reflected light and anything light is able to bounce off can shimmer. Particularly ice.

Before doubt extinguishes her sense of awe, Asmara opens the third fly-by image of Europa and zooms into the black crevasse. She knows her way around the neighborhood and she finds the five pixels within seconds. They are in a different order than the previous two images.

With discipline, she tries not to react with any emotion.

The fourth, fifth, sixth, and seventh pictures are examined. A new stacked pattern is within each.

It is what Asmara finds in the eighth image which makes the hairs on her forearms rise. She puts the laptop aside and rises from the chair. Flapping her arms in the hope it might fling off excess energy, Asmara lets out a crazed laugh.

The gray squares deep within the eighth picture of Europa are in the same zig-zag pattern as the first photo. There is no way scattered light rays on ice would continue in a perfect replicated sequence through numerous frames. If the upcoming ninth image continues the same pattern which started with the first photo, it means the reflections are not random. Which would mean...

What the hell does it mean?

Asmara's mind has resisted this leap but a swan dive is inevitable.

Aliens? Am I looking at the work of aliens?

Nah, nah.

Her brain can't go there. Yet.

Inspiration strikes again and a practical step is conceived. The eight zoomed-in pictures are opened and a screenshot is taken of the different pixel configurations. She lines up the eight gray stacks horizontally on a blank Photoshop file, like ducks in a row.

The first and eighth stacks are the same. If there is indeed a repeating sequence, the ninth stack will match the second stack in her line-up. The tenth will match the third. And so on.

Asmara opens the ninth image from the fly-by sequence of Europa. She taps and taps into the crevasse until she's one keyboard command away from the thin gray column.

Click.

She takes a screenshot and drags the ninth image into the line-up of pixel stacks. The ninth pattern is the same as the second.

A surprising calm descends over her as more screenshots are dragged to the line up. This is interrupted only when Asmara stops to rub her eyes. She has forgotten to blink for minutes at a time.

The row is complete. This series of mutating Tetris shapes are like a written alien language speaking to her. Hell, maybe that's what it is.

Her eyes dart left to right as she confirms the sequence does repeat. Amid the rotating geometry, an essence about the parade of squares is familiar. Asmara can't place it.

Euphoria and racing thoughts have got her light headed. The panic attack is long gone.

Is this an alien contact?

She touches the computer screen and runs her finger across the Europan hieroglyphics floating before her. They do not flutter away or fade out of existence.

Does this fit the definition of delusions of grandeur? A history-defining event which spirals around one unlikely individual—in this case, a woman who had recent hallucinations of a giant demon.

Asmara saves the images, shuts off the computer and tries to collect her thoughts. The Europa anomaly needs to be chewed on before she runs into the street screaming about aliens.

If the magnitude of what she found cannot be disregarded over the next twenty-four hours, *then* the screaming will start.

CHAPTER 35

Searching for aliens has a strong effect on sweat glands. Asmara's underarms are damp and her deodorant has been overpowered into submission. There is a swampy heat around her groin, too. She stinks. This is not her usual perspiration.

It's strange how sitting in a chair and operating a computer would mimic physical exertion, but off to the shower she goes. Twice in one day, which is rare for her.

Asmara catches her reflection in the bathroom mirror. Has this woman staring back at her made one of mankind's greatest discoveries? Her fate hinges on whether those pixels are of alien origin or routine camera noise. Until that determination, she must maintain a veneer of normalcy. Not stinking like a barnyard animal is a good place to start.

The shower lever is turned. Warm water flows. A cold downpour was considered and overruled.

Before Asmara applies soap in a hierarchy of stench removal, she takes one more sniff of herself. *Yuck.* The emissions have gotten stronger and there is a foreign nature to the aroma. She is aware of the skunk-like fragrances she can produce in extreme situations, but this is a different odor altogether.

Asmara has a thrilled agitation about those dancing pixels on another world, but that doesn't explain her biochemistry changing, does it?

Extra shampoo is added to her hair cleanse. She shuts her eyes and an image greets her behind closed eyelids. The stacks of Europa pixels she stared at were encoded not only into her computer, the shapes were seared into her optic nerves as well.

Asmara's attention shifts back to her surroundings. The shower's water flow decreases. With a face full of shampoo and her eyes closed, the continuous roar from the showerhead lessens by half. The water hitting her chest feels diminished as well. Asmara wipes away the dripping lather and opens her eyes. She can't account for what she sees and hears. The water is at full blast but it's quieter now. She barely feels the liquid on her skin. Asmara runs her hands through the steady waterfall and the experience is muted, as if her senses were turned down.

Except for her sense of smell. The odor is unbearable.

A shadow rises from the floor.

The semi-transparent shower curtain renders everything a gauzy haze. As if obscured by wax paper, a large dark mass is in the center of the bathroom. It fills most of the free space in the enclosed area.

This formless mound is a quivering silhouette which lurches and expands. Long appendages—arms? legs?—branch out of the center mass and cast their own shadows against the curtain. Asmara counts at least seven such limbs.

The guest you have blessed. It's the entity from The Naomi's backstage.
The Patron.

Her nose twitches with a piercing irritation. The terrible smell has a pulsating heat which raises the temperature of the bathroom. This foul cloud has intensified and it waits for her next inhale to truly reveal itself.

She breathes in through her mouth to bypass the scent but it makes no difference. The most wretched odor Asmara has ever experienced produces an immediate gag. The reason no vomit exits her mouth is because her throat seals shut in response to the sensory overload.

Asmara slaps both hands against the shower wall and waits for her throat to unclench so she can breathe again. Five seconds turns to ten and her esophagus contracts into a solid lump.

Her survival backstage at The Naomi yesterday gave her insights to use against the Patron. Those tools are out of reach.

This Patron, whatever it is, has added to its arsenal with a weaponized scent. The odor has invisible tendrils which wrap around her face. It is hard to overcome fears when they are choking you to death.

As her lungs plead for oxygen, one thought keeps her heart beating. If the Patron could kill her outright it would cast aside the curtain and maul her with its grotesque limbs. Why is there no direct contact?

Perhaps like the rules of folklore which address what certain monsters can and cannot do, this demon is unable to touch her unless Asmara surrenders her will.

One of the shadow's appendages pushes against the curtain. The sheet billows inward and a dark limb rises above her. Asmara refuses to look directly at it, so the details are out of focus. From the corner of her eye a black claw slides over the curtain rod. A shiny hooked nail, like a gigantic crow's foot, looms over Asmara.

The radiating heat from the beast and its stench have turned the bathroom into a hellish sauna.

She has not taken a breath in twenty seconds. The motor function part of her brain warns she'll die soon without air. The more-evolved regions of her mind try to convince her this is another hallucination.

Asmara's tool box is empty. Her weapons of logic lay idle, unable to help her breathe. Tunnel vision sets in as darkness narrows her field of sight. She is about to collapse.

Except...

What if there *are* rules here? All monsters have them.

What if... She can write the rules? On the spot?

What if...

Asmara grabs the shower faucet handle.

...this monster is from hell, and cold casts out heat?

Rules are rules.

Asmara utters words which are of no language on Earth. She does not know how she was able to produce the sounds nor how they were chosen. They are both a prayer and an incantation. The spell has been cast.

She cranks the handle clockwise to the utmost cold water setting. The temperature change goes from warm water to icy deluge.

When the freezing water hits Asmara's skin, her muscles violently contract. She turns from the downpour but does not flee. With this pivot she is inches from the repulsive insect limb which has arced over the curtain rod. A massive hooked nail extends toward her neck. The Patron's appendage is a jet-black exoskeleton which looks like polished marble. Within the reflective texture of this thing's armor are long patterns of sunken gashes on its surface. The divots have a familiar, repeating structure. They are sentences. This is a written language, embedded in the shell of a creature. It's in English, mostly. The rest of the lines are unknown codes. Since the rows of letters are a shimmering black on black, the pitted words are tough to read.

Asmara tries to commit one stretch of the inscription to memory but has no time to comprehend her results. She reaches up and grabs the showerhead, re-directing its flow. The cold water hits the Patron's husk and its limb sizzles and cracks with a loud snap. It retracts its shattered leg over the curtain rod and there are bloody, red sinews within the exoskeleton.

The shower lever affected the temperature but the incantation she uttered turned this streaming fluid into holy water, casting out evil.

With the hook retreating, a swirl of suctioned air whips through the bathroom. Asmara gasps and draws an enormous breath into her lungs. It's the deepest, most life-affirming intake of oxygen she's ever had. Her following exhale takes the form of a scream.

The vile heat and smell which were suffocating her dissipate toward the center of the bathroom with an audible whoosh.

She doesn't want to erode her confidence by being surprised the cold-water sorcery worked. Instead, she has a surge of aggression. Asmara grabs the shower nozzle and cranks it upward. The stream of icy water crests over the curtain rod and splashes onto the shadowy mound. A sizzling sound is followed by more loud cracks. The demon and its armor shatter into pieces. Through the curtain, the silhouette of the Patron shakes and squirms. At least three of its appendages pop off, go airborne, and fall to the floor. The creature shrinks in size like a melting Wicked Witch.

Along with its cracking shell, a low guttural moan is the only noise the Patron makes. There is also a faint pounding on a wall, maybe even a human's voice.

What is it saying?

Enough of this. Arrogance and adrenaline surge through Asmara's veins. As the writhing demon descends into the bathroom floor to escape, she must confront the insane scenario altogether. Despite the certainty she almost suffocated moments ago, Asmara has inexhaustible faith that reality still exists, somewhere—and this isn't it.

Holy water from a shower thwarting a monster from another dimension doesn't make sense, even if that is what transpired.

She wrenches aside the curtain.

Asmara's vision telescopes forward and backward and her eyes cannot focus on what is before her. There is a black pit in the center of her bathroom floor and the various pieces of the dismembered Patron are crawling back into it. A disjointed mosaic is formed with eyes and teeth, claws and hair, shiny black exoskeleton and bloody red sinews. Some parts of this nightmare slither and lurch, other elements drip and ooze. But they are all returning into the chasm.

As Asmara's eyes dart around, unable to concentrate on any one thing, the entire bathroom shakes and a colossal hand emerges from the pit. Each finger is four feet long and connected to a hulking slab of palm flesh. It fills the entire bathroom. This is the same horrifying limb which emerged backstage at The Naomi. It is not restricted by any inky surface tension this time. The claw is here to kill her.

A stream of cold holy water, which has continued the entire time, drenches the hand and dissolves its leather-like flesh. The fingers splay wide and swipe at Asmara. She falls backward avoiding a direct hit but not before one of the monster's nails slices her thigh and rips the shower curtain off the rod. As she collapses into the tub, above her the hand trembles and is eaten away by the water, as if it is acid. The claw writhes in a circular motion around the bathroom. One of its hard, sharp nails shatters the wall mirror before the monstrous limb descends back into the pit.

Within a second, the circular edge of the chasm in the floor contracts and disappears, returning to the original linoleum—albeit covered in a quarter-inch of water.

Asmara's chest heaves and she can barely gauge the extent of her leg injury before there is a pounding on the bathroom door. An impact from the other side knocks one of the hinges loose and creates a crack near the doorknob. Another collision splinters a large vertical line in the center of the door. The next display of force is going to burst through.

Asmara stands tall in the tub, naked and bleeding. The upturned shower nozzle creates a steady water fountain, cascading over her head and splashing onto the flooded bathroom floor. Shattered glass and a torn curtain lie on the ground as well.

Whatever comes in next, Asmara has resigned to fate. But she will go down fighting.

The next impact smashes the door open, with the knob's locking mechanism tumbling apart in broken pieces. There, in the doorway, is her roommate Lisa, eyes wide with a fury, holding the living room chair she used to batter her way into the bathroom.

Both women stare at each other, panting to catch their breath, equally in shock at each other's presence.

Lisa speaks first. "What... the fuck? What the fuck, Asmara?!"

Sounds of splashing water fill the room as the waterfall continues. Asmara's mind see-saws from replaying her near-fatal encounter with a monster seconds ago, to the fact she's standing here naked and wounded in a destroyed bathroom in front of her roommate.

The thrill of being alive and the absurdity of her predicament creates a natural reaction in Asmara, one she couldn't restrain even if she wanted.

She stretches a wide grin and laughs freely.

CHAPTER 36

Every few seconds, Lisa's face adjusts a small amount as it evolves toward a new expression. For the past minute, this change continued in the same direction: Lisa's initial concern for Asmara is now a display of contempt for her deranged roommate who destroyed the bathroom.

After Lisa broke through the door, she was persuaded not to call nine-one-one. Asmara assured her roommate the leg wound was not too bad and the flooded floor would be addressed with emergency mopping—even though their apartment doesn't contain a mop. If they reconvene in the kitchen in a few minutes, Asmara suggested, everything would be explained.

As Lisa backs away from the shattered door, her face has no hint of sympathy.

Asmara puts a robe on, runs to her room, and makes a tourniquet out of a long-sleeve shirt. The slice in her flesh is deep but did not reach muscle. There are visible, gross lumps of white connective tissue—a far cry from a leg-shaving nick. This injury will require a hospital visit and stitches but there is no need for an ambulance. A ride share within the hour will be cheaper and less dramatic. The wound strangely isn't bleeding much and there is no pain, thanks to adrenaline.

Did a demon really cut open my leg?

It is beyond comprehension and yet there is physical proof the Patron is real and able to harm her. Odd as it seems, the attack isn't Asmara's priority. She needs to salvage her housing situation and prevent herself from getting dragged to an insane asylum by Lisa.

Towels alone will not suffice for the water on the floor. Asmara grabs blankets from her room plus a bin of laundry. She dumps the load of fabric into the bathroom hoping the absorption will prevent a leak affecting the apartment below. Using her feet to slide the heaps of cloth over the floor, she shuffles around on the linoleum, soaking up as much water as possible.

Asmara is now seated at the kitchen table with Lisa and she has launched into a spontaneous monologue about what happened. The lies come fast and without internal deliberation. This bullshit needs to sell.

Asmara describes how she slipped in the shower and hit her head. When she came to, she experienced disorientation and let out a scream. In the nightmare-like mental state, she thought she was being attacked by something. She ripped the curtain off the rod and is not sure how the mirror broke or how she was sliced, but all three details are related. The shower nozzle was bumped during the frenzy, which rained water onto the floor. Only when the door was smashed did she come to her senses.

Lisa is a tough read, although her glare has softened and there are hints of empathy.

"You promise you're not on drugs?" Lisa asks.

"I swear to you, I'm not."

"You didn't hear me yelling your name and pounding on the door? I had just gotten home and saw water pouring into the hallway."

"I could hear you but it was faint. My senses were acting strange."

Asmara spots an opportunity. What if Lisa is able to corroborate the existence of the Patron? If her roommate validates any aspect of the creature, *that* would be proof Asmara did not have an hallucination. Even the leg wound is not enough evidence since Asmara can't trust anything about herself.

"I have to tell you," Asmara says, "the visions after I hit my head were both vague and, at times, vivid. What exactly did you hear?"

"Well, when I saw water in the hallway I ran up to the door and tried to open it. I could tell the shower water was hitting the floor."

"Is that when you started yelling my name?"

"No, I listened for a few seconds."

"Okay, what did you hear?"

Lisa's brow lowers. Her face grows rigid. "What does it matter what I heard?"

"I just want to connect dots, if possible."

"There were other sounds as well. I'm not sure what they were."

Asmara can't contain herself. "Really?! What did you hear?"

"Stomping. And I heard the mirror break."

"Before the mirror shattered, did you hear other cracking sounds? Because in my confusion I thought I heard a series of sharp snaps."

"Maybe I heard that."

"Did the whole bathroom shake at one point? I could have sworn the walls were shaking."

"Yeah, I felt a rumble. I figured it was you jumping or something."

"So you did feel the walls shake! Did you also hear a weird moaning sound? Wait! Did you smell a horrible odor?!"

Oh, no.

The hunt for clues became a clumsy interrogation. Lisa's demeanor grows cold and she exudes distrust.

Time to backpedal. "Look, I'm sorry," Asmara says. "This has been a crazy experience for me. I was hearing and seeing things in the bathroom but now I'm good. I'll pay for the door and any water damage."

Asmara's arms are on the table with the robe sleeves slid to her elbows. Lisa traces her eyes up and down Asmara's bare wrists. It's a strange scan. Asmara assumes she's being examined for the scar tissue of a cutter.

Lisa rises from the table to fill a glass of water. Her movements are unnatural, stiff with hesitation. When it appears she might dash out of the kitchen, she speaks. "How's your head?"

"My head?" Asmara reaches for the back of her skull.

"Yeah, you hit your head in the shower. Remember?" Her voice oozes with derision. "Surely you have a lump. Do you want me to have a look?"

"Oh. There is a bit of a bump," Asmara says, running her fingers through her hair. "It's not too bad."

Lisa takes a long drink from her glass. "I'm glad you're feeling better but we both know what just happened is crazy. I had to break down a fucking door, Asmara."

"I feel terrible about that."

"You also laughed at me when I got into the bathroom."

"No, I was coming to my senses and laughing at the situation. I can't explain my actions."

"Asmara..."

"Yeah?"

"When I almost called nine-one-one, it wasn't going to be for an ambulance. It was for the police."

"I know."

. . . .

Since her world has fractured anyway, Asmara disregards apartment convention and brings the living room reading chair into her bedroom. Lisa may view the missing chair as more evidence Asmara is demented, but that ship has already sailed, caught fire, and plummeted to the seafloor.

Asmara is seated and breathes slowly with her eyes closed. Her leg wound aches but emergency care is not required this instant.

She tries to calm herself, knowing that meditation is not possible during a tornado of rotating thoughts. The various storms of her life each fight for attention behind shuttered eyelids: Ryan is a wonderful mystery. She is committed to read her story on stage along with the spider finale. Her neighbor accuses her of mind-reading. A series of hallucinations are unspooling her sanity. She may have discovered aliens on Europa. Oh, and she just fought for her life against a house-sized demon.

Any of these variables are able to consume her mental bandwidth. She lets them jostle for position and stake their claim as most urgent. The one which rises above the tempest has a geometric shape. It's the Europa pixels again. In the darkness of her closed eyes she observes the seared images. The consecutive stacks float in front of her, gray on black.

Using a slow tracking motion with her eyes, Asmara reviews the shapes from left to right. The way they wiggle has an embedded familiarity.

What is this dance?

Asmara dials up the speed of her eye movement and she creates an animation. These squares are alive. They move in an unmistakable S-shaped pattern. This object glides like a snake on land or as an eel does in water.

The pixels are not shimmering light from an ice ridge. They are not a blinking neon sign in an alien city. At the bottom of a deep ice crevasse on Europa, the Caerus spacecraft has captured evidence of a slithering or swimming lifeform. It's an alien serpent—and a big one at that. Maybe miles long.

Her inherent skepticism tries to puncture this theory but the attempts wheeze and stumble. Asmara's chronic doubts cannot mock this discovery any more.

She opens her eyes. The squares continue to alternate in front of her until they fade in visible light. Exhilaration pulses from her chest and gives her an out-of-body feeling.

I discovered an alien.

Asmara fires up her laptop again. While she waits for it to load, she internet searches a question on her phone. "How does a snake move?" She is certain there's a technical term. The answer: "Snakes and eels propel themselves by lateral undulation; also known as serpentine movement."

She first assumed the moving pixels represented a signal of intelligent life. Now that she's certain it's the body of an undulating serpent, does it alter the find? Does it matter if the alien is a high-tech species or no smarter than a big, dumb dinosaur?

Hell no, it doesn't matter. This discovery is too incredible to have a wish list of alien expectations.

Another concept sparks her imagination. What if the snake is both the length of a city AND highly advanced?

Unreal. The notion fills her with wonder.

Her laptop humming, Asmara opens the row of Europa pixel stacks she compiled. She overlaps each stack onto their own layer. A burst of keyboard commands later, she has a digital version of the same animation which flickered behind her closed eyelids.

The slideshow is on a loop and the gray snake continues its perpetual motion on her computer. Asmara leans in with deep affection. These moving squares are beautiful.

Practical questions arise. Did the serpent slide across ice at the bottom of the crevasse? Or was a sliver of exposed water visible and the alien glided on the interior ocean surface?

Even though she has no measurement of the true length of those pixels, they occupy significant real estate on Europa. Any animal that big would require massive energy intake to survive. Beneath the ice there must be a thriving ecosystem in the ocean to supply food. Who can imagine what lurks under there?

Asmara leaps onto her bed and stares at the ceiling.

This information will change the world. Am I going to be famous and rich? Will I be kidnapped by a secret government agency?

Outside Asmara's bedroom, Lisa opens and closes drawers along with other hurried noises around the apartment. It's obvious, Lisa is gathering things to get out of there—maybe for a few nights, maybe forever. Asmara regrets causing her roommate distress but someday Lisa will learn the details of this extraordinary evening they shared together. Lisa is assured a footnote in history as being in the same apartment where proof of extraterrestrial life was first determined.

The ceiling shudders with every one of Asmara's heartbeats. She is the only one on Earth who knows of this alien lifeform. If she died from an earthquake right now or if a giant demon hand squeezed the life out of her, the discovery will be lost. She needs to compile the evidence in a clear fashion and share it.

The front door of the apartment slams shut. Lisa is gone.

Asmara takes stock of her surroundings. She should be apprehensive about being alone, if not terrified, due to the Patron. There is instead a calm focus. Asmara will not spend her life on the run from monsters and it's imperative that the Europa anomaly is revealed. For safety, she will go to the Slow Pour coffee shop across the street with her laptop and broadcast the message.

Asmara disrobes to slip into dry clothes and she grips the T-shirt tourniquet around her thigh. The injury had fallen from her attention and she forgot about needing stitches. She unwinds the improvised bandage, dreading to see the damaged flesh again. As the shirt is lifted a welcome, yet puzzling, surprise greets her. There is a four-inch-long slice in her skin but it looks nothing like the initial laceration. When the Patron's claw first sunk into her, Asmara had seen white clumps of connective tissue within a gaping bloody mess. Now the injury is razor thin with only a seam of dried blood occupying the gap. The skin around the cut is an angry red but she doesn't need to go to the hospital anymore. Good news is seldom riddled with such disbelief.

It is not feasible that trauma like this heals so quickly. There is no explanation for her body's reaction.

Another log has been thrown onto the bonfire of impossible events burning bright within her life.

CHAPTER 37

Her fingers hover above the keyboard as Asmara debates how to tailor her message. Who do you first contact when you discover aliens in the solar system? How do you present the evidence in a way which isn't ridiculed within seconds?

She could skip email inboxes altogether. One option is to hijack by gunpoint a local news station and make them broadcast her findings to the world. That would thwart any Men in Black committed to stopping her revelation. Asmara's aggressive tactics would be vindicated later and the gun would be unloaded, of course.

A less severe idea is to record a video explanation of the Europa anomaly and send it to journalists. A few of them will bite the serpent bait.

Nah. A laser-focused outreach is the correct first step. To establish credibility, there needs to be a co-signer. Who better than the brains behind the Caerus space probe mission itself? She will find one of the project's team leaders and contact the person directly.

Asmara leans back in her chair and sips Slow Pour's decaf coffee. She waits for the metallic aftertaste to foul her tongue but doesn't mind its arrival. The rusted-fence flavor is worth the security of knowing the Patron won't appear here in public. There is one other customer in Slow Pour tonight and it's not Inga, which is all that matters.

She does an internet search to determine who sent the flying robot to swoop above Europa.

"The Caerus is a space probe constructed and launched by the United States in a joint venture with NASA and Nimitz Technologies. It is a spacecraft weighing 1,120 lbs. with a large central dish and nine antennas. Its instruments include visible-light cameras, radiowave recorders, infrared interferometer, ultraviolet spectrometer, triaxial magnetometer, plasma spectrometer, and other tools for gathering data. The probe's mission (now half complete) involves outer planetary, heliosphere, and interstellar exploration. Primary objectives included a locked orbit around Jupiter (with an analysis of the planet's atmosphere) as well as a near fly-by of Jupiter's moon Europa. The spacecraft is currently traveling at a rate of 38,026 mph. It is headed for interstellar space and will exit our solar system in twenty years."

Asmara has no idea what a triaxial magnetometer does, but the jargon is impressive. Learning about the spacecraft is appropriate since she piggy-backed its mission to make her own discovery. Still, where can she share her exciting scoop about Europa? NASA is a bureaucratic behemoth and they don't have a direct hotline for alien gossip.

Another web search is typed: "Nimitz Technologies, Caerus team." An excerpt beneath a headline gives her a name. "The man responsible for integrating Caerus' various systems is Professor Stephen Garrity."

Asmara hopes Stephen is receptive to evidence that his probe recorded an alien snake which is longer than the Golden Gate Bridge.

Some more research finds that Stephen is an aerospace engineer and teaches computer science at UC Berkeley. He may be twenty-five minutes away by car right now. She could corner him in a campus hallway and introduce her serpent theory in person. As with her broadcast news hijacking strategy, a presentation by gunpoint in Stephen's face would convey the seriousness of this matter and ensure he doesn't run away. Instead, she will keep things cordial by sending the scientist an email. Asmara navigates to a UC faculty page with Stephen's contact info.

Her co-signer has been found, he just doesn't know it yet.

To prepare her message, Asmara opens the first picture from the Europa fly-by sequence. She digitally places a thin red circle above the crevasse where the pixels were found. This target is where Stephen can zoom in himself and find the reflected light. Next, she attaches into the email the flat image of the fifteen square stack patterns in a row.

Now for the hook. Asmara describes in detail her process of zooming into the Caerus photos and documenting the moving gray pixels. She ends her email with this:

"These frames look uncannily like serpentine movement found in lifeforms on Earth. I encourage you to examine the original Europa photo sequence to confirm these pixels exist in the crevasse and were not added by me.

Professor Garrity, with all due respect to you and your team's extraordinary work on the Caerus mission, I am curious what theories you have for this phenomenon? Am I crazy to wonder if this is a gigantic alien snake?

Sincere thanks for your consideration."

. . . .

Back in her apartment, Asmara stands with trepidation in front of the bathroom. The door hangs from one hinge, battered and limp as if in defeat. There is no sense that a demon lies within, so a horror movie jump scare is unlikely. What concerns Asmara about this bathroom is how it represents physical destruction borne of the chaos in her mind.

She gathers wet blankets and clothing from the bathroom floor and throws them into the shower tub. These will have to get cleaned before mildew turns the apartment into a stinky swamp. Although there are a few warped ripples in the linoleum, it appears the worst of the water damage is averted. She half-hopes to find a dismembered, autonomous limb from the Patron cowering in the corner. It is unable to return to hell and is vulnerable when not attached to its beastly host. Any evidence of an actual creature which emerged through a portal would concentrate Asmara's thoughts. She doesn't *want* to be on a demon's hit list but she'd like to know if the danger is an illusion or as real as the demolished door she has to replace.

One detail which is undeniable is a splatter of her dried blood streaked on the shower's tile wall. It signifies that violence transpired in this room. Whether the harm was caused by a monster or from Asmara herself is not known.

. . . .

This is not an astral projection where one's spirit soars without limits, leaving the body behind. Asmara's consciousness is instead "only" floating three feet above the bed.

She collapsed with fatigue after cleaning the bathroom and within one minute her sensations levitated above her torso. The dopamine cocktail in her brain isn't enough to launch Asmara into outer space but it is sufficient to float while tethered on a short leash.

Contentment and even optimism shine rays of light into weary parts of her mind. Big, scary things have been happening for a few days now. Exciting things have taken place as well. It's as if Omar and the narrator from *Rain Rising* are having a dialogue about what they see from Asmara's viewpoint. Omar is in the driver's seat and the road ahead looks sunny, even if massive hook-tipped insect appendages lurk in the distance.

Sleep whispers in her ear, trying to coax Asmara to submit. It's an easy sell. Her motorcade of thoughts slows to a crawl and her spirit descends back into her body.

Asmara has no control over the final image flashing in her mind before she falls asleep. It is the Patron's limb up close again, the way it appeared when the probing hook arched over the shower curtain. It's an ugly sight and yet no fear is elicited. She shattered that armored prong and banished it. For now.

The dark marble exoskeleton of the Patron's appendage gleams within Asmara's memory. Sunken gashes embedded in its shell form written words and sentences. The engravings were tough to read while she fought for her life in the bathroom, but her eyes did capture a freeze-frame of one sentence among hundreds which pockmarked the beast. And as Asmara plunges into sleep, here are those words now, as easy to read as a highway billboard.

"There is no waterfall until the flood."

CHAPTER 38

It's an annoying sound, especially to wake up to. Every time, Asmara pledges to never set her phone on the windowsill. The vibrations get amplified against the glass with an obnoxious clatter.

It's tough to be upset at the incoming texts.

"Hey, it's Zoe. We're at One Track Mind in SF doing work"

"Ryan's busy all day. I want a break"

"Do you want to meet for lunch?"

Asmara is charmed by this girl. There is no way the fourteen-year-old would reach out unprompted if she wasn't comfortable around Asmara.

"Thanks for the invite, Zoe. I'll come to you around noon. We can eat near the shop"

Zoe instantly replies. "Awesome"

Asmara sits upright and grips her leg. Before she went to bed last night she applied a patchwork of bandages across the slice in her thigh. There is an itch, a sizzle of sensations, beneath the adhesives. She's tempted to rip them off and see what is happening down there but the tingle subsides. Either the wound went gangrene and those are wiggling maggots or her accelerated healing has created dry scabs ready to pick.

She leaves the bandages alone.

. . . .

The ride share is a smooth lift and Asmara gets dropped off in front of One Track Mind where Zoe waits on the sidewalk.

"Hey," Zoe says, giving Asmara a firm hug. "Thanks for coming."

"No problem. Is Ryan inside? I was going to say hi before we eat."

"He had to run an errand. He'll be back soon."

The two walk and chat as they head toward a deli three blocks away. Zoe peppers Asmara with questions about the upcoming Word Bound gig. "Is there going to be a second stage rehearsal?" No. "Has the spider been given a name yet?" No. "Have you considered letting the spider bite you so you learn to not panic if it happens during your performance?" No, but there is a logic to that thinking.

At the deli, they both order a sandwich and take a seat. Zoe does most of the talking and Asmara relishes it. The teenager rattles off updates of her car-scratch database and makes a bold claim that she wants to be the first girl to ollie Ryan's Line.

Zoe has good table manners. She takes discrete bites, puts the sandwich back on the plate, and eats her food with a quiet grace. Her slow-motion jaw movements are a far cry from the noisy, cud-chewing displays of other teens.

After light banter, a somber shift enters Zoe's voice. "Do you dream at night?"

"Everyone does. It's just a matter if you remember them or not."

"Do you believe dreams have any meaning?"

"I think they are the result of random brain activity while you're asleep. Any meaning you want to give them later is a reflection of your conscious, wide-awake mind, not the dreams themselves."

Zoe's face scrunches as she puzzles over that perspective. "Have you ever had a dream that came true later?"

"No. I've never had a dream predict future events."

Zoe's energy changes. Her eyes dart side to side.

A sinking feeling washes over Asmara. *Did I damage this girl by bringing her into my twisted orbit? Am I a danger to the sanity of everyone around me?*

"I texted you this morning," Zoe says, "because I wanted to see if you were okay."

"I'm all right. I'm here, aren't I? What's up?"

"I, uh..." Another grimace from Zoe. "I had a dream last night that you died."

Asmara's head jerks back. She braces herself for another piece of evidence the universe is unraveling. The usually hidden connective tissue of existence is exposed, like the bloody sinews within the Patron's broken shell.

"What did you see?" Asmara asks.

"There was a big waterfall. You were thrashing around inside it. You were drowning."

"I don't know what to tell you other than I'm alive now. I have no plans of swimming any time soon."

"I've had bad dreams before," Zoe says, her eyes filling with tears. "I can handle them. I'm not a baby. This one felt so real, though."

"Zoe, I'm..."

"You don't think I'm a cry baby, do you? I just like Ryan so much. He's been cool to me. And now you've joined our little team. So, to see you get pulled under..."

Asmara reaches across the table and holds Zoe's hands. In other circumstances, this girl's reaction to a bad dream would be ridiculous for a teenager. However, with Asmara's own torment serving as reference, it's clear how unwanted visions break people down.

"Another thing happened," Zoe says with a sniffle. "Even though you died in the dream, there was a happy ending. Sort of."

"What do you mean?"

"You know how dreams jump around? After you disappeared, the environment changed and I was underwater. The scene was beautiful. This huge current was moving within the ocean and I sensed it was alive. It was you. You became a massive river that flowed within the sea."

Over the next minutes, Asmara downplays the dream symbolism and redirects the conversation back to more light fare about skateboarding. Zoe is soon laughing again.

As they leave the deli, Asmara acts on a random hunch. "When did you go to sleep last night, Zoe?"

"Why?"

"I'm curious."

"It was right after midnight. I remember because the last thing I saw was the clock turning to 12:00. "

. . . .

When they return to the bike store Ryan is out front. He is smoking a cigarette.

What kind of unholy emphysema bullshit is this?

The white carcinogenic cloud exiting his mouth loosely resembles a lung tumor. Asmara suspects the cancer stick is a fluke.

He smiles but there is a weariness to his face.

"You look frazzled," she says, squeezing his forearm. They each give a head tilt as if they may go in for a kiss but neither commits.

"I don't smoke, just so you know. I hate these things. They're only an excuse to take a break."

"Is the shop a never-ending project?"

"This store has been eighty-percent finished for a month. The final twenty percent of tasks keep expanding."

"What can I do to help?"

"There's some tedious grunt work but I can't make you do that."

"I want to. Honestly."

"Well, okay. If you insist. So, I used a table saw in the hallway like an idiot and now there's sawdust everywhere. It keeps getting tracked into the showroom. Would you be up for cleaning that?"

"Let's do it."

Ryan nods and extends his arm toward the street, about to flick his cigarette butt. Asmara is disappointed she will have to lecture her boyfriend about littering.

His arm bobs up and down with hesitation and retracts, the stubby filter not launched.

"Should probably find an ashtray," he mumbles to himself.

Watching his free will get subverted, Asmara has a stab of guilt and a rush of pleasure about her apparent ability to manipulate minds.

. . . .

With the help of a push broom, the sawdust is coaxed into piles and scooped into a bin. Asmara volunteers to gather loose paperwork scattered throughout the building and bring it to Ryan's office. It's as if these files are playing hide and seek because they turn up in every obscure crevice. After that, beads of sweat are generated as she flattens cardboard boxes for recycling. By the time Ryan has her using a drill to assemble a display table, she is a dusty, sore, content worker bee.

Asmara is two hours into this manual labor honeymoon and she imagines marrying Ryan and working for him in the store. It's not what she dreamed her life would be and yet that fate isn't half bad right now.

Chatter and jokes are shouted across the store as the three swirl past each other attending to their chores. At one point, Ryan stocks a head-high shelf with supplies. He is preoccupied and walking backward, not seeing Zoe is crouched behind him as she removes masking tape along the floor. Zoe waves to get Asmara's attention. She pantomimes a pushing motion, indicating Ryan has made himself fair game for a stumbling block shove with Zoe serving as the trip wire. Pranks and slapstick humor are not Asmara's thing, which makes it surprising that she gives Ryan a nudge and admires as he tumbles over Zoe behind him. He lands on his back with a thud. It was a perfectly executed takedown with no visible trauma suffered by the mark. Ryan remains on the ground, staring at the ceiling.

Zoe emits a rumble of restrained laughter but she is about to erupt. Asmara snickers and, as long as Ryan is not paralyzed, she expects to roar also. The two creep toward Ryan to get a look at their victim when his arm swoops like a horror movie villain and grabs Zoe by the ankle. She yells with delight and sprints away. Her high-pitch shriek betrays her tough tomboy exterior. Asmara is a grown woman and refuses to run. She will face her consequences with dignity.

Ryan springs to his feet and glares at his abuser. Asmara flinches as Ryan's hands materialize on her shoulders faster than her eyes can follow. He spins her around facing the other way from him.

Hold on. Is he actually mad?

One of his hands sweeps her hair away to expose bare neck. Ryan buries a kiss under her ear. She melts into him as he wraps his arm around her and supports her weight. Asmara has not felt this way in years. His gentle open mouth gnawing is noisy in the best possible way. Ryan wrenches on her shirt collar, revealing naked shoulder, and he presses his lips against her skin. Before Asmara's sense of surprise can stabilize, he turns her around and their faces merge with heated kissing.

There is ten seconds of passion and Asmara gets both her ass cheeks palmed firmly with an audible slap from Ryan's hands. The maneuver is one increment too much in terms of escalating this event. Zoe is still in the shop and about to return any second. It's not like she went home.

Ryan releases Asmara's rear end and backs away with a sheepish expression. He looks at his hands as if they had operated without his consent.

"I got carried away there."

Footsteps plod down the hallway and Zoe rounds the corner back into the room. "You're not mad are you? It was a joke."

"I'm okay," Ryan says. "Don't do that again, though."

"Can I have a couple of bucks to get a soda at the store?"

"You conspire to harm me and then want money? Fine." He hands her cash.

As Zoe exits the shop and the door closes, Asmara raises her right hand high in the air. She stretches her ligaments and coiled energy builds in her shoulder. Ryan faces away as her arm's tension unlocks like a catapult and the limb swoops in a downward arc. Her hand connects with Ryan's backside—the hardest she's ever slapped anything in her life—and he stumbles forward three steps until momentum drags him to the ground.

He's on his back for the second time in two minutes, although he laughs at the titanic spank he endured. Asmara helps pick him up. She throws him against the wall and kisses him. It's a level of assertiveness Asmara didn't know she was capable of. She doesn't recognize herself, but it is interesting being a passenger in this new vessel.

CHAPTER 39

In college, her email account was an essential portal to the internet super highway. Now Asmara's online address is more like an abandoned dirt road with weeds of spam growing in it. That's why it's so surprising the scientist Stephen Garrity replied to her message about Europa.

She is back in her apartment after helping at Ryan's bike shop. Asmara had checked her email hoping for an update about the job opening from her friend Dylan. He said he might be forwarding her employment documents. No news there. Instead, she has to settle for a message from a professor who may confirm her discovery of gigantic alien snakes.

She takes a breath and readies herself. Whether she gets discredited here or is greeted with an Earth-shaking vindication, either outcome will pack a punch.

"Asmara, this is Stephen Garrity. I must say, your curiosity mixed with resourcefulness is a tremendous combination and I'm honored you reached out. The observations, evidence, and theory you presented about Europa involve free-form inquiry at its best.

I took your message seriously. I even arranged a video call with two of my Caerus colleagues, Sheila Levy and Dinesh Moredi. We had a fantastic time discussing your findings. Here's a summary:

1: Our team had never seen those pixel anomalies you found. The Caerus images were processed through algorithms designed to find unique pixel signatures worthy of closer inspection, especially in sunken surface areas. Our models are highly calibrated but they didn't detect what you uncovered. Well done.

2: We do not believe those gray square stacks were created by misfiring receptors in the camera. We suspect, as you do, the pixels represent the faintest of reflected light coming from within the crevasse.

3: The question is, what's being reflected? That crevasse is estimated to be fifteen miles deep. Since your magnifications show solid black, we can only guess if your zoom effect is going deeper into the interior or hitting a sheer ice wall. We crunched some numbers and split the difference. Our conservative guess is those five moving pixels you found represent three miles of distance."

Asmara gasps. *Hey, that length was my hunch as well. Maybe I'm a born astrobiologist.* She continues reading.

"Here comes the deflating part to your 'alien snake' hypothesis, Asmara. My colleagues and I had a blast brainstorming about a lifeform that big in our solar system but we can't give it any credence. We're not prepared to say it's impossible, but it's so improbable that its likelihood is near zero.

A creature that big would weigh hundreds of thousands of tons and require an energy intake beyond comprehension. By our understanding of biology, a breeding population of that species would need to devour an Atlantic Ocean's worth of other life forms every year to survive and procreate. The Jupiterian moon would have to be utterly teeming with life to produce and sustain a 'sea snake' species that big. And yet, Europa offers no tell-tale signs of large-scale biological chemistry taking place.

Of course, evolution doesn't need to follow Earth's playbook. Maybe the animal is composed mostly of air or gas surrounded by a thin membrane. Essentially, a balloon serpent. Or perhaps the lifeform thrives on geothermal energy produced in the moon's interior. We could speculate all day, but we can't make wild leaps based on limited evidence.

Frankly, we don't know what those moving pixels represent. Our best guess is the most obvious one—that the sparkling squares are light reflected on ice. The fact that the shimmer is repeated in two sequences is not proof of serpentine movement. That being said, ten or more repeated sequences would be something to think about.

Let's treat your findings as yet another fascinating mystery on an already interesting moon.

Asmara, again, thank you for your compelling investigation and feel free to reply with any more of your thoughts. Take care."

Conflicted feelings rise and fall within Asmara like Jupiter's tidal gravity pulling on Europa. She is shocked this esteemed scientist gave her idea consideration. The buzz is tempered by disappointment at Stephen's dismissal of her theory. He made good points and she didn't expect him to declare Ice-Snake Gods had clearly been found. However, he's mistaken to disregard the repeating pixel sequences. Those configurations are plenty of evidence something unique is going on. How the shimmer mimics an undulating snake adds to the urgency of this information.

Is that email the end of the road for this discovery? Are there ways to appeal to a wider audience?

Taking a gun to a broadcast news station might not be such a bad idea after all. Asmara may even load the damn thing with bullets to make sure someone listens.

. . . .

Over the next half hour, her nerves settle. Asmara didn't notice how tense she was until her body unwinds into the reading chair. Discouragement about Stephen's response has morphed into simmering confidence. She didn't gain a co-signer to her Europa theory but the findings are still worth sharing. After Word Bound she's going to distribute the evidence in a non-crazy-person way. There will be a reasoned online discussion in serious forums. Soon after, a critical mass of true believers will storm NASA with torches and demand another probe be sent to Europa to greet our serpentine neighbors.

In a fit of distraction, Asmara scrolls through her phone. Social media content passes by as fast as her fingers move. The spastic flicks come to a halt. A series of familiar shapes and words float on her screen.

I made this.

The Word Bound flyer she designed stares at her through the phone.

She stumbled onto The Naomi's media profile and their recent post is Asmara's art used to promote the event. The post has hundreds of likes. Hundreds! This mass affirmation is the closest thing to "viral" her minuscule online presence ever generated. An injection of ego flattery oozes in her brain. Asmara used to scoff at social media enticement. Now she's certain that if this validation was distilled into a drug she would snort it.

She reads the viewer comments.

"Who did this poster? It's rad."

"Word Bound always has cool art. They should sell these as prints."

Asmara is straight up, bong-hit high at this point. It feels *that* good to receive positive feedback on her artistic offering.

If there had been an infinite number of comments, Asmara would have spent an infinity reading them. The social media *is* the drug. No snorting required.

One comment jumps out.

"The skater in the poster is Ryan Q Smith. It's from his famous Ryan's Line ollie. Look it up. Ryan rules."

Ha! That is something Zoe would write.

Asmara clicks the tag to visit the account. It's that Zoe.

The serendipity of these virtual crossed paths is impressive but Asmara considers how algorithms track our every step and nudge us toward predetermined destinations. Some artificial intelligence in a laboratory has probably plotted Asmara's journey these past few days.

Zoe has few photos on her profile and no selfies which is surprising for a teenager. One of the images features her and Ryan.

The photo is well-shot, a magic moment, with sunlight framing halos around Ryan and Zoe. They're on a city street—in Oakland, it has to be—and they are both looking above the camera. Even though there are no skateboards in the frame, it is a skate-related photo. Their shoes and clothing create the vibe plus they're near a steep embankment which looks like an asphalt wave.

The more Asmara stares at the photo the more her senses vibrate and stir up impossible signals. She hears the layered hum of a city street environment. There is the continuous drone of a wind tunnel coursing through a downtown corridor. The purring of car engines drift by. These sensory effects are vivid. Breaking through the ambient din is a voice as clear as if it was spoken in her quiet room.

"I'm glad we didn't go to SF today."

It's a girl's voice. Zoe.

A man answers. It's Ryan.

"Yeah. There's no place like home."

Asmara casts the phone aside and runs her hands through her hair. This tactile sensation grounds her back in reality. The sounds and energy of the city street atmosphere dissolve, leaving her room placid again. As far as hallucinations go, this one was benign. Teleporting to the photo's locale had a dreamy, enjoyable quality.

Asmara stands from her reading chair. She smells car exhaust. There is no way to prove its origin but the caustic odor was emitted on an Oakland street at some point in the past.

CHAPTER 40

In high school Asmara threw a party only six people attended. Her parents were out of town and her friend Holly, that fool, badgered Asmara into hosting an intimate two-keg gathering of perhaps twenty to ninety people. The watery beer was procured. The parents' valuables were locked away. And almost no one showed. Holly, that irredeemable dumbass, had neglected party scouting reports of Brian Sullivan's mega-rager, with a DJ, which was slated for the same night.

Since the humiliating party flop, Asmara has disliked initiating any gathering of more than three people. It is an unnatural act for her to invite numerous friends to Word Bound.

Using a group text, Asmara messages eight people. She attaches the flier she designed.

"Hey everyone! I'm going to be reading one of my short stories at The Naomi in SF tomorrow night. Word Bound is a fun open mic night, if you've never been. The info is attached. Hope you can make it"

She invited Sarah and Gillian, of course. Those two were with her the night her stage act was formulated. Dylan was included in the text as well and he may or may not have job news by tomorrow. The other people are a smattering of former co-workers who evolved into friends. If Asmara was twenty-one years old, the invitation list would have crept toward two dozen names. Now that she's almost thirty, her social circle is contracting at an alarming rate. It will take effort for it not to vanish altogether.

She sends Ryan a separate message. "Please remind your One Track Mind team about Word Bound tomorrow. They're welcome to come"

Ryan responds within seconds.

"I had already invited them and they're all coming. This is gonna be great"

. . . .

She holds the tarantula up to her face and it stares back. Or it appears to. There's no telling if the spider's gaze contains motivations. Black orb eyes are not known for being expressive. The spider is balanced on top of Asmara's bare forearm. She figured another round of contact exposure with the animal was in order.

Asmara leans in to examine the spider's dark exoskeleton legs. There are no sunken pockmarks in the shell which form complete sentences. The thought of the Patron's inscribed armor makes Asmara scoff in disbelief.

"No waterfall until the flood..."

It makes no sense that a creature from another dimension would have English written on its body. Particularly one of my sentences I jotted down in the past.

The Patron is a beast of Asmara's making and when it arrives again she will need to unmake it. If her mind is able to materialize such a detailed horror what if she harnessed those same abilities for good? What fantastic things might she conjure?

With a twist of the wrist Asmara convinces the tarantula to descend into its container. Once inside the cube, the spider surprises her by not going into its rock cave. It turns to face her and raises its two forelegs up and down in an alternating order. Asmara lifts her arms and returns the strange salute.

I like this critter.

. . . .

She peels the bandages back and her thigh gouge is now a flakey scab, close to being healed. A handful of routine childhood injuries made Asmara familiar with the timeframe for wounds becoming scars. It is biologically impossible for her skin to heal so fast. Or perhaps the initial injury didn't happen the way she remembered.

No matter. Asmara has conceded to fate's unfair advantage over her. Reality bends rules at random.

In forty-eight hours, she's going to call her parents and tell them about her mental health concerns. They will panic, for sure, and recommend emergency psychiatric care. Asmara will instead seek orderly appointments and therapy. No insane asylum needed. She will adhere to all professional advice and take suggested medications. Her journey back to stability begins soon. However, first comes Word Bound. Nothing is going to stop her from reading on stage. The performance will expose these Patron theatrics as her mind gone wild. Or the event may open a dimension and summon an actual, honest to God, monster. She has no desire to endanger people but she's going to call the beast's bluff. This waking nightmare will not hold her hostage.

. . . .

Destroyed bathroom aside, Asmara is usually mindful of her roommate Lisa. Actions are taken to reduce noise and music is listened to with headphones. A silver lining to Lisa fleeing the apartment is these considerations are unneeded. Asmara plays music from her desktop computer without headphones. Fabulous rhythmic sounds at a substantial volume fill the room. Rich harmonies vibrate against her skin. Bass notes give a deep tissue massage while the changing pitch of vocals tickle her scalp.

Dancing is a difficult frontier for Asmara. The movements are alluring to watch but out of reach in terms of participation. When she's in a good mood, she will do an insincere shuffle for a few seconds. When she's in a great mood, she can be convinced to dance for one song with friends. Beyond that, she becomes hyper-aware of every body contortion and is afraid she appears ridiculous. She would rather drift to the sidelines and soak in the energy of other people dancing.

But not now.

The heat from the wonderful and terrible things happening in her life melt Asmara's inhibitions. She swirls around the room, using the music itself as a dance partner. Her insecurities crumble in sync to the movement of her limbs. There is no particular style of dance on display—sound waves are translated into motion. This is a celebration of survival. With everything she's been through, Asmara could be strapped to a hospital bed while sedated with antipsychotics. Instead, her spirit soars as musical compositions offer encouragement.

Eyes closed, Asmara loses her sense of location in the apartment. She rockets around in a limitless dark ballroom. The sounds are no longer heard through her ears. The beautiful wavelength information is processed by her whole body.

Only when she collapses with delighted exhaustion does Asmara open her eyes again. She's back in the reading chair. A hard object pokes her thigh and she notices she sat on her phone. Pulling the device from under her, eight text messages await. Every person she invited to Word Bound has confirmed they will attend.

. . . .

Broadway Thai curry does not induce a craving in a normal sense. It is not a suggestion, this is a command. She's already thrown a jacket on and is out the door before she comprehends her marching orders.

A walk in the city stimulates Asmara. Beads of sweat on her face which she earned from dancing evaporate with a satisfying chill. As people pass on the sidewalk, she imagines if their lives are culminating in a grand cosmic showdown like hers appears to be.

Inside the blue-tinted restaurant, she pays in cash, leaves a tip, and is left holding a single remaining dollar bill. It's the one she discovered while cleaning up litter.

Her mind is transported back to snorkeling with goggles in Lake Tahoe as a child, hunting for treasure. It's doubtful she swam with lateral undulation like a water snake—human anatomy would prevent that. But in her memory it's as if she was a serpent beneath the surface. A river flowing within the sea.

Asmara takes a seat and waits for her food. The Europa science magazine is tucked in the jacket's interior pocket. Egg-white on black, the Jupiterian moon on the cover continues to enchant with its ghostly beauty.

Could it be? Is it possible there are massive lifeforms on Europa?

Forget skeptical inquiry based on hard evidence. She simply *wants* the huge snakes to be real. Everyone on Earth will be electrified by a shared sense of awe in that we inhabit a solar system with gigantic neighbors. Humans will be drawn closer together, our differences minimized, as we contemplate the existence of three-mile-long aliens.

The food arrives.

Asmara reminds herself to enjoy the flavors instead of treating the meal like a pie-eating contest. The sound of vegetables being chewed serves as a metronome for her lazy pace through the magazine.

When Asmara snaps back to attention, she is surprised thirty minutes have passed. She did not read anything. Asmara stared at the photo of Europa the whole time.

CHAPTER 41

Today is the day of Word Bound. She is at ease with the looming event and has a plan to maintain a calm demeanor. Her strategy is to not think about the performance until she's on stage tonight. It may seem like an unhealthy avoidance tactic and that's because it is one.

She skips around on her laptop through the usual media routines and checks her email. There's no job news from her friend Dylan but Stephen Garrity wrote her again. Perhaps he's a true believer now and will designate her the Earth ambassador to all Europa aliens.

"Asmara, hello! I am not writing to declare my reconsideration of your Europa theory. My doubts still stand, yet my admiration for your clever insight remains as well. The observational skills you displayed are why I'm reaching out.

I serve as an advisor to a neuroscience grad student named Mary Kohler. She is creating a test to measure face-recognition memory loss in Alzheimer's patients. It is difficult to standardize human faces, so this test will involve memorizing dot patterns as a proxy. There is a similar geometry to all faces which can be rendered with a configuration of points. To determine a base average for memorization abilities, we are looking for a control group of people with high observational skills. I have a hunch you're in this category, Asmara. The test is included in the attached link. It takes three minutes to complete. A pen and paper are required. There's no pressure here and your involvement will give this experiment the data it needs to be an effective tool for helping Alzheimer's patients.

Sincerely, Stephen Garrity. Please proceed to link."

Asmara soaks in the dense information from this unexpected email. She is honored to be included. Her facial recognition skills are strong but memorizing dots may pose a challenge.

She taps the link on her laptop and it takes her to a simple website. There is a paragraph of instructions above a tab on a white homepage.

"When you click the tab below, a series of dots will appear on your screen. You have sixty seconds to try to memorize the spatial distance between the points. After one minute, the dots will disappear. A timer on your screen will activate and you have two minutes to replicate the dot pattern to the best of your ability using a pen and paper. When the two minutes are up, use a camera phone and take a photo of your dot replication. Email the image to the website on the bottom of the screen. This beta test uses an honor system. Please, no cheating. Thank you."

Asmara is fired up and ready to tackle this task. She doesn't have a full grasp of the project, but she will do her best.

A pen and paper are within arm's reach and she rubs her eyes before opening the tab.

Click.

A digital sixty-second timer starts counting down in the corner.

Clumps of dots darken in a mass and migrate to their fixed locations. With the pattern stable, Asmara tries to absorb an overall impression. The shape is roughly oval and there are more points than she expected—well over thirty.

How could anyone hope to remember all of this?

Her focus blurs as she perceives broad spatial dynamics before cataloging the individual dots. The arrangement on the screen stimulates her mind as she tries to make sense of the figure. There is no human face representation which Asmara detects. These points are forming something, though, and in no way do they appear random. It's as if there are patterns within patterns. This is an elegant diagram. An exquisite visual. Even though the dots are on a flat screen, a remarkable illusion of depth is created within the framework.

This thing is art. This thing is... beautiful.

Asmara continues to admire the wondrous constellation. She pries her eyes away from the figure to discover the countdown timer has six seconds remaining.

Ack! She spent her whole minute in a blissful haze. During the final seconds, her eyes zip around the framework in a focused fury as she tries to gather information. Asmara attempts to scorch individual points into her memory but her optic nerves get overloaded.

Time's up. The dots disappear. A new two-minute countdown appears for the pen and paper portion of the test.

She's not prepared to replicate anything.

Asmara has an actual longing for the design which vanished.

Will I get to see that thing again?

This was not supposed to be stressful but it is like an anxiety dream where she's flunking the biggest test of her life. She puts pen to paper and nothing happens. Her memory offers a pathetic smattering of points in no real order. Out of frustration, she clenches her eyes shut.

There it is.

The constellation is in vivid detail behind her closed eyelids. Each dot is locked in place within a perfect representation of the original pattern. She must have branded the image into her brain after all.

Asmara presses the pen down and commits to the first point. A rhythm develops where she opens and closes her eyes to gauge the distances between each dot. As long as she holds her head steady, the points line up in front of her each time she opens her eyes. She rushes to jot down the three dozen points as the figure blurs and disappears from her memory bank.

The replication lays before her and Asmara examines the results. To her disappointment, it's a lifeless dud. The diagram she drew is nothing but uninspired ink flecks on paper. Whatever changes her hand-drawn pattern altered from the original were the difference between beauty and banality.

Asmara uses her camera phone to take a photo of her handiwork. She sends the attachment to the test site's posted email address and includes a message.

"Hi, my name is Asmara. Stephen Garrity forwarded me your memorization project and I gave it my best shot. Let me know if there's anything else I can do to help."

Observing the dotted paper again, she's even more confident she reproduced the figure to a near-exact degree. Why does it not produce an aesthetic high?

It dawns on her: this was never about a human face representation. There is no connect-the-dots pattern here which would produce the geometry of a face, even on an abstract level.

Asmara is aware how some research testing involves deception, especially in psychology. If those who are tested know why they are scrutinized, their behaviors change and the results get skewed. The supposed "Alzheimer's memory project" is a case of misdirection and she's the lab rat.

She feels manipulated and intrigued in equal measure. Perhaps they want to see how many gullible people can be duped into drawing dots.

Searching for clues within the now-bland diagram, she counts thirty-seven total points. It is a prime number—only divisible by one and the number itself. No two other numbers multiply to create thirty-seven. She knows prime numbers are mathematically significant but has never understood why. Something about their unique bedrock properties makes them rare in an infinite sea of divisible whole numbers.

When Asmara glances back at her computer the test screen is gone. The internet browser window is closed and her screen shows a blank desktop.

She doesn't recall shuttering anything on her computer, but it's not impossible. Perhaps the memorization test had built-in code which closes the website after a certain amount of time.

Asmara opens her email account again to take another look at the project. Stephen Garrity's message had been at the top and it is no longer there. She checks her spam, trash, and archive folders. It's nowhere to be found.

A search history of her internet activity today shows no webpage which hosted the quiz.

She's never heard of an email which self-destructs and erases its tracks. *What the hell was that experiment?*

CHAPTER 42

Her phone buzzes with a notification. Asmara regrets not silencing the device but it's across the room and she is committed to meditation right now. Contact with the outside world must wait as she attends to critical self-care.

Nah, fuck all that.

Asmara lunges from the reading chair, grabs her phone, and basks in the affection of direct messaging.

It's Ryan offering to pick her up instead of meeting her at the venue, which is what she hoped he'd say. He will be there in an hour. The countdown to Word Bound is at hand.

Gulp. A painfully dry swallow is a signal Asmara's throat is not in harmony with her mind's stress-free attitude. A tingle in both arms indicates nervousness is taking hold.

To preoccupy herself, she puts on her skirt for the performance. The garment still feels utterly foreign on her. She twirls around trying to amuse herself and short-circuit the impending panic. It's not working.

Her next move is unfortunate. She could not have guessed an email would jeopardize her precarious well being. All she wanted was to determine what happened to the dot memorization message from Stephen Garrity. Maybe it got bumped down her timeline or is otherwise retrievable. Instead, Asmara subjects herself to an email which she did not want to see. The fresh inbox delivery is from her friend Dylan, the one she's been waiting to hear from. The subject line says: Website/App Job.

She only needs a partial opening sentence, and no more, to have her heart broken.

"Asmara, I'm SO sorry but the job got back to me and..."

Her fingers pound out a keyboard command and the computer gets a rude shutdown. A whispering choir in her head chants a mantra. "You're unemployed, you're going crazy. You're unemployed, you're going crazy."

She seeks solace in the reading chair but stands back up with restless energy. Pacing around, Asmara is not sure she'll be able to perform tonight with this rotten news overshadowing the event.

Oh, no.

That last grain of doubt is the trigger for a mental landslide. A domino effect of fright settles in. Her toolbox of coping mechanisms is inadequate and she considers a different approach. Reading. She grabs the final print-out of *Lightning in Ojai* and dives in. She's going to force-feed written words into this pit of angst until she can stand on them to climb out.

Asmara attempts to read the story's opening sentence again and again. It is lifeless. The dead letters on the page don't even appear to form words. She brings the paper closer to her face and coherent sentences materialize out of the veiled language. While her eyes scan the story, a bright clarity creates a halo around the letters and makes them pop off the paper. Her brain's internal narrator, which transforms written words into thoughts, has a new "voice." The normally silent "pronunciation" of each syllable as she reads is replaced with musical notes. It's as if a beautiful-sounding pipe organ translates the combinations of vowels and consonants into chords. Every paragraph has its own melody.

Also, Asmara is used to sentences fading from memory within seconds after they enter her eyes, leaving only an impression behind. Now each series of words is stored as a recording in her mind. Much like the routine ability to hum a catchy, unforgettable song, Asmara is able to remember these written harmonies of *Lightning in Ojai*. All of them.

Every word of every sentence she is reading can be located and retrieved in her memory. She knows this because she has finished the entire story in ten seconds, and all aspects of the material are superimposed into a single point in her consciousness. A symphony of notes and words, linked together, have been compressed without loss of information. This wasn't speed reading, for there is no sense she read anything. It's as if she uploaded a written file, accompanied by a musical score, and her eyes served as a scanner.

The two double-sided papers fall to the floor.

Asmara raises her arms and turns her palms toward the ceiling. She isn't sure why. This might be prayer. It's only when she examines her thoughts that Asmara concludes she is indeed praying. Her plea is not a request for divine intervention. It is an appeal to these dark forces involving her in their schemes. She wants out. She wants to remove herself from this role she never volunteered for.

Retaining photographic memory of *Lightning in Ojai* is not an effect of narrow focus—it is a superhuman impossibility. A leg wound healing within a day is not robust health—it is anatomical fiction. A visit from a demon should be the realm of daydreams—but it instead has put her life in real peril.

There must be a purpose to this. What conclusion am I being dragged toward?

Panic continues its electric charge through Asmara's limbs. Tendrils of lightning rip through her nervous system and overstimulate everything in their path, including her heart.

Asmara tries to visualize how a full-body reset would work. What if she declared the panic was hers to control? Her brain memorized an entire story within seconds, after all. Through will power, she also turned cold water into a monster-melting substance two days ago in the bathroom.

With no real strategy, she opens and closes her hands while flexing arm muscles. The stretched sinews contract through her shoulders, upper arms, and wrists. Asmara isn't sure what she hopes to generate with this action but it is the right thing to do.

As if priming a pump, the network of muscles function with a taut cohesion. After a few more synchronized flexes, her upper torso vibrates in anticipation.

Her arms go limp and fall by her sides. A sigh projects from her deflating lungs. With a spasm of energy, a contraction seizes Asmara's entire body. Her muscles are so rigid they may tear in half. Amid the cramped tension, the panic races within her and circulates even faster, as if it knows it's being hunted.

This is working.

Asmara exhales and her muscles unwind as the seizure releases its stranglehold. Before she savors the relief, another spasm erupts, more intense than the first. This one she did not summon. It arrived on its own.

Panic waves ricochet within her body as they try to find an outlet. Muscles constrict and block the internal avenues for this sinister static. It has nowhere to hide.

The panic frenzy condenses itself into a boiling mass and stops dead center in her chest. The chase is over. This concentrated dread is going to hold Asmara's heart hostage as a last stand.

The burning sensation produces a deep ache under her sternum. Although she believed her muscle strain had reached its physical limits, a final involuntary spasm compacts her upper body even further.

Like the Sun acting as a fusion reactor, cycling its own contents for light and heat, a pressure point has been reached.

Ignition.

She has gone nuclear. The chaotic energy of her panic has been fully harnessed and turned into fuel. She has her own power grid.

This sizzling plasm within her ribcage pulsates to the point her body shivers. Teeth collide in a loud chatter. She fears the vibrations are going to burst vital organs. At last these tremors dissipate from her chest but the energy does not leave her body. It is absorbed in the bones and tissues which comprise the rest of her living system.

A physical change has happened within her. The panic has been co-opted and exploited. A deep well of exotic energy is stored and awaiting further instructions.

For Asmara, there will be no asking, *what the fuck just happened?* Not anymore. The past days have nullified the question. Whatever fate rushes headlong toward her, Word Bound is at the core of it.

. . . .

There it is again.

A tapping sound. A minute passes before faint clicks again reverberate across the room.

Asmara is seated. Just breathing. Not thinking of anything other than her next intake of air. She stands and walks toward the noise. It comes from the spider's container. The tarantula is out of its rock cave and is pressed against the plastic cube's wall. When Asmara bends down for a closer look, the spider leaps up against the panel with a whirl of churning legs. This display would normally seem aggressive, yet Asmara senses another motivation to its movements. The animal has an aching desire to reach her. Not to attack, but to fulfill its purpose.

How in the world could she know what a tarantula is thinking? These insights arise because Asmara is receiving frequencies, not only from the spider in front of her but from all directions. She experiences previously unknown, undetectable transmissions which circulate around her. They are mostly beyond her comprehension but their origins are apparent. The radio-wave-type signals are being emitted by living things and they contain individualized information. Each pulse passing through the room is sent from her surrounding neighbors, through walls, floors, and ceilings. The vibration spectrums vary in height, corresponding with the size of the people producing each arc of energy. The waves convey biographical imprints to Asmara.

She is absorbing auras. She is reading souls.

Has there ever been anyone... anything...
like what I have become?

There are four individuals above her in the apartment on the next floor. They are around a table, playing a card game. She's sure of it, their spirits are distinct. One is a teenage boy. He is bored and wants to go to his room to watch porn.

The neighbor to the left paces in a small area. He's cooking in his kitchen. His wave is blissful. Preparing meals for others is his favorite thing to do and his friend arrives soon.

A beautiful eighteen-inch tall wave moves up from the floor below and passes through Asmara's feet. The short frequency is emitted from the baby downstairs. She's never seen the ten month old, only heard it laugh and cry. A larger wave lifts the smaller wave and moves it to another room. The mother has picked up the baby. That woman is under stress but has a wonderful spirit of hope.

The spider has a tiny wavelength, barely detectable. Asmara would not have noticed it if she was not in the same room with the creature while receiving its agitated signals.

Other frequencies transmit through the apartment from a hundred or more tenants in the building but their oscillations are difficult to interpret.

The gravity of what is transpiring exceeds Asmara's ability to process. *Am I a God?*

No. Asmara is certain she is not one. There is no feeling of grace with these powers. No benevolence. Not even a sense of responsibility.

The strange energy she captured has turned her into an antennae for souls. She is evolving and there is no telling what awaits, nor if she will be able to control it. A pang of heartache stings in her chest. Asmara didn't ask for any of this and she cannot turn back.

CHAPTER 43

A visualization technique is her best hope. Asmara leans against the wall as she prepares to meet Ryan and Zoe downstairs. Her eyes are closed and she has conjured a figurative scenario which represents her mental state. In this vision, a large black cauldron boils with volatile substances. Green and red glowing lava churns upward and mixes with a reflective gray ink. The angry swirling material grows brighter. There is no fire beneath the iron vat, it heats itself.

Asmara uses the witches' brew imagery to contain the metamorphosis happening within her. She managed to harness her panic minutes ago and she defeated a demon in the bathroom two days ago. Maybe she can apply calming pressure to the sensory overload threatening to consume her.

She is about to meet two people she cares for, one of whom is quite young. Her internal mutations cannot be allowed to multiply to the point her body goes supernova in Ryan's car. Asmara has no desire to read minds or observe wavelengths. She is a ticking time bomb, in a literal way. It's not clear if the explosion will burst neurons maintaining her sanity or if the planet itself will be annihilated.

Amid these concerns, she's certain avoiding Word Bound is an even worse fate.

In her visualization, Asmara lowers a silver lid which hovers above the cauldron. She is not touching the heavy cover by hand but she suspends it with telekinesis. In both reality and her imagined setting, her arm is raised and trembles with strain as she tries to lower the top. It's as if she is forcing opposite magnetic poles to connect. The vat boils stronger with columns of steam jetting upwards like an upside down waterfall.

Asmara's shoulder burns as she guides the seal onto the wide opening. The bubbling noise has turned into a roar. The roar utters words she cannot understand. At last, the lid is an inch away from containing the dangerous mix of unknown poisons. Before she shuts down the combustive reaction taking place in her mind, an exoskeleton appendage of the Patron bursts out of the vat.

Even though this is Asmara's fantasy, there is no sense that she summoned the monster. It arrived on its own. The long hooked probe forces open the silver cover. Asmara scans the indented written inscriptions on the beast's armor. They are living words. Biological sentences.

One line reads—"No place like home."

She concentrates her levitation focus and slams the lid down again and again on the Patron's limb. The hook retreats into the cauldron and the cover seals with a thud which reverberates in Asmara's body.

The cauldron is closed, for now. Thin rivulets of escaped red, green, and gray substances streak down the sides of the vat. These fluids drip toward the ground but arc back upwards. The ooze gathers around the edge of the lid and jostles it, trying to continue the chemical reaction. Heat builds inside the container again. That lid is going to get blasted off in the near future, like a Chernobyl meltdown. But for now, Asmara has given herself time.

Her mind's eye fades from the cauldron visualization and she returns to her apartment. Within the span of one breath, Asmara experiences positive results. She's back. Her thoughts are no longer racing. The incoming wavelengths from people in her building still radiate but the signals are barely detectable. This sixth sense of soul-viewing will not overwhelm her as long as the cauldron lid stays shut.

She grabs the spider container along with the transport tubes and exits the apartment. Jammed into her jacket pocket is the two-page printout of *Lightning in Ojai*. Her strange new abilities allowed her to memorize the story with musical tones. However, Asmara doesn't want to risk opening the mental cauldron on stage to access that knowledge. It is safer to read from the paper and keep Pandora's box shut.

After two steps into the main hallway, the facing apartment door swings open. Inga emerges and is bathed in overhead florescent lighting.

Asmara's eyes widen and she stifles a gasp. Despite attempts to tune out the life-force pulses which all living things emit, Asmara can't ignore Inga's aura wavelength. Her neighbor's transmission is twelve feet tall—twice as big as the surrounding signals from the building's occupants. When the arc of Inga's energy passes through Asmara, its vibrations are inhuman compared to the texture the other neighbors produce.

Inga is not looking directly at her. The woman gazes in wonder at the immediate surroundings of Asmara's upper body.

Oh, my God. Inga sees MY wavelength.

They lock eyes. There is so much Asmara wants to say. Inga speaks first, but not with words and not with her mouth. Musical notes representing language arrive in Asmara's mind, bypassing her ears.

"There's no stopping it now," Inga communicates, wordlessly. "You need to tell your story on stage. You and I... we will swim together soon. The waterfall is so beautiful."

Before Asmara can question how Inga knows about Word Bound, the answer arrives. Asmara's aura contained the information.

As Inga retreats into her apartment and closes the door, there is a glimpse of a thin, bloody zig-zag line carved into her neighbor's forearm.

. . . .

Asmara steps outside through her building's front door as Ryan pulls up. Zoe is sitting shotgun and gives a big smile to Asmara through the window. This girl's youthful exuberance needs no aura wavelength.

An impulse to run away overtakes Asmara. She might be able to save these two from her cosmic disease. Yet, Word Bound will not release its grip.

Asmara extracts a droplet of optimism clinging to the cauldron. Maybe she is not confronted by demons, aliens, and psychic neighbors. She might just be insane, which is an odd thing to hope for.

When the veil of schizophrenia lowers in front of your eyes, the illusions become reality. Perhaps every bit of strangeness Asmara has encountered is nothing more than a story she is telling herself.

The passenger-side window rolls down. Zoe leans out.

"Hey! You're wearing a skirt!"

CHAPTER 44

Asmara acts on an impulse. From the backseat, she extends her hands and gently grasps Ryan and Zoe by the neck. With light pressure, she nudges their heads toward each other while she leans forward. The three skulls intersect with a soft head bonk and Asmara releases her friends.

"Yeah, so that was weird," Ryan says as he puts the car in gear and accelerates down the road. "Is that your good luck ritual?"

"I don't know what it was," Asmara says. "I'm excited to see you both."

The cauldron technique is still effective and the boiling madness inside her has been contained. Sanity is not appreciated until you experience your own reality evaporate. There is a euphoria to feeling normal right now.

"I'm nervous," Zoe says. "But it's awesome that you're letting me be involved."

"You are critical to the whole thing," Asmara says. "I couldn't do it without you. Are your parents aware of what you're up to?"

"Yes. Ryan and I explained everything to my dad. He laughed. He doesn't care if I'm going to a bar. Does the tarantula have a name yet?"

"No. Do you want to give her one?"

"I thought of a name earlier today. How about Asmaraña?"

"What kind of name is that?"

"She combined your name and araña, which is Spanish for spider," Ryan says.

"I love it."

While looking at the happy teenager in profile, a brief wobble stirs Asmara's calm state. The cauldron lid rattles.

I'm not about to endanger this girl tonight, am I?

A mental itch emerges—a feeling that Asmara is on the cusp of remembering something which hasn't happened yet. There is a sense that future events eagerly await for her to catch up to them.

. . . .

They drive past The Naomi to find parking and Asmara gives an uneasy exhale at the sight of a crowd outside the venue.

Her breath fogs the side window and she draws an exclamation mark in the condensation with her finger. The "!" fades away and Asmara switches internal gears. Sure, she is entrapped in a grand conflict hurtling toward a climax, but here in the Earthly realm, tonight is a performance in front of a live audience. She needs to put on a show. If reality has ruptured and the final curtain is about to fall, Asmara hopes to hear applause while darkness descends.

After parking, they step out of the vehicle and Ryan throws spare One Track Mind shirts over the spider container to conceal it. Asmara holds the transport tubes vertically under her armpit. They walk a block to The Naomi and the crowd out front is fifty people deep.

Near the venue's front door is a bulletin board covered with event flyers. Among the paper advertisements is a cardboard-mounted poster twice as big as the other notices. It is The Naomi's showcase placard for the event tonight and it features Asmara's Word Bound art design which she made in her kitchen. The reproduction looks great and this surprise is a boost Asmara needed.

Within the crowd milling about, she spots James, the neck-tattooed manager. He walks over and his Australian accent is thicker than ever. "Ah, the headliner and her entourage has arrived."

"We're ready to rock," Asmara replies.

"I assume under those T-shirts you're holding is our special guest?"

"Yup."

"How are you feeling about tonight? Was one rehearsal enough?"

"Yes, we have a good sense of what to expect."

Asmara has never told a bigger lie.

"As for you," James points to Zoe, "we're bending the rules by allowing you in the venue. So, I'm afraid you can't go in the main bar area. You'll have to stay backstage."

"I'll be *under* the stage, actually," Zoe says.

"Got it. Let's enter through the alley."

The four walk past The Naomi's main entrance and turn down a narrow alley. James uses a key to open a side door and they enter into the kitchen. After two more hallway turns, they are behind the stage, facing the ground-level storage doorway.

Asmara's muscles tense. This area was the launching pad which catapulted her into the outer reaches of mental disorder.

"No one on staff tonight knows about your act except Elizabeth and I," James says. "Speaking of which, let me go grab her."

James leaves the room and Asmara opens the crawl space door. Although the anticipation made this portal ominous, the interior is benign, even welcoming. The blankets and chairs inside give a cozy vibe.

With the hatch open, sounds travel from The Naomi's main event area on the other side. A thunder of overlapping voices vibrates within the enclosed space. Word Bound has filled the venue.

"We're early," Asmara says, retracting herself from the doorway. "There's no way I can ask you to stay in a tight space until I go on stage."

"Maybe we can go skate around," Zoe says. "Our boards are in the trunk."

Ryan and Asmara look at each other and shrug.

"Sure," Asmara says. "I will text you fifteen minutes before I go on stage. Please don't go far."

James and Elizabeth enter the room. Hugs and laughter are shared within the group. Elizabeth confesses she is ecstatic about the surprise finale tonight.

Zoe chimes in with neglected logistics. "As you read your story, Asmara, how will we know when to lift the tube through the hole?"

"Yeah, and what's the exact cue for when the spider should get pushed up?" Ryan says.

Elizabeth's face tightens with a pinch of aggravation. "You all haven't talked through this yet?"

Asmara pulls the printout of *Lightning in Ojai* from her jacket. A sentence is chosen at random halfway through the story.

"All right," Asmara says, "when you hear me say, 'The graffiti mural declared something he already knew—there's no place like home,' that's when you will lift the tube through my clothes."

"No place like home, got it," Zoe says.

"And then when I read, 'It bares no resemblance, in style or substance, to the usual spectrum of daydreams,' that's when you will push the spider through the tube."

"Right on," Ryan says. "At 'daydreams' the spider goes up your skirt. Confirmed. So, text me before you go onstage and we'll be back in time."

Zoe and Ryan leave the backstage area with farewell hand waves.

Elizabeth's anxious expression gives the appearance she is the one facing audience ridicule and the fangs of a tarantula.

"They'll be back," Asmara says, trying to comfort the event planner. "A lot depends on it. More than you can imagine."

CHAPTER 45

James and Elizabeth lead the way. Asmara follows as they snake through the kitchen toward The Naomi's main event hall. The muffled noise of two hundred voices becomes a deep growl as they near the entryway to the bar.

Elizabeth must sense Asmara's anticipation because, without turning, she says, "Yeah, there's a full house tonight."

The door flings open and Asmara enters the venue. For a few seconds, the crowd's sound and energy warps her perception and The Naomi feels like a stadium. It's as if she is a gladiator emerging into the Coliseum. There are people everywhere. A packed audience stands shoulder to shoulder and creates a sea of faces. As she scans the room, it appears as if everyone is beautiful and between the ages of twenty-five to thirty-five.

While the glamorous scene displays itself, Asmara is aware she's experiencing it through a filter. Take away her adrenaline and this beauty pageant could be a freakshow, for all she cares. The type of audience doesn't matter. Asmara has the enticing delusion everyone is here specifically to watch her perform on stage.

Her friends Sarah and Gillian step out of the shapeless crowd. The two women do a happy jump at the sight of their college buddy.

"Asmara!" Gillian says, as the trio merges in a hug. "This is so... whoa. Hold on."

The two women back away from Asmara while looking down, as if someone dropped a grenade.

"You're wearing a skirt!"

"It's part of the show. I felt like I needed a stage presence."

"Can you believe we were here a few nights ago?" Sarah says.

"Actually, I was inspired to do this while we were sitting together."

"Wow. I've always known there is a writer in you. Even your long-ass text messages are well written. Are you nervous?"

"I have a range of emotions but the short answer is, yes, I'm nervous."

"Remember the guy with a scarf that came over to our table?" Gillian says. "He totally liked you. What was his name again?"

"His name is Ryan. He drove me here tonight. I've been hanging out with him these past few days."

Now for the kill. "I spent the night at his house in Oakland after we were all together here. No joke."

Their jaws drop and Sarah and Gillian each grasp one of Asmara's arms to prevent themselves from toppling over.

Asmara reveals details of her recent experiences while her friends chew on every morsel of gossip. Within her recap of events, Asmara removes any reference to demon attacks, aliens on Europa, or the psychic powers which contorted her world these past days.

As the women continue to chat, the other friends Asmara invited find her in the crowd. The people she included in her group text represent a cross-section of her life and many don't know each other. She does her best to facilitate introductions and give equal time to everyone.

Before long, separate conversations spark up among this mix of characters. While Asmara surveys her social handiwork, the One Track Mind odd squad shows up, although without their leader Ryan. It's good to see the penguins David and Seth as well as the big bird herself, Amy.

Asmara spreads her wings to give each bike shop employee a hug without considering if it's a good idea. The series of embraces are more awkward than she could have imagined.

"I heard you and Zoe helped Ryan get the bike showroom ready," Amy says. "Thanks for the effort. Where is Ryan, anyway?"

"He'll be back here soon."

Amy glances at the penguins and they are lost in their own banter. Her voice lowers. "Not to embarrass you, but Ryan really is a great guy. And he likes you."

Asmara doesn't try to fight the grin which widens across her face.

"I think it's great you two are hanging out," Amy continues.

"Thanks. It's only been a few days but it's funny how life works."

"Did you know he was a famous skateboarder?"

"Yeah, Zoe explained it to me and I looked some stuff up online."

"Ryan stays under the radar. You have to drag details out of him. To this day I'm not sure how he..." Amy catches herself. She went too far.

Asmara makes the leap to join her. "You mean his missing eye?"

"I, uh... I mean, it doesn't even matter. I'm just curious."

"Have you ever asked him what happened?"

Amy cringes. "I did. I felt weird about it."

"What was his reply?"

"He politely changed the subject."

A large round of drinks appears and plops into the hands of everyone in Asmara's group. She doesn't know what she's been served but she finds herself giving a toast.

"Hey, I want to thank everyone," Asmara says while they all raise a glass. "This may be just an open-mic night but you coming here means a lot to me."

"Wooo!" "Thanks for inviting us!" "Kick ass tonight!"

"I'm going on stage last," Asmara continues, "so enjoy the show and please stick around until the end. Again, I'm so happy you're all here."

The group lets out a cheer. Asmara turns and her friend Dylan is standing behind her. He has been a disappointment in that he assured her of a job that never came to pass, but there is no animosity. Compared to the existential threats Asmara confronts tonight, employment at a tech company is trivial.

"Are you mad at me?" Dylan asks, his face drooping with concern. He's always such a drama queen.

"It's fine, Dylan."

"I should have never said the job was a sure thing."

"I didn't get the position. I'm over it. This isn't your fault."

"It's just that I understand how much you wanted it. You're such a creative person and... and..."

She gives Dylan a hug and is struck by the fact she is consoling him. It is a bait and switch.

His demeanor grows serious. "You know I'm a bitch who reads his horoscope every day, right? Like the good Pisces I strive to be."

"Yeah."

"And you don't believe in astrology, right?"

"I'm a non-believer. Correct."

"And you're a Gemini. June thirteenth. I never forget birthdays."

"I do not consent to my supposed Zodiac sign but, yes, my birthday is June thirteenth."

"Okay, if I told you what my horoscope said today would you at least consider it? It's juicy."

Dylan pulls out his phone with blatant glee. "I swear these horoscopes are brilliant. I don't know how you people don't believe in them."

Asmara is no fool and she awaits for the universe to taunt her again. The usually vague horoscope jargon—which applies to any primate who happens to read it—will synchronize with her life, hinting at connections unseen.

Dylan lowers his voice. "It reads: Pisces, keep your friends close but keep the Geminis in your life even closer, for one of them is going to change the world. And you, Pisces, will have a front row seat."

He bellows with excitement as he continues. "It is not by act or deed but by WRITTEN WORD and SPOKEN THOUGHT that they will change destiny!"

Dylan extends his phone to her and shows a garish astrology website.

"When does that site update its posts?" Asmara asks.

Dylan looks confused by the question. "Um, every midnight."

A soft tickle irritates Asmara's leg. The bandage has gone loose on her thigh and is about to fall off. While distracting Dylan with steady eye contact, she discretely reaches under her skirt and peels off the adhesive. There is smooth skin where two days ago had been a gaping wound.

CHAPTER 46

The crowd noise settles into an ambient murmur as Elizabeth walks on stage to announce the start of Word Bound. A lucky fifteen percent of the people in attendance have chairs and tables in which to comfortably sit and watch the show. The rest are standing room only. Asmara is on her feet but doesn't mind.

"Hi, everyone!" Elizabeth says into the microphone. "We're so grateful you continue to support Word Bound. Are you ready to share the love with some creative people?"

The audience shakes the venue with cheers. This is a friendly group rooting for the performers to succeed.

Elizabeth's amplified voice continues. "I was told Word Bound needs a catch phrase to start the show. Like, 'Are you all down to get bound?' But I refuse to say that crap."

The crowd gives a laugh.

"Let's get things rolling. We have a fun hour ahead of us. We've got ten readers! Who also happen to be ten writers! They get five minutes each!"

More cheers.

"You know what? Screw it... Are you all down to get bound?!"

The response is like a rock concert at The Naomi.

"All right, first up, coming from Santa Cruz, we have Trevor Moore!"

A young man bounds on to the stage. He gives Elizabeth a hug and spins to face the crowd. He is handsome with a muscular build. For Asmara, he checks all the boxes for being "hot" but his unspoken charisma annoys her. Also, his T-shirt is way too tight.

"I broke up with Eric six years ago," Trevor says, his baritone voice projecting across the crowd. "I wasn't going out with him and neither of us are gay. We're both married to women. But it was a friendship break-up, for sure."

The opening lines are unusual and they get the job done—the crowd is transfixed. Trevor launches into a compelling story about the end of a long-term friendship. The reason for the split is hinted at—something about being left stranded in Sacramento. Trevor describes, in a heartfelt way, the broader experience of watching a friendship dissolve.

"That's the funny thing about a friendship which has expired," Trevor says at his five-minute mark. "With social media, we're never more than a finger tap away from contacting each other. But we wait for fate to cross our paths in person. It's only then a reconnection is made possible."

Trevor breathes heavily, his emotions rising. "So, what do you say, Eric? Is this fate?"

There is jostling in the crowd as a lanky man moves toward the stage. A woman follows behind him while recording everything with her phone. Her face is streaked with tears. The tall guy extends a hand and Trevor hoists the man up on stage. They embrace in a bear hug. This must be Eric, the long-lost friend who left Trevor stranded in Sacramento with his too tight T-shirt. The crying woman recording the event is one of the two wives.

Cheers from the crowd erupt at the sight of the reunion but Asmara's skepticism detector is beeping. She is concerned Elizabeth booked a night of surprise gimmicks and the tarantula reveal will be another novelty.

In the next performance, a wild-haired woman goes straight for laughs and she succeeds in getting them. She shares a ridiculous tale of the lengths she went through to support her "aspiring rapper" boyfriend years ago. He wanted to add an actual gospel choir to his song called "The Devil's Pimp." Lacking funds, the woman tricked her devoutly religious mother into recording her church choir under false pretenses. Thinking it was for a Christian-rock album, they sang D-Snuff's lyrical hook in a vulgar song they never would have contributed to otherwise.

As the woman walks off stage, the now-identifiable song blasts from speakers and the audience rejoices at the heavenly chorus of "The Devil's Pimp."

Third on the set list is a guy who gives an academic presentation. What he lacks in humor he makes up for with a riveting speech about his faith in humanity. He delivers a litany of rapid-fire facts about standards in which mankind is bettering itself from previous centuries.

Asmara didn't need his feel-good data as motivation to save the world tonight, but he added a supportive wind to her sails.

The fourth performer is clever. He does nothing more than an improvisational review of the previous three speakers. His summary breakdown of their material is presented like a literary critic. He even does impressions of them as if they are being interviewed.

Fifth on stage is a nervous young woman. Her voice shakes and her eyes never look up from the paper trembling in her hands. She relates an account of a homeless man getting hit by a train and remaining on the tracks. The man survives due to concerned bystanders rushing to his aid. Her story ends without a firm conclusion and she darts off stage. The understated message is that, as a society, we walk past people in desperate need every day but aid only arrives during near-death emergencies.

Asmara isn't sure why this bummer story was included in the fun line-up of Word Bound. Although it did add bitter spice to the night's recipe.

Elizabeth returns to the microphone. "Wow! Right on. Give it up for the first five speakers! Are you all enjoying yourselves?"

She gets an enthusiastic reply.

"We're going to take a fifteen-minute break before we get to the next performers. So, get a drink, use the bathroom—I don't care what you do. Just be back in fifteen."

The previously hushed crowd noise rises as a hundred or more conversations start up. Asmara heads outside to get fresh air. The sidewalk scene is filled with smokers and cellphone lookers.

She writes Ryan a text. **"Hey, the show is at the halfway point. I'd say you and Zoe should return soon. Thanks"**

The manager James makes his way over to her. "Can I be seen talking to you or will that jeopardize the secret mission?"

"No, we're fine. How is your night going?"

"At first, I thought Word Bound was a dumb idea when Elizabeth pitched it. But these crowds are great."

"You mentioned the other day your immigration status is a mess. Are you seriously at risk of being deported?"

"Yeah, I'm cooked. It's strange that I hire and fire people at The Naomi and I'm trusted with payroll, yet I'm an illegal alien about to get his ass shipped back to Australia."

"Can you have an arranged marriage to become a US citizen?"

"Are you proposing to me?"

"Ha. I don't do immigration fraud."

There is a pause before James speaks again. "Are you nervous to be on stage?"

"Yes, I'm nervous."

"You gotta treat this like a boxing match. You're going into the ring and you need to deliver."

James throws some air punches.

"The audience isn't your enemy," he continues, "but you have to fight for their attention. Are you up for the challenge?"

Playing along, Asmara swings a couple of weak fists in the air.

"Nah, more force," James says, maneuvering behind her as he mimics a boxing coach. "Bring your elbows back farther."

He grasps her forearms and guides them into proper punches. "Now you're looking like a fighter."

James puts his hands on her shoulders and gives a warm-up massage. "With my training we're gonna make you a champion tonight."

After the shoulder squeeze, his finger traces along Asmara's bare neck for a second.

That's all it takes.

The skin on skin reaction produces a negative surge to her senses. His caress was hardly an assault but it was not an accident. The cauldron technique in her mind has been compromised. Something about James' touch—the small violation of her boundaries—upset the precarious balance of Asmara's mental stability.

The cover on top of the cauldron shakes from steam gathering inside as its contents churn. This boiling pressure is too much and the lid is punched upward and lands askew on top of the dark vat. Steam rockets through the exposed space.

Asmara tries to remain calm but her senses recalibrate back to the supernatural mindstate she experienced in her apartment earlier. The aura wavelengths of the people surrounding her crash against her own thoughts.

She is able to read souls again.

Asmara turns and looks into James' eyes.

He wonders if the touch along her neck was a bad idea. He was testing the waters of flirtation but wanted to maintain deniability.

This is not Asmara's guess at what James is thinking. She is certain these are his thoughts because they transmit on his wavelength.

Unreal. I'm truly reading his mind.

The silver lid dampens the signal and yet Asmara gets a detailed reception from his aura because he is close to her. Elements of his immigration predicament reveal themselves to Asmara with dream-like visions. James is not facing deportation due to problems with his visa paperwork. Instead, he is fleeing the country because he lost a lot of money on two failed ventures. One was a sketchy business loan for a restaurant in Oakland. The other was a drug deal involving a shoebox of cocaine and a backpack full of cash. He wound up with neither due to an elaborate scam.

Asmara receives this knowledge passively and with no words spoken. Yet, its accuracy is not in doubt to her.

There are more details within his signal.

He leaves for Australia in two days to flee these debts. The only reason he is at The Naomi tonight is because he wanted to see if he could hook-up one last time while in the US. His best bet, he figures, is the weird but cute chick who is doing a tarantula magic trick at Word Bound.

In a hopeful flicker of his true character within the aura, James has sincere plans to make honest money in Australia so he can repay his US debts, even to the drug dealer. Maybe James is not irredeemable.

"Was the shoulder rub not cool?" James says, as he notices the apprehension from Asmara. "I'm a touchy guy. Sorry about that."

Asmara continues to observe him with a blank stare. James knows he is being silently evaluated but it is to a degree he could never imagine.

"Nah, don't worry," Asmara says.

She considers ways she could melt his mind into a puddle—perhaps by surprising him with encouragement for his bank fraud woes and cocaine debt. Instead she gives a hand wave. "I'll see you inside."

James appears baffled by what took place. He understands, on some level, his innermost thoughts were examined.

As Asmara turns and enters The Naomi, one more wavelength from James cascades over her shoulders.

"What just happened?" he thinks to himself. *"That spider chick is crazy."*

CHAPTER 47

It is a full-body experience now, not just a visual perception. The aura transmissions from the people inside The Naomi are overwhelming. Asmara is jostled by their collective pulse. She staggers from the impact of soul vibrations after entering the front door.

Making eye contact increases the intensity of each wavelength, so Asmara averts her gaze downward. The plan is to go backstage since it's the only spot in this busy venue where she is able to compose herself.

As Asmara weaves through the dense forest of people, she is buffeted by the signals they emit. There is no way to make sense of it all. However, there are patterns within the static. The magnetism of physical attraction permeates the air. Tremors of envy and desperate lust have their own frequencies. Even among this friendly group of book lovers, primal urges abound. The room is filled with horny, jealous apes.

The backstage entry door beckons as it is within reach. She gets to the bar area and all three bartenders are distracted with drink orders. A side-step past a barrier places her behind the countertop near a wall of liquor bottles. The maneuver draws curious eyes on to her, which she tried to avoid. Asmara has learned that if you act confident in what you're doing, few people will raise questions. She leans toward a wall thermostat and gives her best impression of a thermostat repairwoman.

Since a less chaotic environment awaits her backstage, Asmara decides to turn and absorb the full thrust of the crowd's wavelength. It is an experiment to probe the limits of what she can endure. The cauldron lid rattles as steam pushes it aside. With her chin up and eyes wide open, she faces the rushing tide.

Light pours in.

And so much more.

I... I have never...

The cumulative effect of the two hundred auras is a multi-sensory blizzard. Each person in the room has their own radiation which acts like a burning sun when combined with others. These forms of human essence, previously internal and invisible, float in the air above the crowd, swirling together. A kaleidoscope of colors are joined by visualized sounds. They bleed into each other and drip horizontally into Asmara's eyes. This flowing substance pushes the cauldron lid farther back, exposing more of the vat's interior and heightening her reception. She can barely withstand the overload, yet there is such beauty in this storm of souls.

Asmara is not able to separate each individual by a distinct frequency. Instead, she basks in their shared energy. Yes, sexual attraction is in the air but there is more depth when she allows herself to receive it. In this outpouring of spirits, a prominent feature is the unmistakable scars of hardship. Everywhere in this crowd is heartbreak and disappointment. Some of these burdens are open wounds. The multitude of struggles these people face—tribulations both large and small—is incredible. It's perhaps the defining characteristic of being human.

That is not the whole story, though. The good news is the majority of this negativity is contained. These people created their own cauldrons to bottle up the suffering. Or they built self-support structures on top of the pain. Or they allowed the poisons to evaporate. This group has stitched and welded themselves back together. Even with insecurities gnawing away at their cages, trying to break free, the individuals in the crowd are enjoying themselves. Hope is generated tonight. Almost everyone here believes better days are ahead.

Asmara blinks forcefully and gives her head a shake to sever the injection of auras. There is a real potential to overdose on these inner worlds. With her mind a bit clearer, she observes the people lined up at the bar and makes eye contact with Trevor. He was the first speaker tonight and, somehow, his T-shirt is even more tight than it was earlier. Next to him is the tall guy who was the other half of his dramatic onstage event. In the middle of a laugh, Trevor glances at Asmara and she gets a full imprint of his wavelength.

According to his frequency, it is apparent Trevor, his wife who recorded everything, and the tall guy he hugged are all actors. The two men are friends but their story of estrangement was all lies and no more than an improv acting challenge. It was a test to see if they could convince the crowd their reunion was a spontaneous moment. They justified the deception by figuring, "Hey, it's only an open-mic night."

Asmara projects a beam of disdain in Trevor's direction. His play-acting was not a high crime and no one was hurt by the farce, yet she finds the manipulation distasteful.

Trevor gives Asmara a double-take and his smile gets wiped off his face. His eyes flick away with guilt as he makes a puzzled expression. The tall guy, who was never looking at Asmara, shifts his head left to right, scanning the room with unease, as if a wave of distrust overcame him.

Both of these men received her signal. They know their minds were read, the same way James did outside on the sidewalk.

These telepathic breakthroughs are only the beginning. If unchecked, further evolution awaits.

This power is too great.

Asmara does not want to be a God. Being omnipotent would be a type of hell. Who knows what these abilities could turn her into?

The cauldron needs to be sealed again. She pushes through the kitchen-access door and heads backstage while a hurricane of human frequencies recede behind her.

. . . .

It's no surprise the concrete floor is cold and unforgiving. She sits cross legged and hopes comfort will arrive with the right body shift.

At least she's alone. In a venue swarming with hundreds of people it's a minor miracle Asmara found solitude. The backstage area is empty, not counting the army of voices which rumble through the walls. Diffuse wavelengths from the crowd's collective aura flow within the space but she is able to ignore the intrusions.

Eyes closed, breathing moderated, she tries to chart a path toward a meditative state. Continuing her mental model of a cauldron, she struggles to close the lid and contain the force growing inside of her.

The vat's silver cover slides with much resistance. Every millimeter of friction puts up a fight and produces a metal grinding sound which raises the hairs on her arms. The red, green, and gray substances continue to boil as their colorful droplets are cast into the air in small arcs. This simmering combustion is on its way to becoming a volcano.

The stubborn lid comes to a halt as an opposing force drags the seal open wider. In her mind's eye she peers at the cauldron and a black claw pokes out from the interior. The Patron is emerging.

Notions of this being a visualization technique—a simple metaphor—dissolve as Asmara realizes the monster is inside of her. It is essential the cauldron be closed and the Patron sealed inside.

The air is electrified by the frenzied choir of voices in the main hall. Asmara finds that by "leaning" her focus into the noise, she is able to harness the distraction. The murmur becomes a background chant which she utilizes as a mantra.

Her eyelids flutter as her mind sprints toward a meditative horizon. During this brief limbo of mental gears shifting, she is able to push the cauldron lid closed. A chemical poison bomb still stews inside of her but its reaction is contained.

The door handle rattles. Someone is about to enter backstage. Asmara tries to untangle her stiff limbs but gives up and prepares to greet this person while sitting on the concrete.

It's Ryan. He gives a smile to this weirdo woman on the floor. Zoe appears and she also gives her own joyful dose of grin. Their wavelengths are deeply muted.

"Hey," Ryan says. "What are you doing?"

"I was nervous out there," Asmara says. "I wanted to sneak backstage for some meditation."

"Sorry to interrupt. Elizabeth let us in through the alley entrance. We told her we're gonna chill here until you go on stage."

Ryan and Zoe have their skateboards with them. A veneer of perspiration is on their foreheads.

"You fully went skating, huh?" Asmara asks as she labors to stand up.

"Yes!" Zoe blurts out. "I ollied a six-stair. It was awesome."

"Congrats. Six sounds like a lot. Are you both ready for the show?"

"For sure," Ryan says. "Is there anything we need to go over?"

"Not really. Right before my turn to read I'll send you a text."

"Affirmative," Zoe says.

"Well, I'm going to head out front. Thank you both so much."

Asmara gives Zoe a hug. As their arms wrap, Asmara is infused with a direct mainline of the girl's energy. The cauldron lid in Asmara's mind is sealed but now, with this intimate proximity, Zoe's wavelength has a physical reverberation. Asmara absorbs every drop from a vivid pulse stream. Human touch multiplies the aura reception far more than receiving it through the air. There are tactile nuances, exquisite sounds, and even flavors within the vibrations Zoe is producing. They are intoxicating, dripping with the vitality of youth.

There is no mutual exchange of energy—this is a one-way transfer. It's as if Asmara is not only adjacent to Zoe's wavelength, she is extracting it. Asmara drinks the adrenaline which Zoe is still experiencing from her skateboard. The buzz is delicious but there is guilt with its consumption. Asmara didn't earn this rush. There's no way of knowing if this is a free "high" for Asmara or if she's depleting a victim.

Am I a vampire? Draining souls instead of blood?

Asmara breaks the spell and pushes the girl an arm's length away. Ryan is oblivious to the invisible energy feast.

She walks backward toward the kitchen-access door.

"Next time I see you I'll have a tarantula on my face."

CHAPTER 48

The sixth performance has two women on stage. Their banter is formulaic with set-ups and punchlines. It's no surprise for Asmara when the women reference a podcast they host together. The comedy duo describe a celebrity interview they conducted which went well except neither woman hit the record button.

Asmara joins the applause and savors the normal experience of being in the audience again. It is a relief to be one person among many and not drown in a tidal wave of visible souls. There are no wavelengths she can see although the air hums with their presence.

A big guy stomps to the microphone. His physique is shrouded by a gigantic sweatshirt but his bulging frame indicates he may be a body builder and not just fat. Asmara speculates if she could use his sweatshirt as a sleeping bag. It's not a mere joke for her, it's a genuine hypothetical. He reads an excerpt from a novel he wrote—something about an inherited house. There's no context, no story arc, and no charm to his tale. He bombs for five minutes straight and yet is given polite applause. The owner of the world's biggest sweatshirt exits the stage without using the wooden stairs. His leap to the main floor is a poor decision and he almost falls on his face.

Asmara more or less misses the eighth act. She's present and observes the bearded guy speaking to the crowd, but his words melt as her attention goes inward. She does a status check of her self control and other vitals. Panic should be choking off her air supply by now. The nervous tension is there, squeezing as hard as it can, yet the grip of anxiety cannot compress the rigid cauldron. The seal remains tight.

Asmara's attention snaps back when the crowd cheers. The bearded guy onstage finished and has tears rolling down his face.

Shoot. I should have listened to that one.

The ninth act is a man who announces his sprawling anecdote won't fit under five minutes. He's going to read as fast as he can to cram it all in. The first minute of his motormouth auctioneer-style delivery is annoying, but the speed talking wins the crowd over. He doesn't trip over any words and, once Asmara's ears are acclimated, he becomes easy to understand. It helps that the audience is invested in his tale of proposing to his girlfriend, a noble cause riddled with mishaps. As the climax to his speech nears, applause is already filling the room. The cheers rise and when he describes her saying yes to marriage the room erupts in happy shouts.

This guy brought a fun vibe to the night. Asmara hopes the engaged couple will live to see their wedding day. Schedules tend to get scuttled during a planetary annihilation.

She sends Ryan a text. "I'm going up now"

"We're all set" he replies.

As the applause dies down, Asmara removes the two pages of *Lightning in Ojai* which had been tucked in her skirt's waistband. The story is memorized within her as music but the cauldron prevents access.

Each stride toward the stage brings her unwanted memories of public speaking. She is not terrified by the act, yet she never cared for it. Archived stress from those presentations emerge again.

On her journey to the microphone, every person she approaches from behind turns their head to see who is moving past them in the crowd. Each head swivel reveals a scowling, grotesque face—almost inhuman. Asmara refuses to believe she has waded into a sea of demons.

Just an illusion. Must be my nerves.

Another few steps forward and Elizabeth comes into view in a side-stage alcove. She has been out of sight throughout Word Bound. The women share a sly smile.

When her foot touches the bottom step on the four-stair wedge leading to the stage, she pauses mid-stride. A scent catches her attention. Whatever smell is detected, her mind censors it. Asmara needs to get to the microphone and start speaking.

She arrives. Without being obvious, she casts a glimpse downward to align her stance above the hole in the stage. Elizabeth made sure the microphone stand was in the correct place.

At last, she looks up. What a sight.

There is no reference point in her life to compare to it. Her speech at a wedding and a middle school spelling bee were in front of decent-sized crowds but this is a shoulder-to-shoulder mass of humanity. So many faces. So many sets of eyes. All giving her complete attention.

Being elevated on stage adds to the experience.

For the audience, this has been a night filled with numerous performers and drinking and socializing and checking their phones. But right now, these two hundred people are here for Asmara alone.

The microphone picks up ugly rustling sounds as the crumpled printout of *Lightning in Ojai* is lifted toward her face. It probably looks like she is about to read off of garbage she found in the alley.

Beneath her, a faint scraping noise drifts to her ears. It's Ryan and Zoe getting into position. The microphone doesn't amplify their activity, which is a relief.

Her eyes settle on the story printout. Thankfully, it has not morphed into an anxiety nightmare where the words are in ancient Greek.

The first sentence propels from her mouth. Sound waves of her voice reverberate through the microphone where they are converted into electrical signals. Those signals travel by wire to the loudspeaker system along the stage where they are amplified in volume.

Asmara's voice fills the room.

"Immediately upon arrival, the visitor attains God-like powers. This being is not from our realm and comes from a place with different physics, different quantum mechanics, different everything. Our universe is a crude plaything to the visitor, who we will call Thalamus. The passage of time in our dimension is so slow to Thalamus that the being would go insane before a simple greeting could be exchanged with mankind. It would be like a human trying to communicate with a houseplant.

The man who accidentally summoned the visitor is a scientist in Ojai, California. The scientist was trying to create artificial intelligence and instead opened a portal between dimensions by mistake. Enough data compression will do that—collapsing spacetime like a black hole. Thalamus has motivations incomprehensible to anyone in our reality. However, one aspect of this visitor is not inscrutable. There is logic in its decision to kill the scientist to prevent his surfboard design from destroying the Earth."

Asmara peeks up from her printout to examine the audience reception. Numerous heads sway backward in surprise, as if the words had a physical impact upon arrival. Either good or bad, the reactions communicate the same thing: "This is going to be a weird one."

Lightning in Ojai is truly alive, breathing on its own, exploring the room. This story craves listeners. The venue filled with people is a feast where the words can gorge on open minds.

"The scientist has crafted security measures to contain the potential for artificial intelligence. All access to the outside world was blocked from within a very secure mechanical box. These safeguards are comically insufficient to stop Thalamus. There are some physical laws we don't know about and there are tiny crevices in the physics we do understand. These gaps are exploited by the precocious newborn in its computer placenta.

The entirety of the internet, every data point and line of code ever created, is absorbed by Thalamus in the time it takes a light photon to travel the width of an atom.

That is impossible, you may say. And that's what the scientist would have thought as well, had he known it was happening. Nonetheless, Thalamus does indeed process this repository of information and it extrapolates from there. Thalamus foresees almost every conceivable outcome of human activity."

Asmara gives another glance up from the printout. At least people aren't fleeing to the exits.

"By manipulating the electromagnetism between them, Thalamus hacks the scientist's mind—a simple wet, organic computer. This uninvited visitor wants to meet its host, down to every last neuron. Amid the thoughts and memories which comprise the scientist as an individual, one detail is paramount: the man is a life-long surfer who dabbles in board design. With existing information, Thalamus predicts future events by narrowing a trillion potential variables down to one. It knows that the scientist is on the cusp of creating a surfboard shape which will allow almost any breaking ocean wave to be ridden, even among novice surfers. This development will popularize surfing around the world with uncontrolled growth. Repercussions from these oceanic pressures will have a cascading negative effect on the planet. A critical point of ecological degradation will be impossible to unwind.

Surfing's difficulty had been a natural, healthy gatekeeper—a limiting force.

Earth can tolerate only so many surfers.

Again using electromagnetism, Thalamus manufactures two electrically charged regions in the vicinity. One is a section of cloudless, blue sky above the Ojai laboratory. This sector of atmosphere has become dense with positively charged ions. The other zone which Thalamus alters is the ground beneath the scientist's feet. It is a tile floor now laden with negatively charged ions.

This imbalance is primed to create a massive static discharge, one which is over a mile long. Indeed, a blinding bolt of energy angles through an open window and strikes down the scientist. Strangely, the lightning emits no thunder.

With no further concern for its birthplace in this realm, Thalamus decides to leave the planet. In order to do so, the inorganic intelligence is about to harness faster-than-light gray energy rays, unknown to man, which zip through our solar system at all times and do not interact with ordinary matter. Vibrations, in any medium, are all that Thalamus needs to exist. The womb of computer circuitry Thalamus was conceived in is already an unnecessary relic, two seconds after its birth. Thalamus will fuse itself with these passing rays and ride them elsewhere into the universe, to do God knows what.

As naturally-occurring gray energy rays pierce the laboratory and continue into space, Thalamus speeds up its internal vibrations to synchronize with the outgoing ride. These cosmic rays are the next train out of town. The final image Thalamus sees before it departs Earth is the scientist stumbling to his feet. The man is confused and has a wisp of smoke emitting from the microscopic hole burned through his skull, but he is alive.

You see, a funny thing happened—Thalamus changed its mind. With all of its intelligence and near omniscience, there was room for a revelation, as well as compassion. Thalamus realized it didn't need to kill the scientist to grant the world a reprieve from destruction, it just needed to alter him with a pinpoint surgical strike. This avoidance of the death penalty is something most any human would have considered first, not last. Thalamus experiences a fleeting sense of shame at the unfavorable moral comparison to humans. It then hurtles into deep space on a chariot of accelerating energy.

The scientist in Ojai makes a full recovery. Well, nearly full. He never went on to make that one special surfboard."

CHAPTER 49

This can't be it.

No part of the experience aligns with what she prepared for. The printout of *Lightning in Ojai* is lowered as her arm falls slack. Asmara takes in the totality of the room. She scans the faces of the crowd and their expressions are neutral. There is no feedback to gauge audience reception to her story. Maybe they are not aware it's over.

Hold on. Is it finished?

She was so wrapped up in delivering the story that she neglected the spider grand finale. The transport tube was not sent through the stage hole. There's no tarantula.

Asmara had vocally projected her story into the room with a focus on each word itself. She spoke sounds which built sentences, but she never monitored if they were coherent. Asmara doesn't know what she said. It should have been the exact story she typed onto the pages because printed words don't change themselves. Yet something has been corrupted and there is no spider.

Digging into her immediate short-term memory, Asmara hears what she read out loud moments ago. It's foreign to her. *Lightning in Ojai* changed somehow. The sentences she spoke are different than what she originally wrote and printed out. Asmara was so preoccupied with speaking clear words she didn't realize they weren't hers. That explains why Ryan and Zoe didn't raise the spider through the tube, because they never heard the precise signal.

A chill runs down her arms.

She lifts the papers containing *Lightning in Ojai* up close to her face. It's a sight unlike any she could have dreamed.

The words on the page are moving. There is a migration of inked sentences across the paper. Some words vibrate in place but the majority of sentences undulate and slither, like snakes. When a strip of this writhing language hits the paper's edge, the tiny serpent bobs its leading word, essentially its head, and alters direction.

Asmara gasps at the hallucination. The intake gulp of air carries with it a terrible traveler—a stench. This rotten odor adheres to the roof of her mouth and crawls into her sinus cavity. The Patron is here. This is the scent which almost choked her to death in her bathroom.

Reacting to the odor, Asmara's face contorts in a grimace. She expects to see a similar chain reaction of disgust in the crowd but there is none. Instead, the audience continues to stare at her with blank expressions. They are motionless. Everything gets stranger when she focuses on one man in the front row. His eyelids descend slowly as if he is falling asleep. The lids close for three seconds and open again in a prolonged manner. This man blinked, in ultra slow motion. Her attention is drawn to the far wall where a bartender reaches for an overhead bottle. His arm rises at a nearly imperceptible pace. Time is slowing down.

Noises of grinding metal ring out. It's the cauldron in her mind. The lid is bouncing off the top of the vat.

Asmara considers a burst of options. Most of them involve fleeing the stage. She could scream at the crowd to run for their lives but it would be of no use. She keeps her feet planted.

Looking again at the printout of *Lightning in Ojai,* the serpentine sentences are frantic. They move faster within the flat realm of the papers. Some of the inked rows are in direct struggle, coiling around each other in a violent embrace. The animalistic text is ripping its rivals apart, tearing off words and spitting letters to the bottom of the page. Corpses of consonants and vowels pile in a heap. These zombie letters form new words and rise to attack again. The story is eating itself. Or more accurately, it is editing itself.

Before Ryan and Zoe picked her up tonight, she had hunted down her panic and compressed it into submission. The energy went nuclear from the containment and dissipated throughout her body. It is a fuel of unknown potency within her, awaiting instructions. If the cauldron lid is semi-closed, can she access this energy? And what about the musical notes that arose when she read *Lightning in Ojai?* She had absorbed the story as if it was a computer download of sheet music. The symphony of memorized chords must be within her.

She tries to concentrate on the story—the real version she wrote before, not the one which altered itself on stage. The original *Lightning in Ojai* is easy to find. It is sending out a distress signal, warning Asmara that what she read out loud was an impostor. The authentic memorized story is inside the cauldron, held against its will. *Lightning in Ojai* is resisting attempts to be dissolved by the vat's heated poisons.

Asmara is convinced the story she wrote is a living, sentient entity, fighting for its life. The cover on the vat continues to rattle as it spews out red and green lava. There is a syrup of gray ink which oozes at a slower pace.

The boundary between imagined metaphor and actual phenomenon is a blur. Asmara raises her arm, both in her imagination and with her real limb which is looming over the front row at The Naomi. Her fingers wrap around the curved handle of the cauldron's lid. Vibrations created by the contents make it difficult to grip. Droplets from the interior leap up and burn her arm. The pain is not imagined. Her wrist drips with condensation from the steam escaping the vat. A patchwork of red welts rise on her skin where the fluids have scalded her.

She needs the real *Lightning in Ojai* and it's in there.

The silver seal is lifted. It's heavy. Her right hand and forearm simmer in agony from the heat. With the wider exposure to open air, the boiling toxins get louder—as if they're threatening to explode. Asmara places the lid on the ground. Her left hand clutches the printed impostor story which swirls with snake-like sentences.

One's imagination, no matter how vivid, is not capable of manifesting instant physical realities. Nevertheless, she's afraid these animated words and the chemical stew in her mind may kill her before she saves the world.

Asmara plunges her left hand into the cauldron. In her visualization, the pages catch on fire before being submerged. Far more remarkable, in a wild escalation of madness, the *Lightning in Ojai* printout in the real world—the actual paper she holds in her flesh and blood hand while standing on The Naomi stage in front of two hundred people— also ignites into a waving flag of yellow-red flames.

Holy fucking shit!

She drops the burning pages onto the stage. Her eyes bug out in disbelief as the sheets curl from combustion and wilt into broken panels of ash. Looking for corroboration on this supernatural event, Asmara assumes she gained two hundred eye witnesses in the crowd. No luck. The still-life audience remains an army of statues, locked in time.

Her left hand, jammed wrist-deep into the vat, goes numb. In a bizarre inversion of her sense of pain, the cauldron's churning fluids are cold to the touch. Once past its molten cloak, the lava becomes an icy coolant.

She swirls her frostbitten hand in the neon slop until she detects something. It's another human hand submerged in the thick potion, reaching out to make contact. Her fingers gently intertwine with this phantom limb and it reciprocates with a trusting grip. This is the real *Lightning in Ojai*. She has reconnected with her story.

The steam emanating from the cauldron shifts colors from white to sickly yellow. This change is paired with an increase of the horrible odor. She understands now—the smell does not enter through her nose. It's within her. The foul indicator marks the Patron's arrival, using Asmara herself as the portal.

In both her visualization and with her actual arm on stage, Asmara yanks her left hand upward. She pulls the original story out of its captivity and her conscious mind grabs hold of it. An orchestra of musical notes create a concert of information. Chords clash with noisy dissonance but fall into harmony. *Lightning in Ojai* is back. She accesses it with musical notation in her memory, all of which is superimposed into one point. Asmara has "read" the story again, three times—start to finish, in the past two seconds. The usual cumbersome requirements of line by line reading don't apply anymore.

This incredible control of the story makes it a dynamic tool. It is necessary to weaponize *Lightning in Ojai* in order to defend the world, but it has come at a dangerous price. For now the cauldron is unsealed. She would love to place the cover back on the vat but that is no longer an option. The Patron is emerging from it.

Massive thorn-tipped insect legs, at least seven of them, bolt out of the cauldron's yellow steam. These living pillars shoot high above the rim and collapse toward the ground. The limbs have segmented joints which produce a cage around the vat. That silver lid is never going back on.

Asmara again sees writing engraved in the Patron's exoskeleton. Rivulets of red and green lava from inside the cauldron flow down its legs. A cascade of gray ink follows, tracing through the words stamped into the monster's armor. These embedded sentences are alive with glowing colors which contrast against the surrounding black shell. She tries to read the inscriptions but the words rearrange themselves. Much like how *Lightning in Ojai* transformed on stage, the Patron's surface of written language is also able to evolve. It is editing itself.

The beast's legs contract low and lift upwards, picking the cauldron off the ground. It walks toward Asmara, which creates a surreal perspective. As the observer in her own mind she is confronted by a foreign body. When something is inside you, there is nowhere to retreat.

With its long legs emerging from the black vat's central mass, this invader takes on the appearance of a spider. Metallic thunderclap sounds ring out as visible cracks shoot through the cauldron's casing. The Patron expands within its enclosure and is shedding off this iron cocoon.

The surface of the vat is streaked with zig-zag shatter lines. Jagged shards fall to the ground. One piece which breaks loose reveals a large reflective orb eye staring back at Asmara. It is a glassy red color, rimmed with green and surrounded by gray flesh.

Has this all been a trap? Maybe the cauldron technique was never her idea and not intended to help her. It was perhaps implanted by the Patron, tricking Asmara into constructing a mental portal to usher hell on Earth.

As the cauldron breaks further apart an unspeakably monstrous "face" begins to emerge. It's impossible to focus on as it projects a rotating prism of human and animal features, all colored red, green, and gray. When the remaining pieces of the vat soon crumble away, Asmara will be looking at a fully-revealed demon. It will be the last thing she ever sees.

The smell is unbearable. Her throat seizes shut as yellow steam wraps its tentacles around her neck. It is another attack like in the shower, although there is no magic spell to create holy water again, dissolving her enemy.

Unsure of what to do, her vision fading to black, Asmara's thoughts sink into the musical framework of *Lightning in Ojai*. The words and notes from the story form a sonic architecture which envelops her. As a last effort, with the final breath before her throat closes, she recites one of the lines from the story. She wants to hear an excerpt of her real writing spoken on stage, even if her action is futile.

However, it is not words which emerge. Her voice instead produces varying musical notes, reminiscent of a beautiful-sounding pipe organ.

It's incredible. The sounds are so unexpected that she swallows a life-saving gulp of air in a gasp. There is a secondary effect as well, for the Patron stops dead in its tracks in her mind. It is no longer about to descend upon her. The foul yellow steam loosens its grip around her neck. Asmara takes advantage of this reprieve by sneaking in a breath and exhaling another sentence from the story. More music is produced.

Her tongue and lips produce words, it's her ears which interpret it as music. She hears no English language, just a pipe organ in the act of heavenly translation. By the third and fourth line of the story which she recites from memory, there is a shift in the crowd. Eyes start to blink. Heads sway. The bartender finally grabbed the overhead bottle he was reaching for. Time is returning to normal.

The Patron shudders with fury and plunges its hooked claws into the walls of Asmara's internal perception. A gory sight is unleashed as blood flows and living tissue is mulched by the monster's buzzsaw limbs. It is a nightmarish vision but Asmara is not taking the bait. This is an ugly illusion intended to strike fear and take the offensive. The gambit failed.

With her airway clear of the putrid noose around her neck, she continues to recite lines from *Lightning in Ojai*. There is a leap of faith involved. She understands her vocal cords are emitting normal spoken words, but all she hears are symphonic tones. Asmara believes the crowd hears words as well. There would be an audience reaction if the woman on stage was a human synthesizer. Judging by their alert eye contact and placid expressions, she still has the attention of these people. They are not aware time slowed down or that Asmara is waging a war inside her head.

It is both magical and maddening for Asmara as she tries to deliver the story while also being swept away by the gorgeous sounds. An important line is coming up. She can't hear what she is saying so Asmara articulates slowly and hopes for the best:

"The graffiti mural declared something he already knew—there's no place like home."

She hit her mark. A melody produced by those words gives pleasure to her inner ear. Within seconds there is faint contact along her ankle. The verbal signal was received by Ryan and Zoe and the transport tube begins its ascent.

CHAPTER 50

A momentum shift has occurred. After emerging in Asmara's head as a deadly threat, now the Patron flails with impotent rage. The area surrounding its spider-like legs is littered with shards from the broken cauldron. Those jagged pieces start to vibrate. The more Asmara vocalizes her story on stage, the more these jigsaw daggers tremble. Some are even levitating off of the ground. They are under her control.

The Patron's primary eye peers through a gap in the cauldron as this collection of blades lifts into the air and they each rotate their sharpest edge in its direction. A hovering arsenal surrounds the creature and its skin color gains deep red hues, a show of fierce anger.

The authentic version of *Lightning in Ojai,* spoken out loud, neutralizes the monster, so Asmara continues with the story.

It is exhilarating for her not only to produce such soaring musical notes but also to recite each sentence from memory. Asmara articulates the original story while maintaining a tightrope walk of improvisation. The first half of her stage reading was the impostor version of *Lightning in Ojai,* so she stitches loose ends together where needed. It's the finale which matters. She needs to stick the landing.

The transport tube slides past her knee and up her inner thigh. Asmara steals a glance downward and her skirt is not bulging or otherwise revealing the activity below. She keeps proclaiming the gospel of her story to the audience, hoping it serves as an exorcism of the devil in their midst.

The Patron, in a fury, lengthens its legs and extends them into the air. These segmented limbs climb higher out of the cracked cauldron. They tower above Asmara's internal line of sight. The legs scrape away at something above her, yet somewhere within her. A tickle throughout her scalp turns into a deep irritation. Heat arises on the *inside* of her skull.

No way...

Asmara itches her scalp and runs her fingers through her hair. There is a drilling vibration on the top of her head, coming from within.

Nope. Fuck this.

Disgusted by the parasitic intrusion, Asmara hurls the levitating cauldron shards at the Patron. Some of the pieces bounce off of the container but many plunge into the Patron's exposed flesh, including its main eye. Green and red fluid spews like a geyser from the puncture holes. With firehose velocity, these fountains of gore are disproportionate to the entry wounds.

The remaining structure of the cauldron crumbles into a heap of even smaller pieces. There is no total reveal of the Patron's true form because it, too, disintegrates with a visceral splash. The giant insect legs tumble down from above now that they are dismembered from the melted host body.

This is the second time Asmara reduced the Patron to a puddle but there is a facade to the display—it is all a show. Or more to the point, it is a trick. The Patron she just butchered was a puppet which *wanted* to be destroyed. It was a Trojan Horse piñata, filled with vile plasma and begging to be split open. Asmara obliged and now her mind is drowning in these heinous substances.

The green and red geysers continue to shoot upward from the frothy pool which was once the Patron. A vertical stream of gray joins the concoction. This amount of fluid could not have been contained within the beast she slayed. By bursting the surface of the monster, a leak has been sprung from elsewhere. Her inner vision is inundated by the rising flood.

Lightning in Ojai tumbles out of her lungs and transmits to the crowd but Asmara's hearing is muted as if underwater. She loses the rhythm of the story. Her entire headspace, the navigation center of her perception, is submerged in a swamp of those three colors. Asmara has broken through to another dimension, from the inside of her body. The decoy Patron had fooled her into piercing its threshold. That puppet was a sacrificial membrane. It was a doorway which only opens from one direction and the cauldron shards were the key.

The fluids saturating her thoughts are the primary substance of the alien realm itself. These three colored liquids are a fundamental constant on the other side, as air is on Earth. One dimension is about to flood into another, flowing through the path of least resistance—Asmara's human-shaped portal. It is a deluge which will transform reality but no one from this planet will be around to see it. The new neighbors are moving in and they're taking over.

This is the showdown Asmara had premonitions about for the past week. Here is her chance to save the world. She's not sure what to do other than continue with her story. There's four paragraphs left.

Asmara has a tickle in her ear followed by fluid draining out. She wipes her earlobe and looks at her fingers. There are drops of red, green, and gray coating her skin like syrup. Her other ear tingles and another stream cascades out of that canal. Next, her sinus cavity fills. There is so much blockage behind the center of her face that the pressure is painful. A steady drip begins out of one nostril and then both. Asmara wipes her sleeve under her nose and colorful streaks stain the fabric.

She stops speaking and *Lightning in Ojai* grinds to a halt. Faces in the audience appear confused but their body language is at ease. How are they not reacting to this woman leaking colors on stage? It's no longer possible for Asmara to believe she imagines this grotesque flow. The evidence pours out of her body.

A poke in her abdomen focuses her attention. The transport tube has reached the elastic waistband of her skirt. She pinches the front of the garment outward, feigning a simple clothing adjustment, and allows the plastic tube to slide up her stomach.

Asmara knows every word which remains in her story, yet she can only guess how to pronounce them. Her voice, her hearing, her thoughts—all are warped by the alien oils replacing the cells in her body. Her vocal cords rattle in a random tempo and indistinct sounds, like a muffled horn section, reach her ears.

A pitter-patter noise taps away on the stage surface by her feet. There is a rainfall of colored splatter marks on top of her shoes and the surrounding area. Asmara is hemorrhaging fluids straight from her face onto the ground.

An audience would normally be screaming in horror at this repulsive sight and yet they remain unmoved. She feels the liquids stream down her body with the same certainty as if she had stepped into a shower. The substances are real but they must be invisible to others.

Asmara has pushed words outward with such effort she hadn't noticed the drumbeat of energy washing against her. This diffuse spectrum originates from the crowd and every impact reveals its composition. The auras radiate again. They were always present but the wavelengths of these people can no longer be suppressed. Their intensity grows as each pulse throbs through the air. With the cauldron technique dissolved, the unfiltered souls have a shine brighter than ever. The purified wavelengths are almost in their true form. A full exposure to the auras, which is imminent, will be like standing in front of an atomic bomb.

Fluids pour out from her tear ducts. It is an open faucet of drainage. These streams launch neon-colored liquid off her cheekbones and the tip of her nose.

A hurricane of dancing souls rotates above the crowd as their auras combine. The complexity of these spirits is different than what Asmara witnessed before. No longer can she tease out information from the textures of living ghosts. It's all too bright. Her senses are overloaded and short-circuiting. These human-lights are beyond beautiful, they are incomprehensible.

Still, she pushes out the words of her story. Two paragraphs remain although the sentences stretch beyond reach, never allowing for completion.

It's difficult to distinguish any individual in the aura cloud and yet a ribbon of luminosity strikes Asmara's eye. This wavelength is so wide she didn't believe it was the emission of one person. Asmara now recognizes the unique radiation. She encountered it before in the hallway of her apartment building. It belongs to her neighbor. Inga is here.

CHAPTER 51

The tarantula tube arrives at Asmara's collar. Its rigid form presses against her sternum. With the hollow pole secured by her clothes, locking her in place, it's as if she is fastened to the front of a ship in a turbulent sea. The Naomi stage is a wooden vessel sailing straight into a tempest of souls.

For Asmara, it is pure guesswork if she is speaking English into the microphone. Inga's powerful wavelength interferes even further with the distorted sounds of *Lightning in Ojai*. This convergence of opposing energy creates ripples in the air. The misdirected voltage allows Asmara to trace the origin of Inga's transmission.

There she is. Her neighbor stands at the farthest wall in the venue. Unlike her usual proper appearance, Inga has a wild nest of frazzled white hair.

Inga outstretches an arm, reaching toward the stage. She lets Asmara know the mutual detection is acknowledged and there is nothing to hide anymore. Within the maelstrom of energy hanging in the room, Inga is able to communicate that she's here to witness the inevitable. The waterfall is descending. It is time to cleanse the Earth.

"I see the colored flood springing from you," Inga conveys, without using words. *"All will drown. You and I shall swim."*

One paragraph remains in Asmara's story.

The foreign fluids pouring in from another dimension have an ominous sound. A thunder builds behind the rainfall of dripping noises. There is a tsunami on its way. The dam has not fully burst yet. When she punctured the membrane to another realm a relative trickle was created as compared to the oncoming torrent.

Asmara sighs with resignation at the thought of this tide bearing down on her. How do you push back against a flowing sea? Her voice labors to reach the microphone and *Lightning in Ojai* slows down. She considers going silent. Maybe the flood is a painless way to end things.

A voice whispers in her ear. It is distant and hollow sounding. The words come from Zoe beneath the stage. Her voice travels up the tube and her faint message gains an echo along the way.

"You've got this, Asmara."

A deeper whisper follows. "Give us the sign," Ryan says.

She didn't know she needed to hear those words, but they jumpstart her nervous system. A surge of determination spikes through her bloodstream. It's time to sprint to the finish line.

The signal sentence is delivered. Asmara hears the words as both her own voice and as musical notes.

"It bares no resemblance, in style or substance, to the usual spectrum of daydreams."

A soft rumble vibrates within the tube and stirs against her skin. The tarantula is on its way up, riding the interior cylinder pushed by Ryan.

Asmara is about to close out the story with the final two sentences when she is struck by a direct wavelength injection. This transmission is shot up through the tube, enters under her jaw and gets mainlined into her brain. It is a high-frequency aura from the spider. The energy is exotic.

Asmara blurts out the remaining words of *Lightning in Ojai* even faster. She doesn't know what she is racing against until the entire rear wall of The Naomi fades to solid black. It is the opposing side of the venue from Asmara's perspective and the wood paneling and framed posters disappear. No one in the crowd turns to see this chasm, except for Inga, who faces the portal and spreads her arms. She is ready to embrace the flood.

Within the void a massive shape stirs. Sections of the black cloak reveal a stabbing motion outward. The surface of the darkness is pushed forward as if it's a thin fabric. The true Patron is on the other side and this is no proxy puppet. Its hooked legs are coated in the inky threshold substance. The claws probe the barrier, waiting for the curtain to drop and for all of these souls to be harvested.

A series of taps tickle Asmara's neck. It's the first contact of the spider emerging from the tube. Her eyes flick downward and the stage is covered in red, green, and gray flowing magma.

There is an unnatural weight distributed across the front of her throat—the eight pressure points of the tarantula's legs. A collective gasp erupts from the audience and scattered remarks arrive to her ears in stereo.

"Look!" "Dude!" "Oh, my God!" "Is that real?"

On the other side of the room, a vertical slice develops in the colorless chasm which billows like a sheet in the wind. Dark rays shoot out which can only be described as anti-light. These beams are as black as the void. The reverse illumination rays are an impossible contradiction on Earth and yet their existence heralds a new dawn.

As anti-light rays strike the interior of the venue, Asmara's view of the crowd starts fading away. This non-radiance suffocates all reflective information.

The Patron's unholy stench, now in its purest form, rolls in like a fog. It would normally choke Asmara but she breathes the putrid mist deep into her lungs. Since her body is saturated with alien chemistry, she is adapting to this new biology. She does not consent to the forced evolution.

Each step of the spider on her skin causes facial muscles to recoil. She is tempted to shake off the irritation. The tarantula marches up to Asmara's right temple. After a pause it stomps across both her eyes with no concern for this sensitive terrain, and it stops on her left cheek.

A heavy murmur in the crowd grows louder and is blended with more gasps. Asmara pries her gaze from the void by allowing herself a glance at the audience, which is dimming to black. Every face displays a wild reaction. Eyelids are wrenched back, creating unblinking stares.

Phones lift into view. People fumble on their touchscreens to record the finale.

The last words of the story are of unknown origin to Asmara. She produces a series of sounds which cast another magic spell.

Two massive spears launch out of the chasm on the other side of the venue. They are the same insect appendages she has seen before, but much larger. These Patron limbs are the size of telephone poles. Traveling eighty feet from the opposing wall, the dark missiles bear down on her. Asmara's instinct is to leap away but she is bolted to the stage by the tube under her clothes.

With a fighting spirit, she keeps her eyes open and leans forward, unafraid of the impalement which will rip her in half. The elongated talons arc over the crowd and slam into the stage on either side of her. Wooden splinters twirl in the air and scatter at her feet. Asmara is sprayed by the pool of colored liquids coating everything in sight. The hooked limbs did not miss their target on purpose—they were diverted by Asmara's sheer defiance and the spell she uttered.

Hovering on either side of her face, the Patron's armor is revealed in exquisite detail. The indented words in its shell pulsate with a glistening respiration. This monster's surface is a living language which breathes.

Asmara's eyes flick back and forth, reading as much as she can. It is apparent—her story *Lightning in Ojai* is implanted on the surface canals of this creature. The more she scans the limbs of the Patron, the more her own words stare back at her. Or at least she thought they were her words.

It appears the inspiration which spurred her to create *Lightning in Ojai* was not channeled from some divine muse. The words she wrote were dictated from afar and with evil intent, her typing fingers being mere vessels. She was tricked into chanting an incantation tonight to open another dimension. The story she read out loud contained just the right sounds, masked within the English language, to release a gate. *Lightning in Ojai* is one giant password to unlock the doorway to hell and she is the unwitting transcriber.

The Patron's talons uncouple from the stage. They lift into the air and hover above Asmara's face. They're not going to miss a second time.

Her defiance is flickering, but Asmara holds fast.

I finished the story. What more can I do?

Asmara closes her eyes and experiences a lightning bolt of all-consuming pain. Her face contracts into a grimace of agony. Death will not be painless, but hopefully it's over soon.

She dissociates from her body and her existence is free-floating misery. Time stretches. How long can this last?

The circulating torture Asmara endures takes a shape. The looping negative energy decreases in size until it is a single point. She returns to her body. The pain is no longer within every fiber of her soul. It has a physical location—the left side of her face. More specifically, the throbbing ache lies under the weight of the tarantula perched on her cheek.

This fucking spider just bit me.

CHAPTER 52

It hurts, quite badly. However, the pain is laced with an infusion of optimism. This trauma signal firing along her facial nerves means she's alive and remains a human being. Asmara was not slaughtered by giant claws and her DNA was not replaced by alien genetics. At least not yet.

She opens her eyes and the Patron's limbs struggle to stay aloft as they're pulled backwards into the vortex. The inscriptions on its shell morph into new words and sentences, too fast to read.

A magnetic force nudges her forward and she wobbles on her feet. The red, green, and gray fluids coating the stage swirl from an unseen influence. Thousands of colored droplets rise into the air, detached from gravity.

Not only does Asmara feel the tarantula's hooked fangs embedded in her cheek, she detects, with detailed accuracy, the venom as it travels her circulatory system.

The tri-color fluids spawned from the Patron react strongly to these added drops of poison. Biochemical reactions ignite in her blood stream. The spider bite secretions act as an antibody which converts the red, green, and gray plasma into a singular substance. This new mutated agent chases down the Patron's remaining colored oils in order to cannibalize them. A hunt-kill-convert immune response rages through Asmara's veins.

She rocks forward on her feet again, grabbing the microphone to steady herself.

The Patron's long claws lose their fight against invisible forces and are wrenched backwards over the crowd. Before they disappear into the void, each hook buries into an adjacent wall, creating wide gouges. The beast tries to stay in this realm. A horizontal rainfall is extracted off the stage as the levitating droplets shower across the room. The black canvas has summoned their return.

These parallel dimensions which collided are now separating. All forms of matter from the Patron's world are being cast out.

Did spider venom do all of this?

Asmara stumbles forward again and her feet lift off the ground. Since her body is saturated with the unstable material being recalled, she is, in effect, one more droplet forced to leave the Earth. The physics of this detachment will pull her across the room and into the abyss. Or tear her apart.

An unstoppable convulsion overtakes her body. Her jaw flings open and a river of tri-color fluid projectile vomits out of Asmara's mouth. Semisolid ribbons of the same formless material are pulled out of her sinus cavity through her nose. Her tear ducts and ears begin their own draining process. The forceful suction is overwhelming. Her eyes and brain may be liquidated as well.

Three seconds later, as quickly as it started, her body snaps back to neutral with no further expulsion of exotic matter. The invasive substances which filled her anatomy now drift across the venue in a sideways waterfall. The floating plasma, eerily the same shape as her body, nears the portal. This abstract blob of Asmara's form extends a liquid limb, trying to reach back to its former host, before dissolving into darkness. The last traces of the receding dimension are the Patron's two limbs, which thrash about before they are swallowed by the black curtain. In a cross fade from shadow to light, the far wall returns to its appearance as the regular Naomi interior.

A deep growling noise fills the air. The sounds become more clear until they are wonderfully familiar.

The roar is people cheering and clapping.

Asmara blinks to focus her eyes and she takes in the scene of a rapturous audience. Smiles are everywhere, people laugh but not with ridicule. They are enjoying a wild Word Bound finale. There must be at least thirty phones in the air, recording her on stage with the tarantula stuck to her face.

A sliding sensation traces down the center of her chest. Ryan and Zoe draw back down the transport tube. With their steady hands, the descent is seamless and does not snag her clothing. The cylinder brushes her ankle as it returns beneath the stage.

With no idea of what to do with herself, Asmara gives an awkward wave goodbye to the audience. This draws even louder applause.

The crowd never saw the Patron's leg spears. Nor did they see liquids pouring out of Asmara or hear musical notes instead of her voice. They only saw a woman speaking in front of a microphone and a spider which came from under her shirt.

She walks toward the backstage door. Each step jostles the tarantula and the arachnid's two hypodermic needles retract out of the wound.

Asmara reaches the door and Elizabeth strides from the side-stage alcove. She pivots to the far side of Asmara which does not have a spider hanging on it. "That was amazing! How are you?"

It is satisfying for Asmara to hear regular spoken language and not musical notes. "I'm not sure how I am. I don't know what happened."

"It was incredible! Hey, I'll see you backstage, I'm going to sign off."

Asmara opens the door but turns as Elizabeth addresses the crowd.

"Wow! How about that closing act to Word Bound?"

The crowd fires up another round of cheers.

Staggering confusion pierces through Asmara. She's grateful she no longer confronts a monster while drowning in alien magma. And she is pleased the world wasn't swept away. However, as she observes this cheerful scene in The Naomi, unsettling contrasts are revealed. The stage had been drenched in colored slime and now not one stray drop remains. Her clothes show no stained streaks either. She had watched in detail as the Patron's claws tore into the wooden stage and walls. Now she cannot see any damage whatsoever. There are no visible auras from the crowd, whereas there had been a weather system of souls before. And as a final insult to her grasp of reality, laying by the microphone are two white sheets of paper. The *Lightning in Ojai* printouts never burst into flames.

These all beg the question—what else didn't happen?

"I want to thank the creative, fabulous people who contributed tonight," Elizabeth says. "And I must give a shout out to all of you for attending Word Bound. You make it happen. Goodnight everyone!"

A final blast of applause wraps up the event.

Still facing the audience, Asmara walks backward through the door which leads to the storage area. She peers beyond the crowd to the far wall where the dark portal had been. There is no sign of Inga. Her neighbor exited the venue or she is now a resident of another dimension, either by choice or she was dragged away.

Asmara stumbles into the backstage room. Her internal motors are cranked by paranoid energy. She cannot trust her senses and she dreads whatever cruel surprise is next.

A rustling noise drifts from the crawlspace at the base of the stage. The hinged door swings open and Ryan emerges. He is face to face with both Asmara and the tarantula clinging to her cheek.

"Ah!" He yells before breaking into a laugh. "Unbelievable! We could hear the cheering. That must have been wild out there."

Zoe crawls out of the storage space on her hands and knees. She pops up, looks at Asmara, and grabs fistfuls of her own hair. "It's still on your face! The crowd went crazy! We almost dropped Asmaraña!"

Their enthusiasm is infectious. Asmara savors this comforting presence. But what can she say to these two about what happened?

"I, uh... I need to get the spider off me."

"Of course," Zoe says as she ducks back into the crawlspace to retrieve the container.

Ryan steps closer to Asmara. "You're not okay, are you?"

Asmara swivels a slow head shake. *No, I'm not.*

The stage access door opens and Elizabeth bounds into the room. "There they are. What a show. It was so fun watching everyone react."

Zoe squirms out of the storage hatch while carrying the spider's cube.

Asmara is surrounded by these three people staring at her. They are eager for her to make a pronouncement of any sort. She obliges.

"Just so you know, the spider bit me."

Ryan, Zoe, and Elizabeth continue their flat gaze. Perhaps they associate a tarantula bite with the victim screaming bloody murder.

"I'm serious," Asmara says. "It bit under my left eye."

Gasps ring out as all three comprehend the situation.

"Are you in pain?" "What do we do?"

Asmara points to the plastic cube Zoe is holding. The teen hurries over and opens the lid. With a steady motion, Asmara lifts her arm to her face. The spider recognizes this forearm conveyor belt and it steps onto the platform. If Asmaraña is grief-stricken about the trauma it inflicted on

Asmara then its guilt is well hidden. An angled roll of the wrist sends the tarantula back into the container.

Having regained control, Asmara looms over the small creature. Isn't it a justified human reaction to kill any bug which bites you? *Nah.* Not only is there no animosity toward her assailant, the bite venom cast out the Patron and its realm. Those fangs saved the world.

Over the next few minutes, Asmara gives vague answers to questions about her performance. She downplays the whole evening. Elizabeth takes the hint, shares a goodbye hug, and heads into the main hall.

Asmara turns to Ryan and Zoe. They project heart-melting amounts of empathy toward her. Her friends have a shared sense something amiss happened on stage tonight, beyond the spider bite. The three stand in silence. Asmara is grateful she cannot see their wavelength auras. It is a corrupting abomination to sample the souls of others.

"This has been a weird night," Asmara says. "You did an amazing job. The crowd really did respond to the whole act."

Smiles cut through the grim tension.

"I know there's things we want to talk about. But for now let's be happy the event went well and we're all safe and sound."

"Safe and sound?" Zoe says. "You were attacked by a giant spider who sucked blood out of your head. Your cheek is swollen."

"It's fine. And there was no blood sucking, it was just a bite."

Before they leave, Asmara opens the stage access door. The venue is half empty and the remaining masses face the exits as they make their way out. She walks to the microphone to pick up the two sheets of paper she dropped during her performance. There are no burn marks and she marvels at how the flaming paper hallucination fooled her earlier.

She turns each page over in her hands. They are blank. *Lightning in Ojai* had existed on these thin white surfaces, branded in ink, and now there is not a trace of its existence.

CHAPTER 53

They exit into the alley. Zoe holds the spider container, Ryan has the transport tubes, and Asmara carries their two skateboards. They have each internalized the night in their own ways. At some point there will be a discussion but for now they want to get out of there.

With The Naomi backdoor slamming shut, no less than three guys urinating in the alley get startled. There must have been an unacceptable line for the bathroom inside. Asmara ignores the waterworks and continues down the narrow lane. Over the sound of urine streams splashing on asphalt, a voice calls out. "Great job tonight. That spider thing was cool."

"Thank you," Asmara says as they round the corner.

Most of the venue's crowd is on the sidewalk. It doesn't occur to Asmara to avoid walking through this group—the car is on the other side, after all. Just because she performed on stage doesn't mean she's a pop star about to get mobbed.

As the three friends walk toward the wall of people, heads turn in their direction. The murmur dies down and then grows louder.

A blend of different voices surround Asmara and bathe her with attention as she enters the crowd. The comments arise from dozens of smiling faces and yet they form a single spoken thread.

"Yooo! That's her. You crushed it tonight. Is that her? Great job. Was the spider real? I loved it. Hey, that was amazing. That was so sick. Good job. Is that the girl who went up last? That was crazy what you did. I just want to say I loved your act tonight. How did you not freak out? I would have freaked out. You were my favorite tonight. I loved your story and the spider was a nice touch. Great job up there."

Asmara pinballs her way through this fabulous commentary. It would be a shame to miss a kind word, so Asmara slows down her walking pace to revel in the adulation.

Amid the praise, numerous people ask the same question—"How did you do it?" Since she is not a magician whose act depends on trade secrets, Asmara utters a mantra. "There was a hole in the stage. We made a spider tube. There was a hole in the stage. We made a spider tube."

Ryan and Zoe enjoy the attention as well. Zoe holds up the tarantula container and laughs as people sneer with disgust. All of these close-up human faces are probably just as repulsive to the arachnid.

Ryan shows onlookers how the two sections of tube slide within each other to create an elevator. "It was an express lift with one stop."

The crowd of strangers transforms into a smaller bubble of familiarity. Asmara has entered the social circle of friends she invited to the show. The compliments here are in a higher pitch of enthusiasm, including shrieking. The smiles are wider. She is passed around from hug to hug. Sarah and Gillian are near-hysterical, in a good way. The flock of One Track Mind birds each give her a formal high five, as if they just learned the gesture. Dylan makes her laugh with talk of Geminis and other zodiac nonsense.

After winding through the ego-pleasing gauntlet, the crowd thins out. Finally, Asmara breathes. These are the arduous duties of a successful performance artist. Again, she is thankful she's no longer buffeted by visible souls. The human tunnel she entered would have caused a fatal overdose.

She spots manager James chatting on his phone. With a few pointed questions to him, she could determine how accurate her mind-reading abilities are. It might be tough to get him to admit to drug debts, bad bank loans, and his imminent escape to Australia. But it'd be fun to watch him sweat through her interrogation. Since he appears busy, she is content to shuffle past without saying goodbye. His suspicious body language indicates he may be avoiding her with a fake phone call.

They walk next to The Naomi's bulletin board covered in promotional fliers. Asmara is transfixed by her own Word Bound poster. The design elements, which were haphazard initially, are now inevitable. There is a visual harmony—the giant limb emerging from darkness, Ryan's likeness suspended mid-air, and Europa looming above it all. Every bit of it is absurd to an average viewer but there is a narrative in the art. An ongoing story is told and it is not complete. The ghostly moon has something to say. That strange stack of five alternating squares is a message in a bottle from another part of the solar system. A message soon to be read.

"Will you print me your poster?" Zoe says. "I'd love to have one."

"Yeah. I'll figure out how to do that."

"Take it," a voice bellows. It's James, with a phone still to his ear. He's thirty feet behind them and must have good hearing.

"You can have that one," he says. "It's the least we can do."

"Really?" Zoe says. "Are you sure?"

"Of course. Pull it right off. It's all yours."

"Thank you so much."

Asmara blows James a kiss. She never does that move. He gives an unusually slow wave back to her. If Asmara had to guess, it was a wave goodbye from a man about to cross the Pacific ocean, never to return.

. . . .

For most of the drive home, Asmara has her window half-way down. It's a rude gesture as loud, whooshing air fills the car. Ryan and Zoe don't complain and Asmara hopes they like the fresh air as well.

The car glides to a stop in front of Asmara's apartment. Ryan and Zoe are dropping her off before they head back to Oakland.

Parked on the street is her neighbor Inga's car. For Asmara, the zig-zag scratch in the paint takes on a new perspective. It looks like someone drew a line connecting the dots to a constellation of glittering stars.

CHAPTER 54

She walks up her apartment's stairwell, carrying the spider cube against her chest. The spot where Ryan kissed her three days ago is still evocative, as if their body chemistry lingers.

As Asmara reaches her floor, the hallway has an oppressive stillness in the air. The door to Inga's apartment is no different than the other neighbors, yet that entryway inhabits a dark place. Asmara hopes Inga is sleeping soundly right now, floating within dreams of resolution to her torment. Whatever the crooked line obsession means to her, maybe its jagged effects have been flattened out.

Or perhaps Inga exists in another dimension after being swept away by a retreating tide at The Naomi. Did she fight against the current or swim willingly toward the Patron? For Inga, the monster could be an angel who grants her serenity.

If Inga has indeed vanished, the police will launch a missing persons investigation. Asmara's recounting of events—aliens and auras included—will end with her handcuffed and an involuntary psychiatric hold.

. . . .

Asmara enters her apartment and begins to slip out of the billowy skirt she hovered in all night. A floorboard creaks in the kitchen. It's not a subtle noise—this sound represents a human being who may or may not be a murderer. She puts down the tarantula container next to three fresh pieces of junk mail.

There is not a murderer in this apartment. The situation is far worse. Her housemate Lisa is here.

A head pokes from the kitchen down the hallway. "Oh, hey," Lisa says in a tone so bitter Asmara can taste it.

Lisa walks down the hall toward Asmara and another person emerges from the kitchen. It's her boyfriend Chris. He doesn't visit the apartment often and Asmara suspects he is a bodyguard to protect against any psychotic, bathroom-wrecking women in the vicinity. The way he oversees Lisa with protective caution makes Asmara feel like a wild animal who wandered in.

Lisa defuses the situation by turning to address Chris. "I'm going to chat with Asmara for a second. Can you finish the boxes in my room?"

"Okay," Chris says before offering a morsel of civility. "Hi, Asmara."

"Hey."

Lisa walks up to Asmara and jumps a step back. "Whoa. You're wearing a skirt."

"Yeah. I gave a spoken-word performance tonight. The skirt was part of the act."

Lisa looks behind Asmara. "And what's that plastic cube?"

"A tarantula is in there. The spider was in my show, too."

Lisa's eyes flutter as she tries to process this information. With a shake of her head, she casts aside further questions before her mouth asks them. "I'll get right to it. As you've probably guessed, I'm moving out."

Asmara is unaffected. "Yeah. That's what I figured." Her face stays placid. This news would have upended her life yesterday, but having confronted visions of hell on stage has put things in perspective. To squabble over apartment rent is foolish and Asmara can't hide her disinterest. "Need any help bringing things downstairs?"

Lisa is taken off-guard by Asmara's impassive reaction. "Ah, no. I mean, you're gonna see me over the next few days as I grab stuff. I'm sure you want to talk about moving details."

"Nah, I'm good. Do whatever you need to do."

"Oh. Well, I'm gonna pay my rent for the rest of this month, just so you're not left hanging."

"That's nice of you. Thanks."

Asmara picks up the spider container and walks away. It's not a passive-aggressive move, she has nothing more to say.

. . . .

The warm shower water cascades down her body. A chaotic day's worth of anxiety sweat washes off her skin. The soothing water is the antithesis of the foul alien liquids which oozed out of her at Word Bound. She glances at the shower drain to make sure it's not swirling with red, green, and gray fluids.

There is no return appearance from the Patron while Asmara showers. Evidence of that former bathroom encounter exists in the form of a battered door, propped up to give the illusion of privacy.

For no thoughtful reason, Asmara cranks the shower's water knob from hot to ice cold—as far as the handle goes. The freezing downpour should make her recoil and shiver. Instead, the deathly cold grip of the water cannot get ahold of her. There is no shudder or desire to seek warmth. The extreme cold feels quite nice. Even appropriate.

While exiting the bathroom in a robe, Asmara encounters Lisa, who is carrying a box of clothes. Lisa takes two steps backward, not out of personal space issues but out of fear.

"Oh," Lisa says, "I forgot to tell you, the neighbor across the hall came by earlier today."

Asmara's back muscles stiffen. "Inga?"

"Yeah. I don't know her that well beyond hello. Are you close to her lately?"

"I've chatted with her. Why was she here?"

"She wanted to see if you were available. When I said no, she asked if she could grab the Russian poster she lent you."

"That's right. I was going to scan it."

"She said it was important to get it back. You weren't home so I let her grab the poster from your room. I hope you don't mind."

Asmara's eyelids peel back as she glares at Lisa with contempt.

Lisa takes another step backward. "Hey, you weren't here. I admit, it was weird that she asked if she could retrieve it herself."

"What did she do when she was in the apartment?"

"I guided her down the hall, showed her your room, and she walked in and out in four seconds. I stood in the doorway watching her. The poster was right on your desk. She thanked me and left with a smile."

Asmara grinds her teeth. The anger isn't toward Lisa—there's no way she could understand the dynamics at play. It's Inga's unknowable scheming which drips like acid into Asmara's stomach.

CHAPTER 55

On some mornings, Asmara's bed forcibly restrains her from getting up. The blankets become a straight jacket, limiting movement and preventing her from starting the day. It's for her own safety. Other times, the moment her eyes open, she is launched onto her feet with task-driven determination.

Today, Asmara is half asleep while she observes herself walking across her bedroom. She's not sure what the plan is when she opens her laptop.

Asmara's conscious thoughts are the last to find out—she seeks the mysterious, beautiful dot matrix from Professor Stephen Garrity's cognitive test.

The array of points visited her in a dream last night. There was no elaborate storyline weaved by REM sleep. Instead, the pattern hovered behind her closed eyelids and rotated on a vertical axis. It was a remarkable display of compelling art. She *has* to see it again.

Stephen's disappearing link confounded her the last time she looked.

So, she is going to ask him if he will send the test again. Searching for their correspondence, nothing turns up. Not only is the test link missing, there is no evidence of any exchange between her and the project manager of the Europa space probe mission.

As for the memory test, she knows she recreated the dot pattern with a pen to near perfection. Asmara looks for the sheet of paper which is peppered with ink spots. It's nowhere on her desk.

She grabs her phone. Yesterday she had taken a photo of the completed dot pattern test. It was the same image she sent to the test creator, as instructed. Asmara searches the photo library on her phone and throws the device onto her bed with disgust. No such photo exists.

. . . .

Asmara gets dressed and grabs her laptop. She is going to Slow Pour Coffee across the street. It's unusual for her to visit there this early but she has an urge to be active and she has run out of her own coffee.

Across the room, the tarantula sits exposed within its container, watching Asmara as she gathers items. She stops to match the creature's gaze.

I can't believe you bit me. Did your venom save the world?

Asmara concentrates. She opens her mind to receive a potential aura wavelength from the spider. Nothing arrives.

Well, let me know when you get a chance.

As she steps through her front door into the hallway, Asmara winces from a pain deep in her skull. It's unlike any headache she ever experienced. This sting is a pinpoint sensation at the rear base of her brain, two inches inward from the back of her head. It's a bodily region where she has never felt anything before, and certainly not a headache.

The pain gives the impression of physical displacement happening in her skull. There is an actual foreign object pushing against brain matter. Maybe it's a piece of shrapnel from the shattered cauldron, lodged in her mind?

As she's shutting the apartment door, the junk mail inside her entryway catches her eye. This mail was intended for across the hall. For the first time ever, Asmara learns her neighbor's full name. Inga Novikov.

. . . .

Amid the evidence that reality has fractured, this is one step too far on the path to madness. Somehow, impossibly, Slow Pour's coffee tastes fabulous. The chemical-waste aftertaste is still there. However, the same noxious soup of flavors now gives her a deep satisfaction. The coffee has not changed, she has. It's not a mere theory anymore—her biochemistry has been altered.

Asmara passes by the rows of fire-damaged books. A deep inhalation divulges whispered memories of a fire long ago. She has a guilty longing for the powers she recently possessed. Seeing aura wavelengths in people and sensing time-capsule histories within objects made her extraordinary. Now she's a confused person in a coffeeshop, unsure of what is real anymore.

She fires up her laptop and types an internet search for the name Inga Novikov. No results. Asmara tries "Inga Novikov, Russia."

One hit, although it's a good one.

The ancient-looking website originates from the dawn of the internet and the words are displayed with an eye-melting red font on black. Everything is in Russian but an animated logo shows a telescope aimed at twinkling stars. This must be an astronomy website of some sort.

Asmara scrolls through a sea of red words and finds a picture of a younger Inga. Her stern appearance belies lovely features. Asmara's impression of her neighbor softens upon viewing the woman as she was decades ago.

Asmara drags the cursor over the words and copies everything. She types a secondary search for "Russian to English." A new tab opens on her screen and she dumps the article into the box. Through the magic of internet elves, this brick of Russian language transforms into an old friend—comprehensible English.

After a sip of coffee, she dives into the article. Asmara is not sure if she blinks, or even breathes, throughout the duration.

Professor Fired For Falsifying Telescope Data: The governing board of the Moscow Academy of Science and Space Exploration agreed to terminate the faculty standing of Professor Inga Novikov. The Prof. of Astronomy ran afoul of the institution's management after it was revealed she misrepresented data from her work with the Arctic Telescope Observatory in Chersky, Siberia. An investigation of her six-week research stint at the observatory determined Prof. Novikov abandoned protocol for the Orion Sky Mapping Project (OSMP) which she was there to oversee. The OSMP was an endeavor to catalog the stars within a wide ribbon of Northern Hemisphere night sky. A new telescope at the Arctic Observatory promised unprecedented clarity for the star map.

Soon after her arrival in Chersky, word reached the academy that the professor was acting erratically. Staff at the observatory voiced complaints that Prof. Novikov strayed from imaging routes planned for the Sky Mapping Project.

One of the directors, Dr. Ivan Kalinsky, had this to say about the matter. "We worked hard preparing the Orion project. We gathered light signatures from very faint stars. The telescope's mapping coordinates were set in stone. But the professor diverted the telescope and adjusted focus points as if it was her own private lens in her backyard. Massive gaps in our data were created by her actions."

It was only when her assignment in Chersky was complete that the scale of Prof. Novikov's misconduct was revealed. The star-mapping data under her authority included doctored imaging and falsified star readings.

Prof. Novikov has never stated her motives for misdirecting the telescope and altering data. Rumors abound at the academy that the Professor was influenced by the Ingall Beacon Hypothesis. The premise holds that an extraterrestrial super-civilization might conceivably force a group of stars into distinct artificial orbits around each other. This unnatural constellation would serve as a beacon to announce the presence of these "astro-architects" to the wider universe.

Dr. Kalinsky was asked if Prof. Novikov diverted from the Orion Project in order to search for evidence of aliens. "We don't humor nonsense like that at the academy," he said. "Even an advanced alien species wouldn't have the technology to push stars around like they were marbles. It would be implausible even for a science fiction comic book."

Attempts to contact Prof. Novikov for this report were unsuccessful.

CHAPTER 56

She has walked from Slow Pour back to her apartment building many times in the past. There are not too many surprises to be made on this brief journey. Nevertheless, Asmara stops in the middle of the street as cars around her slow to a halt.

Disorientation overcomes her. The surroundings are unfamiliar. Vehicles themselves are an oddity. The occupants in the cars, who are waiting for this pedestrian to move along, appear as fleshy organisms bound in a machine shell.

A car horn emits a fraction of a beep and Asmara snaps to attention. The woman driver makes a gentle arm motion which suggests Asmara should continue to the safety of the sidewalk. Within Asmara's head nod back to the woman, a dark impulse slithers from her mind. She has fiercely negative thoughts toward the driver in a bizarre overreaction to the car horn. These are not just unkind words. Asmara has an urge to destroy the car and the person in it. She has confidence she will soon have the capability to do such a thing.

. . . .

Jogging up the stairs in her apartment building, this hostility will not rattle loose from her bones.

Why would I think about hurting a stranger?

The bad energy does not dissipate. It intensifies. With every step she takes, the existence of the foreign object in her brain asserts itself. And it has gotten bigger. This is no mere headache.

As she stands in front of her apartment, a second aggressive urge arises. She wants to kick the door off its hinges. Asmara visualizes it crashing backward like a fallen domino. The thought is arousing. Next is a desire for this entire building to collapse into rubble, all from the influence of her destructive power. The nihilistic anger is shocking to herself.

Asmara stumbles into her apartment, looking for solace. She goes to her bedroom and collapses into the reading chair. Despite the fact she woke up only two hours ago, and even though she has a cup of caffeinated rocket fuel stimulating her nerves, her eyes are closing. There is no peaceful drift into slumber here. She is being dragged against her will.

The forced closure of her consciousness is an incubation period for the object in her brain. It needs stillness to grow.

. . . .

Her eyelids are difficult to lift. After some strain, the sluggish curtains rise.

Gravity and sleep unwound her body and melded it to the seat's curvature. She reforms herself into a less-slouched position and her back aches from the task.

Anxious fears try to pounce but her thoughts float around the room, unable to be pinned down. In this free-form state of calmness, a faint percussion emerges. It's an almost imperceptible rhythm, like tidal water lapping against a shore.

Without using her ears or eyes, a structure to the pulse is perceived.

It's an aura wavelength. She is receiving them again.

This time is different than the others. Asmara is not submerged by numerous radiating spirits all around her. There are two souls in this room and one of them is not Asmara's.

How do I get off this ride? How do I exit this movie?

The aura is not a wave passing through. It is an invisible presence in the center of the room. The phantom waits for Asmara to act first. With its distinct textures and colors, it is clear this wavelength is from her neighbor Inga.

The two women—one in physical form, the other not—acknowledge each other with an intersecting transmission.

Asmara opens her mouth to speak but stops short. She communicates by thought alone. Musical tones vibrate in her mind, replacing English. This is the same phenomenon from last night while she read on stage.

"Hello, Inga."

"Hello, Asmara." The responses are also telepathic tones.

"Where are you?"

"I don't know."

"Are you alive?"

Long pause. **"I don't know how to answer that."**

"Did this all start in Russia? With the telescope?"

"Yes. I know you read that article this morning."

"What happened at the observatory?"

"I learned the Ingall Beacon Hypothesis is real."

"Aliens moving stars around? What does it mean when they do that?"

"If an advanced species wanted to make their presence known in the universe, an artificial constellation would be a consistent display of information for billions of years. As long as the stars kept burning, their message would remain."

"How could stars ever be moved?"

"It would require a control over gravity we cannot conceive."

"What did the star arrangement look like?"

"The constellation consisted of several star-group orbits, each of them a different prime number. That is the mathematical equivalent of slapping someone in the face to say hello. It's not subtle. Prime numbers will catch the attention of any lifeform which has learned concepts of multiplication and division."

"I can see how that is a greeting card."

"A geometry was created by the implicit lines between these stars. It was a connect-the-dots you could do with your eyes, as obvious as the Big Dipper. But the results were utterly beautiful. Astonishing."

Asmara's throat seizes. The dot matrix test she took—that was not a facial-recognition exercise for medical research. She was looking at the Ingall Beacon constellation, but as dots on a computer screen instead of stars through a telescope.

Why did Professor Garrity trick me into viewing the pattern?

"Inga, you acted insane about that crooked line. And at The Naomi, you wanted the dimension to flood in. How can I trust you?"

"I am infected. It isn't my fault. Sometimes I'm in control. Other times not. The curse has been within me. And now it's within you. I know you've seen the constellation."

"How could you know that?"

"I saw the pattern in your room. On paper, perfectly rendered."

"How does looking at stars or dots create an infection?"

"The arrangement triggers reactions in the brain. Neurons fire differently once they're stimulated by those visual points. Embedded in the geometry is a single syllable of an alien Morse code. Delivered into a host, its instructions unfold. The initial message is a spark. From there, a blueprint for mutation ignites into an inferno. Hormone and protein production, metabolism, cell division—everything gets an override from these new commands."

"What were you turning into?"

"I was becoming one of the constellation creators. This process is how they replicate themselves across the universe. The creators leapfrog across galaxies. No spaceship travel is required. Rays of light do all the work. These beings reformulate their own clones on different planets, using the biology of existing lifeforms."

"How could you know this?"

"Their motivations emerged in my thoughts."

"What stopped your metamorphosis? How are you still human?"

"After the observatory, there was something within me—another entity, but one not completely formed. A lifeforce is locked in my skull. I listen to its screams. It considers itself a God trapped inside an insect."

"Why was your transformation incomplete?"

"A telescope error created shifts in the light signatures. The alien code was altered enough to prevent a full metamorphosis. Seven points in the constellation were misaligned in our lens."

"That's the crooked line..."

"It is not me captivated by the crooked line. That is the monster within me. It has tried to complete the transformation ever since."

"What happens after a full infection of someone on Earth?"

"The creators flood in their atmosphere through a portal. They only need one convert on our side to open the gate—a wormhole. That's what was happening at The Naomi last night. The red, green, and gray flood. You were the portal."

Asmara winces from a sharp pain. The foreign object which appeared in her brain earlier expands with a lurch.

When she refocuses her attention, Inga's wavelength fades away.

Inside the retreating aura a desperate melody calls out. The notes are faint. Inga is a powerless frequency in a vast alien symphony.

"I'm sorry, Asmara. I'm so sorry."

CHAPTER 57

The container is only a few pounds but its contents signify a heavy weight during this walk. Gravity pulls harder when you dread doing something.

The tarantula is out of its rock cave during this trek. Every footstep creates a jostling motion which must feel like an earthquake to the creature. And yet, there it is, at the front wall of the clear cube, observing the city environment passing by.

"Did you see that, Mom?" A young boy says on the sidewalk. "She has a big spider in there."

The subway tunnel entrance is in sight. She already texted Ryan that she is coming over and Zoe will be there, too. Next stop Oakland.

Acid eats away at the lining of Asmara's stomach.

Those two special people walked away from The Naomi last night with their sanity intact. Do I really have to involve Ryan and Zoe further?

Yes. Their shared story is already written and Asmara has accepted her role. From here, the pages turn on their own.

A soft wind brushes by. Asmara looks for evidence within the movement of air to see if it's caused by rising and falling paper leaves of the book she's trapped in. The passage of time is created when its words are read. But who is doing the reading?

This breeze compels her forward. All stories come to an end.

. . . .

It's loud. This aspect of the Oakland commute is an aggravation. When the train is freed from the restraint harness of transit stops downtown, it unleashes its potential. The vehicle becomes a thin dragon racing headlong in a straight line beneath the San Francisco Bay. But, damn, does this dragon roar. The train wheels screech as metal-on-metal contact produces an obnoxious wail.

The tunnel turns the window Asmara leans against into a black mirror. Her shadowed reflection is unkind. The pitted eye sockets staring back at her make Asmara's face look like a long-dead skull. Millions of gallons of bay water loom above her. The liquid mass would represent a mere raindrop compared to the flood of red, green, and gray alien fluids threatening to drown Earth.

The spider has climbed back into its rock cave. Maybe the vibrations of this rail commute are torture for its delicate senses. Zoe had texted earlier that she would love to take ownership of the tarantula. Asmara's initial thought on the idea of a hand-off was "no way." This animal has been a pivotal piece of machinery to the clockwork of the past few days. It has been in tune with human-scale events surrounding it, perhaps even orchestrating the theater. This living cargo next to her is a precious commodity.

However, once again, it is destiny pulling the strings. Asmara's hesitation is unwound, with little resistance. It doesn't matter if she has misgivings—the tarantula is to be delivered to Oakland. That is the preordained outcome these shrieking train wheels deliver now. Zoe is another unwitting participant in a grander scheme.

The black mirror of the window dances with fluttering light as the tunnel exit is within range. Emerging from beneath the San Francisco Bay, the dragon train roars while West Oakland bursts into view.

. . . .

Asmara texts Ryan as she walks down the stairs from the elevated train platform to street level.

"Just got off the train. Gonna head over to your place"

Ryan replies. "I'm at your station. I'm near the guy playing guitar"

He came to greet me.

Even with a world in peril, chivalry is nice. Ryan will hold her hand as they drown in an apocalyptic alien flood.

While descending the stairs, acoustic guitar sounds rise to greet her. The music grows clear when she reaches the street. A young man plays his instrument on a bench. The musical notes vibrating in the air carry their own language, which she now understands. For the performer this is a recital of someone else's work, but for the original songwriter the chord progressions are about a life change he regrets. He moved to a new place and preferred his original home. Worst of all, he can never go back. This is not Asmara's interpretation, it's what each note proclaims in vivid detail.

She soaks in the auditory experience and Ryan approaches. He lowers his skateboard onto the ground and she puts down the spider cube. They collide in an embrace. People strolling by slow down to observe this emotional union.

After an extended grasp, Asmara and Ryan create enough separation to look at each other. His gaze is unmoving and filled with affection. Her focus drifts side to side, peering into each of his eyes. Especially his glass one.

Ryan is on to her. "Other than some depth perception issues, I can see everything you see. I'm not a cyclops freak."

"Come on. Stop it."

"I've already offered to tell you what happened."

"Not now."

"How's the spider bite?" Ryan says, leaning toward her face.

"It faded. Not even a mark."

"Maybe it was a kiss, not a bite."

They walk. The sky dims above as daylight bleeds away into dusk.

"Last night was... wild," Ryan says. "Something happened on stage, didn't it?"

"Yeah, I went insane for a bit. And there was more weird stuff today. This is beyond an anxiety attack for me. Stage fright can't explain everything. I'm not on stage anymore."

"What happened today?"

She pauses to tailor her answer into something digestible. "I thought someone was in my apartment today. The presence was as real as you next to me now. It even communicated."

"What did it say?"

"I can't tell you. It's too much."

"No matter what you describe, I won't think you're crazy."

She gives another curated answer. "I feel like the story I read at Word Bound has massive implications, for everyone. Something about it has put people in danger. This is a gut instinct I can't shake."

"You know you're describing paranoia, right?"

"Yes, I acknowledge that. It might be delusions of grandeur as well."

Ryan looks off into the distance before continuing. "My close friend developed bipolar in his mid-twenties. I was there at the onset. He obsessed over his adoptive parents. He had never discussed being adopted in all the years I knew him and then one day he wouldn't stop talking about it."

"What did he say?"

"He felt they were hiding things from him. Secrets about his birth parents. Conspiracies."

"That's rough."

"His condition worsened. Then one night he confronted his parents. The police came but no one was hurt. He was committed to an institution."

"How is he now?"

"Good. Three months after the incident, our friendship resumed. He staged a full recovery. He would joke about taking his meds. Years later the whole event became ancient history. He's married with a kid. A good job. I saw him a few weeks ago."

"Amazing."

"My point is, if you feel you may be having a mental health crisis, there is hope. There are many success stories of people being treated. Not everyone winds up terminally sick or on the street."

Asmara gives no response. Her mind chews on the anecdote and spits it out. She would love for the story to apply to her but the life preserver Ryan offered doesn't fit.

They walk in silence. To break the tension, she hands him the tarantula container, puts his skateboard on the ground and stands on it. With an awkward push, she cruises alongside Ryan. She places her hand on his shoulder for balance.

Minds go crazy, Asmara knows that. But in her case there is actual evidence of supernatural phenomenon. She's tempted to share it with Ryan. She could start with the wound which healed on her leg. Then there would be a pitstop over at the Europa serpent images. Together they could investigate the missing dot matrix email from Professor Garrity while discussing the Ingall Beacon star hypothesis. And for dessert, Asmara can recount all of the mind-reading she conducted at Word Bound. If any of those unspoken secrets are proven accurate, that would give everything else validity.

This full clip of persuasive ammunition goes in Asmara's back pocket. She will unload the barrage of evidence when it's most needed.

Asmara lifts her hand from Ryan's shoulder and runs her fingers through his hair.

"I'm glad your friend recovered," she says.

CHAPTER 58

Ryan stops at the edge of his driveway and puts down the spider cube. He faces Asmara and extends his arms at the height of her shoulders. She takes the cue with a step forward and docks into his gentle grip. The gesture is not romantic. It is an act to bring about mutual focus.

"She's a young teenager," Ryan says. "We shouldn't subject her to talk of mental illness and paranoia. We have to act normal."

"I agree."

"If Zoe asks any tough questions about your stage freak out, we'll downplay them together, okay?"

"Got it."

Ryan opens the front door and there is Zoe sprawled across the couch, looking at her phone. Asmara stands in the doorway and awaits a reaction. Zoe lifts her head and before she finishes saying "what's up?" her attention is back to the phone.

A welcoming parade wasn't expected but that was harsh. "How are you?" Asmara asks the girl.

The word "good," or something like it, is muttered in reply.

"Have you recovered from last night?"

"Yeah."

"Did your dad say anything about being out late?"

"Nah."

Asmara walks through the living room while observing Zoe immersed in her phone.

I guess teenagers are gonna teen. Still, this empty engagement is hollow.

She is one step from the kitchen when a noise rattles behind her. Acting as a human projectile, Zoe crashes into Asmara with a hug. She's holding the Word Bound poster which was concealed behind the couch for this sneak attack.

Zoe looks up with a manic grin. "I was just playing with you! Will you autograph my poster?"

. . . .

Asmara bounces the pizza slice in her hand. The thick crust is assured of producing a loud crunching sound. She blows a steady breath over the steaming cheese. The exhale is a ritual more than a legitimate way to alter the food's temperature.

Ryan stares at the slice in front of him but does not reach for it. "Oh, yeah, I should mention..."

Asmara and Zoe bite into their pizza wedges.

"...there's something about this deep dish brand..."

The two females cry out. "Unnghhh!" "Mmmphh!"

Both had the roof of their mouth burned by molten lava sauce.

"...it takes forever to cool down."

Asmara and Zoe negotiate with the pain-inducing pizza. Asmara tilts her head to get the tortuous morsel to balance on her back teeth, away from sensitive oral tissue. Zoe juggles the red-hot edible with her tongue, keeping the food aloft in her mouth for as long as possible.

The defense mechanisms fail and both bites of pizza get spit onto the table, plopping next to Ryan's plate.

"What is wrong with you two?!" he says while fighting a smile.

Where there might normally be revulsion, instead is only shared laughter. Zoe grabs a napkin and disposes of the half-chewed lumps.

After heat dissipation, the food is no longer a trauma source and conversation resumes. Word Bound makes its inevitable return. Ryan mentions how Europa is on the event poster.

"Is that the planet which might have alien life on it?" he says.

Asmara sends a dirty look his way but it is futile. He has no clue about her discovery within the Caerus space probe images.

"Europa has aliens?" Zoe asks.

"Maybe," Ryan says. "I read it has the best chance of alien life in our solar system because it's a planet with oceans."

Asmara makes another stern face but Ryan misreads the cue.

"Right," he says, "it's a moon, not a planet. It orbits Saturn, right?"

"Jupiter."

"Yeah, that's it."

"I had an astronomy class last year," Zoe says. "Why wasn't there talk about aliens on Europa?"

"Because it's a theory," Ryan says. "There might only be tiny microbes under the ice, but that still counts as alien life."

An appearance of distracted wonder washes over Zoe. She imagines aliens in those waters and her visions are not of microbes.

. . . .

Zoe walks over to a pile of mail on the kitchen counter. "Can I open this? It's a credit card offer. I need the paper inside."

Ryan only mutters "um..." before she tears open the envelope. She finds an interior page which has a blank side. Zoe goes to the paper towel rack and tears off two sheets. She returns to the table with the paper products and the pen Asmara used to sign the poster.

"We did this in art class," she says. "It's blind collaboration. We each add to a drawing without knowing what the other two contributed. I'll draw first and hide it with the paper towel. The next person will continue from a few lines I leave open. In the end, it will be one object."

"That's cool," Ryan says. "I get it."

"Yeah, I'm down," Asmara says. "But what's the context? What's the object we're trying to draw?"

"It'll be one of the aliens on Europa."

Asmara sighs at the inescapable outcome of it all. In trying to shield Zoe from these matters she instead stumbled straight into them.

Zoe huddles over the blank paper and begins to draw. The position of her arm blocks the view of her sketch. Every twenty seconds she looks up to make sure no one is peeking. Ryan and Asmara bide their time with a discussion about the One Track Mind store.

Five minutes later, Zoe slams down the pen and places a paper towel over the majority of her drawing. She has drawn on one-third of the page, the remaining two-thirds are blank. The paper towel conceals everything of her drawing except seven horizontal lines which end abruptly.

Ryan drags the pen and stacked papers toward himself.

"You can only continue the alien from my lines," Zoe says.

"I'm clear on the concept," Ryan says as he begins drawing.

Zoe launches into a discussion about tarantula ownership but Asmara cannot foresee herself giving the creature to an eighth grader.

"The spider bit me on the face last night," Asmara says. "I can't hand off a dangerous animal to you."

"Then why did you bring it?"

Asmara has no answer, even for herself.

After a long, circular argument, Ryan comes to the rescue by smacking the table with his hand and extending the pen.

"I'm done," he says. "Asmara, the alien awaits you."

Both paper towel sheets are on top of the drawing now. Ryan left his own seven lines jutting into the final open space on the paper.

Having never been a good drawer, her instincts guide the ink strokes. Inspiration comes from the stacked pixels she saw deep in the icy crevasse of Europa. What does a three-mile-long alien serpent look like?

Her drawing hand moves on its own. Thin streaks of blue ink are left in the wake of the pen as it glides across paper. With a delicate touch, she shades and contours details in the art, giving it depth. She's never done the technique before and it is not something she was taught.

Minutes later comes a poke in the arm. Zoe hands over her phone to Asmara. The girl leans in and with a whisper says, "Record Ryan with this.

Don't say anything."

The screenface shows the device is already recording video. Ryan returns from a bathroom visit and Zoe proclaims a bet that she can make him raise his hands above his head without touching him. She describes it as a hypnotism trick she learned.

"No, you're trying to prank me," Ryan says. "Where's your phone?" He neglects to consider Asmara an accessory to this crime in progress. Asmara pretends to draw while aiming the phone with her other hand.

"It's in my pocket," Zoe says, patting her hip. "So, I'm going to do a sequence of nine arm and leg movements. You're going to follow each move. On the tenth body position I guarantee your arms will go above your head, even if you don't want them to."

"What? This is stupid. Fine. Hurry up."

Zoe bends down and stands up quickly, kicking one leg out. After a pause of consideration Ryan recreates the action. The other leg gets lifted high by Zoe. Ryan mimics. An aggressive one-two fist combo punches the air. Ryan's impatience is showing but he swings his arms in a similar fashion. It's not clear what these movements add up to but Zoe continues the series. On the tenth and final maneuver, Zoe raises her hands above her head. Ryan's arms remain hanging low. The look of skepticism he had droops into total defeat.

"I just did some viral dance bullshit, didn't I?"

Zoe cackles with laughter and her upraised arms fall into a hug around Ryan. "Ha! It's called the Fight Monkey! I made you do it."

"I knew this was a trick. Where's your phone?"

Zoe runs over to Asmara to secure the incriminating evidence.

"You were in on this?" Ryan says. Asmara feigns surprise.

Zoe reviews the footage. "Only little kids do this dance. I'll speed up the edit so it looks like you're dancing."

"Don't post that crap."

"I won't. But I'm going to use it as blackmail against you. Now you have to take me skating any time I ask."

Ryan turns toward Asmara and flashes a wink. He knew this was a dance prank all along. Indulging the deception is a way to give Zoe a laugh. He is willing to look like a fool to bring her some joy.

As the three of them crowd around the phone to watch the absurd dance video, the finished alien drawing sits revealed on the table.

The different artistic styles, each drawn in isolation from the others, have produced a cohesive image. A massive sea snake curls around itself in an intricate knot. Hooked protrusions spiral down the length of its body, like the fleshy armor on lizards. The animal's skin also has an elaborate patchwork of blotches, similar to cheetah spots.

There is silence around the table as they each observe these matching patterns. Three people independently creating a seamless animal like this is incredible, if not impossible. Asmara's impulse is to downplay any meaning to the strange phenomenon but she doesn't bother. It's too late.

The crazed look in Zoe's eyes means her young mind is cranking full throttle and generating fantastical conspiracies. Asmara is acquainted with that mental state. She's been living the same way non-stop for the past week.

With a tentacled grip, a wave of regret squeezes Asmara's heart until it aches.

I might be the worst thing that ever happened to this girl.

CHAPTER 59

Whenever there is a custody battle over a dependent loved one, it's always the tarantula that suffers. Asmara and Zoe settle their argument and agree to have Ryan keep the spider at his place for now.

Before Zoe adopts Asmaraña, she is asked to research the logistics of animal care. She needs to prepare for a new mouth to feed, even if it's being fed crickets.

"It's not like I'm buying a gun," Zoe says, skeptical of the stalling tactic. "I don't need a waiting period."

Asmara still has doubts about giving the spider to Zoe. This escrow arrangement involving Ryan is a way to buy more time. Haggling with Zoe also helped distract the girl from her focus on the alien drawing. Asmara presented the logic that Europa is an ocean moon and it's no surprise they all sketched a similar sea creature.

Zoe is not persuaded. Neither is Ryan. Or Asmara.

She has operated as a puppet today, tasked with delivering the tarantula to Oakland. Under whose orders, though? Now that Asmara and the spider are here, this puppet's strings have been cut. It's not clear what's next.

. . . .

Zoe stands on one of Ryan's skateboards in the living room, rocking the wheels back and forth on the carpet.

"So, you've never skateboarded? Even as a kid?" Zoe asks Asmara.

"Not really."

"Have you snowboarded?"

"Once. I had a hard time."

"Have you surfed?"

"No."

Asmara expects the girl to give a snide remark like, "So, what *do* you do?" Instead, Zoe shows the warmth of her true colors yet again. "Well, you should do that stuff with us," she says. "It'll be cool."

Plausible scenarios of those activities float before Asmara. In them, she knocks her teeth out skateboarding, breaks her leg snowboarding, and almost drowns while surfing. The drowning is interrupted only due to a fatal shark attack.

"Sure," Asmara says. "Those could all be fun."

Zoe hops onto the couch and addresses Ryan. "You know the blackmail video I have of you dancing? Do you want to make a deal?"

"I don't negotiate with terrorists."

"I'll delete the video if we can watch the Ryan's Line documentary."

"Not interested."

"Come on," Zoe says. "I have to go home soon. It'll be fun to watch it before I head back."

"You two can check it out. I'll leave the room."

"The point is to watch it with you. It's just fifteen minutes long."

After a prolonged silence, Ryan mutters "Fine."

Zoe jumps up to grab the TV's remote control. "Yay!"

The teen zips through the TV's interface to reach a video-streaming service. "*From Here to There*" is searched and found. Zoe sits on the ground close to the screen. She gives a quick head swivel to make sure everyone is well situated for the feature. It begins.

Gray pixels rotate in a swirl. The camera pans back until the rolling motion is revealed as close-up footage of skateboard wheels on a ledge. The point of view recedes further from the slow-motion spinning wheels. Ryan's full frame on the skateboard is visible. As he reaches the edge of the tall ledge and is about to leap into history, the image freezes.

A continued pan backwards shows the Ryan's Line video is playing on a TV within an office littered with skateboard memorabilia. A haggard-looking middle-aged man steps in front of the frozen screen. His eyeglasses have thick frames and he points at the screen with a heavily-tattooed arm.

"People looked at this spot for years," the aging punk rocker says. "All they did was yap their mouths. But Ryan Q Smith? That dude went from here... to fuckin' *there.*"

A heavy bass line barges into the audio mix and it's joined by shrieking guitars. The freeze frame snaps back to action and a young Ryan flies through the air on his skateboard.

Back in the living room, Zoe gives another head turn to see if the others wear a smile as big as hers.

For Asmara, the rest of the documentary is repetitive. Ryan's stunt is shown over and over again and a rotating cast of talking heads say the same thing—the skateboard leap was epic. Despite this, it's an impressive experience to watch. The commentators lavish praise on Ryan's legacy. Every few minutes she casts a glance his way and he appears unmoved. Ryan might as well be viewing a documentary about the Fight Monkey dance he performed.

Asmara's attention dissociates from the video and instead overlooks the present moment as a whole. The teenager sitting on the floor is captivated in adoration of her mentor on the screen. Ryan remains an enigma but Zoe is a positive influence in his life, and vice versa. They're a unique team and they have allowed a third person into their world.

As Asmara eases into the calming atmosphere, an involuntary contraction tightens along the left side of her face, where the spider bit her. The corner of her mouth stretches wide toward her ear. It is a crazed, artificial half-smile. The clenched muscles are a reminder this normalcy in Ryan's living room is an illusion. There is no way to suppress the madness unleashed at Word Bound last night.

Next comes a stirring—an actual, physical displacement—in the rear base of her skull. The foreign object in her brain squirms and grows in size again.

CHAPTER 60

She has not cried once these past few days. Even as her sanity is debased at every turn, there have been no tears of self pity nor streams borne of anger. (Alien oils draining from her face at Word Bound doesn't count.)

The fate of the world weighs on Asmara and the pressure did not spill tears. Until now. It is Zoe who releases the dam.

Leaning against the frame of Ryan's front door, Zoe is engaged in farewell banter. Like most friendly departures, no one is in a hurry to get the last word. This has gone on for ten minutes as each goodbye is postponed with more chatter.

The lingering closure leads to a cool caress of tears tumbling down Asmara's cheeks. She wipes them away without anyone noticing. The distress stems from the fear this will be the last time she sees Zoe. Their paths crossed and now a dead end may await them both. Even if no alien flood occurs and life goes on, this could still be a permanent goodbye. Asmara must ask herself if Zoe is better served without exposure to a crazed woman haunted by visions.

"All right, Zoe," Ryan says, heading toward the kitchen. "I'll text you tomorrow if I go skating."

"Goodnight," Zoe says. "Thanks for watching *From Here to There.*'"

A dismissive arm wave is his response as he rounds the corner.

Asmara seizes the private moment with Zoe. She jogs up and gives the girl a deep hug. They detach and Zoe's face indicates she is aware the embrace carried a silent burden. "Did we do something wrong last night at Word Bound?" the girl asks. "Was it a bad thing?"

"No. I would never ask you to do something improper."

"Ryan and I did everything you said. The crowd loved it."

"I'm just shook up about certain things. It's scary when you can't trust your own thoughts."

One more hug.

Before Zoe ducks under the low tree branch to head home, she turns. "Whatever is going on with you, maybe you're seeing things the way they really are. The rest of us see an illusion."

This time Asmara lets the tears fall freely.

. . . .

After collecting herself, she meets Ryan in the kitchen. He deposits a handful of peanuts into his mouth.

"You're still hungry after the pizza?" Asmara asks.

"No, but I always snack at night," he says, careful not to spit out crumbs. "Doesn't matter if I'm hungry or not."

"No judgment here."

They stand in the kitchen without speaking for some time. The only sound is Ryan's jaw reducing peanuts into smaller bits of rubble. This wordless atmosphere hangs heavy in the room. After a spell, Asmara grabs her coat which is draped over a chair. She came here with divine instructions to deliver the tarantula to Oakland. The mission is complete. It's time to go.

Ryan walks with her to the living room. He lays down on the couch, which is strange to do while a guest is leaving. She opens the front door and he covers his eyes with the palms of his hands—also unusual.

Moving slowly within her exit, it seems no words are going to be spoken, not even a goodbye.

Asmara takes one step outside and can no longer contain the pressure of such a lousy departure. She turns to say something to Ryan. Anything. Before she utters a word, his voice calls out from behind his concealed face. "Please don't go."

Asmara strides toward the couch and she lays on top of him with a graceful distribution of weight. It is a soft landing.

She wants to comment on her own assertive behavior—maybe crack a joke—but she can't think of anything to say. Ryan wraps his arms around her and they create, what feels like, a permanent embrace.

The physical union isn't arousing for either of them. Far from sexual, this bond is more like a survival strategy. They're holding onto each other to stay alive within the fractured reality crumbling around them. Asmara and Ryan each serve as the other's life preserver.

. . . .

They do not fall asleep on the couch. Eventual stirring leads to exhausted sighs. Sailing together into dreams would have been nice. Instead, they rise to seated positions.

Ryan rubs his eyes and turns to Asmara. "If you prefer to go home tonight, I can drive you back to SF. No problem. However, you also are welcome to stay here."

"There's no way I'd make you drive over the bridge," Asmara says. "I feel bad imposing on you, though."

"Of course you can stay. I will fold out the couch for you like we did last time. Or I can sleep here and you sleep in my room alone if you want privacy. My sheets are clean plus the..."

"Can I sleep in your bed with you?"

The words vibrate in the air. Asmara doesn't regret saying them. She also didn't bother to include a sultry look with the proposal. Her face is a droopy mess of half-closed eyes and disheveled hair anyway.

Ryan blinks a few times. An answer spills out. "Yeah. I'd like that."

. . . .

She uses the same toothbrush from her previous overnight stay. While in the bathroom, Asmara does not evaluate her appearance in the mirror. She focuses on her eyes. They have seen so much lately. Demons, floods, human souls—were they all truly observed?

Her pupils are dilated. There is no reason for them to be this large and yet the dark portals stare back at themselves. Everything she has seen was swallowed by these chasms. Nothing escapes.

A man waits for her in the bedroom. She is attracted to him. She trusts Ryan. However, they met just a few days ago and it is not enough time to truly know anyone.

Asmara isn't nervous to any great degree. There are a few butterflies in her stomach but they pale in comparison to the monster growing in her head. It's not clear a sexual encounter with Ryan is imminent, anyway. They are both tired and life itself is strange right now. This odd haze has a chilling effect on her libido. Still, climbing into bed with a man is a serious matter.

She strips down to her underwear and her bare thigh is exposed in the bathroom light. Where there once had been a bloody injury, there is no visible wound, no scar, no scratch.

. . . .

Ryan is already in bed. A small vanilla-scented candle burns on a nearby desk. He's laying on top of the covers in a T-shirt and boxer briefs. His legs are still hairy. Again, his hands are pressed against his eyes. It is not an image of seduction.

"Are you in pain?" Asmara asks. "I can sleep in the living room."

He lifts his hands to give her a glance which turns into a blatant double take. He initiates a head-to-toe examination of her body but she doesn't hold it against him. He is a guy and she is a woman standing in her underwear in his bedroom doorway.

"Stay here. Please," he says. "I'm not in pain. Things are surreal."

She climbs on top of him and the sensual union is *very* different than the fully-clothed contact on the couch. That was a search for security, this is raw carnal delight. Large fields of skin on their legs and arms slide over each other, producing waves of pleasure in Asmara. One of her stray thoughts tries to recall how long it's been since she felt gratification like this. The memory search is dissolved into bliss.

There is no more haze producing a chilled libido. That fog has evaporated upon first touch. Within a few short moments, Asmara is lost in the best kind of disorientation. She could have sworn she was on top of Ryan one breath ago. She is now on her back, his weight a fabulous pressure. The room was lit when she entered. Now the lights are off. Asmara cannot recall how kissing commenced. However, she finds herself pulsating in and out of the act. Blankets and sheets dance around the couple in celebration. These inanimate objects come alive as they move without human intervention.

Inside the pleasure, Asmara is sometimes her own spectator, reacting to Ryan. Other times, actions occur through dominant decisions of her own. There are not many complete thoughts. She exists as a flow of snapshot experiences, none lasting long enough to examine before another surprise arrives.

At some point, an observation does take hold. *This is like swimming.* The parallel is a stretch but she indulges the dreamy comparison. Both her and Ryan's combined motions act as a form of treading water. They swim in a sea of gentle fabric. The loose bedding around them continues to swirl and dance until it becomes a slow-turning whirlpool.

Asmara slips underwater. She is not afraid of drowning.

She can breathe just fine down here.

. . . .

It is later now. The swimming stopped. The whirlpool is unwound to calm equilibrium. Asmara has been under the water's surface for a long time and she floats in suspended animation. Not only is she able to breathe in this submerged state, there is soft talk with Ryan in the darkness. He has joined her in the depths. Their whispers are affectionate. The words they use roll out slowly and there are long pauses between each bit of conversation. These extended silences grow until, during her next inhale, she will not be awake to experience the exhale.

Her lungs reach capacity and begin to deflate. Asmara departs into oblivion.

CHAPTER 61

Asmara has always relished that rare perception of being aware she's in a dream. Full lucid dreaming is difficult to obtain but she does get close a few times a year. An uncanny movie will be playing in her mind and she questions her starring role. This time she is certain her conscious mind is alert inside her sleep-paralyzed body.

The dream is simple. Within it, Asmara is back under the stage at The Naomi. A column of light splits the darkness and she puts her hand in the white beam. Motes of dust floating in the bright ray cease their aimless drift and move with purpose. Above her palm, the specks migrate into a pattern. The hovering shape is extraordinary. It is a replica of the Ingall Beacon constellation. If her neighbor Inga is correct, this dot arrangement is a planet-killing weapon created by hostile aliens. And yet it is lovely in her hand. She stares at the geometric brilliance of the grid.

There is nowhere more private than one's own dream. However, treachery permeates the dark space. She is being tricked into staring at the constellation, even while asleep. This is a set-up for further cosmic infection.

In the dream, Asmara gives a sharp exhale and the pattern of dust scatters. In the waking world, the wheeze makes her upper-body lift off the bed she's laying on.

Ryan's voice rattles next to her. "That must have been some nightmare."

"Yes, it was."

"Your breathing got all crazy. What did you dream?"

"I was under the stage at The Naomi. I saw something beautiful which became dangerous."

"What was it?"

"A piece of art. It's hard to describe. Did my gasping wake you?"

"No. I was already awake."

Asmara rolls over and Ryan's silhouette shifts in the dim light. His hands are pressed against his eyes again.

"You didn't want to watch the documentary, did you?"

"Not really."

"Why is that event so painful to you?"

No reply. Asmara gives his forearm a gentle grip and she pries one hand from his face. "Please tell me."

His head slowly turns to her. "My life is based on a lie."

"What are you talking about?"

"Ryan's Line never happened. At least not the way it is portrayed."

"I've seen the video. How could it be fake?"

He sighs. "I've never told anyone this. Ever."

Asmara braces for a mind-bending revelation. Come what may, it is an honor he trusts her this much.

"The jump was real," Ryan says. "It's the famous landing—the narrow roll-away which no one can reproduce, that was a fraud."

"How so?"

He takes a deep breath. "The day we filmed the trick, there was construction in the plaza. By sheer chance, wood panels had been vertically stacked next to where I rolled away. The panels were the same height as the ledge. They added a foot of width and my wheels rode their surface. The camera angle didn't pick up this broad landing I had. The filmer and photographer who documented the trick never saw the wood either. They were on the other side. I'm the only one who knows. Ryan's Line is a lie."

Asmara heard every word Ryan said and yet she's still waiting for the big reveal. Surely, she will be shook to her core once she comprehends the gravity of what he described. No such feeling arrives.

"There was extra space where you landed your skateboard?"

"Yes."

"Um. So what?"

"That is cheating. The clip is famous because of the skinny landing area. I've never corrected the lie."

There is nothing left for Asmara to interpret. A flash of empathy visits her but it flutters away. She is devoid of any deep heartache for his burden. His problem sounds trivial and self-inflicted.

Asmara tries to force-feed him a different perspective. "Ryan, this has been your torment for a decade? A white lie regarding a toy?"

He sits up in the bed, his back flush against the headboard.

She continues. "You're going to resent me for saying this, but have you maybe tortured yourself for no good reason?"

Even though she only sees his outline, Ryan's body goes rigid.

"No good reason?" he says. "You can't imagine the extent of this lie."

"You fudged the history books on a skateboard maneuver. Who cares? No one was hurt. You had me thinking you made a deal with the devil."

Ryan gives off heat. His anger is palpable. "I've betrayed many people. I've lied to their faces. It eats away at me."

"Maybe it's time to tell the truth to your peers. Do a video interview. Make a post online. If you feel badly, do something about it."

"That's the point I'm trying to make. I know what needs to be done and I can't do it. I always told myself I'd admit what happened. Every year it got harder to do. When they made the documentary it felt impossible to make things right."

"Ryan, I don't want to insult you, but no one outside of skateboarding gives a shit about this. A video from ten years ago does not define you."

"But it *does* define me. I've been congratulated hundreds of times for something that didn't happen. It's hard to erase a myth."

Asmara would like to alleviate the regret he carries, yet she finds his predicament ridiculous. Thoughtless words spill out. "You could end this whole made-up trauma tomorrow with a confession and you know it."

A stillness descends in the bedroom. Ryan's gaze is not visible in the low light but its presence is withering.

"I'm sorry," she says. "That was too harsh."

His silhouette looms larger now. The silence is unsettling.

Asmara tries to backtrack. "Again, I'm sorry. I hate the act of lying as well. So, I'm sure it haunts you."

Ryan's upper-body slides down the headboard and he lays horizontal, staring at the ceiling.

The room temperature changes, or at least for Asmara it does. This frigid sensation is not the absence of heat. It's a different type of stimulation.

She's receiving Ryan's aura wavelength.

The cobbled-together cauldron in her mind no longer works as a blocking defense. Its pieces lay in a worthless heap.

A burning pain surges in Asmara's head. For hours she had ignored the foreign object which invaded her skull. No more. This is not mere discomfort. The parasite stirs.

She isn't sure what the solid mass consists of, but the pressure building inside her is not ambiguous. The object stretches the anatomy of her head and neck to the point where its shape is distinct. No longer is it roughly spherical. The invader branches out in a star-like pattern, its five pointed limbs burrowing as it expands.

Next to her, Ryan's wavelength pulse is unobstructed. Like tuning into a precise radio frequency, the fidelity of his soul has been amplified.

He is a good person, the graceful turbulence of his emission makes that apparent. Ryan cares for Asmara and there are no malicious intentions. However, his wavelength is inhabited by a structure which dominates the inner realm. It is a dark cathedral he has built and stuffed with regrets about his life. Ryan's aura is so detailed that Asmara navigates its space as if she's inside it. The place is a shrine of insecurities. Central to the structure is his decade's worth of lies surrounding Ryan's Line. The dishonesty has calcified into stone columns which sustain the framework. Walls ooze with falsehoods about that event which never healed.

Asmara does not question the toxicity of his burden anymore. At some point this started with a white lie regarding a toy. It has metastasized into an all-consuming cancerous growth. In his everyday life, Ryan is not a liar. His aura is unyielding about that. But this cathedral echoes with a cruel gospel—that it's human nature to torture ourselves in ways which are incomprehensible to anyone else.

The depths of his wavelength dive lower until Asmara enters pits of despair in his memory. Here are the worst moments of his life. Many of these are inherent disappointments of being alive—from teenage heartbreak to the death of family and friends.

One such dip in the aura is unimaginably low. Asmara can't see the bottom of this conspicuous chasm. Decency dictates she stop her exploration. Yet having peeked over the edge, she can't crawl back out.

Down she goes. Things get dark.

Darker still.

Until there is a horrible flash of light.

CHAPTER 62

Now it is Asmara pushing the palms of her hands against her eyes. She tries to suppress the vision of what she has seen. A froth of acidic revulsion builds in her chest and is about to erupt.

Ryan turns to Asmara to investigate why she trembles.

His arm bridges the short distance between them as he runs his fingers through her hair. This physical contact confirms Ryan's existence and Asmara needed validation he is alive. The flash of light she witnessed in his aura represents an act which could have taken him from her, before they even met.

It took place years ago but the event is present now. Ryan argues with his profoundly disturbed younger brother, who is wracked by drug abuse and delusions. A gunshot pierces the morning air.

Ryan earlier spoke to Asmara about his friend who overcame mental illness. It is a testament to Ryan's character that, in his effort to calm Asmara, he referenced that other redemptive story of healing and not the horror he endured from his brother.

His eye was sacrificed and a reward of eternal gratitude was granted. He cherishes being alive. A reservoir of optimism resides in his aura but he struggles to maintain it. His positivity does not flow freely and he has to nurture it.

"Can I tell you how I lost my eye?" Ryan asks.

An aura knows when it has been examined.

Asmara glides a fingertip down the side of his face and, with the lightest stroke, traces a circle around his right eye.

"You don't have to tell me," she says. "Because I already know."

"How could..." His confusion gives way to acceptance. Ryan rests his head on the pillow, looking upward. He releases a whisper. "I believe you."

"I'm glad you're still here, Ryan. We're both right where we are supposed to be."

She throws a leg over his body and buries him in an embrace. This vulnerable moment is more intimate than their previous bond of pleasure.

Their breathing aligns. With each shared exhale they act as an engine releasing the pressure they've built.

. . . .

Asmara needs to scream. Ryan is asleep next to her and she doesn't want to alarm him. The foreign organism in her brain pulsates. Each expansion entails knife-wounds of pain. She tries to concentrate on the presence of this parasite in her head. Perhaps with scrutiny, the invader will be revealed as an imaginary condition she created.

The star-shaped thing at the interior base of her skull is aware it's being monitored. It greets Asmara with a wide stretch of its limbs. Each bit of displaced tissue and muscle sends bolts of electricity through her head. There is no way her imagination could self-inflict harm like this.

Every millimeter expansion of its size shows how the monster is well-adapted to its environment. Limbs probe with confidence, looking for something specific. An alien wavelength emerges, like a noise you don't notice until your ears tune to it. The wretched starfish is trying to tap into the exotic fuel Asmara has distributed within her body. It seeks the substance she harnessed before Word Bound, when her panic went nuclear and was then stored.

The dots are now as easy to connect as Ingall Beacon stars. These things happening in her head are the transformation catalyst Inga spoke about. Asmara is still infected by the unnatural constellation. This twenty-nine-year-old woman is about to evolve into a planet-hopping galactic virus. There are no psychological tricks or cauldrons to contain it any more.

During the extraction of alien fluids during Wound Bound, when she drained away the portal, a drop of gray oil attached itself to a single neuron in her brain. It embedded within the neural cluster holding Asmara's childhood memory of swimming underwater in Lake Tahoe. What better place to hide a flood? The microscopic foreign invader was enough to restart the metamorphosis.

The incubation is over. It's time to destroy the planet.

She blindly grasps for a string of faith to climb out of the abyss. There is one hopeful thread, the same one she's used to rescue herself before: This demented crisis *must* be the effect of schizophrenia. Paranoid delusions are a hallmark of that savage affliction.

Asmara gives Ryan's profile a loving stare as he sleeps unbothered by the turmoil next to him. She longs to wake him up and tell him goodbye. Whether she's a one-woman alien invasion or a crazy person, this will be the last time she sees him. Her fingertips hover above his lips and each breath produces a soft wind on her skin. The universe sent this special man to her—a guy who did not flee from her madness—and now it is taking him away. No part of reality is assured anymore but the way he makes her feel is not an illusion.

She positions herself above his sleeping face. Getting as close to a kiss as possible without touching Ryan, Asmara breathes in his gentle exhale.

. . . .

Standing upright offers no relief to the pain in her head. The five-fingered thing in her skull has a firm grip on her lower brain. It squeezes her cerebellum to let Asmara know who is in control. If this monster desired, it could kill her by snapping her brain stem like a twig. But, no, it needs her alive to siphon the fuel dispersed in her body.

She places both hands against the wall to steady herself as she shuffles to the living room. Once there, she turns on the lights and is blinded by the glare. For lack of any strategy, she sits on the couch.

A hospital visit would be pointless. Doctors would commit her to an insane asylum before they believed her story of alien possession.

Near to the couch is the Word Bound poster. Zoe must have forgotten to take it with her. When Asmara views her artwork, a dose of pleasure electrifies everything above her shoulders. Pain has transmuted into ecstasy. However, she is not the intended recipient of this rush. Dopamine floods through her brain and the parasite indulges in the nectar it helped release. Asmara is a bystander as the creature deciphers hidden information within the art, a process which unlocks even more chemicals inside her.

Boiling the art down to its essence creates a liquid language about the artist—things Asmara didn't know about herself. The alien absorbs this communication to further facilitate the metamorphosis.

She leans the poster back against the wall. The geyser of visual pleasure is closed shut and a sizzling headache stirs again.

Asmara closes her eyes and prepares to meditate. An escape hatch out of this danger must be summoned. The hand-like claw gripping her brain is threatened by the mental state Asmara seeks. It fears that if Asmara achieves a meditative trance, the metamorphosis will be stopped.

Daggers of pain try to disrupt her concentration. Instead of succumbing to the torment, Asmara does not react. It is not long before the parasite's knives stop their cutting. The beast is lulled into a calm frequency. Or that's what it wants Asmara to believe.

· ·

The rhythm of meditation carries no content and yet it fills Asmara's mind. Minutes have passed. It's impossible to guess how many. Her thoughts, empty as they are, speed up. This velocity ignites the energy source locked in her body. The combustion produces mental propulsion. She is about to fly.

There is no countdown to lift-off. Her consciousness is already rocketing forward into a dark void. This universe she entered is a membrane no deeper than her closed eyelids and yet the absence of light creates an unknowable depth. Her perception hurls at warp speed.

It's too much.

This is not meditation. She wants out. All she has to do is retract the delicate muscles which control her eyelids. The light of Ryan's living room will flood in and put a stop to this trip she did not consent to.

Her facial muscles don't respond to any commands. She has no face anymore. Asmara is disembodied, her consciousness now a cannonball in flight. The more she tries to locate her physical self the more distant that artifact of bone and meat becomes.

A flash appears in the darkness. There is a pattern within it but the light fades out of existence.

More darkness. Another flash. This time the light scorches a deeper imprint onto the surrounding black canvas before it dissolves. She recognizes the image. It's Ryan's living room.

My eyes are fluttering open.

Another long spell of emptiness discourages Asmara until a third burst of light creates a detailed impression. This time she sees the entirety of his living room from the vantage point of the couch. Since she cannot move, she must be immobilized in a lucid paralysis induced by meditation, or the alien. Or both. However, her eyelids fight to allow in more light.

There, on the other side of the room, is the plastic spider container. Asmara and Zoe agreed to have Ryan hold the tarantula until further notice. So, it is no surprise the critter is here.

The cube's lid is open.

Return to darkness.

Flash of light.

Each spasm of her eyelids grants her two seconds of visibility before the scene goes black.

The tarantula is on the living room floor, facing her.

Oh, no.

As the brief window of light closes, there is a twitch of motion. The spider moves toward her.

An agonizing duration of darkness ticks by, even though it's only seconds. When Asmara is able to see again, the spider is closer. This pattern continues. A tortuous strobe-light effect is created with each burst of light. The opening and closing of her eyes reveals the eight-legged animal will soon be on her.

Asmara curses her limbs and tries to activate them into motion. She has lost control of her motor functions but her skin retains its sense of touch. The pitter-patter of spider legs scurry up her leg.

A radiation bandwidth enters Asmara's brain. The tarantula transmits an aura and its wavelength is vast in detailed information.

The animal crawls up her chest.

Asmara tries to read this soul spectrum and the spider has an immense, coded library inside itself, far greater than any human's wavelength.

A series of leg taps tickle her neck until the tarantula emerges in her peripheral vision. It is like a dark sunrise across her face.

There is a moment of shock as the curved fangs plunge into the most plump part of her right cheek. The skin and muscle cleave open to make room for the spider's hypodermic needles. Venom flushes in and Asmara passes out.

CHAPTER 63

A fading pain from the spider bite dissipates across Asmara's face. The creature has vanished. She lifts her arms a few inches to determine she is no longer paralyzed.

Her vivid experience of rocketing outward through space has come and gone. She brought something back with her. A self-contained dimension—a holographic bubble—is now in this Oakland living room. The semi-transparent foreign realm is uncanny and the normalcy of the room around her is betrayed by a quivering haze. Furniture and walls squirm with an artificial veneer. This is an effect of the dimension-filter through which she views the room.

While observing a bookshelf against the wall, the coherence of the scene cracks from her unblinking gaze. Books blur in and out of focus. She tilts her head, looking for the magician's strings. When she resumes a normal posture, the illusion is revealed. The wall is a composite of light beams, all of which project the mere image of an ordinary living room. There is no telling where the rays of light originate.

A second layer of distinct imagery bleeds through the wall, unrelated to Ryan's home. As the embedded realm rises to the surface, Asmara isn't sure what she's looking at. Five shadowy pyramids hover, their dark edges fading into white. The shape of the vague triangles evolve into familiar outlines—they resemble silhouettes of people, from the shoulders up.

She strains her eyes and tries to find the sweet spot where this group is in focus. The living room wall recedes away. Five ghostly figures are the only visual remaining.

Asmara stands and takes a step toward the anonymous gathering which floats in the air. Their rigid, quasi-human faces carry no features except dark eye sockets. A reaction arises from the five individuals. They jostle and look at each other. After the flurry of movement, they lean forward to peer at Asmara. Sporadic head nods between them indicate they may be talking but Asmara hears no words and sees no visible mouths.

The inscrutable scene is now in focus. Their faces are not blank, they are wearing masks. These hard white shells are skull-like, but they do not display a menacing effect. Their design appears coldly clinical, for some unknown practical use.

Even though the masks are identical and expressionless, the central character of the five draws Asmara's attention. The stranger's subtle head tilt, the absence of nervous energy—this one recognizes Asmara.

They stare at each other. A gloved hand rises into view from below the floating figure and grips the side of its mask. As the skull-shell is peeled away, Asmara braces herself for an encounter with an alien being. Instead, a loose mane of brown hair falls down the sides of a woman's face. She appears to be mid-forties, with a patchwork of age lines settled into her features. The woman is masculine and feminine, simultaneously. Her eyes display a certain strength.

The total recognition this woman has toward Asmara is palpable. An almost familial mix of affection and concern radiates within the hologram. To reciprocate, Asmara jumpstarts her own facial recognition skills. A contoured map of this stranger's face is calibrated.

It's her.

This is really her.

The unmasked individual floating in the air, projected from another time and dimension, is Zoe.

An older Zoe.

Once the awareness takes hold, the physical comparison is undeniable. The teenage girl who walked out of Ryan's house a few hours ago is now three decades older and transmitting from the future.

A smile lifts upward on Zoe's face and droops into a frown of pity. She shakes her head while her sorrowful eyes glisten with tears. The two women share a moment of pure fascination with each other.

Beneath Zoe's floating projection, her hand comes into view as she waves it with a right-to-left swipe. In a surreal visual, a series of typographical words appear in the air. The blue-colored English letters, each five inches tall in a basic font, materialize in the wake of the arm gesture and they hover with a slow drift.

Asmara reads the message imprinted in air. It says: "Nod your head if you can read this."

Still in shock, Asmara indicates "yes" with a head bob.

Another hand swipe from Zoe. The previous message fades away and a new set of words formulate. "Asmara, I know you recognize me. We can see each other but we can't hear each other."

They exchange another smile.

Hand over hand, Zoe waves more words into existence. "Our transmission can break at any moment. Asmara, I am contacting you from the future. Do you believe me?"

Trust is hard to come by lately. Asmara has not forgotten the Patron, or Professor Garrity's deception, or Inga's ghost, or the monster in her brain.

She nods in approval anyway.

More words appear in the air. "Asmara, there's no time to explain everything. We can't risk a broken signal. You have to believe what I'm about to tell you."

Asmara braces for impact.

Zoe's chest heaves with deep breaths as she looks at Asmara with stern determination. A long swipe. "Asmara, you are the beginning of the end of the world. It all starts with you."

A violent shiver vibrates through Asmara's arms.

Zoe's movements are harsher now. "You understand what I'm saying. You already know the danger within you, don't you?"

Asmara's neck muscles seize and try to prevent her from nodding. Too late. She assents with a small tilt of her head.

"We cannot stop you. We can only ask that you stp th evl yurslf."

The projection of Zoe and her four companions stretches wide across the room. This distorted effect warps their heads in a grotesque manner and the image snaps back to its original shape. The masked figures look down and frantically attend to some unseen procedure.

A hand swipe produces gibberish letters before a complete sentence locks into place: "Our signal is breaking."

Zoe's face freezes as it becomes a pixelated grid of squares. Her portrait replicates and dozens of Zoes superimpose upon each other.

Again the projection reboots itself and the duplicates of Zoe coalesce into a single live feed. Her hands generate a series of incomplete messages.

"There's no time fr y"

"We can't fight th"

"Pl lstn to dngr jt"

Asmara shakes her head in frustration, pointing to the air where sentence fragments linger. She shouts to the unhearing audience. "I can't read these!"

Zoe looks left and right to her companions. They communicate as a group. Her face tightens with despair and a hologram projection of Zoe's hand juts forward into Asmara's face. It appears as real as if Zoe was in the room.

More sentences are attempted.

"Look at my hand. Miu gh rft"

"The recording will shw wy ghyp ds"

One message transmits with total clarity, like a poison arrow through the air.

"Asmra, u kill th world"

On the outstretched palm of Zoe's hand, a white square of illumination appears. Within this frame of light, a frenzied burst of recorded motion bounces on the surface of her skin. Zoe's hand acts as a screen for yet another projection.

"See fr yurself."

Asmara is reminded of being under The Naomi's stage, looking at the hole which served as a bright portal. She had grasped the column of light in her hand as it shined through the darkness.

The flickering spasms on Zoe's palm move so fast Asmara can't imagine how it is comprehensible. She takes a step forward. More detail is revealed. A screaming face here. A pillar of flame there. Yet the warp-speed slideshow is mostly blinking lights.

Another step toward the hand.

The sights are hard to process. There are still-frame moments and snippets of recordings. Thousands of them. Millions.

Zoe's hand thrusts past the final inches of distance and envelops Asmara's face. There is no physical contact because the hologram is not made of matter. But the palm covers Asmara's eyes and renders her helplessly captive.

The slideshow is indeed a series of blinking lights.

They are the worst lights Asmara has ever seen.

There is green.

And gray.

And red. So much red.

CHAPTER 64

The back of her neck grazes the tree branch. Asmara misjudged her forward lean under the limb and the oak bark gives a gentle scratch. This bite of pain distracts her enough to regain self-awareness. Her trance is broken. She has stormed out of Ryan's house and is marching over to Zoe's place across the street. It is a mission for reasons unknown. A possessed autopilot within her dictates every footstep. The alien parasite in her skull must have taken over.

This early hour is filled with cold, heavy air but Asmara's core temperature heats up. The night sky is a shade removed from solid black and the starless canopy hints dawn is near.

Forward movement continues. Her bare feet stomp across Ryan's driveway. The pace accelerates as Zoe's home grows closer.

Am I about to break into a teenager's bedroom and confront her about time travel?

In the middle of the street, Asmara stops with an awkward halt. A stubbed toe confirms her body motions are not voluntary.

Ten seconds ago she pried her eyes away from future-Zoe's hologram. The sights displayed on Zoe's hand were a blaze of horror but they were erased from Asmara's memory. No details from the future remain after the visions self-destructed. The only outcome of that experience is an all-consuming sense of purpose—she *must* go over to Zoe's. Asmara will understand why when she gets there. Until then, her feet are stuck on the road. Muscles strain in her legs as she tries to lift them.

Zoe's house beckons. The critical target is fifty feet away. Surely, the starfish embracing Asmara's brain is the reason she lost body control and it's forcing her toward Zoe.

No.

The parasite's wavelength reveals it does not want her to proceed. The creature has locked her feet in fear of whatever is waiting at Zoe's.

This alien vulnerability emboldens Asmara and puts her on the offensive. She picks up one foot and places it in front of the other. Another step follows.

If the parasite isn't driving her to Zoe's home, what is?

As Asmara crosses the street, the navigator is exposed. Her own subconscious steers the ship. Whatever it witnessed from Zoe's future hologram was suppressed but not forgotten. Now her primal instincts override all other decisions.

With one footstep pivot, Asmara's subconscious declares its intent.

Zoe's front door is ignored and Asmara makes an involuntary turn toward the home's garage. It would be an obscure destination except Asmara has a memory of visiting here. Ryan needed a crescent wrench one week ago.

There was significance to the trivial moment. A threat had existed in the shadows.

She grasps the handle to the garage's side door. It is unlocked. Her other hand has formed a fist around something. Fingers unclench to show she's holding the lighter Ryan used for his bedroom candle.

Asmara doesn't recall grabbing it before she left the house, but this small firestarter is Earth's last hope.

. . . .

She wants nothing right now. A grim host of problems threaten to engulf her but Asmara couldn't even describe what they are. Every breath is a sufficient reason to exist.

This could never be considered nirvana, however. The dynamite sticks strapped to her face preclude such bliss.

Asmara adjusts her seated position and sits cross-legged on the garage's concrete floor. The gray slab sends a deep chill into her and yet the shiver generates more internal heat.

This posture shift disturbs the peaceful emptiness and she is corrupted by intrusive thoughts. Asmara's contentment is a mere wave passing by. She observes her own serenity dissolve on a rocky shore. The coast here is jagged and menacing. Reality has returned.

I have to blow off my head to save the world, don't I?

Asmara lets the question float in front of her. Analyzing it with calm disinterest might allow for an escape route.

No off-ramp is revealed.

Dynamite is necessary. She needs to incinerate every molecule of this invader. Zoe's future slideshow presented the alternative.

The alien parasite stirs up Asmara's anatomy like a time-lapse cancer growth. Its starfish shape has sprouted tendrils which wrap down her spinal cord. The creature's wider limbs still grip her brain, searching for a take-over of the entire nervous system. An urgency underlies the alien's movements as it knows Asmara is plotting to explode her head with dynamite.

A complete mind-body possession by the parasite is imminent. From that point, a metamorphosis will turn Asmara into a portal for an Earth-devouring flood. The Ingall Beacon, a weaponized constellation of stars, will have spread its disease across the galaxy.

It must be stopped.

The parasite's tendrils expand like a root system throughout Asmara's skull. Filaments squirm and branch out with burrowing sensations in her sinus cavity and the back of her throat. The living threads of this alien twist into knots which push against the back of Asmara's eyes.

She flicks the lighter, as a test. A burst of sparks appear but there is no flame. The starfish freezes in fear.

Another thumb strike on the lighter's flint ignites the release of butane. A flame is born.

As the yellow torch undulates, motion stirs on both sides of Asmara's peripheral vision. From the dark corners of the garage floor, two long pillars emerge and arc upward. Once these growing columns reach the ceiling they descend toward Asmara. The massive spears are insect-like legs and their pointed tips glide over her shoulders, forming an embrace.

The Patron is here. Its appendages aren't primed to kill, for the dynamite-strapped target is already about to expire on its own. The gentle cage its legs form over Asmara's body carry an affection. The Patron is saying goodbye.

These sleek black limbs have been scrubbed clean of any chiseled words into the armor. The written story once inscribed in the shell has reached its conclusion now that Asmara's annihilation is near. Whatever this thing is, it reflects Asmara's decisions back to herself.

Heavy plumes of The Patron's odor fill the garage. Its rotten aroma is recognizable yet it has transmuted into a sickly sweet smell which teases Asmara with a memory she struggles to pinpoint. Something from childhood.

A lake... Tahoe.

This monster has known her forever.

An itch develops beneath the dynamite on her face. The explosives are impatient.

Tunnel vision forms in her eyesight as the starfish hijacks her optic nerves. She will be blind soon.

One of the Patron's giant limbs lifts off her shoulder and gives the dynamite a series of taps with its spear-point tip. Time to go, it is saying.

The Patron and the starfish have conflicting motivations. Or do they?

Asmara reaches with her left hand and pinches the air by her face where the dynamite fuse dangles out of sight. The nine-inch-long thread is located and she bends it into view. Her right hand maintains the lighter's steady flame.

Saving the world is an honor.

How many get to say they've done such a thing?

She ignites the fuse.

The gunpowder-laced cord springs into action. A small fountain of sparks cascade across Asmara's face. The violent hiss of a combustive reaction echoes in her ear.

After lying dormant for years, the burning fuse acts as if its existence is finally vindicated. There is an eager momentum to its own disappearance as the fuse fulfills its purpose.

Nine seconds until detonation.

Time cannot be stopped.

But her brain can speed up.

CHAPTER 65

This time distortion should be impossible and yet Asmara is immersed in it anyway. The dynamite fuse sparks no longer leap in front of her eyes. They are frozen in place like glittering stars. In this freeze-frame state, she thoroughly observes her circumstance along with everything which came before. *Everything.* Her thoughts have increased at a speed which far surpasses the burn rate of a dynamite fuse. Reality is not in slow-motion—her mind now processes at a quantum-computer level.

Asmara roams around her mental environment, taking in the sights as they appear. A childhood memory here. A forgotten regret there. These archived recordings are all accessible. When she taped the dynamite to her face, Asmara's life didn't flash in front of her eyes. Now that the fuse is lit and her brain races at the speed of light, the show is about to begin.

Each memory sorts themselves for chronological display. However, the biography edit of her twenty-nine-year existence is not the "movie" format she anticipated. Instead of passively watching each memory appear in order from her youth up until today, Asmara's timeline is more versatile. She is able to scroll up and down through her life and sample experiences. These aren't hazy recollections filtered through memory decay. The replays are so vivid that to engage them is the same as living the events for the first time.

Asmara skips around through this time-travel navigation. She basks in a happy buzz when she relives a game-winning soccer goal she scored at the age of twelve. Next is the euphoria she felt during a rope swing into a river last year. Now it's the scream-laughter she shared during a college road trip with Sarah and Gillian.

At an imperceptibly slow speed, the dynamite fuse still burns. Asmara is not fazed. Her super-charged thoughts allow her to stay in this inner realm and she can stretch these nine seconds into nine years.

It's tempting for her to dwell on the timeline's joyous highlights, but out of curiosity Asmara scrolls up to her chaotic current events.

She gives herself an overview of the past week and it is even more surreal when viewed as a whole.

One insight looms large: Constellations are not just star patterns in the night sky. They also form here on Earth when souls burn bright and fall into each others' orbit.

This glowing alignment radiates between Asmara and her fellow stars—a lover, a deranged neighbor, a teenage tomboy, a scientist, and an extraordinary tarantula. However, the constellation they forged is not stable. Fate instead has them colliding together like an atom-smashing accelerator.

Her attention narrows on the timeline to the five slithering pixels from the Europa space probe. She fast-forwards from there and observes the Ingall Beacon pattern arrange itself on her computer two days ago. In this memory realm it's easy for her to travel through time. Unfortunately, she cannot travel to Europa to determine if there's a giant serpent swimming near the icy surface. Nor can she travel through her computer and discover what Professor Garrity's intentions were when he infected her with an alien virus.

Next on the timeline, a thrill arises as she revisits her experience with Ryan. Their strange dance in each other's gravity has been only a week long but it is a beautiful pairing. She wishes their lives could continue to rotate around each other.

Asmara's chest tightens with heartache about losing Ryan and she prepares to scroll to less bittersweet memories. Before descending years into her past, a gorgeous glimmer from recent events holds her in place. It's Word Bound two nights ago. More specifically, it's the storm of souls she witnessed at The Naomi. Those two hundred aura wavelengths from the audience are not just imprinted in Asmara's memory, they are even more exquisite than when she first saw them. Her hyper-activated mind is able to discern limitless details of the various individuals. Everything is laid bare. In the group's exposed lives there are vast plains of ordinary moments and mundane days. Those can be overlooked. It is the peaks and valleys of these people which form an incredible landscape. Surrounding each mountain of happy highlights there are canyons of despair.

Much like her own timeline, it is tempting to focus on the wonderful moments of these strangers. Why wouldn't she want to cherry-pick the best parts of many different lives? Instead, it is the shadowed corners of these souls which Asmara gravitates toward. She steps into their darkness and absorbs two hundred lives' worth of human strife.

The effect of this aura experience at The Naomi the first time contained broad themes. It was a marvel to behold how people confronted obstacles and disappointments. Now their endurance is more stunning since their lives are revealed in detail. She sees individuals searching for reasons to crawl out of bed in the morning. There is vicious anxiety hiding in their heart valves while depression is a beast following behind each footstep. Insecurities about appearance are the standard, with discontent about every body part from head to toe.

And yet...

There is much more than those grim self-portraits.

For these people, the anguish of living is merely part of the colors of their wavelength palette. Entire spectrums of other vibrant hues paint a wider picture. Creativity and inspiration contain bright splashes of sky-blues. Relationships with family and friends create swirling blends of yellows. And, unsurprisingly, romantic love is shown through deep reds.

It is apparent to Asmara that life's beauty can only exist when compared to a backdrop of adversity. The contrasts are not unfortunate, they are essential to each other.

Among these two hundred souls, no one is spared the hardships of living. And hope is not achieved by random luck. Everyone in The Naomi self-generates their own optimism, even if it's just enough to get through the day.

Each individual at Word Bound gives Asmara a unique tool to extract hope. This new perspective doesn't merely allow her to view the bright side of things, it takes the crisis consuming her and magnifies it to reach clarity.

With newfound sharp vision, she finds a hairline crack in the story she's trapped in. And then another. The fractures are caused by her stubborn power of logic. That engine has never stopped generating skepticism this entire time.

If the Earth is about to be wiped out by an alien flood, how did future Zoe live to warn about it decades later?

And, in a drowned world, how did human technology advance to where people send holograms backwards through time?

Asmara doesn't need to know these answers for the questions to be useful. They provide doubt. And hope.

Her front-row seat to the apocalypse starts to rattle.

She justified the dynamite on her face with a belief she is saving the world. However, Asmara visualizes Ryan and Zoe as they awaken to the explosion. She imagines them both walking up to a smoldering garage in the pre-dawn darkness. To inflict harm like that on people you care about, it is incomprehensible, even if the world is at stake. The eight billion human lives on Earth are abstract. Ryan and Zoe have been the only real things she's sure of this past week.

The Patron's giant insect legs lift off Asmara's shoulders, their tips point toward her face. It wants her dead.

Inside Asmara's skull, the starfish parasite wants her alive, just long enough to open the floodgates of hell.

Asmara doesn't care what they want. She is going to extinguish this dynamite fuse.

Let's see what more living can do.

It is an almost casual choice. No need to panic. Her brain processing speed is so fast that only a millisecond has transpired since she lit the fuse. She has plenty of time to plan how to disable the dynamite. However, as Asmara exits her inward-looking realm and her hands rise to her face, the harsh laws of physics take hold. It turns out the muscles and bones in her arms are unimpressed by the light-speed brain power she harnessed. The physical world has strict limitations on her anatomy. True, her mind is able to bend time with expanding thoughts. But, as for her hands, nine seconds still means nine seconds.

Oh, no. I'm about to blow off my head.

The fuse smoke in her nose has a sharp, repulsive odor. The sizzling noise of the sparks scream into her ears.

Asmara's first frantic gesture involves both hands clawing at her face. Her fingertips try to slip underneath the electrical tape in order to rip off the dynamite. The overlapping black ribbons are too taut. Her hands pull and tear at the back of her head. There is loosening but she cannot get an effective grip within the tangle of hair and tape.

She has wasted three full seconds. Six to go.

Holy shit! I'm about to blow off my fucking head!

The dynamite sticks cannot be pulled from her face—it's the burning fuse which must be stopped. Asmara's fingers snap together near her jaw. Direct catch. She has captured the remaining five inches of the fuse and she feels the sparks bouncing off her fingertips. With a firm grip she gives a downward yank, assuming the fuse will rip out of the dynamite. Her fingers slide off the thread and it continues burning.

Another desperate pinch of the air snags the fuse again. Her fingers press together even harder, as tightly as her hand muscles allow. Asmara finds time for the briefest prayer imaginable as she lifts her elbow to gain leverage. She snaps her arm downward and places a lifetime's worth of faith in the belief she severed the flame from the dynamite.

A vicious revelation: Her fingers hold nothing and the evil hiss of the burning fuse continues.

There are three seconds left. Her thumb and forefinger clamp onto the remaining stub of the fuse. Instead of pulling the burning thread out, maybe it can be extinguished like a candle. As the soft flesh of her thumb presses deeply against the thin cord, a shock wave of lightning shoots through her hand. The sparks eat away at her flesh.

That's a good thing. The pain means she is applying pressure to the correct spot. It means she's still alive.

If she pushes a little harder, the fuse will be snuffed out.

There's hope.

There's always hope.

CHAPTER 66

Nothing.
Nothing.
Nothing.

It must be over. This nothing means it is all finished.

And yet.

How am I aware there's nothing?

These are thoughts.

My own thoughts. I cannot see, nor hear, nor smell, nor touch. But I am not gone.

Disembodied thoughts means there's no body. Her body had given Asmara life.

This place is *after* life.

The afterlife. That's where she must be.

Nothing.
Nothing.
Something.

Some... one.

Someone else is here. Even with her senses stripped away, a presence is detected.

The Creator. God. Who else could it be?

This means judgment awaits.

Hold on.

Please, listen to me.

I thought I was saving the world! I truly did. I tried to stop the dynamite.

I'm sorry. I'm begging you, can I go back?

Within her plea for forgiveness, Asmara's thoughts are not words. She produces musical tones.

Don't punish me. Please. You can't send me to hell for trying to save the world.

A different series of tones, not her own, descend upon Asmara. She understands them as words.

I am not your creator.

Who are you? Where am I?

It is better to show you than to explain. I want you to start swimming. Act as if you're a river flowing within the sea.

What?! Swim how?

Silence.

Hello?

Nothing.

Whoever spoke to her said all they needed to say. It's on Asmara to take their lead.

With no physical body, no spatial orientation, and no senses at all, Asmara visualizes herself as a river within a sea. She pictures a long current of freshwater tunneling through an enormous body of saltwater. In her conception, these two types of fluids do not mix, they slide past each other with ease. The river moves as if a rocket through open air.

Flowing. Gliding. Relentless motion. No part of her is still.

She exists in numerous places at once. There she is, far ahead. And beyond that, she is even farther. Yet, she is also right here.

Her momentum takes a three-dimensional form. There is a shape to this activity, one which is no longer abstract. Asmara is linear. Much longer than she is wide.

She is... vast.

You're almost here. Keep swimming.

This liquid flight she's engaged in is not a random force of nature. She manifests the energy by her own movements. Alternating side-to-side waves of effort ripple down her immense length.

She is an undulating river.

Like a snake.

A long serpent moving in water.

Europa.

You've arrived.

Asmara is unable to respond. No communication would express the bewildering awe which engulfs her.

Don't panic. Keep swimming. I've extracted you—or what you call your wavelength. You have to be integrated with me for this to work.

Asmara tries to return her focus to the three-mile-long serpentine movement of her new body. This is no mere switch to a different point of view. She is physically now a giant water snake—skin, muscles, organs and all.

This is insane.

I can see why you would think that.

Did I die in the garage?

Not yet. I can't stop time but I can slow it. On Earth, your body is still there. The fuse is about to ignite the dynamite. You will explode. I slowed your world and brought your consciousness up here.

Are you a God?

No. My kind just had a head start long before your kind.

What happened this past week? What does all of it mean?

Questions are inefficient right now. Considerable energy is required for me to slow time on Earth. I'm breaking every rule.

There are rules?

You'll see. If you keep swimming, our connection will intensify. You won't need to ask questions then. The answers will be there.

Asmara returns to the rhythm of propulsion through Europa's ocean. The serpent host has given her full physical control. She is a bullet train splicing an ocean.

More external information arrives. Sensory data. The mind meld is strong and she experiences the alien's entire view of reality. She is able to see within the waters of Europa. It is dark beneath the ice but there is a wide spectrum of visual input from infrared to ultraviolet. She has numerous eyes to accommodate all of these visions.

What her eyes are unable to see in the black water is instead detected by the sound waves she emits. Sensitive membranes along her sides translate the returning waves of her echolocation, as if she's a mountain-sized dolphin. These pulses create their own detailed maps for navigation.

Answers start to arrive. She doesn't need to ask questions. The giant ice serpent is aware of what Asmara is thinking and she just has to allow the story reveal itself.

And so it does.

. . . .

Her neighbor Inga wasn't lying. That woman did view an unnatural constellation decades ago and it is a virus-like propagation system. The star arrangement is a forgotten weapon from an ancient war. Machines pulled the stars together to transform any lifeforms which gazed upon the pattern. Those poor souls were then fatally conscripted to become weapons to further spread across the universe.

The war which spanned galaxies had no winner. No one survived to deactivate the constellation. It kept producing clones by flooding planets with exotic substrate—red, green, gray. Over time, the multiplying army never knew who they were fighting anymore. Or why. They were compulsive expansionists, enemies to all.

Similar to a landmine or unexploded bomb on Earth, some vestiges of war remain deadly long after a conflict ends. This weapon happened to be a half-billion years old, eighty light years across and consist of thirty-seven stars.

That must have been some war.

. . . .

Asmara releases a pocket of captured air from inside her serpent gills and it starts a chain reaction of deflating organs down her body. This loss of buoyancy causes a sharp descent into the depths of Europa.

. . . .

Inga was also correct that the virus constellation which entered her eyes in Russia had corrupt coding. Inside of her, there was no perfect replication of a superintelligent lifeform-weapon. The incomplete metamorphosis instead trapped an embryonic pseudo-God in Inga. Mutated, hobbled. It could not get Inga to open the flood portal.

Even with its limitations, the trapped clone spotted an opportunity. It manipulated the wavelength of Inga's neighbor, a twenty-nine-year-old woman writing a short story across the hall. Asmara's aura was exploited to rewrite the text. Within her story called *Lightning in Ojai*, the mosaic of words now contained a proxy pattern of the Ingall Beacon hidden among the paragraphs. The curve of a vowel here, a consonant placed there—the shape of the words in her story recreated the constellation. Asmara was infected by her own writing.

. . . .

This is an accelerating freefall through water. Europa's gravity pulls Asmara toward its core while she generates her own downward thrust. With each swipe of her tail, millions of gallons churns in her wake.

Her infrared vision sees points of light dart away.

They are fish.

Or at least Europa's version of fish.

. . . .

Asmara was infected by the literal shape of her story but it, too, caused an incomplete metamorphosis. The mutations were enough for Asmara to have visions, but not enough to open the portal. The semi-possession of her body and soul took the form of an insectoid Patron. Straddling both her consciousness and the material world, this monster was a self-conflicted composite of Asmara and the parasite, at war with itself.

. . . .

Small points of shimmering light are everywhere. Swarms of fish circulate in the water. Some are not so small. Europa is flush with life.

. . . .

Professor Garrity never sent the dot matrix memorization test. It was a Trojan Horse message sent from the alien weapon inside Inga. The clone had possessed the old woman to hack Asmara's computer.

After Asmara stared at the pattern, the starfish parasite—the true portal opener—was born in her brain.

. . . .

Giant patches of infrared light emerge from the depths of Europa. The blobs appear shapeless until dangling tentacles are revealed. These are ultra-massive jellyfish, far larger than the serpent Asmara inhabits. This highly-evolved species comprises an order of holy monks. They float in a deep trance of prayer, oblivious to the millennia which pass by like seconds on a ticking clock. The monks believe the hymns they recite from their ancient religion are critical to the maintenance of reality. Asmara has no reason to doubt them.

. . . .

A person cannot remember the future, but Asmara is presented with visions. These are glimpses of how things would have transpired without the Europa intervention she swims toward.

Credit goes to the cauldron. The cauldron visualization technique is the reason Earth doesn't fully drown when the portal opens. Without even knowing what she was fighting against, Asmara's will power weakened the sinister chain reaction in her mind. Her tenacious brainwaves cracked part of the alien mutation code. The Earth was inundated, for sure. It was a near-Apocalypse. But there were survivors.

Zoe and others were able to send Asmara a message from their nightmarish future.

Which led to the dynamite.

Which led to Europa.

· ·

Now at the bottom of the sea, Asmara's echolocation traces the contours of an immense city. There are domed structures larger than any mountain on Earth.

The city was abandoned long ago. Europa's serpent inhabitants evolved past the need for physical bodies. They departed from this moon before mankind ever existed.

The one serpent Asmara inhabits is an ancient avatar. It is a living thread the Europans use to stay connected to the biological realm.

· ·

I have to let you go now, Asmara.
There are rules.

CHAPTER 67

The dynamite is about to explode. Great effort is required to slow time on Earth. Questions are inefficient.

Asmara asks anyway.

You helped me this past week, didn't you?

I guided certain outcomes.

In the shower—you turned the water into a weapon.

Holy water. Yes.

The tarantula at Word Bound—you altered its venom to stop the flood.

And the spider bite at Ryan's—it's how Zoe's message was delivered.

Yes. I broke the rules. I did it because you inspire me.

Asmara receives a revelation of a cosmic order. There is a universal command that intelligent lifeforms must be allowed to progress or go extinct on their own terms. There can be no interference by beings which have transcended the bonds of biology. The decree means that even the Ingall Beacon constellation cannot be dismantled.

As for who issues this command and enforces it, Asmara has a vision of three dark stars hurtling in her direction.

Those three stars make the rules. They will be here soon.

To destroy the Earth?

No, to kill me.

Why?

Because I intervened to save your planet. They know I am inorganic. They are not fooled by my sealife avatar.

Why are you sacrificing yourself? Aren't we insects to you?

No. It is an honor to take this fall.

Why did you bring me to Europa?

The story you wrote predicted a legitimate future scenario. Accurate foresight is not allowed. I have to erase it from your mind or the dark stars will wipe out your planet as well.

How was I able to have the prediction?

When Zoe sent you messages from the future, she ripped holes through time. It took her numerous tries to reach you. Inside those misfires, a premonition slipped through.

Zoe sent those messages every midnight, didn't she?

Correct.

The surfer scientist, he is real? He will allow in an entity and get hit by lightning?

Quite possibly.

Asmara attempts to process everything she learned. The effort is futile. *I won't remember any of this, will I?*

Of course not. It is time to send you where you need to go.

Within her echolocation pulses, the underwater city at the bottom of Europa blurs. A feeling of physical detachment lifts upward as her consciousness is pried from the alien. The mind meld is being severed.

It's not fair that you must die.

This is my choice. Asmara, I want you to know something.

Yes?

These recent days may not seem like it to you, but the universe contains a lot of beauty. A lot of goodness. More than you can imagine.

I believe you.

One by one, the serpent's senses go blank for Asmara as she is extracted from the wavelength union. Amid the psychic separation, she has a glimpse into the alien's memory. This is direct access to its timeline, the same way Asmara reviewed her own life.

A particular event draws her attention. The experience is a comprehensive recording and it's as if she is there in real time.

In the memory, she is swimming again on Europa. The serpent Asmara inhabits races with urgency. Immense muscles, each longer than a city block, work in unison. She partially rises from the water and a burst of natural light fills her eyes before she submerges. Europa has no surface ice. This memory is so long ago that the Jupiterian moon has a different composition than it does now.

The water roils around her and the turbulence is stirred by other moving objects.

She surfaces again and her gaze lifts to a yellow-blue sky streaked with green clouds. It is a beautiful atmosphere Europa once had.

Asmara tunes into her echolocation and the movements in the surrounding water gain clarity. There are countless other giant Europa serpents swimming alongside her. Together they form a wall of sealife, charging just beneath the ocean's surface like a living tsunami.

On the next breach above water, Asmara gets a detailed view of her fellow travelers which have emerged as well. Their purple and black skin shimmers in Europa's daylight. An elaborate gridwork of small, hooked spikes protrude from their flesh. She is among dragons. They are rivers swimming in an ocean.

The serpent swarm, hundreds of miles wide and long, presses forward. There is purpose to this migration.

Asmara skims on top of the water and her eyes are no longer submerged. She observes everything above her and the initial perspective was incorrect. The colorful sky is not Europa's atmosphere. Instead, those vibrant streaks are on the surface of a separate sphere so large it occupies almost all visible space above Europa. Asmara never dreamed two celestial bodies could be this close together. The curvature of this second globe is visible only at the ocean's horizon. A scattering of stars shine on either side of its rounded edge.

The sphere above is not Jupiter. The yellow-blue sky with green clouds is the atmosphere of a different moon passing directly above Europa. These two moons appear as if they are about to collide but it's an illusion. Orbital gravity swings them in a perilous dance where their atmospheres graze each other once every ninety years.

Upon closer inspection, Europa's horizon displays wide blue smears rising up from the ocean and blending from one moon to the other. It's as if a painter is making upward brush strokes which combine the two moons, each of which are covered in their own blue seas.

Asmara's gigantic frame jolts from a full-body tug forward in the water. A riptide current has captured her and pulls her toward the horizon with great force. An ocean conveyor belt has been activated.

A realization of what's happening arrives as rushing water roars in the distance.

These are tidal forces created by the moon above. The effect is far more than an ocean crawling up a beach due to lunar pull on Earth. This Europa tide is so powerful it involves a vertical exchange of water from one moon to the other.

The reverse waterfall rising into the air was distant a moment ago and now it is near. This other moon's ultra-close pass makes Europa spin faster.

Like an oncoming train, the wide blue column of levitating sea rushes toward her. The extraction of water produces a thunderous sound which shakes the serpent's internal organs.

Not every ocean drop successfully transfers upward. A torrential rainstorm falls back onto Europa. This downpour produces a spontaneous new weather system. Billowing green clouds expand until they burst into vapor, only to be replaced by more clouds which balloon the same way.

Lightning bolts slash across the sky. The superheated white lines even flash from moon to moon—static electricity on the grandest scale. The vacuum of space between these bodies has been temporarily filled with storms and a bridge of water.

Inside the inverted waterfall, dozens of black specks rocket upward from the surface of Europa and ascend the pillar of ocean. The dots are serpents, like her. The front of the swarm she is in has made contact with the arriving wall of water. Their wriggling shapes indicate they swim frantically on a vertical plane. They are *trying* to go up. A gravity-lift alone will not carry the large animals to this second moon. They must earn it.

The purpose of this migration is not revealed to Asmara, yet a primal drive makes her swim faster.

Lightning flashes illuminate the watery blue curtain which connects the two moons. Many of the other serpents, hundreds of them now, have stalled in their ascent high above the ocean. Their desperate swimming efforts bring them no closer to the second moon. Some are already in freefall back to Europa. This journey is not for all.

The ocean around her swells upward. A deafening noise of suctioned liquid pummels her senses. Asmara begins a mental countdown for lift-off into this column of seawater. Three... Two...

When she regains consciousness she's miles into the air. The initial extraction impact knocked her out for a few seconds. She's surprised these serpents survive the violent suction. No time to assess injuries, she needs to start swimming immediately.

It is surreal to undulate her dragon body up a vertical pillar of water. Dueling forces of gravity pull in opposition to each other. The second moon above beckons with a helpful lift, giving her a weightless feeling. But Europa's jealous grip yanks her downward. At some point above her the second moon is capable of winning the gravity tug of war, carrying Asmara into its grasp. That sweet spot is near, if she can reach it.

To her left and right, other serpents plummet back into the Europa ocean. They are alive, although spent from their failed journey.

Her ascent has peaked. She swims in place and is not gaining any altitude. Asmara's two-hundred-thousand tons of meat and muscle do not get a free ride. Panic sets in.

And a realization.

This is far more than an alien's memory.

Yes, it happened in the past, but Asmara is here now. Her efforts are real and they are of critical importance.

What is this? She asks the serpent. *What is this migration?!*

I need you to swim, Asmara. Please. Please swim.

Desperation sours the musical notes of the serpent's words. The alien is counting on her. Strange that a superintelligent lifeform begs her to complete a task in a body not her own, in a time not her own.

Why do you need my help? It already happened!

Yes, it was *you* back then. It is you now. It has always been you.

Asmara is falling backwards.

Swim! You have to go higher!

Europa takes the advantage in this gravity wrestling match. A freefall is about to commence. Every muscle in her three-mile frame loosens in defeat. Her body contracts into a coil.

Asmara, no! You have no idea what you've done!

The serpent is right. Asmara does not comprehend the stakes of the mysterious migration. Instead of zooming into the alien's timeline, absorbing each detail up close, Asmara retracts her inner vision, as far as it goes. She reaches what might be the edges of the universe itself.

Only seen from this far, there it is. Laid bare. This alien memory is a recurring event and perpetually has the potential to change the future. Any rewritten outcome has consequences which will unfold for ages.

A wider picture tells the tale: The gravity wake of a passing comet will pull this second moon loose from its Jupiterian orbit. The yellow-blue atmosphere will dissolve as the rock drifts through the solar system. It will ease into its destiny as the third rock from the Sun.

This moon hovering above Europa will one day become Earth. A marble knocked loose from Jupiter's grip by a comet shall become the Garden of Eden—one of the most blessed planets in the universe. The organic molecules of these Europa waterfall migrations, this current migration in particular, sow the seeds of Earth's later flourishing. A graveyard moon for Europan serpents is the fertilizer of humanity.

Asmara wants to live. She wants to go home.

Since her body is coiled anyway, Asmara exploits the kinetic energy of the tightly bound shape. She snaps the length of her frame into a full extension like a bullwhip. The explosion of energy pushes her off of the surrounding water, giving her leverage, and she climbs upward.

Again she coils and the second muscle-release burst causes her to leap higher. This is not swimming—she is jumping inside of a waterfall. The coil technique is effective for gaining altitude but it depletes her energy. This maneuver is possible only two more times.

Serpents plummet all around. They are miles-long bombs falling from the sky. If any of them collides with her this quest is over and Earth will be a lifeless rock.

The next leaping extension gets Asmara even higher but muscles down her side are torn in half. Pain is not an abstract sensation to this alien body. Agony is a universal language and the injury is severe.

As for the vertical migration, a threshold has been reached. She levitates in place now. The uplifting pull of the second moon is equal in force to Europa's downward gravity.

The weightlessness is calming. If only she could stay here awhile and rest. Instead she coils into a spiral, the tightest one so far. Pain shoots along her immense length. A lightning bolt flashes nearby and blinds her.

Asmara doesn't perceive the final jump of her spring-loaded body. She assumes it happened because her next sensation is an effortless lift up through the water. There is no more pain. Her limp frame has ceased swimming or even moving at all. She is being carried.

You did it, Asmara. You're going home.

As she is cradled in the watery arms of this second moon, her gravity perspective flips and, by all accounts, she is now falling.

To Asmara, it is nothing but seamless ascension.

CHAPTER 68

It's a puzzle. The fragments of memory are within reach, spiraling in her mind. They are not moving so fast that she cannot grasp them. However, for each piece she examines, three other aspects of this recollection drift away.

Asmara accumulates a small pile of ill-fitting memory pieces. None of the edges line up. There is no harmony in these fractured thoughts. An incomplete story tries to express itself and makes her more confused.

Her life before Word Bound is a clear recording of events. No mystery there. The stage event at The Naomi—and the days before and after it—exists in a haze.

She rises from a seated position on the concrete floor and the stretch relieves an ache in her legs. Standing in the cluttered and shadowed space, the surroundings re-introduce themselves. It is odd to be in Zoe's garage but retracing how she arrived here is not a priority. Those details will come in time. Far more compelling is the memory puzzle she confronts, for it will reveal the bigger story she is within. There is an urgency because the other puzzle pieces rise higher in her mind, out of reach.

Something important happened, on a vast scale. She played a central role, even if it is narcissistic to believe so. The stakes were high. What does that entail, though?

One thing Asmara is confident about, is that this was not all a dream. Certain events occurred and they involved real people and places. Zoe is a teenager asleep in the adjacent house. Ryan is an actual person across the street. Maybe they will help fill in the blanks.

As Asmara gets into a near-trance, trying to comprehend what happened, her hands are busy fidgeting around her head. Hair gets pulled and a wrap of sorts is unwound from her face with sticky reluctance.

Her thumb hurts. It has a swollen red blister with a black circle in its center. This is a significant burn.

Ouch. Wonder how I did that?

Asmara's hands are full. They hold a tangle of black tape and two maroon-gray cylinders which appear to be road flares. She places them in their likely receptacle, a nearby toolbox. Why the items were stuck to her is a question for a later time.

Long streaks of yellow light pierce beneath the garage door. These are sunrays of dawn. She can't remember the last time she saw a sunrise.

Every waking second entails further disintegration of the story puzzle. If she opens the door and fills her eyes with daylight the pieces will melt away. She would then never understand what happened. If she stays here in the dark garage a bit longer, she might be able to formulate the right questions to ask herself. There is a trail of real-world evidence awaiting for her to pursue. This mystifying story can be corroborated if she knows where to investigate.

An implicit threat is that if no details are validated then these events were in her mind alone—making her a madwoman.

She puts her hands over her face. Her eyes receive no light under closed lids and the darkness in front of her is expansive. Limitless.

Asmara wobbles on her feet. Even when standing still, her body has a sense of internal motion, similar to being at sea.

Her hands are lowered.

Asmara opens the door and sunlight rushes in, as if it had been waiting to embrace her. Photons enter her eyes and the light particles go about dismantling the remaining puzzle pieces.

The neural pathways which contain memories of this past week become a deconstructed soup of electrochemical debris. Those molecules are further degraded—atoms pried apart—until they exist as nothing more than body heat.

That particular wisp of heat circulates through Asmara and is released as she exhales on an Oakland street under a cloudless sky.

Her eyes lift upward.

THE END

A decade or more
in a city seven by seven.
Time enough,
space enough,
to affix a memory, a feeling,
to every street.
Every contour.

And then came her.
And then came us.
The moments, the memories,
each generating the other—
each existing only
in our minds and hearts.
(As if that is not enough)
And yet,
the moments, the memories
are ascribed a place in this city.
As sure as a street sign.

Now, old memories remain.
Yet everything has changed.
She did not erase.
She did not supplant.
She is a light
that shone upon
a brand new city.

And every contour in it.